John & Jackie

"…this story is particularly poignant for me. It cuts very close to the bone, and it is told with painful realism."

—Prism Book Alliance

"It is definitely worth reading if only to experience a true love affair."

—MM Good Book Reviews

"This was such an emotional read, a tearing apart of your heart and pasting it back together kind of read… This is a story not to be missed."

—The Novel Approach

Into This River I Drown

"…this is another outstanding read by one of my favorite authors… It touched me deeply."

—On Top Down Under Reviews

Tell Me It's Real

"It *is* real. The characters are real. The dialogue is real. And the actions are real."

—Live Your Life, Buy the Book

"TJ Klune is awesome wrapped in crazy, regurgitated as spectacular… definitely in my fave books of 2013. I laughed, cried, I laughed while crying, and most of all I fell in love with all the characters."

—Pants Off Reviews

By TJ KLUNE

Burn
Into This River I Drown
John & Jackie
The Lightning-Struck Heart
Tell Me It's Real

BEAR, OTTER, AND THE KID
Bear, Otter, and the Kid
Who We Are
The Art of Breathing

Published By DREAMSPINNER PRESS
http://www.dreamspinnerpress.com

THE Lightning-Struck HEART

TJ Klune

DREAMSPINNER PRESS

Published by
DREAMSPINNER PRESS

5032 Capital Circle SW, Suite 2, PMB# 279, Tallahassee, FL 32305-7886 USA
http://www.dreamspinnerpress.com/

The Lightning-Struck Heart
© 2015 TJ Klune.

Cover Art
© 2015 Paul Richmond.
http://www.paulrichmondstudio.com
Cover content is for illustrative purposes only and any person depicted on the cover is a model.

ISBN: 978-1-63476-367-7
Digital ISBN: 978-1-63476-368-4
Library of Congress Control Number: 2015905843
First Edition July 2015

Printed in the United States of America
∞
This paper meets the requirements of
ANSI/NISO Z39.48-1992 (Permanence of Paper).

To those that have patiently waited for me to find my footing again, I say thank you. This book is for you.

CHAPTER 1
The Villain Monologues

"AND NOW, I will tell you of my plans to take over the Kingdom," the evil wizard and total douchebag Lartin the Dark Leaf said with a cackle.

"Please don't," I said. "You really don't have to."

Of course he didn't listen. Villains never do. That's why they suck. A lot. It didn't help that my arms and legs were bound with vermilion root. That shit is hardcore. No lie.

"You see, back when I was a child, I always knew that I was different. That I was meant for *greater* things than what my father had planned for me." Lartin looked out toward the cave entrance almost wistfully, as if thinking of his childhood days. What a dick. "He always looked down on me with scorn because I never wanted to be an ironsmith. He always said that—"

"Do you think he realizes we don't care?" Gary asked me. He sounded really bitchy when he said it, but if you were a hornless gay unicorn, you'd be bitchy too. "Like, seriously. Don't care. At all."

I shrugged as Lartin looked at us in disbelief. "He has daddy issues."

"I don't have *daddy* issues," Lartin said, sounding annoyed.

"So that gives him the right to monologue?" Gary snorted. When he did, little pink and purple sparkles shot out his nose. Being a unicorn is awesome like that.

"He's a villain," I said. "It's what they do. They have to broadcast their entire plan when they think they've won because no one else will ever listen to them."

"Lame," Gary said, glancing at Lartin. "Girl, I really don't care. Unbind my legs before I scratch your eyes out."

"You don't have fingers," I reminded him. "You can't scratch anything."

"He's lucky I don't have my horn back yet," Gary muttered. "There'd be so much goring, it'd be unreal. It'd be like Gore City up in here. These roots are chafing. He should undo them."

"Are you going to undo them?" I asked Lartin.

"Uh, no?" he said. "You know I captured you and you're my prisoners, right?

"Did he?" I asked Gary.

"Well, we *are* tied up," Gary said. "And not in the fun way."

"I don't want to know when you've been tied up in the fun way," I told him.

He rolled his eyes. "Sam, you are such a prude."

"Guys?" Lartin said. "I have a plan? That I need to tell you about? You need to listen."

"I am *not* a prude," I said to Gary. "Just because I don't talk about... you know. *Sex* stuff. That doesn't make me a prude."

"Your face just turned red when you stuttered on the word sex," Gary said. "I almost believed you."

"I didn't *stutter*."

"You kind of stuttered," Lartin said. Because he was an asshole who I was totally going to kick in the balls before the day was up. "Can I get back to my story? I really think you'll appreciate the many facets of my character once you hear it. I'm dynamic and—"

"When were you tied up?" I demanded. "Unicorns aren't *allowed* to be whorish. You're supposed to be all virtuous and pristine!"

"Oh please," Gary said. "How do you think I was created?"

Huh. "Honestly? I always thought unicorns were made from sunshine and rainbows and good feelings. Like you just appeared one day in a field filled with flowers and a big fat sunbeam falling all around you. And there'd be butterflies or something." That sounded way pretty. And realistic for unicorn creation.

Gary squinted at me, nostrils flaring. "Seriously? No, you idiot. My parents had hardcore unicorn sex. Like boned for days. They're very adventurous that way. Up in trees, down by rivers, near graveyards at midnight. There really isn't anywhere they haven't spread the love."

"Oh my goodness," Lartin whispered. "Is this really happening?"

"Gross," I said. "That's just gross."

"Hey! Unicorn sex is a beautiful thing!"

"Yeah, but that's your *parents* you're talking about. That's wrong on so many levels. And why haven't I met them? Or heard about them?"

"They're touring the Outer Reaches with their swingers group."

"Swingers?"

"Yeah. Like partner swapping. Maybe orgies. I don't know."

I was horrified, and I'm sure it showed on my face. "Dude! What!"

"Prude," Gary said.

"I'm not a prude! I just don't see why we have to talk about sex all the time. Or your parents being in orgies!"

"Well, I guess you can't understand what you've never had," Gary said, a mean little curl to his stupid unicorn lips.

"You're a virgin?" Lartin said.

"You bitch," I said to Gary. "And *no*, I'm *not* a virgin."

"You so are," Gary said, because apparently this morning he'd eaten sass for breakfast. "A twenty-year-old virgin."

"No! There was that one guy! At that thing! With the people!" My argument was sound.

"That didn't count. He kissed you, and you came in your pants, and then you proceeded to tell him how his hair reminded you of your father."

"It *did*. It's not *my* fault he had dad hair!"

"*I'm* not even a virgin," Lartin said, sounding smug. "The ladies all want up on Little Lartin. There is so much sex to be had when I'm around."

Gary glared at him. "You call your dick Little Lartin? Dude. Wrong."

"I don't have *time* for all the relations and courting and wooing bullshit," I said. "I'm a *wizard*. I have *quests*."

"Uh, you're an apprentice," Gary said. "And you're sent on errands."

"You know how you wanted to dye a strip of your mane purple?" I said.

"Yes. Because I'd be beautiful."

"Well, too fucking bad," I said savagely. "I'm not going to do it. You're just going to have keep it white. Forever."

"You promised!"

"That was before you were a jerk!"

"Oh my gods," Gary said. "Lartin. Get over here and untie me. I want to kick Sam in the fucking face."

"No! He's going to untie *me* so I can hex the shit out of you. Lartin. Get your ass over here and untie me."

"Um," Lartin said. "I don't know if you guys understand the point of being captured. Like… I captured you? Right? And so—"

"No," Gary said. "Not *right*. You caught us off guard because we were looking for wormwood in the Dark Woods, and we just happened to stumble into your camp, and you took advantage of a situation. That doesn't count as capturing. That counts as being an asshole."

"When were you tied up?" I asked again.

"You're still on that?" Gary asked. "Ugh."

"You brought it up."

"Fine! It was that centaur we met last year. In the elf realm."

"You said you were just *friends*!"

"We were. We were just the kind of friends that tied each other up and pushed our penises together."

"What was his name again?"

"Octavio," Gary said with a dreamy sigh. "The *hands* that half man had."

"I have hands," Lartin said. "I've tied you up."

"Is he hitting on me?" Gary whispered loudly.

"Are you hitting on him?" I asked Lartin.

"No! I was just pointing out similarities of the situations."

"I think he was hitting on you," I told Gary.

Gary looked back at Lartin and sized him up. Then he did that thing that I swear only unicorns can do. His blue eyes got impossibly big. His eyelashes lengthened as he fluttered them at Lartin. His mane was luminous in the darkened cave, and he purred, "Well aren't you precious."

"Ew," I said. "Seriously."

Lartin blushed. "Oh, stop it."

"Does Little Lartin want to come out to play?" Gary asked, batting his eyes.

"I wish I were anywhere else but where I am," I said to no one in particular

"Maybe," Lartin said, trying for coy but somehow landing on straight-out creepy.

Gary giggled. He *giggled*. "Well, *maybe* I should tell you that my tongue is fifteen inches of the best thing you'll ever have."

"Yuck," I said. "That just sounds excessive."

"I've never done it with a horse," Lartin said. "Sounds... illuminating."

"Oh, you shouldn't have said that," I told him.

"*Horse?*" Gary snarled. The pretty unicorn act dropped immediately. Red sparks shot from his nose. "Did you just call me a *horse*? Listen here, you two-legged bag of shit. I'm not a motherfucking *horse*. I am a *unicorn*, and I am *magic* and a beautiful creature made of fucking sunshine and rainbows and good feelings."

"I knew it," I whispered.

"Get your ass over here so I can stomp on your face," Gary said to Lartin. "Untie me, lie down on the ground, and let me stomp your face."

"You don't have a horn," Lartin pointed out.

"That's just rude," I said. "I didn't point out that your nose is really big. Why would you say something like that?"

"Sam," Gary said tearfully. "He called me a *horse*."

"Hey," I said. "Hey. Look at me."

He did. His eyes were wet, and I wanted to punch Lartin in the spleen.

"Who is the most beautiful unicorn in all of Verania?"

"Me," Gary sniffed.

"And who has the prettiest mane?"

"Me."

"And who is a badass motherfucker who'll gut a bitch?"

"Me!"

"Damn right."

"Sam?"

"Yeah?"

"We'll find my horn, right?"

"I promise," I said. Because we would. It was important to him so it was important to me. It'd been stolen long ago, years before I'd met him. He couldn't even look himself in the mirror without cringing. That was unacceptable.

"And we can dye my mane purple when we get out of here?"

"First thing," I said. "I already bought the dye before we left the city."

"You love me," Gary sighed.

"I do."

"Okay, I feel better now."

"Good."

"So, are we going to finish, or what?" Lartin said.

I rolled my eyes. "Fine. Do your villain thing."

"This is so stupid," Gary muttered.

Lartin's eyes lit up. He posed in front of us again. "So it was my *father* that—"

"Daddy issues," Gary coughed.

Lartin glared at him.

"Sorry," Gary said. He wasn't sorry. "I had something in my throat."

"My father said that I would never—"

"We didn't lose that bag of wormwood, did we?" I asked Gary.

"Nah," Gary said. "It's still in the satchel on my back."

"Good. Morgan would be pissed if we forgot that."

"He's going to be pissed already. We were supposed to be back yesterday."

"We would have," I said. "If *some* people hadn't decided to tie us up in a cave."

Gary and I stared at Lartin.

"You guys are the worst prisoners *ever*," he muttered. Then his eyes went wide. "Did you say Morgan?"

"You shouldn't eavesdrop," Gary said. "That's rude. We weren't listening to you, so you shouldn't be listening to us."

"You're apprenticed to *Morgan*?" Lartin squeaked. "Morgan of Shadows?"

I grinned at him. "The one and the same."

"Oh no," Lartin moaned. "You're Sam of Wilds."

"Such a sexy name," Gary sighed. "Have I ever told you that?"

"Thank you," I said, pleased. "It sounds very rugged, doesn't it?" I'd worked very hard on earning that name. It'd change again when I was a full-on wizard, but it was good enough for now.

Gary laughed. "Yeah, but then people meet you and you're all skinny and adorable, and they're all like *whaaaa*?"

"I think you meant to say muscular and dangerous," I said. "You got your words confused again."

"No, I'm pretty sure I got them right. As I always do. To be muscular you have to have muscles."

"I have muscles!" I tried to flex, but my hands were bound behind me, and it didn't work out so well. "Okay. Shut up. But I *am* dangerous."

"Yeah, okay," Gary said.

"I am!"

"Honey, you're pouting. That's not dangerous. It's adorable."

"I'm not pouting," I said as I pouted.

"Aww," Gary said.

"Aww," Lartin said.

"Shut up, Lartin!"

"Okay, so can we leave?" Gary asked.

We both looked at Lartin.

"You're Sam of Wilds," he said.

"No shit," I said.

"Do you know how much you're *worth*?"

"Oh, not again," I groaned.

"I could totally ransom you!" Lartin said excitedly. "It would fund my world domination plans for the next six years!"

"Morgan's going to be so mad at you," Gary said to me.

"It's not my fault!"

"Well, you do get captured a lot."

"I suppose."

"And everyone knows your name."

"Right? How weird is that?"

"Totally weird."

"So much gold," Lartin said as he paced back and forth. "Pounds and pounds of *gold*."

"Hey, Sam?"

"Yes, Gary."

"Has Morgan ever paid a ransom for you?"

"Nope. Not once."

"And why is that?"

"He said that if I was dumb enough to get caught, then I'd have to figure my own way out."

"Ah," Gary said.

Lartin stopped. "Never paid?"

"Not once," I told him. "Can you let us go now?"

"No!" he snapped. "I am sick of this! You are going to sit there, I am going to tell you my plan, and then I'm going to get so much gold that I won't be able to *carry* it all."

"Then how are you going to move it?" Gary asked.

"Move what?" Lartin looked perplexed.

"You just said you were going to get so much gold that you weren't going to be able to carry it," I said. "So how are you going to move it if you can't carry it?"

"Oh," Lartin said. "Well, shit."

"Wow," Gary said. "If that's how well you think things through, I can't wait to hear your plans for world domination. I'm sure they'll be positively riveting. And well thought-out."

"Burn," I said. "You just got so burned. You'll have scars from all the burn."

"I'll buy a cart!" Lartin exclaimed. "And a horse." Then he went back to being a complete douche. "Or I'll just keep the unicorn here and he can pull it for me."

"Oh, bitch, say that to my face, bitch," Gary snarled. "Come on. I dare you."

"I wouldn't say that to his face," I said. "Even if he dared you."

But Lartin the Dark Leaf was an idiot. The wizarding clan of the Darks usually were. So it was no surprise when Lartin stepped forward and said, "You'll pull my cart. *Horse*."

That's when the nine foot half-giant named Tiggy roared and burst into the cave.

"Sam," he rumbled. "Gary."

"You're so dead," Gary said to Lartin. "You don't even know. Tiggy! Smash him!"

And since Tiggy loved Gary so, he moved forward to do just that.

"Wait, Tiggy," I said.

And since Tiggy loved me so, he waited.

Gary looked murderous. "Sam," he growled. And if you've never heard a unicorn growl, let me tell you: it's delightfully frightening.

"Your angry face is awesome," I said to him.

He preened. "I've been practicing. Watch." He glared at me, eyes narrowing, teeth bared. "See?"

"I got chills," I assured him.

"I smash now?" Tiggy asked.

Of course, Lartin tried to mutter off some defensive spell. Little green lights arced around Tiggy before they dissipated.

"You're not a very good wizard, are you?" I said. "Giant, dude. Their blood is like the antimagic. Come *on*. You learn that on your first day of wizard training!"

"I smash now." Tiggy looked very pissed off. He usually was when his two favorite people in the entire world were captured. Come to think of it, maybe it did happen a lot.

"Just hold on, Tiggy," I said.

"No, don't hold on," Gary said. "I want to see his insides on the outside."

"So bloodthirsty," I said in awe.

"I would prefer there to not be any smashing," Lartin said. "If I'm being totally honest."

But Tiggy was done with the situation, so he smashed Lartin the Dark Leaf. Multiple times. Into a variety of objects. Like rocks. And cave walls. It wasn't a very pretty sight. What with the blood and stuff. And the brains.

When the smashing was complete, Tiggy came over and snapped the vermilion roots that bound me and my magic. As soon as the roots fell, I felt a surge of green and gold and yellow flow through me. "So much better," I muttered.

"Always get caught," Tiggy grumbled as he tended to the roots at Gary's feet.

"Now that's not specifically true. I'll be honest, though. I've grown as a person this time around and will pledge to avoid capture in the future." That was not the complete truth. I would most likely get captured again. It was sort of my thing.

"Who's my big strong man," Gary cooed at Tiggy.

Tiggy blushed. "Me."

"Yes, you are. I knew you'd come and rescue me. I was like a princess waiting for her hero!"

"So pretty," Tiggy said, running his big hand gently through Gary's mane. "My pretty princess."

"Can we leave the cave now?" I asked. "You guys can flirt later."

"It's okay, Tiggy," Gary said. "Sam's just dealing with some issues. He recently came to the realization that he's a twenty-year-old virgin prude."

"I am *not*!"

"I told him about Octavio," Gary said. "Sam couldn't even say the word *sex* without stuttering."

"Sam never gonna find a boyfriend," Tiggy said. "No one gonna take his flower."

"Don't talk about my flower!" I snapped at them as I checked the satchel on Gary's back. The wormwood was still wrapped safely where I'd left it. So at least this wasn't a complete loss. "And I don't *need* a boyfriend. I am an independent man with priorities. I'm going to be the youngest wizard to pass his apprenticeship, and then I'm going to do great things. Big things!"

"Oh?" Gary said. And he grinned evilly. Evil unicorn smiles are the sign of wicked things about to be said. I hated them. "So I suppose a certain knight doesn't factor into those priorities whatsoever? Like maybe you want to be the youngest full wizard just to impress him?"

"You shut your whore mouth," I growled, trying to not sigh dreamily at the thought of bright green eyes and a beautiful smile. And wavy blond hair. Like, the waviest. I wanted to touch it with my face. "I don't even know what you're talking about."

"Uh-huh," Gary said.

"You want mouth full of knight," Tiggy said. "Knight take your flower and eat it."

"Tiggy!" I shouted, scandalized.

"Such a prude," Gary muttered.

"I hate you both. So much."

And to prove my point, I stormed out of the cave.

But they obviously didn't believe me, because they followed me.

Like I knew they would. I'm lucky that way, I guess.

CHAPTER 2
Please Don't Make My Nipples Explode

ONCE UPON a time in the Kingdom of Verania, there was a kickass boy born in the slums of the City of Lockes. His parents were hardworking, and at times, life could be difficult, but they were alive and had all their teeth. Which was very important.

The mother had been a gypsy, olive-skinned and beautiful. She could smile sweetly to hide the steel in her eyes. Once, a man had tried to rob her in an alley. The man no longer has testicles.

"What happened to his testicles?" the boy asked when he was four.

The mother grinned. "I threw them in the sewer."

The father groaned. "I'm glad our child knows that story now."

The father hailed from the north, deep in the mountains where snow fell year-round and people wore unfashionable things made from yak skin. He had auburn hair and a deep laugh that sounded like thunder in the fall.

"I'm not wearing that," the boy said when he was seven.

The father sighed. "It's what my people wear. It'll keep you warm." He tried to push the weird furry coat thing at the boy again.

The boy said, "It's August. And I don't want to look like I'm the poster child for what happens when a human has relations with a yak. Come one, come all! See the incredible yak-child!"

"Sam," the father growled. It was a low sound that always made the boy smile.

"Sam," the mother laughed. It was a husky sound that always made the boy happy.

The mother was Rosemary. The father was Joshua.

They lived in the slums, yes. They didn't have much, yes. But they were *happy*.

We were. I swear it on all I have.

My mother worked at a little flower shop at the end of a broken brick road, singing as she tended to the wildflowers in a language that sounded almost like birds trilling. She told me once that the songs were old, older than Verania. Her *mamia*, the grandmother of her clan, had taught her the songs under the stars in a field far from the City of Lockes.

My father worked at the lumber mill. He was a big man, able to carry a three-hundred pound Veranian oak log over his shoulder without breaking a sweat. He told me once that in the north, there were beautiful trees made of ice and that could be shaped into the most wondrous things. Like dragons and horses and swords with the sharpest blades. At night when he couldn't sleep, he would carve little trinkets. A heart for my mother. A raccoon for me. Little toys for the children in the slums who never had such things.

Like most other people around us, my parents couldn't afford to send me to the schools, so they taught me themselves at night, bringing home old and outdated books on math and art and history. After I started learning at the age of four, it only took three months to point out mistakes in what was supposed to be factual.

I didn't miss the smile my parents exchanged over my head.

We were happy.

I had friends. Well, sort of. I had *acquaintances*. Boys and girls that ran with me through the streets. The castle guards knew my name, and sometimes they'd give me bread and meat and I'd share it with the others. Sometimes I'd accidentally do something illegal like setting a cart on fire that belonged to a rich man who'd hit a boy named Eric because he hadn't gotten out of his way quick enough. The guards would look the other way because surely little *Sam* would *never* do anything like that, no matter how loudly the man protested. As a matter of fact, the guards said, Sam was spotted on the other side of town when the cart was supposedly set aflame, so it *couldn't* have been him.

Of course, it probably didn't hurt that it'd been one of the guards that'd given me the accelerant I'd used to start the fire. They didn't like assholes, either.

Everything was good.

Sure, I had dreams of something bigger. I'd lie in my bed at night, listening to the slow, deep breaths of sleep my parents took in their bed across the room. I'd stare out my window, and if I'd crick my head *just right*, I'd be able to see stars above the stone buildings across the way.

And didn't I wish upon them?

Of course I did.

That's how these stories go.

I wished for many things, like children do.

I wished for money.

I wished for the biggest turkey leg.

I wished for a bow and arrow.

I wished for my parents to be happy, always.

I wished to find that one person who would understand me forever.

I wished to become something great.

I wished to become someone special.

I wished that people would remember my name because I would be *good* and *kind*.

I wished for Derek Michen to kiss my face off (that one was when I was nine years old and was absolutely positive he was the love of my life. He *did* kiss me two weeks later, but then he also kissed Jessica, David, Megan, Rhonda, and Robert. Derek turned out to be a bit of a whore).

At no point did I wish to be magic.

Sure, I had gypsy blood in me.

Sure, I had northern blood in me.

But fuck all if I knew anything about *magic*.

So imagine my surprise when I was running from a group of older kids after having recovered a bag of cloth they'd stolen from Mrs. Kirkpatrick (a kindly old woman who lived next door and had even less than we did), when I turned down a blind alley that dead-ended into a brick wall and promptly whirled around and caused said group of teenage miscreants to turn to stone.

Awkward. To say the least.

"Oh crap," I said as I saw there was nowhere else to run. I was eleven years old, still scrawny as all fuck. I had great big expressive dark eyes that I'd inherited from my mother that I'd used to get myself out of more than a few situations, but I didn't think the bigger kids would appreciate my full-on patented Look-How-Precious-Sam-Is look. Adults were charmed by it. Girls swooned over it. Some boys did too.

Stupid motherfucking teenagers who stole from old ladies weren't affected by it at all.

"He's down here!" one of them shouted.

I heard the beat of many feet pounding the ground behind me, and I thought to myself, *Well, I really wish this wasn't happening.* So I turned around, ready to accept my fate (most likely either a severe ass-kicking or murder; either way it would hurt like a bitch). As I turned, something flickered across my vision, a bright green *something* that reminded me of spring grass and trees swaying in a summer breeze. There was this sharp *pull* deep in my brain and I took a stuttering step backward, and that's when the group of eleven teenage assholes turned to stone with a loud *crack* that shook the alley and caused pigeons to screech and take flight.

I said, "Hey."

Like, full-on stone. Their leader, a delightfully repugnant fifteen-year-old named Nox, stood in the front, his face frozen into an angry snarl, paused midstep, left arm stretched out front, right arm swung back.

I said, "Huh."

Of course, people had heard the commotion and poured into the alley.

I said quite loudly, "I didn't do it!"

One of the castle guards that I knew quite well said, "Of course you're here, Sam," followed by what sounded like a long-suffering sigh that dragged out for at least thirty seconds because he was a big fat drama queen.

"I don't even know what happened!"

"Uh-huh. You don't know what caused these dickholes to be turned to stone after they were chasing you."

"Honest!" And then I gave him the Look-How-Precious-Sam-Is at one-hundred-percent wattage and he melted right in front of me.

"That's not going to work this time," he said.

Well, almost melted.

"Shit," I muttered, dropping the look. "Pete, I swear, I don't even know what happened here. They *stole* stuff from Mrs. Kirkpatrick and she's old and it's not *fair* because she's so nice and I just wanted to help her." I sniffled as I tried to stop the tears from falling. I was very scared because I thought I was going to get arrested and thrown into the dungeon where I'd have to eat rats and poop in a bucket.

"Ah hell, Sam. Don't cry."

When someone tells you not to cry, it's pretty much impossible *not* to cry.

So I cried and Pete wrapped an arm around me as we waited for my parents to get there.

They looked scared as they came down the alley, but they hugged me close as I cried all over them, telling them I was sorry and to please not let me poop in buckets because I somehow turned teenage dickbags to stone.

"I'm not even going to pretend to know what you're talking about," my dad said as he kissed my forehead, because he was so awesome.

"I won't make you poop in a bucket," my mother said as she ran her fingers through my hair, because she was so cool.

That's when Morgan came.

I didn't know who he was at first. Sure I'd heard of him. He was the King's Wizard and he could do stuff like create fire tornadoes and make your face melt off. Rather, that's what the kids in the slums told each other because we were epic like that. I think I'd even started the rumor that he could make your nipples explode with a single thought. Judging by the looks of sheer horror on the others' faces, it was one of those things that sounded better in my head rather than out loud. Most things often did.

So I didn't know who he was, not by looks alone.

All I saw was a man with a black beard that came down to his chest and an epic pile of hair that stuck out all over the place. He was tall, almost as tall as my dad, but whip thin, with long, elegant fingers that traced over the boys of stone in the alley. He was wearing a long black robe and pointy pink shoes that were just killer. I couldn't even begin to guess how old he was. Maybe thirty. Or three hundred. When you're eleven, anyone older is just *old*.

When he spoke, his voice was light and melodious, almost like he was singing his words rather than speaking them. It was glorious. "This certainly is a surprise."

"Is that—" my mom whispered to my dad.

"I think—" my dad breathed back.

"I like your shoes," I said. Because I did. They were pink and pointed, and I wanted a pair like that so bad.

My mom and dad groaned.

Morgan looked at me and cocked his head. "Thank you, little one. I made them out of the tears of a succubus and a lightning-struck tree stump I found under the Winter Moon. I like your face."

I grinned. "Thank you, big one. My parents made it when they got married. I was a honeymoon baby, whatever that means."

My parents choked on either side of me.

Morgan chuckled and said, "Very well put. Are these your parents?"

"Yes," I said proudly. "This is my mother, Rosemary. You can call her Rose. And this is my dad Josh."

"Surname?"

"Haversford, sir," my father said.

Morgan looked at my mother. "And you, dearie? Surely you haven't always been Rosemary Haversford."

My mother shook her head. "It is a name I adopted when I chose to leave the clan and marry my love. I was born Dika Tshilaba."

"Ah," Morgan said. "I see. Your *mamia* was Vadoma, then."

My mother looked surprised. "Yes, my lord. You've heard of her?"

He gave a mysterious smile. "Perhaps."

And because the conversation was boring and I had questions, I said, "So. Anyway. How many tears did it take from the succubus to make the shoes? Like six? Or fifty? How did you make the succubus cry? What's a succubus? When is the Winter Moon? Is that tomorrow? Can I make those shoes tomorrow? I do like the pink. I would look so awesome if I had those. Everyone would be like, hey, Sam! Where'd you get those shoes? And I'd be all like, don't you wish you knew?"

My dad said, "*Sam*," in that tone of voice that said I was in so much trouble when we got home.

I glared at him and rolled my eyes.

Morgan laughed, and my parents were shocked. "Feisty one, isn't he?"

"My apologies, Lord Morgan," my father said in a rush.

"Lord?" I said loudly. "You're a *lord*?"

He put a finger in Nox's stone mouth to touch his tongue. "I suppose I am."

I gaped at him. "You're Morgan of Shadows!"

"So I've been told."

"Oh, sweet mercy!" I cried at him. "Please don't make my nipples explode!"

His bushy eyebrows went almost up to his hairline. "I wish I could say I've never heard that one before, but strangely enough, that's likely the sixth time someone has said that to me in the last week."

"Wow," I said excitedly. "I started that rumor like three weeks ago! And you've heard it *six times* already? I am *awesome*."

"*Sam*," both my parents said in that tone of voice that said I was in the most trouble I'd ever been in in the history of my life.

"My lord," my father said. "Please excuse my idiot child. He was dropped on his head repeatedly when he was a baby."

"Hey!" I growled at him. "You said you only did that twice. What do you mean *repeatedly*?"

"It would certainly explain a lot," Morgan said. "Does he ever stop talking?"

"No," my mother said. "Never."

"Hey!"

They all looked at me.

I was suddenly nervous because I remembered that this was Morgan of Shadows, and while most of the stuff said about him was probably crap, there had to be truth in there *somewhere*, and I didn't want to be murdered by having my spleen removed with a magical knife or whatever he supposedly did to bad guys.

"I'm not a bad guy," I said to him, trying to reassure him. Or me. Or the both of us.

Pete, my sweet guardian guard said, "Well, not all the time."

I glared at him. He stuck his tongue out at me.

"Did you do this?" Morgan asked. "Turned these boys to stone?"

I wrung my hands together. "I don't know. I don't even know how it happened. I was running from them and they chased me and then *bam*. They were all rock people."

"Why were you running from them?" he asked.

"They stole Mrs. Kirkpatrick's bag of cloth," I said. "She's old and doesn't have a lot but she likes to make things like ugly mittens and pants for obese people and it wasn't *right*. They shouldn't *steal* from nice old ladies who make big pants so I went and took them back so people could eat all the food they want and still have clothes to wear."

They all stared at me.

"Well! It's true! And they chased me down this alley and were going to punch me in the throat so I turned to take it like a man because that's what my dad taught me. That you should never run away from your problems if you don't have to. Or don't want to. Or if you're trapped by a dead end."

My father looked down at me with such fierce pride on his face that my heart stuttered in my chest.

Morgan frowned. "And then they just turned to stone?"

I shrugged. "Yes?"

"Okay, then," he said, clapping his hands in front of him just once. "Turn them back."

"Excuse me?" I might have squeaked.

"Turn them back."

"*How?*"

Morgan shrugged. "That's up to you to figure out."

I frowned at him. "That's not helpful at all."

"No, I suppose it isn't." But he wouldn't say anything else.

I looked up at my mom and dad. They both had narrowed eyes that told me in no uncertain terms that I better change the assholes back from stone or I was going to be grounded for at least the next month, if not longer.

I grumbled at them but pulled away to stand in front of Nox. By now, a large crowd had gathered at the mouth of the alleyway, which made things all that much worse, because I could hear my name getting whispered over and over again. I was pretty sure I was going to make a fool of myself and be pooping in a bucket by sundown.

Since I didn't know what I was doing at all and figured I might as well try and fake it as much as possible, I raised my hands, palms out toward the stone teenagers, and shouted, "Malakasham!"

Morgan said, "What."

"Flora Bora Slam!"

Morgan said, "Flora Bora Slam?" It sounded like he was choking.

"Abra Wham!"

Morgan said, "What are you doing?"

I squinted up at him. "Saying magic words until magic happens?"

"Magic words?"

"Isn't that how magic happens? You say magic words and magic stuff happens. Like people turning to stone and exploding nipples."

"I'm pretty sure it wouldn't be because of Flora Bora Slam," he said dryly.

"Pfft," I muttered. "Like *you* know." Oh, but wait. He was the King's Wizard. "Okay, so, you *would* know."

"Flora Bora Slam," he said again, rolling his eyes.

"Well, I'm all out of ideas."

He looked incredulous. "*That* was your idea?"

"Yes. It might have gone better in my head."

"I have a feeling that sums up your life perfectly."

Since I was too young to understand I was being insulted, I beamed and said, "Thank you!"

"Colors, Sam. Do you remember seeing any colors?"

I frowned. "Colors? What do you mean? I didn't see any...."

I'd caught his attention. "Sam?" he said quietly.

"There was... green," I said. "Like. This green that was out of the corner of my eye. It reminded me of trees and grass."

He nodded and something akin to wonderment flickered across his face. "Earth. Stone. Can you find it again?"

"I don't know how I found it in the first place."

"But you know of it now," he said. "Look for it."

And I did. For the longest time I did. I looked all over. Up and down and left and right. The sky, the ground. The buildings. My parents. Morgan. The crowd. The stone boys. I didn't see it anywhere and just as I was about to tell Morgan so, something danced just out of the corner of my eye and it was *green*, it was so *green*, and I thought, *Hello. Hello, there.*

Morgan took in a sharp breath. "You found it. I can feel it. It's so... *expansive*. How have you never...?" He shook his head. "Can you grab it?"

And I could. I *did*. I would learn later that I didn't find it right away because I was looking too hard for it, but the moment I stopped pushing, it started pulling. I touched the green and it was warm and kind and I said, "Yes. Yes."

And I pushed. Hard.

The alley shook again and people gasped and shouted as they took steps back. There was another *crack*, and the group of stone boys turned back into flesh and blood and bone.

Nox, who'd been caught midyell, continued, "—gonna fucking kick your ass, Sam!" before he squeaked and came to a stop, seeing the alley had quite a few more people in it than he remembered.

My dad growled, "If you touch my son, I'll cut off your arms and beat you with them."

"Wow," I said in complete adoration. "That was graphic and amazing."

My mom said, "And I'll cut off your legs and shove them so far up your anus that you'll taste your feet at the back of your tongue."

"Dudes," I whispered to everyone. "That's my *mom*."

Morgan said, "And I'll make your nipples explode."

"I started that rumor!" I told Nox. He didn't look very happy at that. As a matter of fact, he looked downright frightened. It was a good look on him, all blond hair and bright eyes. If he wasn't such a dick, I'd have thought him handsome. But he *was* a dick.

(But he was still sort of handsome.)

"Please don't make my nipples explode," Nox whimpered as his gang of jerks cried behind him.

"Don't steal from old ladies who make ugly mittens and pants for obese people," Morgan said, "and I might consider not exploding your nipples."

They agreed immediately and fled the alley in a cloud of teenage angst and hormones.

"You're so rad," I told Morgan honestly. "Almost up there with my mom and dad. Not the same level because no one ever will be. But, dude. Like, so close."

He smiled at me. "Thank you, Sam. I'm glad you think so because I have a feeling you and I are going to be spending quite a bit of time together for the foreseeable future."

"You want to be my friend? Okay, that's cool with me. But you have to come over to my house at least three times a week." I took him by the hand and started pulling him out of the alley, reminding him that he still hadn't told me what a succubus was and that we'd really need to come up with code names for each other, like Wolf Fighter and Star Explosion. He told me he already had his code name in Morgan of Shadows. And then he said that one day I'd have my own code name and everyone would know it. I asked him how old he was. He said two hundred and forty-seven. I told him I knew he was so old.

The next day, there was a package delivered from the castle. Pink, pointy shoes in just my size. I wore them every day. I also wore the ugliest mittens that Mrs. Kirkpatrick made especially for me for getting her cloth back. They were hideous and I showed them to everyone.

Three days after the shoe delivery, we were moved into the castle and I became the apprentice to the King's Wizard. My mom worked in the King's garden and tended to as many flowers as her heart desired. My father was given a position in the forestry service, reporting directly to the King. When All Hallowed Day came the next winter, he was put in charge of the gift giving and every child in the slums was given a carved wooden toy.

To say it caused an uproar is a bit of an understatement. A boy from the slums who would become the next King's Wizard. A family plucked from obscurity and made the faces of the ideal dream. Some people were happy for us.

Others resented us completely and fully. Still others were jealous of the position I was in, having trained years upon years to be considered in the position of Morgan's apprentice.

But I was blissfully unaware of all the talk because I was too busy being kickass and learning magic, and it wasn't until I turned thirteen that I realized I hadn't felt the need to wish upon the stars in a very long time.

CHAPTER 3
Face Full of Sass

WE STROLLED triumphantly back into the City of Lockes, only a day after Lartin the Dark Leaf met his gross end in a cave in the Dark Woods.

Pete was on duty at the castle gates. He'd gotten older and fatter, there were lines around his eyes, and his hair was mostly gone. But he was still the best castle guard ever.

"Oh, you are in so much trouble," he said when we came into sight.

Okay, maybe not the best ever. Like eighth best.

"Hush, my good man," I told him. "I'm strolling in. *Triumphantly.*"

"Yeah. You were supposed to be *strolling in* here two days ago."

"Bah."

"You gonna tell me what happened?"

"Not in the slightest."

"Morgan is going to have your head."

"Told you he was gonna be pissed," Gary said as he came to a stop in front of Pete. Pete pulled out some bits of apple that he always saved for Gary. "You're my favorite," Gary told him. "Sam got captured again."

Pete smiled wildly.

"You fickle bitch," I said. "Everyone's your favorite when they give you something."

"Can't hear you," Gary said through a mouthful of apple. "Too busy eating deliciousness that was saved just for me."

"I want apple," Tiggy said, and so Pete pulled a Marcanian Red out of his pack. It was the size of his hand, and I knew he'd brought it specifically for Tiggy. Tiggy grinned and took it from him. "I love you, tiny human." Tiggy patted Pete's head before biting the apple in half, core and all. "I save Sam from capture."

"I'm glad you all are so easily swayed by fruit," I said with a glare. "Your loyalties are shockingly disloyal."

"Morgan wanted to see you as soon as you got back," Pete said. "You know how much he hates waiting."

"Scale of one to I'm-fucked?" I asked.

"Eh," Pete said. "Beyond fucked, maybe?"

I groaned. "Not my fault."

"It never is," Pete assured me. "Best get in and get it over with."

"You'll protect me, won't you?" I asked him, giving him the big eyes.

"Get in there," he said with a grin. "I'll see you later for dinner at the castle. Supposed to be some big to-do tonight."

I hadn't heard anything about a feast before I'd left the week before. It was a good thing we'd gotten back when we did. If I'd missed the celebration, it would have reflected badly on Morgan. "For what?"

Pete shrugged. "Promotions, I think. Of the knights. Maybe a certain knight in particular?"

And my mouth went dry and I'm pretty sure I had half a boner. "Sweet molasses," I breathed.

"Priorities," Gary reminded me before glancing back at Pete. "Sam said he doesn't have time for a boyfriend, much less Knight Delicious Face."

"Remind me why you call him that?" Pete asked.

"Uh, pretty simple, Pete," I said. "He's a knight. And his face is delicious."

"And you've told him this?"

I found the ground interesting to look at. "Shut up, Pete. I don't care. Shut up. I don't even know you. So shut up with your mouth."

"Sam a sad Sam," Tiggy said succinctly.

"Sam," Pete said kindly. "Maybe you should just take a chance, you know? What's the worst that could happen?"

I laughed bitterly. "Um. The worse thing that could happen is that he would laugh in my face and then hit me with his shield and knock me to the ground and then step on me as he walked by me."

They all stared at me.

"What? You said the *worst*. He doesn't even know my name!"

Gary snorted. It came out blue and yellow this time. "I'm pretty sure he does. You're next in line for King's Wizard. *Everyone* knows who you are. And then there's the fact that you both live in the same castle and see each other every day when we're here. And the fact that there's pining involved."

"That doesn't mean he *knows* me! He doesn't even say hi to me at all!"

"That's because you run far when he show his face near your face," Tiggy said.

"That is not even remotely true."

"I hope not," Pete said. "Because here he comes right now."

I had run twenty feet before I realized he was lying. I turned and they were all laughing at me.

"You assholes," I said with a scowl. "We need to go see Morgan. I want to get the yelling out of the way so I can sleep for hours and hours."

"Think about it!" Pete called after us. "You're not getting any younger."

"Fuck yourself!" I called back sweetly.

YEAH, MORGAN was pissed.

My arrival was announced as soon as I entered the gates of Castle Lockes. I tried to get the announcer to shut his face, but he had already blown his horn and yelled out my name, so I instead focused on tamping down the urge to shove said horn down his throat.

It took Morgan less than twenty seconds to come storming into the lobby of the throne room. I was dutifully impressed, especially when he came in with long red robes flowing, looking all kinds of badass. I told him as much as I looked down at my road-weary clothes, trousers and boots covered in dust. My jerkin was torn at the sleeves. I was not presenting very well. No wonder people were giving me weird looks.

"Two days, Sam," he said, voice flat.

"And I am aware of that," I said. "And I have a perfectly good explanation."

"Oh really?" he said, cocking an eyebrow. "It wouldn't potentially have anything to do with the fact that there's a dead Dark wizard in a cave in the Dark Woods?"

I winced. "Ah. Huh. I was kind of hoping news would not travel that fast and I would have a chance to totally lie to you about not being captured."

He looked unimpressed. He pulled it off very well.

"In his defense," Gary said, "Lartin was a jerk who called me a horse and bound us with vermilion root so he totally deserved to be smashed to bits."

"Not helping," I muttered.

"I smash him good," Tiggy said. "He look like squashed tomato."

"He was monologuing!" I said to Morgan. "You know how I feel about villains *monologuing*. Seriously, just do what you're going to do and stop telling people about it."

Morgan rubbed his head like he was getting a headache. Which, to be fair, he often did around me. So I was completely unsure if he *actually* was getting a headache or if it was more of a Sam, You Suck kind of thing. "My life," he muttered. "This is my life. I chose this to be my life. By choice."

We all smiled at him because he was so lucky and he totally knew it.

He sighed. "Here's what we're going to do. You're going to hand over the wormwood because I'm assuming you wouldn't show your face back here unless you got it. You're going to go see your parents, and then you're going to bathe and sleep because you look like shit. You are going to wake up quiet and refreshed and you will stay as such as we attend the feast tonight. You will stay in my sight at all times, and tomorrow, I will kick your ass. And then we'll figure out what to do in case the Darks seek any kind of retribution for the fact that one of their own is dead. Do we have an understanding?"

"Mostly," I said. "I'm not so sure about the ass-kicking part—"

He arched a dangerous eyebrow.

"Complete," I said. "Complete understanding. I'm so understanding, I can't even get more understanding than I am right now."

"Good." He reached out and grabbed my neck, pulling our foreheads together. I felt our magic mingle, and I breathed a sigh of relief. It felt so good to be home. "I'm glad you're back," he said quietly. He pulled away and turned to Gary to rub his right ear in the way that made his back leg shake and kick. Gary sighed happily, and Morgan asked Tiggy to come with him because he wanted to show him something in the lab. Tiggy took the wormwood from the pack on Gary and muttered quietly to Morgan as they disappeared through a stone archway that led toward the lower quarters of the castle where our laboratory was.

Gary yawned, ears flicking back and forth. "I'm gonna head to bed. Tell your mom and dad I'll see them tonight." He pressed his snout to my cheek and I protested the wet kiss, but only because that's what we did. It wasn't so much a secret that I secretly loved it.

"Later," I told him, and he went the opposite direction.

I went through the throne room, where tables were being set up in preparation for that night's feast. Festive lanterns were being hung overhead, greens and yellows. Blues and reds. People bustled back and forth. They called out to me in greeting, and I waved tiredly as I pushed through toward the gardens at the back of the castle.

I knew my parents would have today off, and since it was not yet eleven, they'd be out in the garden, Mom drinking her tea and Dad stretching out in the sun. If anyone had earned it, it was them, so I was happy to see I wasn't too far off the mark when I went back out into the sunshine.

Well, Mom wasn't drinking tea, and Dad wasn't relaxing in the grass. They were both sitting at an iron table glaring at me.

"Dammit," I muttered. I fixed a big smile on my face and waved at them. "Hey, guys! Fancy meeting you here."

Mom was not amused. She stood up and stalked toward me. She at least had the decency to check me over first to make sure I wasn't injured before she injured me by smacking me upside the head. "To be fair," I told her, "it wasn't my fault."

"It never is," she said, lips in a thin line, dark eyes flashing. I took more after her in looks with dark hair and eyes, but I was caught in between her and Dad in skin color. My mother was olive and my father was snow, and I was somewhere in between, like I'd been in sunlight all my life. But I was tall like him, though I decidedly lacked the bulk he carried around, no matter how hard I tried to build it up.

"Gary said I was skinny and adorable," I told her because I'd just remembered. "I told him I was muscular and dangerous."

She rolled her eyes as Dad came to stand beside her. "You are skinny," she said in that melodious accent of hers, words falling out of her mouth like musical notes. "And you *are* adorable, but I still would like to wring your neck."

"Aww," I said. "I love you too."

"Not funny." Dad scowled. "We were worried."

"You know I can handle myself," I said, trying to keep any and all hurt out of my voice. They were my parents. They were supposed to worry. "I'm not a little boy anymore."

"We know," Dad said. "But that doesn't matter. We're going to worry no matter how old you are. Especially when you get yourself captured. Again."

"Gods," I marveled. "How fast does news travel around here? This *just* happened!"

"And a Dark?" Mom asked. "Seriously, Sam? When are you going to learn?"

"Hey! I learned! I learned so hard."

"Gary and Tiggy all right?" Dad asked, because they were family as much as I was.

I nodded. "With all their pieces attached and everything."

"You need a haircut," Mom said, changing the subject and causing me emotional whiplash. But she was right. It was getting to that point where it was starting to curl over the tops of my ears and I looked like I was twelve years old.

"I'll have it buzzed before I come back down," I assured them. "Gotta look my best, you know? Speaking of, I need to go crash for a few hours because I am pretty sure I look like death."

They both got this gleam in their eyes at the same time and I knew I was about to get a face full of sass. "Oh, that's *right*," Mom said with an evil smile. "There's that *thing* tonight."

"For the *knights*," Dad said. "For a *specific* knight."

"I am going to ask that the King grant me a secession from your parentage," I warned them both. "He will say yes because he thinks I'm wicked awesome and I'm the future King's Wizard. And then I will curse you both so hard. You'll have extra fingers. Coming out of your faces."

"Make sure you wear that red tunic tonight," Mom said, ignoring me completely. "It brings out your eyes and skin so well. And those tailored black pants. Shine your boots."

"And don't buzz your hair totally," Dad said. "Leave some length. Makes you look more distinguished."

"For the feast," I said, because I refused to believe my parents were attempting to pimp me out.

"Yes," they both said, "for the feast." Totally pimping.

"So many curses," I mumbled. I hugged them both and promised I'd see them later that night. I turned and headed back into the castle, wondering if I'd have enough time to grab something to eat, but deciding against it in favor of sleep.

So there I was: looking like crap with what I'm sure were large bags under my eyes and dirt smearing my face. Grumbling to myself about parents and Morgan and best friends who got snarky and murdered evil wizards to protect me. Yawning so wide that my jaw cracked.

Of course, since I was looking my absolute worst and talking to myself like a crazy person, I ran into the one person I didn't want to run into. Ever. Well, that's a lie. I totally wanted to run into him while I looked absolutely amazing and he'd say something like "Hey, Sam, I have this extraordinary fascination with your equipment. Let's go somewhere and I'll show you what it feels like to have your balls worshipped."

But there was no sexy running-into. There was a flail of limbs and a questionably manly squawk as my face collided with a chest undoubtedly built from pieces of my dreams, and a surprised grunt that fell from lips that angels themselves must have had a hand in creating.

Knight Ryan Foxheart. Soon to be Knight Commander Ryan Foxheart. The dreamiest dream to have ever been dreamed. The current holder of all my masturbatory fantasies. ("Oh, who's a bad knight? *You're* a bad knight. You've been so bad that I'm going to joust with your butthole.")

He said in a surprised voice, "Sam."

So I said, "Meep," because apparently Knight Delicious Face *knew my name* and any and all command of the Veranian language was gone at such an impossible thought. It made me have *feelings*. Massive, throbbing *feelings*.

"You okay?" he asked, sounding worried, and I thought that maybe if he had one flaw, it was that his voice wasn't as deep as what someone of his size and stature should have. But then I remembered that it was the most perfect voice I'd ever heard, and he was always so *soft* and *quiet* that it didn't matter to me in the slightest.

And, of course, that's when I realized my face was still pressed against his chest because he was a single step above where I stood and that he smelled *amazing*, like sweat and metal and horses and hay and grass and leaves and fires, and I really needed to stop doing that before we had an inappropriate situation on our hands. So, in a move graced with pitch-perfect dignity, I pulled back sharply, slipped on the stairs, and fell onto the stone ground, knocking my head a bit. Because my life couldn't get any more embarrassing.

"Holy crap," Ryan said from somewhere above me.

I opened my eyes and things were slightly fuzzy around the edges. But then my world was filled with the most beautiful green eyes to have ever greened. A lock of hair hung down on his forehead, and I knew I must have been rattled because I was giving very serious consideration to reaching up and brushing it away. I mastered control of my faculties just in time to stop my hand from moving, but that desperate action left all my brain function on my arm and away from my mouth. Which is the only explanation for why I said in a breathy whisper, "You are way too pretty to exist in this world with us mere mortals." I somehow managed to stop myself from calling him Knight Delicious Face. It was close.

And he *smiled*. Like I had *amused him*. There were full-on white teeth just *inches* from my face, and the corners of his eyes crinkled so endearingly that I wanted to wax poetically about his every feature so that he'd smile at me for the rest of our lives. Bards would be singing his praises for *centuries* by the time I was done with him.

"Think you hit your head," he said, and I felt his breath on my face. He must have had eggs and coffee for breakfast and there is no reason why that smell should have been as hot as it was. I would never be able to have that combination again without going full mast. He had *ruined* breakfast for me *forever*.

And we just *stared* at each other, faces so close. I was a magical being, so I had no qualms admitting that the moment was *magical*.

Which is why it ended less than seven seconds later when another voice said, "*There* you are. I've been looking all over for you. What the hell are you doing on the floor?"

I closed my eyes and reminded myself of my place.

Because I *had* a place.

And it most certainly wasn't near the level of the man behind Ryan.

Prince Justin descended the stairs.

Prince Justin, the King's only son.

Prince Justin, the future King for whom I would serve as the King's Wizard.

Prince Justin, who looked like he was carved from marble by the loving hands of a true artist. All severe lines and planes and muscle and perfectly coifed brown curls that fell ever so elegantly across his head as if they had nothing better to do than make sure Prince Justin looked better than anyone else.

Prince Justin, Ryan Foxheart's boyfriend.

Prince Justin, who *abhorred* me.

"Well, look who it is," Justin said, sounding like he'd just stepped in a pile of dog shit. "Surprise, surprise. Another fine mess you've got yourself into, eh, Sam? The *stories* we hear about your negligence are just *astounding.*"

I opened my eyes and Ryan was still above me, but the smile was gone, replaced by a frown. I wanted to tell him to bring the eye-crinkles back because they were so nice, but I somehow managed to keep that little tidbit to myself. Justin could have me executed. And if there is one thing I didn't want, it was to be executed.

"Leave him alone, Justin," Ryan said. "It was my fault. I wasn't watching where I was going."

And that was a big fat lie. Which was awesome.

Ryan pulled himself away, and I wanted to tell him to come back and make Justin leave, but then I thought of my head being chopped off and so I let him go.

I was surprised when he extended a hand down to me and watched me with an earnest expression.

Fuck Justin. This is all I would ever get, so I was going to take it. I reached up and his fingers circled my wrist. His skin was so warm, his palms callused and rough. His grip tightened on me and he pulled, the muscles in his forearm flexing in a way that was stupidly attractive. He pulled me up until I stood before him, and I didn't think I'd ever been this close to him before. I was terribly amused to see I was taller than him by an inch or two, and the fact that he had to look up at me to meet my eyes would no doubt play a further part in my You've Been A Bad Knight scenario as soon as I got to my bed.

I am going to masturbate to you so hard later, I thought while looking at him. I blushed then because I realized that made me super creepy and I didn't feel sorry about it at all.

It was about that time that I realized at least a minute had passed and we were still standing very close to each other. He hadn't let go of my wrist, and I swear he was about to say something when Justin coughed sarcastically behind him. I pulled my arm back quickly and took three steps back, putting a respectable distance between us.

"Are you quite finished, Sam?" Justin asked. "You look just awful. Maybe you should consider cleaning yourself up before you show your face again. I don't want people thinking my Wizard is from the slums."

I ground my teeth together. "I *am* from the slums." I avoided looking at Ryan. I didn't want to see the pity that was probably on his face. I wasn't ashamed of where I'd come from. In fact, I was proud of it. And no one, not even Justin, could make me feel like shit because of it.

He arched an eyebrow.

"My lord," I added.

"Well. I suppose as someone who was plucked from dirt and obscurity and essentially handed *everything*, you wouldn't understand the trials and tribulations of royalty."

"Yes, my lord." *You horse's ass.*

"I think that's enough," Ryan said. I glanced quickly at him and that angry frown had returned. Justin had come to stand right next to him. Their fingers were intertwined, and I was embarrassed. Ryan had probably had it with me taking time away from him and the Prince, so I took another step backward. I didn't want to go to my room. I wanted to go see Gary and bitch and moan and braid his mane and have him tell me that Justin was a giant cockfucker and I was so much prettier than him.

"Sorry," I muttered. "I'll just...."

And I turned to leave.

"Sam."

I stopped and closed my eyes. I was tense as I took a deep breath because that was the second time he'd said my name and it was just awesome, but it made walking away all that much harder, and I wished at that moment that I'd never heard of Ryan Foxheart.

I plastered a fake smile on my face as I turned back around. "Yes?"

He was watching me, so I lowered my eyes and stared at my feet. "Are you going to be there tonight? There's this... thing. At the feast?"

And what the hell was *that*? I looked back up at him in surprise. He was staring resolutely at me. Justin was rolling his eyes and looked extraordinarily bored. "Yes?" I said. "Yes. Uh. I sort of have to be. Like. It's required. Because of the whole. You know. *Wizard* thing."

Ryan coughed. "Oh. Okay. Good. Because of the wizard thing. So."

Wow. Did I sound like an asshole. "Not that I don't want to go," I said hurriedly. "I totally do. Want to go. For the feast. And the other stuff. With the promotion? That you got? Oh, and good job, you." I gave him two thumbs-up, and I just *cringed* at how awkward I was.

"As enlightening as all of this is," Justin said, "Ryan and I have plans. This is a big day after all. Not that you knew anything about it seeing as how you can't even be bothered to return when you're supposed to. There's going to be some changes when I become King. Big changes."

So that was a threat. I gave very serious thought to hexing Justin so that his face melted, but was somehow able to restrain myself. "My apologies, my lord, for taking up your invaluable time." I bowed again and hurried (read: ran) away.

"AND HE was just so *amazing*," I said as I braided Gary's hair. "Like so selfless and awesome and he smelled like leaves and I think his eyebrows should be declared a treasure of the Kingdom."

"Oh my gods," Gary muttered. "This has been going on for forty-seven minutes."

"Did I tell you he *knew my name*?"

"Sixteen times."

"Oh. He said it *twice*."

"Holy fuck on a stick."

"He is." I sighed.

"What happened to your priorities?"

"I still have them," I said, weaving a strand of crocus my mother had grown through the braid. They were purple and matched the dye I'd put in before I started braiding. "I just like looking at nice things. And want to touch them with my mouth."

"You want to lick his balls," Gary said, just to see me sputter and flush brightly.

"Shut up," I managed to say, pulling the braid tightly and causing him to wince.

"I don't see why you don't just tell him."

"That I want to lick his balls?" I squeaked.

"Among other things."

"Um. Because he's dating the Prince? My future King? That in itself should be reason enough for me to never open my mouth in front of him again."

"Honey, you'll never know unless you try," Gary said quietly. "I have a feeling you'd be surprised by the answers you get."

I scowled at him. "Look. I know what you're trying to do. What all of you are trying to do. Okay? I get it. But it's not funny anymore. He's with the Prince. Who can offer him things I would never be able to. Justin is a prick, but he's gorgeous and super rich and has an epic nose and I'm sure his penis is just gargantuan. He's also going to be the fucking king and I'm a lowly wizard's apprentice who can't even stop himself from getting captured every time he's allowed to go out into the world on his own. And I would *never* do that to anyone. Hurt them like that. It's wrong. And you talk like there's a chance. But there hasn't ever been one, so I'm going sit here with my funny little dreams that are going to *stay* dreams, and one day I'll be over it because I was able to do it on my own." I was breathing heavily by the time I'd finished and my hands were shaking.

Gary turned his head and pressed his nose against my cheek. "Oh, sweetheart," he sighed. "You are so much more than you give yourself credit for. I promise you: you're destined for great things, because all those wishes on the stars you made will finally come true. And you'll meet a man who will sweep you off your feet and you won't even be able to remember Ryan Foxheart."

"Yeah," I muttered. I twisted the final braid. "All done."

"How do I look?" Gary asked, posing obscenely.

"Like the fiercest unicorn who ever lived," I said honestly.

"You're too good to me," Gary said. "Now, I want you to get some sleep. You okay to get to your room?"

I shrugged and looked at my fingers. There was purple dye on the tips.

"You just want to stay here with me?"

I shrugged again because I totally wanted to stay with Gary.

So Gary curled himself around me, and I put my head near his throat. He whispered sweet things in my ear until I drifted off. And when I dreamed, I dreamt of stars.

CHAPTER 4
I'd Swallow Anything for You

"HOT *DAMN*, boy," Gary crowed as I entered the throne lobby. "You looking *fine*."

And I was. After pouting and bitching to Gary and generally feeling sorry for myself, I decided that was complete and utter bullshit. I was awesome and epic and no one had a right to make me feel like crap, not even Prince Justin. So I decided to go all out.

My hair was too floppy on my head, so I'd sat in front of the mirror and sheared off the sides, buzzing it close to my scalp. I left some length on the top and spiked it up with a soft rubber that I'd bought at Market. By the time I'd finished, my neck looked longer, my cheekbones higher. My eyes brighter. I winked at myself in the mirror and then realized that's what douchebags did, so I vowed to never do it again.

I pulled on the black trousers that showed off my ass. And apparently my balls, because they were that tight. I wondered just how many awkward conversations that would lead to.

I wore the red jerkin Mom had suggested, cinching it tight at the waist. The sleeves clung to my shoulders and arms.

I shined the fuck out of the boots.

Needless to say, I looked like a high-end prostitute when I was summoned from my room.

"I would let you stay the night and then have you for breakfast," Gary said.

"That is… strangely nice," I admitted. "Thank you. I would also have you for breakfast as well."

He sighed. "Too bad you're like my older sister. We could have been something special."

I narrowed my eyes at him. "*Older*? You're seventy-six!"

"Boo, you whore," he said. "Now it's your turn to tell me how amazing I look." He pranced around me in a tight circle.

"You don't look seventy-six at all," I said.

He glared at me. "Try again."

"You look wonderful."

"I knew there was a reason I kept you around."

"Joy. Sustaining your ego is my life's work."

"Make sure you don't sneeze or fart tonight, okay? Your pants are so tight, I'm pretty sure they would rip. Wouldn't want Knight Delicious Face to get a sample of the goods along with everyone else."

I groaned. "If you look close enough, you can see everything. It's like I'm an advertisement for circumcision."

He looked closely. It was very disconcerting to have your gay unicorn best friend studying your penis that intensely. Finally, he gave his verdict. "It's a very nice penis."

"Thank you." Because it was.

"Not as big as mine, though."

"Good-bye, self-esteem and fuzzy feelings. It was so nice to make your acquaintance."

"Bah," Gary said. "Knight Delicious Face won't know what hit him."

"Uh, yeah he will. His boyfriend."

"Want me to trample him?"

"As awesome as premeditated murder of royalty would be, I don't feel like causing the death of the King-in-waiting. That just might be against the law. Or something."

"I can make it look like an accident," he said. "I've done it before."

"Remind me never to piss you off."

"You piss me off all the time."

"To the point of murder," I amended.

"I would never kill you," he assured me. "Maim. But never murder."

"Most people think you're sweet and fluffy. It's all lies." The throne room sounded crowded, if the noise from the other side of the Great Doors meant anything. I tried to peek through the doors, but I couldn't see anything. Damn superior craftsmanship.

"Just tell me when," Gary said. "I'll handle the rest."

"Tempting. But no. I don't even care about stupid Ryan Foxheart and his stupid gorgeous hands or his stupid perfect boyfriend. Tonight is all about me."

"So glad you think so," Morgan said, coming up from behind me. "It will certainly make things that much easier."

I turned to my mentor. He was wearing dark blue robes adorned with the King's crest stitched neatly on the back. He'd braided flowers into his beard that matched Gary's. They were absolutely adorable, and I had to stop myself from pinching Morgan's cheeks and sighing at him. He didn't like it when I did that.

But wait. "What will go easier tonight?" I narrowed my eyes at him.

He shrugged. "You did say tonight was all about you. I'm sure something will come along to help facilitate your desire."

"Morgan, I swear to the gods if you've—"

Shifty wizard was shifty. "Oh look. We're being called in."

And we were. The Great Doors opened and horns blared and the throne room fell silent. A thousand pair of eyes rested upon us. I always hated this part.

We walked down the center of the throne room, an embroidered red carpet at our feet. Above, the lanterns glowed brightly, the walls covered in banners red and blue, the colors of the Knights of Verania.

Mom and Dad sat near the front, Tiggy next to them at the end, towering over everyone else. They all grinned at me, and Tiggy said, "I like your trousers," quite loudly, which of course caused me to blush and almost trip over my own feet as titters rose up around me, along with a few appreciative looks. Luckily, Gary was prancing regally next to me and I dropped a hand to the slope of his neck.

Morgan just rolled his eyes.

I'd done this countless times before. Stood in front of large crowds. I didn't know why this time was making me feel as awkward as it was. Maybe it was because I had more eyes on me than normal. I tried to think of a way to subtly cover my crotch without bringing attention to it, but came up blank.

The knights entered in next from doors on either side of the throne room. They lined the outer edges of the room, armor shining and bright, shields polished and swords sharpened. I didn't see Ryan, but I obviously wasn't even looking for him at all, so it didn't matter.

"He'll come in after the King," Morgan whispered to me.

"I have no idea who you're talking about," I whispered back.

"He's lying," Gary whispered. "You can tell because he's sweaty."

And before I could respond with what I'm sure would have been a devastatingly witty retort ("Your whole *body* is sweaty!"), the crowd rose to their feet, and the knights snapped to attention as Good King Anthony of Verania and his son, Grand Prince Justin of Verania, were announced.

"He's not *that* grand," I muttered.

"Mediocre at best," Gary agreed. "His hair is pretty fabulous, though."

"Yeah, if you like that sort of thing."

"Most people like hair," Morgan said. "His is curly and dreamy. Now shut up."

The King was wearing long flowing robes made of the finest materials with red and blue jewels sewn into the edges. The crown on his head was uniformly gaudy and ridiculous: gold and diamonds and rubies and sapphires. He'd let me hold it once when he'd gotten drunk off of apple wine. It weighed like fourteen pounds. That coupled with the five-foot-long scepter, and he looked like he should own a couple of brothels rather than be a king. He'd laughed so hard when I told him that after *I'd* gotten drunk on apple wine. It's not every day someone called him a pimp. And apple wine is deceptively strong.

He saw me waiting next to Morgan and winked at me as he approached the throne. Naturally, not really knowing my place at all, I winked back salaciously. I could appreciate the older man. I had eyes, after all. He was all tall and barrel-chested and rocked a mustache that curled at the ends. Gary and I agreed he was a total KILF.

"Sam," he said as he stood in front of his people. "Glad you made it back in one piece."

"Was there ever any doubt, my liege?" I said.

He grinned. "With you? One can never be too sure."

"You wound me."

"Nah. I'm pretty sure Morgan will take care of that for me. I thought I heard him muttering about tanning your hide when you finally got back."

"There will be a suitable punishment," Morgan agreed.

"I should have stayed in that cave."

"And Gary," the King said warmly. "You are like the sun on an otherwise dreary day."

"Your mustache looks like it would tickle," Gary said. "It's gotten longer."

"And thicker," the King said.

"I am so grossed out right now," I said. "I never really got the flirting thing."

"That much is obvious," Gary said.

"I meant between the two of you. Someone certainly rolled in a pile of sass before they came to the feast today."

"It's merely a mutual agreement on each other's aesthetic attributes," the King said.

"That and the fact that you are like a walking daddy fetish," Gary said.

Justin made a strange noise next to the King, and I looked up to see him glaring at us. Specifically me. I smiled back. His scowl deepened.

"Maybe we should move on to the reason we're here?" Morgan said, not unkindly. It was probably for the best. We tended to get distracted very easily, even if there were a thousand people staring up at us, no doubt listening to every word we'd said.

So the King stood before his subjects and gave a long and winding speech about unity and love and the power of Verania, blah, blah, something, something. I'd heard it a billion times before so it was easy to tune out. I scanned the crowd, picking out familiar faces, friends and enemies alike. Not everyone in Verania appreciated magic. Some went so far as to see it as a thing of evil, a demon's gift, but they were few and far between. We lived in a more modern age of science and free love.

But there were a lot of faces that I didn't expect to see. Usually, it was the old and rich, the top tier of society with their fancy clothes and sticky perfumes.

And some of them were there.

But much of the crowd was younger than normal.

And much of them were male.

The sons of the old and rich.

Something wasn't quite right.

It wasn't until I heard the King say Ryan's name that I listened back in, because he was saying things like *brave* and *selfless* and *kind* and *caring* and how at twenty-five, Ryan would be the youngest Knight Commander in history. "He is the true definition of knighthood," King Anthony said. "From his peers to his superiors—"

"And your penis," Gary whispered to me.

I quietly kicked him in the leg. He snorted out orange sparkles.

"—Knight Foxheart has been constantly commended and singled out for his courage and valor in the face of what could often be seen as insurmountable odds."

"He is definitely mountable," Gary whispered to me.

I silently punched him in the throat.

And then Knight Ryan Foxheart was announced and the crowd turned toward the Great Doors. They opened and I'm pretty sure choirs of angels were singing and at least fourteen women in the room became spontaneously pregnant because gods*damn*.

His armor was new, infused with lines of red rock across the breastplate to signify the rank of commander. His sword hung heavy at his side. His shield was strapped to his back. His eyes were wide, his hair slicked back. He was completely and truly beautiful.

"He certainly fills out that uniform," Gary whispered.

"I'd like to fill him out," I whispered back because my resolve to get over him had gone by way of fickle wind. Which was to say I wanted to tap that ass because he was hot like fire.

Morgan kicked us both.

Ryan walked with grace and confidence, but I'd been watching him for a long time. The tense line of his jaw. His hands curled at his sides. The tiniest stutter in his steps.

He was *nervous*.

And it was *adorable*.

And for some reason, his eyes were on *me*.

And they stayed on me until he stood before the King.

Because of course they did.

I didn't even know what to do with that. I'm pretty sure I was sweating in my tight trousers. "Today has been so weird," I side-whispered to Gary.

"I think the word you're looking for is erotic," he said back. "Today has been so erotic."

And then Ryan looked toward the King and knelt on one knee, bowing his head.

"He looks good like that," Gary murmured in my ear. "Right where he belongs."

I choked on my tongue. And spit. And air. And coughed quite loudly. It echoed around the stone throne room.

Every single person in the room turned to look at me.

"Sorry," I said to everyone with a little wave. "Sorry. Bug flew in my mouth. Unavoidable. My bad. Please continue with the… knight. Thing."

Gary snickered.

Justin was not amused.

My parents had buried their faces in their hands.

Tiggy was giving me a thumbs-up.

Morgan looked resigned to his fate.

King Anthony glanced at me fondly.

And Ryan's eyes were still trained on the ground, but I saw him fighting back a smile. I wanted to tell him I'd swallow anything for him just to see him smile, but I realized that didn't sound promotion-ceremony appropriate, so I managed to bite it back down and instead thought of what spell I could use to modify everyone's memories to forget the last four minutes had ever happened. I didn't know if we had any eye of eagle back in the lab. I thought we'd used the last of it after that thing with the fire geckos. Fucking fire geckos.

Eventually, everyone looked away from me, convinced I wasn't about to do anything else completely stupid.

King Anthony turned back to Ryan and pulled his sword and by the power of the Kingdom of Verania and words, words, words, he now decreed Knight Ryan

Foxheart to be Knight Commander Ryan Foxheart, in charge of the Eighth Battalion, and didn't *that* make my heart stutter a bit. Because the Eighth were kept close to the castle to ensure the safety of His Highness. The Castle Guard of the King. Of the Prince.

And of the King's Wizard.

And any apprentice said Wizard would have.

I was so completely and utterly fucked.

Because this was an oath to the King. An oath was the most important thing a knight could ever do. It meant that he was giving his life over to those he pledged to. Oaths were rarely broken and if they were, it was only done because of extraordinary circumstances. Essentially, Ryan was giving everything to the King, everything that made him who he was. And since I was technically an extension of the Crown, he was doing the same for me.

Mostly.

And so everyone stood and cheered for Knight Commander Ryan Foxheart and he gave that goofy grin of his, the one that was crooked and sweet and caused my heart to do a weird little dance in my chest. Especially since it was directed at me for some reason. I decided right then that his jawline was fantastic and that his forehead was the best forehead to have ever forehead. And also? Muscles. (Not that I could see them under the knight's armor, but I had a very vivid imagination and I was not ashamed to use it.) The smile faded as he turned toward the cheering crowd.

Then the King decided to drop two bombshells in such quick succession that I'm pretty sure it caused everyone within a four-mile radius to collectively shit themselves.

The first?

The King said, "And I am so very happy to say that just this afternoon, my only son, Grand Prince Justin of Verania, asked for the hand of our new Knight Commander in marriage. And I could not have given my blessing more proudly. Once Prince Justin assumes the throne, Ryan will be the King Consort of Verania."

Everyone gasped.

Gary said, "The *fuck*?"

My parents looked upset.

Tiggy looked murderous.

The Prince smiled widely.

Morgan was frowning.

Ryan's face went completely and utterly slack.

And it was *silent*.

So, being the bigger person that I am, I decided to break the silence even as my own heart was breaking. Because that's what awesome people do. They step the fuck up and make sure things go right. So I said, "Yaaay."

It came out sounding like I didn't mean that at all.

I took a different approach.

I slow clapped.

No one joined me. They obviously didn't know how slow clapping worked.

I cleared my throat.

Tried again. "Hurrrraaaaaaay." It was a little more believable.

I slow clapped some more.

And glared quite viciously.

Eventually, people got the idea and joined in. The applause wasn't as resounding as it should have been, but what the fuck did I know. I was too busy writing sad ballads to unrequited love in my head and planning a life where my hand would be my boyfriend.

That is until the King made his second proclamation.

Of doom.

His smile was downright gleeful. "And luckily enough, our very own Sam of Wilds returned just in time for tonight's festivities. Given the romantic mood of late, I've secretly been putting out my feelers and have invited some of the City of Lockes' most eligible bachelors so that he himself may be as lucky in love as my son and future son-in-law. Immediately following the feast, the ballroom will open and we shall dance the night away, all in the name of romance. You better hurry, boys! I'm sure tonight his dance card is going to fill up rather quickly. I mean, have you seen those pants he's wearing? If only I swung that way, I'd snatch him up myself!" He chuckled loudly, obviously pleased with himself.

That asshole.

The audience gasped again.

And some of them *leered* at me. With their *bodies*.

Gary said, "The *fuck*?"

My parents looked shocked.

Tiggy looked confused.

The Prince was positively *beaming*.

Morgan watched me warily.

And Ryan?

Well.

He stood. Took a step toward me. Stopped. Hung his head.

Someone in the audience said, "Yaaaay."

And then started slow clapping.

CHAPTER 5
I Don't Want to Dance with Your Dead Grandma's Ashes

"YOU *KNEW* about this?" I seethed at Morgan after dragging him out of the throne room, Gary and Tiggy trailing behind me. "Are you out of your fucking *mind*?"

"I am positive I have no idea what you speak of," Morgan said. "And even if I *did*, you were the one that said tonight was going to be all about *you*."

"What happened?" Tiggy asked.

"The King wants Sam to get covered in man juice," Gary said.

"Oh," Tiggy said. "Your flower gonna get eaten?"

"Nobody is taking my flower!"

"And no one ever will if you keep calling it that," Gary pointed out.

"Not the time," I growled. I turned my glare back to Morgan. "You. *You*. You are in so much trouble, I don't even have *words* for how much trouble you're in."

"And yet, you seem to be finding enough words for all of us," Morgan said.

"I am not in the mood for your shenanigans!"

Morgan sighed. "Is it really that bad? The King just wants you to be happy. He's pleased with what Justin has, and you know he thinks of you as family. He wants the same for you."

"What about you? You've been his wizard for his entire *reign*. And for his *father's*. Why don't *you* have to do it?"

Morgan shrugged. "Simple. I'm asexual."

I blinked. "What?"

"Asexual. I don't find the act of sex appealing. I'd much rather have the emotional connections I do have, not the intimate ones I do without."

I nodded. "Yep. Sounds good. I'm asexual too. Let's go announce that right now so this whole night will be over and done with." I made to march back into the throne room, but Morgan snagged me by the collar and pulled me back in.

"You're not asexual, Sam."

"Don't judge me! You can't tell me how to live my life! Let me spread my beautiful wings so I can *fly*."

"He's not asexual," Gary told Morgan. "He has wet dreams and moans dirty things about chest hair."

"That was *one* time." Okay, more like six times.

"More like six times," Gary said, and I decided we seriously needed to set up some personal boundaries.

"You vile betrayer."

"Ryan Foxheart naked while lying in a vat of fruit and cream," Gary said.

"Whoa," I breathed, because *whoa*. Then I shook my head. "Dammit."

"It was way too easy," Gary said.

"And did you know about *that*?" I demanded of Morgan.

"No," Morgan said quietly. "Sam, I would never do that to you. I know that… certain feelings… run deeper than others. I was just as surprised as you. By right, the King does not need to seek my counsel in everything."

"Pfft," I scoffed. "Feelings. I don't have *feelings*."

I had so many feelings. None of them were good.

And then Morgan hugged me, which was such a rare and absurd thing that I had no choice but to hug him right back. He said, "I won't force you, Sam. I told myself a long time ago that nothing for you would ever be forced. But sometimes, for the good of the Kingdom, we must make decisions we do not like. So, we can either walk and hide away in the labs, or you can stand tall and true and show all of those people in there that Sam of Wilds is not a man to be caught and tamed."

"You eloquent bastard," I groaned.

SO I did. I fixed a smile on my face and entered the throne room.

The crowds were merry and jovial, people laughing and eating and drinking. The drinking part sounded awesome, and I decided that should be a priority. For the rest of the night.

Until I bumped into a solid wall of men.

"Is this a line for the buffet?" I asked Gary.

"That's one way of putting it," he said. "If you're the buffet."

"Oh my goodness," I whispered because he was *right*. They were all lined up in front of *me*, patiently waiting for me to address the first in line so they could all get their turns. There had to at least be twenty guys waiting to talk to me.

"So much alcohol is needed in my mouth right now," I muttered.

"On it," Gary said, leaving Morgan to act as a chaperone. Apparently, being twenty years old meant nothing. My position required an elder to watch me at all times in courting situations. Which was as stupid as it sounds.

"Um, hi?" I said to the first guy in line, because they were obviously not going to leave me alone and I wanted to get this over with. He was tall and muscular with a scar going from his chin to his ear that I supposed made him look rather dashing. Too bad he was eyeing me like a piece of meat.

"Sam of Wilds," he purred, taking my hand and kissing it as he bowed. I thought I felt the flash of tongue. "I would be honored if I could be your first… dance." And then he winked. I guess it was meant to be playful and seductive, but I was pretty sure I was being molested.

"Okay, Captain Bad-Touch," I said, pulling my hand back. "That's quite enough of that."

He stepped forward and started to crowd me, and I rolled my eyes, because really? *Really*? I smiled sweetly up at him and said, "You do realize that I can turn your dick into so much running pus with just a flick of my wrist, right?" I actually really couldn't, but he didn't know that.

His eyes widened, and he took a step back.

"I don't want to dance with you because you're kind of rapey," I said. "It's the eyes."

Morgan snorted from somewhere behind me.

Captain Bad-Touch left with an angry look on his face, muttering something about me being an uptight bitch.

Rude.

The second, third, and fourth guys in line all tried to give me presents.

Morgan choked behind me as the third guy handed me his late grandmother's ashes and said, "I want you to have her because after we get married, it will be the three of us, and I want you to get used to the weight of her since she'll always be around."

"You are so epically strange," I told him.

He grinned at me and told me his grandmother liked to waltz, so she'd be dancing with us too. But then he seemed to get jealous of me and said he really didn't like it when other people danced with her.

I gave him back his grandmother and said that I didn't want to come between them, and maybe it was better if they just danced with each other. He nodded, looking relieved.

I made a mental note to find King Anthony later and kick his royal ass.

Gary came back with a bottle of apple wine and pulled me away from the crowd. I liked Gary again. I liked him even more after I slammed back two mugs full of the wine. I told him as much as Tiggy and my parents joined us.

He huffed and said, "You are such a lightweight."

I laughed because he was the funniest unicorn I knew.

He reminded me he was the *only* unicorn I knew.

I asked if I could meet his parents, and somehow that led to a ten-minute conversation about the swingers trip his parents were on, and I told him I didn't want to swing with his parents because I didn't want to end up being Gary's stepmother. I also told my parents that if I ever heard of them swinging, I would send them to the dungeons.

Mom told me she wouldn't even dream of it because she didn't want to poop in a bucket. This, of course, led to reminiscing about the good old days. Until I got distracted by something shiny.

"A man licked my hand," I told my mom and dad as the wine proceeded to loosen my lips.

Dad grimaced and said, "That doesn't sound very comfortable."

"If you had tried to lick my hand when you courted me, I would have had *mamia* throw you into a fire," Mom told him.

"So violent," I whispered. My parents were hardcore.

"Which one?" Tiggy asked. "I smash him."

"Everyone I love would kill for me," I announced loudly.

The men waiting in line winced. I heard a loud bark of laughter above the sounds of the feast and saw the King sitting with Justin and Ryan. Justin was smiling at his father, and Ryan was watching Justin. I was too far away to tell, but it was probably with love and adoration and he totally couldn't wait to get married to Justin and have his babies, who would end up being the most beautiful creatures to ever exist. They would end up taking over all of Verania and putting all the less beautiful people into camps where they'd be forced to do hard work like chopping down trees and peeling potatoes.

"And I just said all of that out loud, didn't I?" I asked when I saw my little band of misfits staring at me. They nodded and so I said, "Crap. I don't even care. Look! I'm good. I have tight pants and great hair. Nothing else matters." They were completely convinced even as I slurred my words.

"Maybe hold back on the wine for a bit?" Morgan said, taking the third cup away.

"Thank you for telling me about your asexuality," I told him seriously. "You are like my sun and moon and I want you to know we can share everything with each other. Since you told me a secret, I will tell you one. I was making stuff up that first day when I said Flora Bora Slam."

"You don't say."

"Totally off the top of my head. I know it sounded believable, but I can't go on anymore without telling you I had no idea what I was doing."

I saw his lips twitch. "Lightweight."

"I make you smile," I said in awe. "I'm going to be great at wooing Ry—a man. A man who is not a knight. And who knows I exist and appreciates my qualities and face."

"You have your work cut out for you," he assured me, turning me back around and pushing me toward the crowd.

"Yes, yes. Wouldn't want to disappoint the future Mrs. Sam of Wilds. Hello, boys! Daddy's back. You may all sigh in relief as one."

They did not sigh in relief as one. Some looked rather scared.

Being drunk made everything easier.

And I suppose it didn't hurt that the next guy in line was better than all the ones before. His name was Todd and he was an earl or a duke or something, and he said, "I would ask you to dance, but I don't know how to dance, so maybe we can just stand near each other and talk awkwardly."

I gaped at him. "Dude. Way to down sell and keep expectations realistic."

He shrugged nervously. "It's better than upselling and tripping on your feet."

He had big ears that stuck out. His hair was brown and his eyes were brown and his freckles were brown, and I told him all of this because I felt like he should know.

He said he was well aware.

I said, "Now we have to dance."

The blood drained from his face. "You're not going to send me away like the others?"

"Do you want me to?"

He gulped. "Maybe? Because awkward talking I can do. What if I accidentally trip and fall and knock you down and then you turn me into a rambunctious tea cozy?"

"Oh my gods," I said.

"You could!"

"You're scared of me!"

"Um, yes? A lot of people are scared of you. You're pretty intimidating."

I looked at Morgan, who I just *knew* was dreading what was coming. "I'm a scary badass motherfucker," I told him proudly.

Morgan sighed. "Yes, yes. Very much so."

I glanced back at Todd. "I promise I won't curse you to suffer Black Death or become a rambunctious tea cozy. While you're stepping on my feet, you can tell me all the stories people tell about me."

Todd said, "Oh no."

IT DIDN'T hurt that Gary snuck me more apple wine while Morgan wasn't looking.

"Just don't throw up on anyone," he warned me.

"Sometimes I just want to blow raspberries on your stomach to hear you neigh," I replied.

"Please don't tell anyone else that tonight," he said.

"Not even Captain Bad-Touch?"

"Especially not Captain Bad-Touch."

"I'm going to go dance," I whisper-shouted at him.

So, of course, as soon as the King opened the ball with a wave of his hand and the brash clang of horns, I stalked over to him, bowed as low as I could without falling over, and demanded he dance with me.

The King laughed, then removed his outer robe and took my hand, leading me to the dance floor.

"I like the ruffles on your shirt," I told him. "But that is the only thing I like about you right now."

He began a waltz and I was nice enough to let him lead. It was close, though.

"You're mad," he said with a kind smile.

"I think I just told you that."

"I want you to be happy."

"I *am* happy." And I was. Mostly.

"Happier," he said.

"I'm the happiest I've been."

"Are you?"

"Stop. I've been drinking. No analyzing. Did you know a man licked my hand because you told him I wanted him to take my flower?"

The King tripped but recovered gracefully, as kings are wont to do. "I can assure you that combination of words never came out of my mouth." He was turning slightly red.

"He still licked my hand."

"Who was it?"

"Captain Bad-Touch. I don't know. Scar on his face. Rapey eyes."

"Ah. That would Duke Waller of the Outer Banks. A shame, really. He came so highly recommended."

"I would recommend him for euthanasia," I said. "And I don't want to know the criteria you came up with to vet out any less desirables."

"I did nothing of the sort," the King said. "I just had your stats and the date and time of the ball written on every tavern bathroom wall within a sixty-mile radius. There was no vetting."

"Remember that one time I laughed at a joke you told?"

He grinned at me. "I do."

"This is not going to be like that time."

He laughed enough for the both of us.

I bit my lip. And then opened my mouth. "Is"—*Ryan*—"Justin happy?"

The King's smile softened. "I think so. Love can do that to a man. Just look at them."

And I did. I didn't want to, but I did. They were dancing on the other side of the floor and they moved gracefully together. They were of an even height, and I was pretty sure that Justin's hand was *almost* touching Ryan's ass, which I absolutely was not staring at. Ryan had changed out of his armor and wore white trousers and knee-high black boots, almost like he was going riding. His black jerkin stretched tight against his chest and arms. And yes, they *did* look happy. Mostly. Maybe. I couldn't quite figure out the look on Ryan's face.

Ryan must have felt us watching them because he looked over and caught my eye. He frowned again, and I looked away quickly.

"I suppose," I eventually said.

"He makes Justin happy," the King said. "And I hope Justin can do the same for him. It's been a long time since I've seen Ryan smile."

Which, odd. Because I'd seen it a few times. Earlier that night, even. And that morning.

"I still don't know what that has to do with me," I said.

The King sighed. "Sam, ever since the day Morgan brought you to the castle, I knew there was something special about you. It had nothing to do with your magic or whatever Morgan thought you would one day be. It had to do with the size of your heart. You have so much to give to people and I think you sometimes hide it behind your wit and words. I want you to find that someone who makes you feel complete, who allows you to let your guard down and just *be*."

"I have you," I said honestly. "And Morgan. And my parents and Tiggy and Gary. What more could I possibly need?"

"Someone to call your own," he said.

"I have priorities," I said weakly.

"Do this, and I'll agree to fund your proposal for more teachers being hired in the slums."

I narrowed my eyes at him. "You cheater."

He smiled at me.

The King and I danced on.

AND I did dance with a few of them. The King wanted me to try, and there was no way I'd ever let him down. Not after all he'd done for me and my family.

That didn't mean I'd let him off the hook so easily.

It was awkward and weird, and I found out I *really* hated dancing with strangers who were trying to get up in my business, so I filled in the silence with vivid descriptions of how we'd have at least ten kids and that I knew a spell that would allow us to get pregnant so we could take turns just popping out the ass babies. I'm pretty sure a couple of them all but ran by the time we'd finished. I waved after them.

And then Todd came over with his ears and nervousness, sputtering about how he couldn't even *fathom* how ass babies would work and I thought, *Okay. Okay, why not?* I was drunk and reckless and why the fuck not. I looked good (mostly). I felt good (kind of). Why the fuck not?

I said, "Dance with me." I waggled my eyebrows at him.

He flushed. "You were dancing with the *King*."

"I had to. I needed to yell at him."

He looked horrified. "You're going to lose your head!"

I rolled my eyes. "Yeah, because *that* happens so often around here."

"I can't really dance. I told you this. Remember the awkwardness? It's *awkward*."

I shrugged. "Dance with me awkwardly, then."

Maybe I thought I saw the hint of a smile. And maybe I thought it was a nice smile.

So he bowed in front of me, and I laughed at him.

He took me by the hand and led me to the floor.

From there, he seemed unsure where to put his hands.

Because I liked seeing him blush, I said, "Anywhere."

He went full-on red, but one hand went to my back and the other gripped my fingers and we moved.

He stepped on my foot.

I said, "Well, then."

I counted out the waltz.

He followed, staring down at our feet.

The song ended and another began, and I said, "You haven't run away yet."

He said, "No, sir."

He was nineteen. His parents were in the King's Court. His father was a businessman who owned hotels across Verania. They made lots of money.

He said, "So I can provide for you." He wouldn't meet my eyes as he said it.

And I laughed at him again. I told him I didn't need to be provided for. That I didn't want to be.

"What *do* you want?" he asked me curiously.

Ah. Now that was the question.

"Many things," I said, and he left it at that.

He was a better dancer than he gave himself credit for. Mostly.

But still felt... off. Because it was so *nice*. Just... nice.

The alcohol buzz was dampening. Things felt a little heavier now.

A third song was about to begin when Todd said, "Shall we—"

"Mind if I cut in?"

And I *froze*.

Todd flushed again and sputtered, "Sure. Yes. Of course, Knight Commander. My apologies." He disappeared as if he'd never been there at all.

Ryan Foxheart took his place.

His hand went to my waist and it *burned*.

His other hand took mine, and I felt every scrape of his fingers against my skin.

I could feel the heavy muscle of his arm under my touch.

This was not *nice*.

This was an inferno.

The music swelled.

We moved. I didn't have to count for him.

He said, "You've been busy all night." There was no smile on his face and a heat to his words.

And because I had enough of a buzz still going, I deflected and said, "Congratulations. On everything." The words came out light and sweet.

"Thank you. You danced with him twice."

"What?"

He moved as he always did, with beautiful precision. He was leading and I didn't even try to fight it. "The others. You sent them away after one song."

"Or they ran."

His lip twitched and the skin around his eyes crinkled slightly. "Or that. But he didn't."

"No, Todd didn't," I agreed.

"Is that his name?"

"It is. He's very nice."

"Is he?"

"Yes."

"Because you like nice."

"Perhaps."

We danced on.

"I'm not nice," Ryan said suddenly. "Not all the time."

"You're a knight," I said, because that almost meant the same thing.

"Knight Commander," he said with a glint in his eyes.

I rolled my eyes. "I'm so impressed."

"You don't sound like it."

My mind wandered. "You know, I think this is the longest conversation we've ever had."

He arched an eyebrow at me, and with that single motion, a fire burned in my belly like I'd never felt before. "And whose fault is that?"

I grinned at him. "Mine. You scare me."

"Why? Because I'm too pretty to exist in this world?" He threw my words back at me, his voice teasing and soft.

"Because you're scary," I managed to say.

His eyes never left mine. "Why did you dance with him twice?"

"Because he was different."

"Why?"

"Well, for one, he didn't lick my hand like the first guy did."

Ryan's hand tightened in mine. "Is that so?"

"Sure. It's been a weird night."

"I know."

"You didn't know, did you?" *About the marriage,* I couldn't say.

He didn't need to ask. He just shook his head. He said, "Todd didn't lick your hand. Why else?"

I laughed. It felt like it was edging toward bitterness. "He told me he didn't know how to dance. I thought it was sweet. And he didn't run screaming after the ass babies."

Ryan chuckled darkly. "Why sweet?"

"It was honest. When's the wedding?"

"We haven't decided. When are you seeing Todd again?"

I narrowed my eyes. "I never said I was."

"Why not?" he asked, jaw set. "He's sweet. And honest."

I felt dizzy. "I don't have time for such things. I have priorities. Goals to accomplish."

"So do I," he said, and it was like he was trying to tell me more than those three words, but I wasn't in the mood to understand anything.

"I suppose. I guess we'll be seeing a lot of each other."

"That so?" he said, and I thought he pulled me closer.

"Yes," I said and I didn't allow my voice to drop. "I'm the apprentice to the King's Wizard. You're the Knight Commander of the King's Guard. Seems as if we'll see each other more often than not. Especially after you're married to the future King of Verania. I will be his wizard."

"Will you run this time?" he asked, and when had his face gotten closer? I could feel his breath on my cheek. It was hot and moist and mint and wine. "I try and I try but you run away. Every single time."

Suddenly, I felt very out of place. Or rather, I *remembered* my place. My skin was too tight, and I was sweating. The song was ending, and I pulled away. He didn't release my hand. I could hear him being called by someone and realized tonight was supposed to be about him. He needed to mingle and kiss ass and make out with his fiancé in darkened corners because he was getting married.

"Thank you for the dance, Knight Commander." I bowed to him because rank and custom made it so.

"Dances," he said, voice pitched so low I could feel it crawl over me. "Plural. Because we went through three waltzes. Not one. And definitely not just *two*."

Oh shit.

Ryan bowed back to me. I pulled away and his fingers trailed against mine.

I NEEDED air.

The stars above were bright as I moved into the garden. Lanterns hung from metal poles, lighting the paths near the roses and the tulips.

I took a breath and let it out slowly.

Footsteps came up behind me. Of course they would follow me out here. They would follow me anywhere.

"Had to escape to hide your raging erection?" Gary asked sympathetically.

"You know," I said, "I came across a spell in Morgan's Grimoire. In one of those back pages for the truly evil shit? It called for the dust of unicorn bones. I'm thinking about trying it out." I kept walking.

"If it makes you feel any better," Gary said, "I don't think I've ever seen dance fucking before. It was illuminating to see a live demonstration."

I walked into a tree.

Tiggy and Gary laughed at me, because that's what best friends do.

"I don't even know what you're talking about," I said as I picked tree bark out of my mouth. "Todd was very nice."

"Todd," Gary mocked. "Yes. Todd."

I ignored him. "Tiggy, did Morgan say when he was sending us out again?" Because being in the castle for the foreseeable future seemed like a Very Bad Idea.

"Two weeks," Tiggy rumbled.

"That motherfucker," I muttered. "He's doing this on purpose."

"Kind of like how Ryan was dancing all up in your business on purpose," Gary said.

"You shut your mouth!"

"Dance fucking!" he hissed at me.

"I don't even know what that *is*."

"It's when you're all, like, dancing, but it's so easy to tell you'd much rather be *naked* and dancing. And by dancing, I mean fucking."

"That's so stupid. And we *weren't*. We were talking about his *wedding* and about *Todd*."

"Who Todd?" Tiggy asked.

"Big ears," Gary said. "Couldn't dance."

"He precious," Tiggy said. "Turned color of strawberries at all things."

"Yes," I said. "He *was*. And maybe I just wanted to dance fuck with him, not Ryan."

"Yeah, keep telling yourself that," Gary said. "Todd was an appetizer. Ryan was the main course covered in dessert."

"I thought I was the buffet?" I asked, confused.

"You were. It's... that... okay, too many food metaphors. I'm trying to be subtle here."

"You're a talking unicorn," I said. "Sometimes when you poop, it comes out as rainbows and smells like cookies. There is nothing subtle about you."

"It magical," Tiggy said succinctly.

"The *point* is," Gary said loudly, "when you were dancing with Todd, it was cute and clumsy and juvenile. When you were dancing with *Ryan*, I thought the entire room was going to choke on the tension."

I groaned. "That's the last thing I need. Because if you could see it, then others could too, and that's how *rumors* start, and I seriously don't need everyone knowing how I want to do... stuff... to him."

"Stuff," Gary mocked. "Prude. And trust me when I say it's not just on you. He's right there with you. You should have seen the glares he was giving Todd when you went through a second dance."

"Lies," I said with a scowl. "All lies. You know what? No. I don't even want to talk about this anymore. I don't even care. I'm over it. Past it. Moving on. I'm going to march back in there and tell Todd that he's going to take me out on a date and it will be awkward and nice and that'll be that."

Gary and Tiggy stared at me.

"What?" I asked.

"How can you not *see* it?" Gary asked incredulously.

"See what?"

"Gaaah!" he shrieked.

Tiggy shushed him soothingly. "It okay. Pretty Gary. It okay."

"You guys are so weird," I muttered.

"I love you," Gary said. "But sometimes I want to kick your spleen in."

"The feeling is mutual," I assured him. "I don't even—"

"Sam?" a voice said from behind us.

Because of course.

All three of us turned.

Ryan stood there next to a stand of my mother's violets, the light from a nearby lantern falling perfectly across his face.

"Well fuck me upside the head," I said.

He said, "What?"

And I said, "Absolutely nothing," because my *mouth*.

"I heard screaming."

"And you came running? Of course you did." I sounded like I was in pain.

He shrugged. "I thought somebody might need help."

Apparently being noble and righteous is a turn-on for me, so I might have drooled a bit. "That was just Gary," I managed to say. "He does that sometimes. With the screaming."

"It's true," Gary said with a dramatic sigh. "I seem to suffer from a very serious condition called obliviousness by proximity. It causes screaming and the occasional uncontrollable need to stomp stupid wizards for being stupid."

"And it's completely fatal," I said with a glare. "So maybe make with the dying."

Gary ignored me. "You just happened to be in the garden?" he asked Ryan.

Ryan stared back. "Exactly."

"Finding a rosebush to make out with your fiancé?" His tone was gentle, but I'd known Gary a long time. He was not being gentle.

"Gary," I hissed.

"Completely alone," Ryan said.

"Is that right? It seems a betrothed knight commander wouldn't need to be alone."

"You would think."

Gary's eyes narrowed. "I'm pretty sure I don't like you."

"My world is crumbling," Ryan said.

I might have laughed. Because *sass.*

Gary wasn't as amused. "Gary knows how to kill a bitch."

"You probably should run," I told Ryan. "When he starts referring to himself in the third person, it usually means he's about to go into one of his unicorn rages."

"Unicorn rages?" Ryan asked.

"There's glitter involved," I said solemnly. "Glitter and sarcasm. You'll be emotionally eviscerated. Not physically, because we haven't gotten his horn back yet. Count your blessings."

"Don't think I need it to kick your ass, though!" Gary snarled, prancing backward and forward. Glitter started sprinkling in the air around him, sloughing off from his back and sides. We could never really quite figure out where it came from. Gary had said it was because his insides were so festive. I'd told him that was way lame. "Bring it on, pretty boy! Gary gonna bring the *pain.*"

"It would probably be more threatening if you weren't angrily raining glitter," Ryan said. "It's hard to be intimidated when you're so shiny."

"This is amazing," I whispered to no one in particular because no one was listening to me.

"*Shiny?*" Gary said, outraged. "I'll show you *shiny*! When I am finished with my emotional onslaught, you won't even understand the *concept* of self-esteem, much less how to have it!"

Tiggy said, "This gonna be ugly."

"You're adorable," Ryan said, and he was adorable for *using* the word adorable. Especially since he sounded like he *meant* it.

And Gary must have heard it too. Especially since unicorns can tell when someone is lying. "I'll *murder* your face and—wait. What?" Gary stopped prancing.

Ryan shrugged. "You're adorable. With your angry glitter."

And Gary *blushed.* His whole *face.* Never before in the strange and sordid history of our super-best friendship had I *ever* seen him blush. "Aww," he said. He scuffed the ground with one hoof. "You just hush, you." And then he *giggled.*

"What is even happening right now?" I said.

"Isn't it obvious?" Gary said. "Ryan is in love with me. We're going to run away together. Now shoo." He turned back to Ryan, dismissing me completely. "Now," he said. "Tell me more about myself."

"It's a love for the ages," Ryan agreed with a small smile.

"You have to hand-feed me grapes," Gary demanded. "Peeled frozen grapes. I will not accept anything less. I am the light of your life and you shall treat me as such."

Ryan rubbed a hand along Gary's nose and I was so pissed off because I wanted him to rub *my* nose. So I said, "Gary, you whore! He's getting *married!*" Like I actually thought Ryan would fuck my unicorn best friend. Right? *Right?*

I heard the wicked curl in his tone even before I could comprehend Gary's words, and only then did I realize just how much of a diabolical mastermind my best friend could be. He had *planned* this. Getting to this point. He was *evil.*

"Sam," he said with a glance back at me. "Weren't you saying something about marching back inside and asking Todd out on a date?"

And the somewhat cheery atmosphere died a quick and painful death.

I cursed Gary in my head. My fingers actually twitched with the beginnings of a banishing spell that could potentially send him to the ends of the known world, but I somehow was able to stop myself. Barely.

Why, though? It shouldn't matter what Gary had said. I owed nothing to Ryan. He definitely owed nothing to me.

So I said, "Yeah, sure." Because I was. Because I had *options.*

Ryan took a step back from Gary and dropped his hand.

And then he said flatly, "You'll need a chaperone."

I rolled my eyes. "Because that makes sense. It's not like he can hurt me. I'm taller than him and can set him on fire."

"It's to protect your virtue," Ryan said through gritted teeth.

"My *virtue?*"

"Oh," Gary said to Tiggy. "It's so much more fun being on this side of things."

"Why Sam loud?" Tiggy asked.

"It's his default setting," Gary said.

"It's to make sure you stay safe," Ryan said. "You're important to m—to the Kingdom."

"To the Kingdom," Gary whispered.

"Right," Tiggy whispered back, "the *Kingdom.*"

"I don't need anyone to protect my *virtue*," I snapped. "If I wanted to go out and fuck the first guy I saw, then I could. Or maybe I'd feel adventurous and find a lady! Maybe *both*. At the same time."

"Sam, honey," Gary called, breaking through the anger. "Remember you love the *mens*. No lady bits. Though you seem to have an unhealthy appreciation of boobs."

"Okay," I said. "Point. Breasts are fascinating."

Ryan was pissed. "You're not going to *fuck* anything."

"Whoa."

"What?"

"You just said *fuck*."

"So?"

"But, you're a *knight*. You can't say things like *fuck*. You're supposed to hug children and rescue kittens and slay fantastical beasts. You can't say *fuck*. It's unbecoming of someone of your position."

"And you can?" He was back to being bemused.

I grinned. "You bet your fucking ass I can. I'm a wizard."

"Apprentice," Gary whispered.

Murder is bad. Murder is bad. "*Regardless*, I am my own man. I don't answer to anyone but myself."

"And me," Gary said.

"And Gary," I allowed. Because it was true.

"And Tiggy," Tiggy said.

"And Tiggy." Because that was also true.

"And your mom," Gary said. "And your dad. And Morgan. And the King."

"Okay, them too." I was not my own man at all.

Ryan smiled. It was not the nice one I'd seen earlier. "Good. I'll ask the King about it, then."

Mother*fucker*. "You fight dirty, Foxheart," I grumbled.

"Hey, if I have to go through with it, then so do you," he said, which brought significantly more questions than I wanted to deal with. Like did they ever ditch the chaperone? Did they run away and fuck in the forest? Was Ryan a virgin? A sweet, sweet virgin with a big, fat—

Nope. Nope, nope, nope. So not even going there.

"Not for much longer," I said lightly. "Pretty soon, it's married life for you." That was easier to think about.

"Hey, Ryan?" Gary asked. "If you're so concerned with Sam's... *virtue* and importance to the *Kingdom*, why don't you volunteer to be the chaperone? As Knight Commander of the King's Guard, no one is more qualified than you to ensure the safety of his butthole."

I muttered two dark syllables as the green fluttered around the edges of my vision. I snapped my fingers and Gary's mouth was bound with shining twine. He glared at me while Tiggy laughed at him. Gary was a unicorn, so his magic would counteract my own in a few short minutes, but it shut him up for now. It was time to end this, and Ryan would laugh and I would laugh (while slowly withering on the inside), and then I'd go back inside and find some way to move to a different continent.

And then Ryan said, "That's a good idea. I'll tell the King immediately." He turned tightly on his heel and started walking toward the ballroom.

Because. What? "*Hey!*"

"Don't worry," he called over his shoulder. "It'll be a great first date. You'll see."

And then he was gone.

"What in the *fuck* just happened?" I breathed.

Gary's magic finally negated my own and the twine fell away and disappeared. "I fell in love with Ryan, you got jealous, then I fell out of love with him because he seemed needy, you tied me up, I got half a chubby because it reminded me of Octavio, and now you have a date with Ryan. Oops. I mean Todd. Gosh, I'm beat. What a long night. Tiggy, take me to bed or lose me forever. Bye, Sam! Bye! Good night! Bye!"

And my night ended with me standing alone among my mother's flowers saying "Wait, *what*?" as I looked up at the stars and wished for impossible things.

CHAPTER 6
Ducks, Blueberries, and
Accidental Almost Hand Jobs

TWO DAYS after the Weirdest Night in History (and yes, it even beat the night forty years ago when the wizard Carlton the Dark Moth somehow managed to replicate himself sixty-seven times and then proceeded to have a self-orgy out in the town square of Meridian City), four invitations for dates came to the castle.

I ignored them at first. I was busy in the labs, trying to catch up on writing my own Grimoire before Morgan chewed my ass. I was at least two chapters behind, and getting trapped in a cave by Lartin certainly hadn't helped.

A wizard's Grimoire is his legacy to the world of magic. Or at least that's what Morgan had told me time and time again. At first, I didn't see why we couldn't just *share* his, but he had just smiled at me, handed me his book, pointed out a relatively minor spell to turn an apple into an orange, and told me to knock myself out.

Which is exactly what I did.

When I woke up four days later with my eyebrows singed off, Morgan had told me that a Grimoire's spells were meant to be tailored to the individual wizard who wrote them. Morgan's Grimoire was in tune with Morgan and his magic. Since he was my mentor, his magic was intertwined with my own, which is why I only lost my eyebrows and not a hand or a foot.

Magic isn't just the wave of a hand or the utterance of a word. Morgan best explained it in that a wizard is like a conductor to a symphony. It's the specific timing, the cadence, the movements that allow the magic to occur. Without a conductor, the beat could be lost and dissolve into a blaring cacophony.

Without a knowledgeable wizard or a guiding hand, the magic could be fatal to the caster.

Morgan had shelf after shelf of Grimoires of the wizards that had come before him in the Verania line that would one day go to me. I tried not to think about that part. It felt like way too much responsibility.

So I experimented in ancient tongues. I conducted the magic, listening to it sing. There were colors here. So many colors that it was easy to get lost in them. To be overwhelmed by them. Morgan had said once that he'd gotten so far into the colors that the edges of reality had started to bleed together, like the world was melting around him. He'd made a mistake and almost didn't make it back out. He never clarified what he'd seen in those moments. What he'd heard. He'd recounted the story to me as a warning of the addictiveness of magic. It was so easy to go too far.

Morgan never let me. He kept my boundaries contained and controlled. Every now and then I'd wonder how I could ever know how far my magic could go if it was always boxed in, but I never pushed. Morgan knew more than I did. I trusted him to know what was best for me.

"You're going to need to answer these invites."

Well. Most of the time.

"Fall off a cliff," I told him pleasantly, not bothering to look up from my Grimoire, where I was jotting down a particularly difficult and complex equation that would allow me to create fireworks out of corn kernels. You know. The important stuff.

"I did that once," he said. "I was being chased by a particularly pissed-off manticore. He knocked me off the cliff and into a river all because I'd inadvertently insulted his mother. To be fair, she was a magnificent bitch who had tried to eat me the week before, so I was justified. I woke up four days later without any knowledge of who I was and spent the next six months working in a traveling carnival."

I gaped at him.

"I was the bearded lady," he said. "At some point during those four days that I was passed out, I'd somehow managed to grow a pair of breasts. It was an odd and trying time, but I came out stronger because of it."

"Only you would learn a life lesson from being a bearded lady with amnesia," I said.

"Everything is a life lesson," Morgan said. "Like these invitations from potential suitors."

"Your segue was clunky and I am embarrassed for you."

"This won't go away if you ignore it. You know better than anybody that when the King sets his mind to something, there will be follow-through or fallout."

I rolled my eyes. "I have better things to do."

"Like dance with a certain knight for fifteen minutes?"

I gritted my teeth. "Not my fault. He wiled me. With his ways. I was desperate to escape, but was duty bound as my position of your apprentice to save face. For you."

Morgan laughed. "Because you've cared about that in the past. Clunky segue incoming. The King has appointed said knight as your chaperone for any upcoming outings of a romantic nature."

"Kill me," I begged him. "If you have any respect for me at all, you will end my life right this second."

Morgan shook his head. "I am too fond of you to see you go."

"Sentimental bastard." I paused, considering. "I am sort of fond of you too. Though right this second, I couldn't tell you a single reason why."

He flipped through the invites. "Pick one. Pick all of them. But at least pick one. And when you go out, remain vigilant. The Darks are probably still pissed, even if it was scum of the earth like Lartin. If I think any of this is interfering with our work, I'll pull the plug. But I'll know if you're throwing it on purpose, Sam. You know as well as I do what will happen if you can't find a proper cornerstone for your magic."

I groaned. "Not the cornerstone thing again. I don't need someone to help anchor my magic. And even if I did, I have you. And Gary and Tiggy. And my parents."

He shook his head. "It's not the same thing. Especially now that you've come of age."

"This whole thing was your idea, wasn't it?" I accused him. "The King tried to take credit for it, but you did it."

He shrugged. "Mutual exchange of ideas."

Fine. "Is there one from a man named Todd?" I asked.

"There is."

"Send the response. Throw the others away."

"No sex on the first date," Morgan said. "Don't give up all the goods. Save some of it for later. You have to keep him coming back somehow. The gods only know it won't be from your sparkling personality alone."

"I feel like you not existing would be an okay thing for me right now," I said. "Also, I've started a new chapter on the Grimoire that deals specifically with memory alteration and breast augmentation. Take that for what you will."

"A threat?"

"A threat," I confirmed.

He smiled at me. "You are going to be an amazing wizard. Mark my words."

I DIDN'T see Ryan again until he was to act as my chaperone three days later.

I was totally okay with that.

Because I had a *plan.*

Fuck Ryan. I didn't need him.

"It'll be the Date to End All Dates," I told Gary as he nosed his way through my closet. "And yes, before you ask, it is capitalized just like it sounds. Great plans should always be capitalized."

"Why is that?" Mom asked as she came into the room smelling of earth and lilies and lichen.

"To ensure their success," I said, posing in front of the mirror.

"I don't think that's quite how it works," Dad said, coming in behind her. They went and fussed over Tiggy, who pulled them into his lap where he sat on the floor. We didn't know much about where Tiggy had come from before Gary met him, but he'd been touch and attention starved. My parents had unofficially adopted him almost immediately, and he adored them both.

"You just have to believe," I said as I flexed.

"I believe you should work out more if you're going to keep doing that," Gary said. "Because it's making me feel sad for you."

"Do we like Todd?" Mom asked.

"We do," I said.

"Sort of," Gary said.

"No. Not sort of. If I have to do this, then he's good enough. He's nice. And has these ears."

"Ringing endorsement," Dad said.

"I have priorities," I said.

"As we've heard a thousand times," Mom said as Tiggy brushed a finger through her hair.

"I need to finish the Grimoire," I said as if she hadn't spoken at all. "Then I have to find a binding for it. Morgan says that a wizard's Grimoire needs to be bound with great care, either by the skin of an enemy defeated in battle or a material hard-won in the face of adversity."

"I think I prefer the material hard-won," Mom said. "It sounds less... brutal."

"And that's why I have *priorities*," I said.

"Maybe you should prioritize getting a new wardrobe," Gary said. "Your clothes remind me of sadness."

"I'm an adventurer," I said. "I have no time for fashion."

"You are a wizard in the King's Court," Dad reminded me as Tiggy pressed his big nose into his hair.

"Apprentice," Gary said. "Just make with the magic and conjure up some clothes."

I frowned. "That's frivolous."

"And?"

"You know how Morgan feels about frivolous magic. Magic is important. It's not meant to be for something mundane."

"You tied my mouth shut with shiny rope," Gary said.

"That was important. I didn't want you talking anymore. That wasn't frivolous."

"How is the corn kernel firework spell coming along?" Dad asked.

"Great! I think I... and I see what you did there."

"I did nothing," Dad said innocently.

"Except lie. You liar. How cool would it be to have corn in the growing season ignite into fireworks to let you know when it's ready to be picked?"

"Unless the fireworks light the corn on fire," Mom said.

"And burn down villages," Dad said.

"And make people homeless and dead," Gary said.

"You smell good," Tiggy said to my father.

"Sam of Wilds's Amazing Firework Corn," I said. "It's been capitalized, so now it's a good idea."

"It's like all our wishes for the future have come true," Dad told Mom. "Remember when you were pregnant with him? I would whisper into your stomach that he would make exploding corn when he grew up."

Mom leaned in and kissed him gently. "Those were the days."

Tiggy wrapped them both in a hug. "I love you guys," he said.

"Get out," I said. "All of you. I just realized I only have ten minutes until I go on my first date and I need to have a freak-out before I go downstairs."

They complied immediately. I had trained them well.

"You'll do fine," Mom said as she kissed my cheek.

"Don't tell him about the corn," Dad said as he hugged me close.

"If he hurt you, I smash him," Tiggy said, patting my back.

"Have fun on your date with Ryan," Gary said.

"You bitch," I said.

Gary leaned in and put his forehead to mine. "I put clothes out for you on the bed," he said quietly. "Try to have some fun, okay? Don't freak out too bad. Wake me up when you get home if you need to."

"I'm going to mess this up," I groaned.

"Probably. But that's okay too. I'll still be here."

"I love your face," I told him seriously.

"It's a pretty good face," he agreed.

And then I was by myself.

"Well, fuck," I said as I looked back in the mirror. "You can do this. You got this. You're golden. It's just a date. Only a date. A first date. With a man. Who is nice. And being chaperoned by another man. Who is... someone I am not thinking about. Todd. Todd. Todd. I like his ears and his freckles, and he stumbles over his words and it's awesome. I might want to kiss him. Maybe I will even blow him." My reflection's eyes went wide. "Okay, sorry. Sorry. No blow jays. You haven't practiced yet. Mental note, practice blow jobs. Okay. Good talk. Let's do this."

Gary had laid out gray trousers that were soft and worn thin paired with a green tunic that was a little tight across the chest. Trusting my hornless gay unicorn best friend, I just went with it. I quickly dressed and checked out the result in the mirror.

"I am a sex god," I said in awe. "Well. Kind of. Okay. Not really. And self-esteem is quickly deflating. Feeling sad now."

There was a knock on my chamber door.

Shit.

"Just a minute," I called.

I used that minute to have a complete meltdown. It went well, as far as meltdowns go.

I opened the door, resigned. Pete was on the other side, looking far too amused.

"I don't even want to hear it," I grumbled.

"I wasn't going to say a word," he said.

"You," I said. "Not saying a single word."

He shrugged. "Well, a few words. Your date for the evening has arrived and is waiting in the lobby. And the Knight Commander is there too." He was struggling not to smile. "There might be some... posturing involved."

"Posturing," I repeated.

"Intimidation tactics, even," Pete said.

"Who is Todd trying to intimidate?" I asked, sounding shocked.

Pete covered his face with his hands and groaned. "I worry for the future of this kingdom."

I rolled my eyes. "I'm going to be a part of that future. I think we'll be just fine."

"Because of your level of awareness?"

"Exactly," I said, smiling at him. He knew me so well.

He muttered something that sounded like "we're all doomed," but I couldn't be sure as I was too busy shutting my chamber doors.

TODD DIDN'T seem to be posturing in the slightest as I descended the stairs. In fact, he looked downright terrified.

Ryan stood right next to him, a bland expression on his face.

Morgan was leaning against the wall, humming quietly to himself.

"This was a bad idea," I breathed.

Which, of course, they heard. They snapped their gazes to the stairs.

"Eep!" Todd said.

"Sam," Ryan said.

Morgan just smiled enigmatically.

"Heeey," I said, giving an awkward wave.

Then we all just stood there.

For, like, two whole minutes.

Just staring.

Morgan cleared his throat pointedly.

Todd said, "Um. Yes. Right. My cue. Thank you, my good man." He took a step forward. And then another. "Sam! You look—"

I waited.

"—just... grand," he finished.

"Thank you, Todd," I said. "You look very nice." And he did. He wore a tight waistcoat over a white shirt and a silver cravat. "Your ears are still awesome."

And he flushed.

Ryan scowled.

Morgan rolled his eyes.

"These are for you." Todd handed me a tiny mesh bag. Inside were a collection of beautiful seashells shining gold and yellow and white. They were Rovian shells, specifically, that I needed for a spell I had yet to complete. I hadn't had the time to gather them myself. The nearest coast was ten miles away.

I glanced up at Morgan, because this had to be his doing. There was no way Todd could have known about these. Morgan winked at me.

I looked back to Todd, who watched me with a concerned look on his face. "These are perfect," I said quietly. "Just what I needed. Thank you."

And he smiled, low and sweet. "I collected them myself."

"That makes them even better," I said honestly.

"Shall we?"

I nodded and he led the way out of the castle, Ryan trailing behind us.

This was nice. It was a nice start. Everything was good.

Everything would be fine.

EVERYTHING WAS not fine.

Well, it started off fine.

But then it escalated very, very quickly.

The carriage ride was made in near silence. I climbed in first, and Todd sought to follow and sit next to me. Ryan cleared his throat and shook his head. Todd must have gotten the message because he quickly moved to the other side of the carriage, eyes wide.

Ryan sat right next to me, crossing his considerable arms over his considerable chest.

And stared at Todd.

Because I'd never met a silence that I didn't at least attempt to fill, I said, "So, this is… festive."

Todd said, "Quite."

Ryan stared.

Silence.

I said, "Where are we off to this fine evening?"

Todd said, "Antonella's. It's the restaurant in one of my dad's hotels. It's new and very high class."

Ryan stared.

I said, "At the hotel, huh? If the evening goes well enough, maybe we could just get a room after." It was a joke. An awful, awful joke.

Todd whispered, "Sweet gods."

Ryan glared.

Silence.

So I said, "I was just joking. I'm not really going to fuck you on our first date." For *clarification*.

Todd said, "Sweet *gods*."

Ryan glared.

Silence.

I couldn't help but say, "Well, maybe a hand job if you're lucky. I've got nice—"

Ryan put his hand over my mouth.

Todd was sweating.

I thought about licking Ryan's hand.

Todd said weakly, "It's going to be a lovely evening."

ANTONELLA'S WAS classy. Bright and shiny and new. A string quartet played softly in the background. Crystal chandeliers hung from the ceiling, the candles lit and flickering.

We were led to a table away from the others, a booth in a cozy corner. I knew this was the point where Ryan would have to bow out and keep his distance. It's not like I was on a date with *him*. At the very least, he should have given us some semblance of privacy.

Instead, he loomed over the table, standing with his back to us….

I said, "Go away."

He said, "I'm on guard."

I said, "I don't need you to be."

"King's orders."

"I'm going to throw breadsticks at the back of your head. You're going to be so embarrassed because everyone is going to see you getting hit in the head with breadsticks."

"Try it and see what happens," he said with a sneer.

Todd said, "So."

And then I remembered Todd was there.

I was such a dick.

I sat down and put my full attention on Todd.

That seemed to make him more nervous.

I smiled at him.

That seemed to make him even more nervous. I needed to calm him down.

I said, "I was kidding about the hand job thing."

"Oh dear," he said.

Ryan snorted loudly.

I ignored him. "So. Todd."

He nodded, throat working.

"How is your... life?" Smooth, that. And all encompassing.

"It's good," he said quickly. "Um. So good. Father is talking of retirement soon, and I'll be taking over operations of the hotels."

"That sounds exciting. Especially for one so young." I picked up a glass of water to sip.

He flushed. "I hope so. It's a lot of responsibility." And then it seemed like he wanted to take that back. "But not so much that I won't be able to see you! If we are to marry, then I will make as much time for you as you require."

I sprayed water onto the table and coughed. "That's... good. That's... if we *marry*. Whoa. Like. What?"

"Sorry!" Todd said like he'd offended me. "Sorry. I didn't mean *if*. I meant *when*."

I knocked over the glass of water onto the table. It spilled all over Todd.

"Oh shit," I said. "I'm so sorry. I'm not usually this awkward." Well, that was a lie. This was about par for the course. I scooted over in the booth and took a cloth napkin and started dabbing the water off of Todd. It took a minute before I realized I was rubbing his crotch. I stared in horror.

"Oh *gods*," Todd moaned.

"*Sam*," Ryan snapped. "What the hell?"

I looked up at him with wide eyes. "I'm not giving him a hand job!" I shouted. "I'm just trying to get him dry!"

The restaurant went silent as everyone looked over at us.

"I said that really loudly, didn't I?"

"Sam?" Todd squeaked. "Could you... move? Your hand?"

I looked back down, and my hand was still in his lap. "Sorry," I said, patting his crotch a couple of times. "My bad."

Todd looked like he was about to faint.

Ryan didn't bother turning back around or moving away from the table.

"No more sneak hand jobs," I told him. "I promise. My virtue is still intact."

"I highly doubt that," he said.

"So much sass," I said. "How come no one knows you're so sassy?"

"It doesn't often come up in conversation," he deadpanned.

A waiter came over, looking somewhat apprehensive. "Is everything okay, Duke Goldwaithe?"

"Duke Todd Goldwaithe," I said, trying it out. "Mrs. Sam Goldwaithe."

Everyone stared at me.

I waved my hand at them. "It's a thing Gary and I do." Mrs. Sam Foxheart sounded *amazing*, but I didn't think now was the right time to say that out loud. Or ever.

They still stared.

"Gary? My best friend? The hornless gay unicorn? The fiercest diva in existence? Nothing? Ryan, you know who I'm talking about. After all, you were practically fondling him at the celebration."

He looked like it hurt him to acknowledge that yes, he did in fact know the fiercest diva in existence. "There was no fondling," he said roughly.

"There was fondling," I told the waiter. He looked terrified. "And demands of peeled frozen grapes. It was, like... this whole *thing*. You aren't laughing. Maybe you had to be there."

The waiter just nodded.

"I'm starving," I said. "What's for dinner?"

The waiter cleared his throat. "Pan-seared duck breast with blueberry sauce and roasted potatoes."

Uh-oh. "I'm—"

Ryan said, "Sam is allergic to duck. And blueberries."

I said, "What?"

Todd said, "Oh dear."

The waiter said, "So he's allergic to the full meal."

"Not the potatoes," Ryan said.

I said, "*What?*"

Todd said, "You're allergic to *blueberries*?"

Ryan said, "And the duck."

"I swell up," I said to Todd. "I look like a mountain troll. It's really weird. I don't want to do that on the first date. That's like a fourth or fifth-date thing. Or a never thing. Because of the swelling."

"Blueberries," Todd said.

"We have other things," the waiter said.

"Everything on this menu says duck," Ryan said as he plucked it from the table

"It's sort of a theme night," Todd said faintly.

"You have a duck theme night?" I asked. "That's epic. And deadly. If you're allergic."

"Maybe not a lot of other things," the waiter said.

"Basically everything on the menu will kill him," Ryan said.

"Blueberries," Todd said.

"How did you know that?" I asked Ryan.

"There's potatoes and bread," the waiter said. "And blueberry wine. Wait. We have water."

"Potatoes and bread?" I said with a frown. "But the *carbs*."

Ryan said, "I know things."

Todd said, "Oh my gods. Are you going to swell *now*? Is just breathing the duck and blueberry air going to kill you?" He sounded like he was panicking.

"It might," Ryan said. He didn't sound like he was panicking.

"It won't," I said, reaching out and patting Todd's hand.

"It might," Ryan insisted. Sort of panicking. Barely panicking.

I rolled my eyes. "You and Gary are such drama queens. I'm not going to sniff it up close." I glanced at Todd. "Though, there will be no making out later if you eat duck. You'll make my tongue swell." I waggled my eyebrows at him.

Todd choked on air.

"So," the waiter said, "I'll bring you potatoes and bread."

"And more water," I said. "Because I spilled it on the table. And then it turned inappropriate when I tried to clean it up. I'm going to have to work out even more now tomorrow to make up for all the potatoes and bread. Okay. I feel bad. That was a lie. I'm not going to work out at all. That sounds just awful."

The waiter practically ran away.

"I like him," I said. "Very quick service. Good job, Todd."

"Thanks?"

Ryan said, "Are you breathing okay?" He leaned down, hands on the table, until he was level with me. "Take a deep breath."

I did. And then, because I was an asshole, I started gasping and grabbing my throat.

They both freaked.

I laughed at them.

They weren't amused.

"Calm the fuck down," I said. "We're having fun."

"You're ridiculous," Ryan growled at me.

"And how do you know things?" I asked him, narrowing my eyes.

He shrugged. "I just do."

"That's a nonanswer."

"You want to make out with me?" Todd asked.

"Let's see how the evening goes first," I said. "You're off to a good start. Mostly. Maybe not the Food of Death thing."

"No making out," Ryan said.

"Eep," Todd said.

"Go away. I'm on a date."

He turned and glared at Todd. He tried to look intimidating. It must have worked because Todd was intimidated. "No making out," he said.

"No making out," Todd agreed quickly.

"Ryan, the tip of your sword is poking me," I said. Because it was. I don't know why he thought he needed to come fully knighted-out. Talk about going overboard. "You're getting it all over me."

And then Ryan *blushed.*

I said "Oh crap" in a slightly strangled voice. I didn't think it was possible for him to get any more attractive. But he had done so exponentially and it made my insides burn.

"Sorry," he muttered as he pulled it away.

"Sure," I said faintly. "Sure." I wondered how to go about asking him to poke me with his sword again.

Todd said, "Blueberries?"

The waiter came back with potatoes and bread.

And it was around that time that we were accosted by Dark wizards. Really. With the way everything else had gone so far, it should have been expected.

"None of these touched any duck or blueberries," the waiter said.

"That's very kind of you and it looks lovely and holy shit I'm pretty sure we're about to get in a fight."

The waiter's eyes widened.

Todd slunk lower in his seat.

Ryan whirled around, drawing his sword. Didn't even question me. I liked that in a man.

I stood.

Four Dark wizards had entered the restaurant. I knew them because of the crests they wore on their robes, similar to the one Lartin had been wearing. The one in the front was thick and squat, like a tree trunk. His eyebrows were amazing, almost covering his entire forehead. His eyes fell on me and he scowled.

"Sam of Wilds!" he shouted. The restaurant fell silent as people looked back and forth between us.

"I like your eyebrows," I told him. "Way to buck societal norms of how eyebrows should normally look. Down with the system and all that."

"Sam," Ryan said in warning.

"What? *Look* at them and tell me you didn't think the same thing."

"We are here to have our revenge!" the Dark wizard snapped.

"Oh no," I groaned. "He's going to monologue."

"You have taken one of our own from us. Lartin the Dark Leaf was a magnificent wizard who had grown up with the weight and expectation of a father that—"

"They do this," I told Ryan. "Villains. Every time. Whenever they capture me, they monologue. I don't understand *why.*"

"You need to stop getting captured," he said, flourishing his sword like a badass. "I don't think my heart can take it anymore."

"Are you even listening?" the squat wizard asked. "I have this whole thing to say before the revenge part happens."

"It's not like I do it on purpose," I said to Ryan. "I can't help it if people want to get all up on this."

He rolled his eyes. "That must be it. They just can't stay away from all of that." His eyes traveled up and down my body.

"So much *sass*," I said in awe. "You're like a sass master. You and Gary should have a sass-off to see who would be crowned Queen Sass. Fair warning: he would win. But you could be Princess Sass."

"Guys?" the Dark wizard said.

"I'm not a princess," Ryan said with a scowl.

"I notice how you didn't say anything about being a queen," I pointed out.

"I don't like losing," he said.

I smiled at him. "You can be the queen," I allowed. "Just don't tell Gary I said that. Friendships have ended for a lot less than that."

"They do know we're here, right?" Squat Wizard asked his fellow Darks. "Like, I'm not invisible? I didn't accidentally cast an invisibility spell on myself while walking over?"

"I can see you," one of the Darks said. "You're not invisible."

Squat Wizard looked relieved. "That would have been embarrassing. You know? Like barging in here and saying 'I'm here to have revenge' and not realizing I was invisible. And then having to make myself visible and say it all over again. It wouldn't sound as realistic the second time around. Very forced and unbelievable."

"This is almost worse than monologuing," I told Ryan. "One time, I was kidnapped by a group of thieves when I was fifteen. They thought they could use me to break into the castle vaults. The leader went on for four hours about how perfect their plan was. But he'd forgotten to bind my magic and I turned them into deck chairs on accident."

"On accident?"

"I was trying to turn them into lawn chairs," I explained. "There's a difference."

Ryan laughed quietly. "I hadn't heard that one."

I tried to ignore just how awesome his laugh was. "It was before you came to the castle. A few months, anyway."

Fifteen-year-old Sam had seen twenty-year-old Ryan for the first time and had immediately run upstairs and jerked off. It had been a revolutionary and enlightening experience that essentially answered the question that yes, I was indeed very, very gay. I didn't share that with Ryan and the Dark wizards because now was not the time or place. Or never. Never sounded good too.

"Maybe they're trapped," one of the Darks said. "Like in a fog of magic. And they can't hear you anymore."

"You think?" Squat Wizard asked. He raised his voice and called out, "Can you hear me?"

I rolled my eyes. "I'm trying to have a conversation here. I'm on a date."

"With a knight?" Squat Wizard asked.

My face felt hot. "Uh. No? No. With Todd. Say hi, Todd." I pointed back at Todd, who looked like he wished I hadn't done that. He gave a small wave to Squat Wizard and said, "Heeeeyyy."

Squat Wizard frowned. "Sorry. I just thought you were with the knight. You haven't said a single thing to Todd since we got here."

"I'm protecting him," I said defensively. "He's nice."

"Nice?" Squat Wizard said. "That's not a ringing endorsement."

"You're nice," I told Todd. "That's totally ringing. I like your ears."

Todd blushed.

Ryan said, "Everyone has *ears*, Sam. Gods." He was all growly.

"I'm aware of that, *Ryan*. I am being complimentary!"

"Is that what you call it?"

"Hey, just because *you*—"

"Oh boy," Squat Wizard said. "I totally get it now."

"Get what?" I asked.

The Dark wizards laughed.

I cocked my head at them.

They stopped laughing.

Squat Wizard said, "You're being serious."

"About what?" I was confused.

"Wow," one of the Darks said. "That's gotta be super uncomfortable. For everyone involved."

"It's so obvious," Squat Wizard said. "Like, the most obvious thing I've ever seen."

His Darks agreed.

"What is?" I asked.

"My head hurts," Squat Wizard said.

"People say that around me a lot," I told Ryan. "Must be my magic or something."

"Or something," Ryan agreed. "Like all the talking."

"Her Majesty, Queen Sass," I announced to everyone in the room.

No one seemed to get the joke because they didn't laugh.

"Tough crowd," I muttered.

"I think they're more concerned with imminent death," Ryan said.

"Oh. Right. Well. Can't have that." I looked back at the Darks. "This has been fun. Maybe come back and see me some time? You guys seem nice." I gave them the ol' Look-How-Precious-Sam-Is big eyes and big smile at full blast. Ryan made a strange noise at my side, like he'd been punched in the stomach.

Squat Wizard smiled back and said, "Aww. You too, Sam. We'll just get out of your hair and let you enjoy your evening. So sorry for interrupting. Remember—"

One of his Darks tugged on his shoulder and leaned over to whisper in his ear.

"What now?" Squat Wizard said. "Uh-huh. Uh-huh.... You don't say.... We did what...? Uh-huh. Uh-huh.... Oh. *Right*." He turned back and glared at me.

"Dammit," I muttered. "I thought that would work."

Ryan choked out a laugh. "I can't believe it almost *did*. Has it ever?"

"Once? No. Four times."

He sighed. "You have got to stop putting yourself in these situations."

I rolled my eyes. "I'll get right on that."

"Sam of Wilds!" Squat Wizard shouted. "You took the life of Lartin the Dark Leaf. A fine, upstanding Dark wizard who loved long walks through the forest and the smell of vanilla-scented candles and eating pudding. You have taken his life, and now we shall take yours. And that of the knight since he has chosen to stand with you. Maybe even little Todd there."

Morgan was going to kill me.

A flicker of green off to the side. Maybe some gold.

There was a reason I didn't use my magic much out in public, something that he and I had agreed upon when he'd tested me shortly after finding me with the boys of stone. He didn't want people knowing the extent of my power. Ryan hadn't heard about the thief-chair thing because Morgan had gotten there first and changed them back. No one knew about it, and I was a bit foolish to have spoken of it. Because I was strong. Very strong.

Stronger than Morgan.

Stronger than the Darks.

In fact, Morgan thought I might have been the strongest wizard he'd ever heard of.

And that *scared* him.

And it scared me too.

It scared *him* because he was always worried about what people would try to do to me if they found out. There were always others out there that wanted nothing more than to harness all the power they could get their hands on.

It scared me because I was always worried about what *I* would do to *people*. I had turned a group of boys to stone with just a *thought*.

So we agreed to keep it quiet as much as we could. Until we knew more.

It'd been ten years. The only thing we'd really learned was that we still didn't know where my limits lay. There was always a ceiling to magic, a point where it could go no further. Magic is bound by laws much like physics or mathematics.

The problem is those laws didn't seem to apply to me, and I hadn't yet found my ceiling.

Which is why I needed a cornerstone.

A cornerstone is the first stone set in the construction of a foundation. All other stones are set based upon the placement of the cornerstone. It determines the position of a structure.

Magic is the same. It needs a set foundation in order to properly grow. It was possible I didn't know my ceiling because I didn't know where my foundation began. I could use Morgan or Gary or Tiggy. My parents. And I did. But it was getting harder and harder to use them the older I got.

Hence the matchmaking.

"It'll be worse," Morgan had told me once. "When you feel threatened. Or when those you care about are threatened. It'll be harder to control."

The Darks were threatening me. That was fine. I was used to being threatened. I could deal with it.

But they had also threatened *Ryan*. And that was not okay.

Oh, and Todd. They had threatened Todd too.

That was important.

Still.

I stepped forward, and Ryan said, "*Sam.*"

People moved then. They must have seen something on my face because they just *scattered* out of the way, shoving their chairs out, scrambling until there was no one between us and the Darks.

I said, "You can leave now. Or I'll make you leave. Your choice. To be honest, though, you won't like it if I'm the one to make you leave." I could see the green clearly now. And the gold.

Squat Wizard laughed. "Says the apprentice."

The other Darks smirked behind him.

Ryan came up to stand beside me. He pulled his shield from off his back and took a fighting stance next to me, eyes narrowed.

Something settled somewhere in my head, locking into place. My shoulders eased and my magic felt tighter. More focused. More in control.

Through the haze of green and gold, I thought, *Oh no.*

But the thought was lost as I pulled the green and gold to me. They were the top colors, the earth magic. Other colors shifted in and out (reds and blues and purples and indigos).

The Darks moved. They muttered to themselves and magic began to build.

They were broadcasting. Every single move. Like I wouldn't know.

There were people here, I reminded myself. Innocent people.

And Ryan. Ryan was at my side, and nothing could happen to him.

Which is why when the Dark on the right launched a blue fireball at me, I held my hand out in front of me and pulled it in. It hovered in the air, inches from my palm. It would have been so easy to fire it back at them tenfold, igniting their hair and clothes and skin. But others would get hurt. Others would suffer.

So I pulled it into myself.

It felt odd, another's magic mixing with my own. But mine consumed it, making it a part of me. There was a bright flare in the green and gold and then it settled.

The fireball was gone.

I lowered my hand.

And the Dark wizards just *stared*.

"Um," Squat Wizard said. "What?"

I closed my eyes. I tilted my head to the side, stretching the muscles, popping my neck. Took a deep breath. Let it out slowly.

I opened my eyes.

The Darks took a step back as one.

"I gave you a chance," I said. "You should have taken it."

I could have killed them easily. It was well within my right to do so. They had attacked us first and there would be no repercussions for such actions. I would be justified and no one would say a thing against me.

My fingers tingled and I thought just how *easy* it would be. A couple of old words I'd never spoken aloud before, a flick of my wrist, and I *knew* their hearts would explode in their chests.

But I was not that person. I was not a murderer.

So I thought *tae* and *dao* and *fie* and raised my hands to conduct my symphony.

There was green. So much green because the earth was green and the earth was all around us. I moved my hands down, then *up*. There was a crack of wood as columns of rock shot up through the floorboards, molding up and around each Dark before they could move. I curled my hands into fists. The rock covered their legs and arms and went up to their necks and I almost thought to just *keep going* or maybe *collapse the rock in on itself* and it'd be over, all over for them. But then Ryan was *right there* and I could hear him breathing, could feel his hand coming to my neck and squeezing just once so I *stopped*.

The haze of green and gold faded.

I closed my eyes.

I took another breath.

Let it out.

Opened my eyes.

Everyone was staring at me.

"Huh," I said. "I've never done that before." I looked over at Ryan, who still had his hand on my neck. "Can you remind me to write this into the Grimoire when we get back? If Morgan doesn't murder me first?"

Ryan said in a hoarse voice, "Ungh. Yeah. Yeah. I can do that." His pupils looked dilated. He squeezed my neck again before pulling his hand away.

I beamed at him. "Thanks."

He said "Ungh" again.

Squat Wizard said, "My *gods*. How did you do that?"

I shrugged. "I'm a wizard." Ha, and Gary wasn't even there to correct me. He was going to flip when I told him about this.

The Darks all gaped at me.

"Oh," I said with a wince, "and can you totally just keep this a secret? Like, from everyone? That would be so cool of you. I'd owe you one." I glanced around the room, trying to look each person in the eye so they could see how sincere I was.

They all just nodded.

I felt relieved.

It was going to be fine.

IT WAS not fine.

The next day, there were headlines being called out on the streets in the City of Lockes.

"THE APPRENTICE TO THE KING'S WIZARD SINGLE-HANDEDLY TOOK DOWN AN ARMY OF DARKS WITH THE POWER OF HIS MIND ALONE! WITNESSES SAY HIS EYES GLOWED WITH AN UNHOLY AND SOMEWHAT FLATTERING LIGHT! FIRST DATE WITH THE GOLDWAITHE MOGUL'S SON CONSIDERED TO BE A ROUSING SUCCESS! IMPENDING WEDDING ANNOUNCEMENT EXPECTED! READ IT HERE FIRST!"

Fuck.

CHAPTER 7
This Garden Made of You and I

"I CAN so totally explain," I said when Morgan threw one of the newspapers at me the next morning. I was in the lab jotting down the Rock Column Thing (pending a new and much more awesome name) I'd done the night before into my Grimoire. I thought I'd gotten the basics behind it, but it would take time to go more in depth, and I'd only been at it an hour or so.

"Can you?" Morgan said lightly. But I was not fooled. He was *pissed.*

I looked down at the paper, the *City of Lockes Gazette.* They'd totally chosen to use a photo from when I was going through my awkward phase at sixteen when my face hadn't quite decided if it wanted to be somewhat handsome or a complete train wreck. I wrinkled my nose. "That's so not flattering. Gods, they did that on purpose."

"Undoubtedly," Morgan said.

I scanned through the article. "*...filled out his outfit quite nicely...* Well that's super, I suppose. *...accompanied by the dashing and immaculate Knight Commander Ryan Foxheart as his chaperone...* What a bunch of kiss-asses. Dashing *and* immaculate? I am so going to make fun of him to his face for this. *...on a date with Duke Todd Goldwaithe of the Goldwaithe Hotel conglomerate....* Not one mention about his ears? Travesty. *...attacked out of nowhere by forty Dark wizards....* That's just not true at all. Whatever happened to journalistic integrity? Excessive liberties, I must say. *...took down the Dark army with a wave of his hand....* I suppose it was a wave. Little more complex than that. Way to marginalize. *...while the Knight Commander looked on in beautiful astonishment....* What does that even mean? Did an editor even go through this? Come on. *...they appeared intimate and comfortable as they stood side by side against the rising tide of Dark wizards. Could there be something there? This reporter won't even begin to speculate, but yes. There probably is....* Oh boy. So, ha-ha, fun fact: I might have something to tell you in just a moment. Consider that a teaser, but you totally can't get mad because it's not my fault. *...Earl Terrance Goldwaithe released a statement, saying damage is minimal and that he is pleased that his future son-in-law was able to defend the restaurant and his son....* Well that was nice of him. I will offer to cover the damages, of course, it's the least I can do—and his future *what*-in-law?"

I might have screeched the last part as I continued reading.

"*Earl Goldwaithe told this reporter, 'Just how lucky is my son? I will never have to worry about his safety again. His husband-to-be can obviously handle anything thrown his way. I'm pretty sure little Todd will be in excellent hands, if you know what I mean.'*"

Yeah, definitely screeching.

I looked back up at Morgan with panicked eyes.

His face was in his hands. He was moaning "My life, my life, my life."

"I'm not marrying Todd!" I shouted at him.

Of course, that was the moment Gary, Tiggy, and my parents burst into the lab.

Gary said, "Why did I have to hear about your engagement from the cook?"

Tiggy said, "You still have flower or did Todd eat it?"

Dad said, "Are you sure, Sam? That was just the first date. At least go on one more before you propose. I'm sure he's nice, but he can't be *that* nice."

Mom said, "Or fifty more. Or seventy. I feel really old today and that's not a good feeling."

I hit my head against my desk repeatedly.

"Sam," Morgan said, pulling his face from his hands. "The Darks. Where are they? And why in the name of the gods did you not wake me the *moment* you stepped back into the castle?"

"Well, see, that's a funny story," I said.

"Is it?" he said. "Amuse me."

He didn't sound like he was in the mood to be amused.

"Okay. But, like, you need to listen to the whole thing first, before making judgments. And I know you, so I know your judgmental face. Yep. There it is. Right there. That face. Stop it." He stopped. Sort of. "So, there I was, having a nice first date and did you know they have theme nights? And the theme was duck and blueberries. Or something. I don't even know. But I'm allergic to those and then Ryan was going to force-feed me *carbs*, and Todd may have been under the impression that I was going to give him an accidental hand job, so when I spilled the water on him, he got all wet. And then Ryan had to be all, like, *I'm a knight, you must listen to me and do what I say all the time everywhere ever*, and I was, like, say whaaaaat? And then Todd got flustered because Ryan poked me with his sword, which is *not* dirty, by the way, and then four—*and only four*—Darks came in and they started to monologue! You know how I feel about that! But then they threatened Ryan with death and I was, like, *bitch, please. You don't know who you're messing with.* Oh, and they threatened Todd too. Can't forget Todd! But they *did* know who they were messing with and they *still* decided to mess with us, and so I made rock rise from the ground and trap them completely and instead of bothering you because I know how cranky you get when you're woken up, I had Pete come and take them to the dungeons, and they're in the special cells that block their magic, so that's good. And here we are now! All of us. Together. In the same room. This is nice. We should do this more often. So, good night!"

I ran for the door.

Morgan waved his hand.

It closed and locked.

"It's ten in the morning," he said.

"Motherfucker," I sighed.

I turned back.

They all stared at me.

I waited.

Then:

"You gave him an accidental hand job?" Gary shrieked at me. "How did you do it *accidentally*?"

"That was long story," Tiggy said. "I don't know what happened."

"I swear to the gods that only you find yourself in these situations," Mom said, shaking her head. "Maybe I should have eaten more meat during the pregnancy. Did I fail you? Should I have eaten more yak?"

"Why would they have theme duck and blueberry nights?" my father asked. "That just sounds ridiculous."

"It *was*," I said. "Even the *wine* was blueberry."

We both made faces because he was allergic too.

Morgan said nothing. Didn't even have his judgmental face on.

I looked at the others. "Can you guys give us a bit? There are things Morgan and I have to discuss."

They looked between the two of us, but eventually Mom herded them toward the door. The door opened and then shut behind them as soon as they'd gone through.

It locked again.

I gulped. "So, were you amused? You don't look amused. You look—"

"Sam."

I stopped talking.

We were quiet, for a time.

Then, "How long?"

"What?"

"How long did the spell take?"

"From inception to completion?"

He nodded once.

I frowned. "Five seconds. Maybe as much as ten, though not more."

"And the words spoken?"

I winced. "Ah, see. Um. I didn't actually *say* the words. I might have just... thought them?"

He went very still. "What words did you think?"

"Um. *Tae. Dao.* And there was some *fie*. Yeah. Definitely some *fie*."

"Some *fie*," he repeated.

"Yes."

"Sam."

"Yes?"

"There's something else. That you haven't said."

I groaned. "Gods, I hate how you can do that. It's creepy."

He waited.

"Okay, so one of the Darks *might* have shot a blue fireball of doom at me and I *might* have absorbed it instead of deflecting it."

"You did what," he said. No inflection at all. It was really admirable. I wondered if that level of dryness came with age or merely having dealt with me for close to a decade. Probably a combination of both.

"Yeah. It was an ordeal." I sighed the weary sigh of the put-upon.

"And your body didn't reject it?"

I shook my head. "No. It felt strange at first, but then I felt it meld with my own magic and that was that."

He stared at me.

I did my best not to fidget.

My best was not good enough. I started to fidget.

He said, "You could have been hurt."

"I know."

"You could have hurt others."

"I *know*. But I didn't. I wouldn't. I'm not that kind of person." I felt heart-stung at what he was implying.

"I know you're not," he snapped at me. "And I have never suggested otherwise. My *gods*, Sam. Do you have any idea what could have happened?"

I laughed bitterly. "Yes, Morgan. I am well aware. You don't think I know? You've drilled it into me enough. How easy it is to be consumed by magic. How easy it would be to let it take over. Especially me. And don't think I don't know it. Don't think I didn't feel it when they stood in front of me, threatening Ryan, saying they were going to kill him. Don't think I didn't want to kill them right then and there, that I didn't just want to wipe them from the face of the world so they could never make threats like that again. I could have turned that fire back on them. I could have pulled the rock over their faces and let them suffocate. I could have broken their beating hearts from their chests. So don't think I don't know. Because I *do*. I *know*. But I made a choice and I stopped them from hurting anyone."

"And yourself and Todd," Morgan said.

"What?"

"You said they threatened Ryan. Surely they threatened you and Todd too."

"Of course," I said quickly. "Yes. Todd and I were threatened as well. Poor Todd. With his ears."

"But it was just Ryan that made you act."

"What? No. Of course not."

"So let me get this straight," he said. "They threatened you and Ryan."

"And Todd," I said.

"And Todd," he agreed. "And then you absorbed another wizard's magic and called upon the earth and encased them in stone."

"That's about the gist of it."

"Is it."

"Yes." I smiled at him.

"You said something earlier." His look was calculating.

My smile faded. I hated calculating Morgan. "I said a lot of things earlier. It's kind of my thing."

Morgan said, "So, ha-ha, fun fact: I might have something to tell you in just a moment. Consider that a teaser, but you totally can't get mad because it's not my fault."

"I really hate your photographic memory," I said. "So, so much. And that voice you just used? If that was you trying to do an impression of me, I am insulted. I do *not* sound that high-pitched and whiny."

"I was trained as a master impressionist," he said, completely serious.

"Okay, so maybe I *do* sound that high-pitched and whiny. That's disheartening."

"I am devastated for you," he said. "So. You teased me. Give me the rest. I wait with bated breath."

"You can't get mad," I said.

"Whenever you start stories like that, I usually end up mad."

"Crap."

"Sam."

There was no point trying to lie about it. Morgan would know. "I think Ryan might be my cornerstone." I closed my eyes and waited for the yelling to commence.

It never came.

I gave it a minute, just to be sure.

Nothing.

I opened one eye. Then the other.

Morgan just looked sad. "Oh, Sam," he said quietly.

That was worse than yelling. It was *pity*. And I *hated* pity. "I know, I know. It's not… ideal. And it's not… happening. I know. I know this. But you have to believe me when I say I didn't know. I didn't mean for it to happen. I was just *there* and he stood by my side and something just *clicked* in my head. And then when they threatened him, all I could think was how I would never let them do that. I would never let that happen. But it's okay, because it's not permanent. We're not bound. I just need to keep my distance from him and find someone else. Todd is… nice. I'll go on more dates with him. I'll go on so many dates that you won't even have to worry about it. You won't even—"

"Sam."

"Shit," I muttered. "I fucked up. I'm sorry."

He sighed. "You didn't. It's not as if you did it on purpose. That's not how it works. You can't force something like that."

"I know. It's just…."

"What?"

"It's just of *course* it's him. You know? The one person I can't have. Of *course*. Because that's how my life works."

"There doesn't have to be romantic involvement in a cornerstone, Sam. You know this as well as I do. Mine was certainly never romantic."

"Because you're asexual," I said, treading lightly, because things made so much more sense now. Morgan *never* talked about the past, at least not something this personal. A wizard's cornerstone is private. The details of the relationship are usually only for the two involved. Most were romantic, but not all.

"Yes," Morgan said. "But that doesn't mean there wasn't love involved. Because there was. That's something the Darks can never understand, which is why they have never subscribed to the idea of cornerstones. Their magic is erratic for a reason. They have nothing to build it off of. It's also why they're so dangerous. And here you are, wrapped up in five of them in the last week alone."

"What can I say? They must like me."

"Sam," he said in warning.

"I don't know!"

"It's about the *connection*. I said it doesn't always have to be sexual or romantic and I meant that. Mine... well. She was like me. Asexual. And I loved her very much."

I held my breath, not wanting to break the moment.

He smiled, and for the first time since I'd known him, I saw a wistful curve to it. "She laughed at me when I told her what she was. What she did for me. I was seventeen at the time. She was almost thirty. An odd pair, we were. But we made it work. She helped me build the foundation I needed, and we were very happy. By the time she passed, my magic was solid and strong. The decades we'd spent together made sure of that."

I felt the sting of tears at the softness of his voice. "What was her name?" I asked, my voice slightly rough.

"Anya," he said.

"She sounds wonderful," I said.

He reached over and patted my hand. "She was."

"Maybe you could tell me more about her some day?"

"Sure, Sam. I think I'd like that. She would have loved you."

"It can't be Ryan," I said quietly. "It can never be him."

Morgan cocked his head at me. "And why is that, little one?"

"Because... I just." I looked away. "It could never be... platonic. With him. From me. I would always... want. And that's not fair to him. Or me. Because I can't have that. And I would never do anything to hurt him or Justin."

He grabbed my hand and held it tightly. "And Todd?"

I shrugged. "He's nice."

"And his ears."

"His ears," I agreed.

"But?"

"I don't know. It doesn't feel the same."

"You can't force it."

"I know."

"Maybe...."

I looked up at him. "Maybe what?"

"Maybe you need to get out of here for a while," he said slowly. "Clear your head."

I laughed. "You'd let me go out? After everything that's happened in the past few days?"

"You'd have to stay away from the Darks."

"Yeah. That's a given."

"And keep your magic under wraps."

"I usually do."

He nodded. "Okay. Let me do some digging."

"Are you going to tell me where I'm going?"

He shook his head. "Not yet. You're going to have to trust me on this. It's probably time this happened anyway."

"Oooh," I said. "Ominous."

He squeezed my hand again before he pulled away. "I'll see to the Darks. I doubt we'll get anything from them, but it doesn't hurt to try. I want you to write a detailed account of what happened last night for posterity. It'll help should there be… questions, down the road."

The door unlocked and opened. He slipped through and it closed behind him.

I DIDN'T leave the labs until well past nightfall, not trusting myself or anyone around me not to say or do something stupid. Gary, Tiggy and my parents all knew me well enough to know that it was best to steer clear of me for a little while. I'd find them tomorrow and tell them what I knew. Well, *most* of what I knew. I didn't think I needed to bring up the cornerstone thing again. That way lay heartache and misery, two things I could do without at the moment.

I detoured through the kitchens, grabbing some fruit and cheese as the cooks fussed over me. They gave me warm bread and milk and told me I was precious and handsome and I was so brave to have taken on an army of Darks with only a knight at my side. I told them that's not what happened at all. They laughed and cooed at me, not believing a single word I said. I stuffed the cheese and bread in my mouth to avoid having to say anything further.

I went out to the gardens. The spring air was warm and redolent with my mother's flowers. The lanterns were dark, but the moon and the stars shone down from above and fireflies flickered in and out, lighting my way.

I was in the deepest part of the gardens, a place where very few ventured. I considered it to be my own little secret, though others surely knew of it. Here the flowers were more experimental, more wild. They grew from the pots and plots, vines thick and thorns sharp. Had I been here in daylight, the flowers would have been open and wide. As it was, they were curled up against the dark, but that was okay. I wasn't here for them.

I lowered myself to the ground and lay on my back in the grass. The night sky above was clear and bright, and while the moon was beautiful, yes, I had never been drawn to it. Not like the stars.

I had wished upon them as a child and had wished upon them as an adult. It was upon these stars that I had rested my hopes and dreams, my anger and frustrations. I wished because as a child, that's what you're supposed to do. You don't know any better. I wished because as an adult, sometimes you don't know what else to do. You know better, but you don't care.

I could see the constellations of my childhood, and the stories that came with them: David's Dragon. The Lightning-Struck Man. The Pegasus. Vhan's Fury.

I hadn't spoken to any of them in a very long time.

I said, "I don't know what to do."

Because I didn't.

I was twenty years old.

I was son of Joshua. Son of Rosemary.

My best friends were Gary and Tiggy.

Somewhere inside of me was the capacity for great magic, both light and dark.

I was the apprentice to the prodigious Morgan of Shadows.

His magic was legendary. Had been for centuries.

And someday soon, I'd be stronger than him.

If I wasn't already.

But he'd had his cornerstone at the age of seventeen. She'd helped him build his magic into what it was.

I couldn't let myself go Dark.

Todd was… nice.

I liked his ears. His nervousness.

But he could never be my cornerstone. No matter how hard I wished it so. I could never twist and shape him into being what I needed. It wouldn't be fair to him. Or to me. Especially if I ended up hurting him because I lost control.

And Ryan… well. That was always going to be a mistake. Because he was promised to another and regardless how I felt about the Prince of Douchedom, I would never do something like that to Justin. And not as if Ryan would anyway. He had a fucking prince. I was nothing more than an apprentice.

Justin looked like a god.

I looked like a peasant.

Justin was royalty.

I was from the slums.

Justin was—

"Oh my gods," I groaned. "I am so pathetic."

Fuck that, because that wasn't who I was.

I was awesome.

I was epic.

I was a badass fucking wizard's apprentice who would one day change the way people looked at magic.

I was going to rescue people from the slums and make their lives better.

I was going to open a shop where anyone got to come in and hug puppies for free and leave with a balloon, ice cream, and a compliment. "Here's your pistachio cream. I made you a balloon animal in the shape of a walrus. You have very nice knuckles."

I was going to finish my Grimoire, and five hundred years from now, people would be studying it and thinking to themselves, *Wow. That Sam was pretty neat. I wish I could have been his best friend forever.*

Because I was Sam of Wilds.

Maybe I didn't look like I was a god.

(More like the gods had a sense of humor.)

But I could do things that were almost godlike.

I could create. I could rejuvenate. I could *make something out of nothing because I was godlike—*

Yikes.

"Curb the ego, Sam," I muttered to myself.

But I *was* something, okay? I *was*. I'd come from a place where not much hope resided, and whether by accident or design, I'd changed the shape of my future and not just for me. For my mother. For my father. They had given me everything they had, and I was able to give them something back.

That should have counted for something.

And it did.

But still….

There was an ache in my heart.

To know my cornerstone was here and I could never have him.

It wasn't the be-all and end-all.

There could be others.

I would find them. The one for me. It would all be okay.

And so I looked back up at the sky, took a breath, and wished upon the stars.

I wish I could find that one person made for me so that way I can show them why I was made for them.

Selfish? Maybe. Sad? Definitely. But I knew—

"Sam?"

I squawked attractively.

Okay. That was a lie.

There is no way to squawk attractively.

It was rather unattractive. Arms flailing, legs kicking. It was just awful.

"Didn't mean to scare you," Knight Ryan Asshole said, sounding amused.

I sat up and glared at him. "I wasn't *scared*."

"You screamed like a frightened little girl."

"I squawked like an indifferent tall *man*." Because that was a sound and logical argument. "What are you doing out here?" I hadn't seen him since we'd been escorted back to the castle the night before by Pete, who'd kept laughing at me like I'd done something hysterical.

He shrugged and glanced away. He looked tired. He was dressed down more than I'd ever seen before, wearing trousers and a soft-looking tunic with embroidered edges. It was open at the throat, and my mouth went dry. "Just… checking things out."

"Things."

He rolled his eyes. "Yes, Sam. *Things*."

"Well. I hope *things* are okay." I paused. "Are they?"

"What are you asking?"

"Honestly? I have no idea. You startled me and my brain isn't working yet."

"Scared you," he corrected.

"Ass. How did you know about this part of the garden?"

He fidgeted. "Well."

I waited.

"Your mother… might have showed me?" He sounded embarrassed.

"*Did* she?" I said, already plotting revenge.

"A long time ago," he said. He brushed a hand over the furled petal of an orange wildflower. "I needed it, I guess."

"What? Why?"

"Said it was a good place to come if I ever needed solitude. It gets… loud. In the castle."

"Understatement. Why do you think I was holed up in the labs all day today?"

"Yeah. Uh. About that."

"It's okay," I said with a straight face. "I know it's hard being dashing and immaculate."

He groaned and buried his face in his hands. "Of course you saw that."

"Do you ever go anywhere and not be dashing and immaculate? It must get tiring. You know. With all the dashing."

"You think I'm dashing?" he asked, dropping his hands, eyebrows arching.

It was suddenly very hard to breathe as I realized he was towering over me and that my penis found that to be very attractive. "What? Just. What? Shut up. With your. Face." *Smooth. Real smooth.* "Just quoting your adoring fans."

"I don't have *fans*," he snapped.

"Wow. Bitchy. And wrong. You do. You have fans. They have clubs. Did you know that? There are actual legitimate Ryan Foxheart Fan Clubs in Verania. They meet and talk about your eyebrows and when it's better if you part your hair left or right and how fantastic you look when you pose everywhere you go."

"I don't pose!" he said like it was the most outrageous thing he'd ever heard.

I pushed myself up off the ground. "First of all, lie. You totally do." I lowered my voice just a tad to do an extraordinarily accurate impression of him. "Hi, my name is Ryan Foxheart. Oh no! There's *danger* afoot! Let me pull out my sword and pose." I mimed pulling a sword from my side and cocked an eyebrow. "Notice how dashing I am. And immaculate. And today, my hair is parted on the right. Wink."

"Oh my gods."

"Spot-on, right?" I thought about putting the sword away, but then I realized there wasn't one and that I was still posing. I stopped that immediately. "I bet it was like looking in a mirror."

He was flustered. It was awesome. "*No.* That's not even close to what I sound like."

"But the rest of it, then, huh? I knew it!"

He scowled at me. "You aggravate me."

"I aggravate everyone. It's part of my charm." And this conversation was weird. I didn't even know why we were having it. Why I was allowing it. I'd sworn to myself to stay far away from Ryan Foxheart until Morgan sent me out again. And yet, I'd left the labs for less than an hour and here he was. It was unnerving.

"I wouldn't call it charm exactly," he said.

"Oh? What would you call it?" I asked and thought, *Walk away walk away walk away.*

He didn't answer. Instead, he said stiffly, "Todd seems… nice."

And that was a change of subject I almost couldn't follow. "Huh?"

"Todd," he said slowly, as if I was an idiot. "Your fiancé."

My eyes bulged. "My what now?"

The scowl deepened. "Your future husband. It was all over the news." He looked angry, and I had no idea why.

"I'm not getting married!"

"Then why would they print that?"

"Because the freedom of press has gone too far in this country? I don't know!"

"They can't just print whatever they want!"

Poor, sweet foolish child. "Uh. Yeah. They can. It's called sensationalism. They were calling you dashing and immaculate!"

"I *am* dashing and immaculate!"

"Aha!" I cried. "I knew you did that shit on purpose. Oh my *gods.* That's so embarrassing for you. My impression was so right it's not even funny. I am going to tell all your fan clubs."

He grinned and it was evil. "And how do you even know about the fan clubs?"

ABORT. ABORT. ABORT. Because he didn't need to know that I went to one *once* while in disguise. That was just ridiculous. And creepy. "Gods. It's late. Look at the time. Actually, I can't because I don't have my watch. I assume it's late. So."

"It's barely ten." He took a step toward me.

"Late," I insisted. "I'm tired. *Some*one decided to keep me out till the wee hours of the morning last night."

"You were attacked," he said, "by Dark wizards. *Again.*"

"It doesn't happen as often as you might think," I said, taking a step back. "I just have one of those faces that people want to shoot things at." And I immediately made that dirty in my head.

"That's one way of putting it."

"Seriously," I said, eyes wide. "You're not even Queen Sass anymore. You're like the God of Sass. You created all the sass the world knows. Why don't more people know this? Instead of *dashing and immaculate*, they should be describing you as *sassy and bitchy*. I am going to write a letter to the editor first thing in the morning. It must be reported on immediately."

"Maybe you can bring that up at the next fan club meeting too."

"Hey! I don't even know what you're talking about, okay? I *hear* things when I'm on my travels. I don't even *care* about stuff like that." I cared so hard. I had actually gone three times to the fan club meeting. They knew me as Mervin. I had a backstory and everything. It was my turn to bring muffins next time. I was considering poppy seed. Or cranberry. Fun.

"So you're not marrying Todd?" he growled, taking another step toward me. "That's probably a good thing. He was going to kill you with ducks and blueberries."

"I'm *not*. Trust me on that. I like his ears but really, that only goes so far."

He grimaced. "You and his *ears.*"

"They stuck out. I thought they were adorable."

"If that's your qualifier for a relationship, then you're screwed."

"That's the idea, isn't it?" I said, trying to grin salaciously. I think I missed the mark and went directly to constipated.

He grunted and closed his eyes. "You can't say stuff like that."

"Why not? Gary says I'm a prude. I don't think I am. I can talk about stuff like that. It's not *that* hard. Or. Well. It could be. Ha! See? I just made a sexual pun, and everyone knows that sex puns are the highest form of humor. Fuck you, Gary! Sex and fucking and balls!"

Ryan actually took a step back at that one, which was good because somehow, he'd gotten really close. "Sam," he hissed.

"Hmmm. Maybe *you're* the prude. Dicks and fornication."

"Sam!" He was turning red again, and my *heart.*

"What!"

"Don't marry Todd," he said. "When you marry, it should be for love. Nothing more. Nothing less."

And that hit me right in the gut, because it couldn't possibly be any clearer than that. "Ah," I said through the blood roaring in my ears as I took a step back. "Congratulations."

"For what?" He looked confused.

"For marrying Justin. You must love him very much. Right? That's what you just said." And I knew he was my cornerstone then because I wanted nothing more than to blow something up with a few choice words, but was able to stop myself. Hurray for personal growth and damning realizations.

He said, "Sam." It was strained.

"What?"

"I don't...." He looked away.

The mood had changed very quickly. "It's okay," I said brightly. Probably too bright. "When I get back, I'll figure something out." And, well. I hadn't meant to say that.

So of course he pounced on it. "Get back?" he asked, snapping his gaze to mine.

"Uh. Yes? I mean. I'll be going out again. For a while."

His face went carefully and explicitly blank. "Oh. For how long?"

For as long as it takes to no longer hurt to have you this close.

I shrugged. "Don't know this time. Will probably be awhile. Morgan's sending me... away."

"Where?"

"Sorry, Ryan. Doesn't work like that. Wizarding business."

He narrowed his eyes. "I'm the Knight Commander of the Castle Guard. You live in the castle. Therefore, you're my business."

That irritated the fuck out of me. "Even the *King* doesn't always get to know what Morgan and I do," I said. "Maybe you should remember that, *Knight Commander.*" Which was a lie. I pretty much told the King everything. Morgan would just smack me upside the head while the King laughed at me.

"And how long will it take for you to get captured again?" he said. "What then? Wait until I ride in to rescue you?"

I laughed at him. "Oh fuck off. You've never had to rescue me. Not once. As a matter of fact, if anything, I rescued *you* last night. You just stood next to me, all dashing and immaculate. Remember? While I had all the magic?" I wiggled my fingers at him.

And his eyes glazed over as he watched my fingers and said, "Ungh."

I frowned. "What's wrong with you?" I didn't think I'd accidentally cursed him.

"Nothing," he said in a rough voice. "Just. Lightheaded. It's fine."

"If you're sure."

And then we just stood there.

I didn't know if we were fighting or not. I thought I was mad, but I also thought I was really turned-on. I wondered if those were sort of the same thing. And while I *knew* why I was turned-on (I mean, hello, proximity: he was like *right there* and I could *smell* him), I couldn't for the life of me figure out what I was supposed to be mad about.

"These are very confusing times," I said.

"No shit," he muttered.

"No cursing," I scolded him. "You're a knight. You don't get to do that. You gave up that right when you swore your oath to the King. You have to lead by example now. So say stuff like 'fudge toast' and 'mothercrackers' instead of 'shit whore' and 'fuck storm.'"

"I can assure you I have never felt the need to say shit whore or fuck storm in my life," he said.

I gaped at him. "But you just *did*. There are little *girls* in your fan clubs! They are young and impressionable." And they could be very mean, I knew from the eight times I'd gone to the meetings. Well, one of them was mean, anyway. She told me that I obviously knew nothing about Ryan Foxheart because his favorite color was burgundy and he one day dreamed of owning a sheep farm. Her name was Tina and she was a bitch, and I hated her stupid face. His favorite color was *scarlet*, and he wanted to open a *bakery*.

(Really, none of that was true. It was just the sort of things we discussed in the meetings.)

He grinned at me again, and the butterflies in my stomach turned into dragons and laid waste to my innards.

"Not that I would know," I said quickly. "I just assumed that only little girls would go to those things. Right? Because anyone else would just be weird." Very weird. Also, I'd been to sixteen meetings and I was thinking of running for fan club treasurer next time. There was already a girl in place named Deidre, but I would destroy her in the next round of elections. She was twelve. I was a wizard. I couldn't lose. "Look. This has been... fun." Lie. This had been nerve-racking and I needed to go masturbate. "But I have to go. I've got stuff to do before I head out again." Masturbate. "Wizard stuff. Like... secret wizard stuff." Masturbate.

Ryan's smile faded. "You're really leaving?"

I sighed. "It's... complicated. It's better this way."

"For who?" he asked.

"It doesn't matter," I said quietly. "Ryan. Look. It's…. For what it's worth, I'm glad we're friends now. Right? We're friends?"

He looked down at the ground. "Yeah, Sam. We're friends."

This made me happy, even if it felt bittersweet along its edges. "Good."

He looked back up at me, and there was something akin to desperation in his eyes. "You just… you have to come back. Okay? You have to."

I was shocked. "I will? Er. I will. I'm going to be the King's Wizard, after all. To your husband."

"Yeah," he said. "I know. When will you leave?"

"Soon," I said. "A week. Maybe a little more."

He nodded tightly and turned to walk away. He made it a few steps before he stopped again. He looked up toward the stars above and I followed his gaze.

He said, "I wish—"

And I said, "Don't."

He turned back to look at me.

Everything hurt. "You can't," I managed to say. "You can't say your wish out loud. Not when you look up at the stars. If you do, it won't come true. And I can't… I can't allow that to happen to you."

He watched me.

I watched him back.

Finally, he looked back up to the stars and closed his eyes, and I knew he was making his wish. I hoped that whatever it was, that it would one day come true.

When he was done, he opened his eyes and I couldn't look away.

But that's okay because neither could he.

And right then, I hated that we were friends.

It was easier to watch him leave when he didn't know I existed.

CHAPTER 8
Turning Noses into Dicks and Other Stories

EIGHT DAYS later, Morgan said, "I'm sending you north."

I paused from where I'd been scribbling in my Grimoire. "Oh?" was all I could think to say. Because this wasn't just north. I knew he meant *north*. Which, to be perfectly honest, was intimidating as all fuck.

He must have seen that flicker of fear across my face because he shook his head. "No. Not for that. Not yet. You're not ready, Sam."

Thank the gods because he meant *north*.

The cold lands from where my father had come.

Where Morgan's mentor resided in a castle made of ice.

Randall. The scariest motherfucker ever.

Morgan rolled his eyes. "He's not that bad." Like he could read my mind.

"Not that *bad*?" I wheezed. "He's the one who decides who moves on from apprenticeship by conducting the Trials! He's the one who can make or break my future. Oh, and there's the little fact that he *hates every fiber of my being*."

"He doesn't *hate* you, Sam. I've told you that a thousand times."

"Uh, pretty sure he does. I don't blame him, either. You were there the first time I met him. You stood *right there* when I accidentally turned his nose into a penis. He couldn't figure out how to reverse it for *three days*. And he was officiating a wedding the *next* day. He had to marry a bride and groom with a dick nose! He told me that one day he'd have his revenge. Oh gods. What have I done to you? Do you really hate me that bad? Did I disappoint you so badly that you want to subject me to the absolute worst thing you could possibly think of?"

Morgan was trying hard not to laugh, the bastard. "It could have happened to anyone," he said. "Granted, it happened to *you*, which is not all that surprising."

"I was *fifteen*," I said with a scowl. "Of *course* I was thinking about dicks. You know what? No. I blame you. Puberty was an awful, awful time, and you made me do magic. This is all your fault."

"Trust me," he said. "I tell myself that every day."

"Har, har. No. I'm not going. I'll go live in the woods and become the scary story that parents tell their children about. Be careful, little Tommy. Old Man Sam lives in those woods. If you don't eat your vegetables, he'll come when you're sleeping and steal your feet."

"To be fair, it wasn't the first thing you'd turned into a penis."

"Ugh."

"Like that turkey."

"Shut up."

"Or the King's wine glass."

"Do you remember the look on his face? I thought he'd literally shit himself."

"Or the—"

"I get it," I snapped. "I had dick on the brain."

"I love our little talks."

"You're really going to make me go, aren't you?"

"It'll be good for you," Morgan said kindly. "Give you some time to clear your head."

"With the wizard of all wizards. Like, the *head* wizard."

"Yes, Sam."

I had to make sure. "I'm not ready. For the Trials."

"I know. And that's not what you're going for. At least not yet. Hopefully, that's still years away."

Randall was the oldest wizard in existence, and I swear he was hanging on just so that he could one day have his revenge against me. Morgan said he was at least six hundred years old, that the amount of magic in him kept him from passing through the veil, but I knew otherwise. I was going to get there, he was going to turn me into a giant dick, and then he was going to die, cackling as he did so.

Granted, that would mean he wouldn't be in charge of my Trials, the process from moving on from an apprentice to being a full wizard. The youngest wizard to pass the Trials had been forty-two. Morgan had done so when he was sixty-seven. I wanted to take the Trials by the time I hit thirty.

But between not having finished my Grimoire and a lack of a solidified cornerstone, that dream was slipping further and further away.

I sighed. "You told him, huh? Through your secret wizarding network that you still haven't told me about."

"It's called a letter in the mail," he said.

I narrowed my eyes. "It takes a month to get to Castle Freeze Your Ass Off."

"I'm aware. And don't call it that when you get there. It's Castle Freesias. You know how Randall gets when you're mouthy. You need to try and curb some of your more natural urges."

"I'm aware. His jaw twitches whenever I speak."

Morgan grinned. "That's because you let the words fall out without rhyme or reason. He's a bit more economical that way."

"That's code for he hates me."

"He's worried about you."

I looked up in surprise. "He is?"

"Regardless of what you think, he cares about you, Sam. And we're... concerned."

"Concerned," I repeated.

"This cornerstone business can be trying on an apprentice," Morgan said. "Especially one of your... unique caliber. He will teach you in ways that I cannot. I'm too close to you. I'm biased and might not be able to see the full picture. And in the long run, that will cause more harm than good. For the both of us."

"Because you love me," I said, sounding smug.

"More like you grew on me," he said. "Like fungus."

"How long?" Because Randall was on the other side of Verania and I highly doubted he would be coming to me.

"A month to Castle Freesias," he said. "Four months there. One month back."

"Six *months*? Morgan, I don't have *time* for—"

"You do," he said, bringing himself to his full height. "And you will. Because this isn't a suggestion. I am the King's Wizard. You are my apprentice. This is an order."

"You know, that ooh-scary-look-at-me voice might work on other people, but I've seen you vomit pink goo after that selkie scratched you and you told me you wanted to hug me for days. It doesn't work on me anymore when you have demanded I snuggle with you."

"I had a *fever*," he said. "There were hallucinations!"

"Riiiight. That's what we're going with. And if I go, Gary and Tiggy go too."

"Because you're codependent and can never do anything on your own."

"Rude. You're just jealous because you're not invited on the Super Awesome Road-Trip Fun-Time Extravaganza."

He sighed. "You capitalized that, didn't you?"

I smiled because he knew me so well. "When do we leave?"

"Five days," he said. "It'll give you enough time to prepare. And I'm serious, Sam. You stay on the roads. You stay out of the Dark Woods. You stay away from Dark wizards. You avoid any and all shenanigans. You get to Castle Freesias. You learn what you need to. You get back. I want no deviations to that, you understand?"

I laughed at him. "Come on. It's me you're talking to. What could possibly go wrong?"

MOM SAID, "You're going *where*? And for *how* long?"

Dad said, "I'll make sure you have plenty of yak fur to wear because you are a wuss and can't handle the cold."

Gary said, "You want me to walk to Castle Freeze Your Ass Off? Are you out your damn *mind*? I just got my hooves painted!"

Tiggy said, "You gonna get captured again. I go to keep you safe, tiny human."

Morgan said, "Just stay out of trouble. For me. For my sanity. I beg of you."

AND I did. I tried to stay out of trouble.

Too bad trouble found me even before we'd left for the north.

Dragons are funny like that.

"WORD ON the street is that you're leaving," Justin said as I left the labs.

And I'd done so well in avoiding him. Goddammit. I plastered the largest fake smile on my face and turned to look at the Prince.

Of course he looked as perfect as usual, leaning nonchalantly against the stone wall, arms across a built chest, a bored look on his handsome face.

"Your Grace," I said with a nod of my head. "I wasn't aware you went out to the streets. Much less listened to what's being said on them." And I was slightly annoyed that *someone* had been talking when they shouldn't have, which meant that Gary probably ran his big fat unicorn mouth down at the nail salon where he went to get his hooves touched back up after he'd scuffed the ground in anger. He and the owner, Ming Win, were thick as thieves, and I just *knew* they were plotting together in that language Ms. Win spoke that sounded like the fluttering of bird wings.

"When it pertains to my wizard, I tend to listen," he said.

Man, did *those* words grate. I was not a fucking possession. "Apprentice," I said.

He glared at me. "What's that now?"

"Not a wizard. I'm an *apprentice*. But thank you for your concern."

"Are you leaving?"

"You've never asked me that before."

"I've never had a reason."

I cocked an eyebrow at him. "And you do now?"

"Ryan," he said.

"Ryan," I said blandly, even though my heart was thundering in my chest.

"He's a bit… distraught."

"Is he?"

"Has been ever since that night."

"And which night would that be?"

"When you two went on a date." He smiled. It was an icy thing. "Sorry. When you went on a date with *Todd*. How is Todd?"

"Uh. Fine? He's fine. He's good." Actually, I really had no idea how Todd was because after Morgan had said he was sending me north, I'd sent a missive to Todd explaining how his ears were awesome and I liked his freckles, but that I had to leave for months and that it wasn't fair to him to wait for someone like me. I told him to find a nice man who could eat blueberries and ducks and maybe when I got back, I could take him out for a drink and we could be friends.

He'd responded two days later with a letter of his own.

> *Sam—*
> *I figured this was coming the moment the Knight Commander got into the carriage with us. Father will be disappointed, but I understand. Your world is magic and mystery. Mine is hotels and theme nights. Those should probably not mix in any romantic capacity. The results could be disastrous.*
> *Safe travels,*
> *Todd*
> *PS: So when are you going to tell the Knight Commander you're in love with him? Because, honestly? That was PAINFUL.*

I had immediately burned the letter because it was all *lies* and attempted to construct a voodoo doll of Todd. I got stuck on the ears and abandoned the whole project in favor of glaring at the ash remains of the Letter of Evil. I thought about writing again and taking back every nice thing I'd ever said about his ears, realized that was petty and untrue, because his ears were adorable.

And truthfully, I felt kind of bad.

So, no. I hadn't heard from Todd. Nor had I expected to.

But fuck Justin in the face.

"He's busy," I said. "Hotel stuff."

"That so?" Justin asked. "Good for him. Well, since you're obviously not doing anything—"

"That's not true, I have plenty—"

"—I think it's a good idea for you and I to spend some time together. Just the two of us."

I would have rather had my balls torn off. "Say what now?"

He sighed prettily. "Sam, you are to be the King's Wizard one day. I am going to be the King. You will be my advisor, as wrong as that sounds. We should at least spend some time together before you leave for months on end. I mean, who knows if you'll even come back? I would just feel *awful* if something happened to you out there in the big, wide world and I never had a chance to say we bonded."

"Somehow, I get the feeling you wouldn't be that upset."

He grinned. "Nonsense. I would be broken to pieces."

"I can tell. Your words are too kind, my Prince."

"Now, what should we do? What could you and I *possibly* do together?" He tapped the side of his face, thinking malicious things. Then his eyes lit up. "I've just had the most *wonderful* idea."

"Uh-oh," I muttered under my breath. "Hold on to it. I have a feeling those are a rarity."

"How's that now?" he asked, stepping away from the wall.

"Nothing, Your Grace," I said sweetly. "I'm sure whatever you've thought of is perfect."

"Oh, it is. Shall we?"

I WAS completely and utterly fucked.

I figured as much when Justin got that glint in his eye that meant he was about to be a fucking jerk. Yes, I was not a fan of his (and I was most certainly *not* a member of his fan club—of which there were inexplicably several—though the two clubs met every other month or so to talk about "Rystin," their favorite couple, while I would sit in the back seething that combining Ryan and Justin to make Rystin was stupid, but what if Ryan Foxheart had met a guy named Sam Haversford? It'd be HaveHeart! *It practically wrote itself.* This, by the way, being the twentieth meeting I'd attended). But I liked to think that maybe deep down in the black and murky confines of his soul, Prince Justin was an okay guy.

I was wrong.

"So, this is the sparring grounds," I said unnecessarily. "And we're alone."

"Are we?" he said, sounding surprised. "I suppose we are."

"You're a Prince. And we've somehow managed to make it out of the castle and out of the city undetected to the sparring grounds. Which are empty."

"How strange. Well, it's Wednesday and the knights will be on the east end, going through their exercises."

"And we're west," I said.

"West," he agreed.

"You probably shouldn't murder me," I said out loud, even though I totally meant to keep that in my head.

He laughed. "I'll keep that in mind."

Wow. That was reassuring.

He walked over to a massive shed standing at the edges of the field. There was a metal padlock on the doors.

"Oh no," I said. "It's locked. We should go home."

"Bah," he said. "You have your magic. Unlock it."

"I left my magic in my room," I said, like that was a real thing.

"Oh. It's good I have the key, then."

"Super. Good. We're going to spar, aren't we?"

"We are," he said easily, unlocking the doors. "It'll be good to measure each other's strengths with weapons. Heavy, sharp weapons."

"Remind me, what place did you finish in your sword-handling division at the last summer celebration?"

"Hmmm?" he said, pulling the doors opened. "I didn't think you paid attention to such things. Oh, Sam. I don't like to brag. It's so unbecoming." He reached in and pulled out an estoc longsword. He spun it easily in his hand with a ridiculous flourish. "First place. Four years running."

"Yeah," I said. "I'm going to have to take a rain check. I just remembered that I made plans with someone to not be here and be wherever they are."

"Nonsense," Justin said. "Gary's with Tiggy in town picking up supplies for your trip that no one is supposed to know about. Your parents are at work. My father is meeting with certain heads of state to discuss new trade routes, Morgan by his side. And Ryan is overseeing the knights' exercises. Who else could you possibly know? Pick a sword, Sam. Your training is about to begin."

"Training," I said stupidly.

"Indeed. After the disaster at Antonella's where you proved you are not in control as you'd like everyone to think, you really believe I'd let you go out into the world without knowing how to use a sword? Come, Sam. That would just be irresponsible."

A low-level fury rolled through me, and I did my best to push it away. "That's very kind of you, sire. I'm sure your tutelage will prove to be enlightening."

He smiled. It was all teeth. "Undoubtedly." He tossed me the estoc without warning. I fumbled gracelessly, narrowly avoiding grabbing the blade. It was heavier than I thought it would be.

I never understood the point of sword fighting. It felt too visceral. Too barbaric. It usually always resulted in bloodshed in close proximity. Magic wasn't like that. There was no need to incapacitate by injury when it could be avoided.

Of course, that little dark voice inside that spoke through the magic reminded me just how close I'd come to encasing the Darks completely in rock. How I could have burst their hearts or set them on fire.

I did my best to ignore that voice. No good would come of it.

Except for setting Justin on fire.

That'd probably be good.

Just his shirt.

I'd put it out.

Eventually.

He reached back in and took out another sword, similar to the estoc he'd given me. He handled it easily. My body and arms weren't conditioned like his and Ryan's. I wasn't dashing and immaculate. Yet another reason they were obviously perfect for each other.

Wow. That sounded bitter.

He left the shed doors opened and turned toward the sparring field. There were wooden dummies shaped in the approximation of a man at one end, covered in nicks and cuts from sword practice. I thought we'd start there (wondering why we were really starting at all), but Justin didn't even glance at them. He led me to the far end of the sparring field, the grass bright and green under our feet, the sky clear and blue above. There was a breeze, and I could smell the trees and the flowers and maybe even a hint of salt from the sea at the ports ten miles away. On a hill in the distance, a large flock of sheep grazed, white among the green.

It was almost nice.

Company excluded, of course.

Because he said, "No magic."

I said, "What?"

He stretched his neck from side to side. "No magic. It isn't fair."

I snorted. "I've never used a sword. Let's talk about *fair*—"

"We could always use our fists," he said, and there was a sour tang to the air now. His jaw had tightened and there was a flash of something in his eyes that hadn't been there before.

"What is this?" I asked him quietly.

"A lesson," he said, brandishing the sword again

"In?"

"Humility. You see, Sam. If I didn't know any better, I'd think you didn't know your place."

"You'd think wrong."

He took a step toward me. I took an answering step back. "Is that right?"

"Yes."

He raised his sword. Settled into a defensive position. "Sword up, Sam. It's time to begin."

I brought the sword up, holding the handle with two hands. It was awkward. The blade shook slightly.

"Now," he said. "Most think it's about brute attacks. Quick and heavy. Bashing down your opponent. Skin split and blood spilled."

He swung his sword out in a flat horizontal arc. I managed to jump back. Barely.

I said, "Justin."

He said, "But unless your opponent is weak, sheer brute force will only result in exhaustion. And that could lead to mistakes. Mistakes not normally made."

He brought the sword up and over his head, bringing it down toward me. I raised my own sword defensively over my head. The blades clashed. The vibrations from the impact rolled down my arm into my shoulder. The metal scraped as he pulled his sword back and away.

"It's better to dance," Justin said, taking a step back. "Waiting for your opponent to attack and attack and attack. Eventually, he'll tire until he can barely stand and that's when you move in for the kill."

There was green, flicking off out of the corner of my eyes. It felt heady and strong, and I knew just how easy it would be to hold on to it, sink down under it and just *push*.

Instead, I said, "I'm not doing this. Whatever this is."

I dropped the sword. It fell to the ground.

Justin's eyes narrowed. "Pick it up."

"No."

He brought the flat end of the sword up and before I could move, slapped me across the thigh with it. There was a flare of pain as the muscle seized, but I kept my face blank.

"Pick it *up*," he snarled.

So much green. It was everywhere.

"What do you want?" I asked him. "I've never done anything to you. In fact, I've done everything I could to stay out of your way."

"And yet I find you there again and again," he said. "My father. The King's Court. The castle, the city, the country. Everyone knows of Sam of Wilds. The little boy from the slums who *by accident* found himself a spot in royalty though he'd done *nothing* to deserve it."

"And you have?" I asked him, cocking my head. This felt hard. Dangerous. I didn't care. "What exactly did you do? You were *born* and it was given to you. That's all. That's all you've *ever* done, and you're in line to be King. And a king I don't know if I could serve."

He took a step back. "You don't have a choice."

I smiled at him. "There's always a choice. I am not bound to you. Not yet. I haven't taken my oaths. I haven't been through the Trials. You don't own me, Justin. I could walk away from you and never come back."

A king without a wizard to advise him was frowned upon. A prince whose wizard apprentice had walked away was unheard of. There weren't many of us. He needed me more than I needed him.

There was a false bravado that pushed itself through the real fear I saw on his face. "You wouldn't."

"Watch me."

"Your parents," he said. "You'd never see them again."

And that… well. That didn't sit right. "Are you threatening my parents?" I asked him, my voice low.

"You're the one that said he'd walk away." He took a defensive stance.

"What is this?" I asked him again. "Why all the theatrics? What do you want?"

"Stay away from Ryan," he said. "I don't care what has happened between you. I don't care what you think he is to you. You stay away from him."

Ah. Because that makes sense. Unless he knew about Ryan's position as my cornerstone, which would mean Morgan told him or someone else. Which frankly didn't fly. Morgan was a man of secrets. Cornerstones were private business.

So the only thing that remained was my ridiculous crush on a man I would never have. And that I hadn't been as subtle as I thought I'd been. Not-that-subtle and I were more than passing acquaintances.

"It's not like that," I said quietly.

"Bullshit," Justin snarled. "I've seen the way you look at him. The way he looks at you."

I laughed bitterly. "I assure you he sees me as nothing more than an annoyance. I didn't even know he knew my name until the day I got back from the Dark Woods."

"Trust me," Justin said. "He's known who you are for far longer than that."

And before I could even begin to process what *that* meant, I said, "I'm leaving. For at least six months. You won't have to see me."

"I know," he said. "I've had to see the look on his face ever since you told him."

"He's my friend," I said. "Nothing more."

"He's *mine*."

"I know. Trust me. *Everyone* knows."

He raised the sword again and I said, "*Don't*."

I thought *fier* and my fingers twitched and flexed and there was red and orange and I thought to push and push hard, but I pulled most of it back.

Justin gasped as the sword in his hand grew scalding. It fell to the ground, charring the grass underneath.

He said, "I'll see you in the *dungeon* for this—" and I ignored him because the sheep began to bleat loudly among a low rumble.

I turned toward the hill where they'd been grazing.

They were running toward us, frantically calling out. I didn't see a shepherd, unless he was on the other side of the hill.

Birds called out overhead. I looked up and they too were heading the direction of the sheep.

I felt the first ripple of *something* in my chest, like a pinprick of magic, dancing along my skin.

"What the hell?" Justin said, coming to stand next to me.

"Do you feel that?" I asked him, because the ground felt like it was shaking, almost like an earthquake.

"What is it?" he asked.

"I don't know. It looks like—"

Then great wings appeared over the hill, rising up and falling down.

"It looks like a motherfucking dragon," I said weakly. "We should probably run."

And so we did.

I was not a fan of the Prince. He was cocky, arrogant, rude, and apparently had brought me out here to beat a lesson into me about wanting to secretly bone his boyfriend. (My *life*.) I had no reason to care for him aside from the fact that he would be my King one day.

But that's all it took.

Because he *would* be my King one day. Even if I walked away, even if I left the City of Lockes, I would always be a part of Verania, and he would be my King.

So my only thoughts were to keep him safe.

I glanced over my shoulder.

I really wished I hadn't.

Because the dragon had crested the hill. It wasn't as big as I'd thought it'd be, which meant it was still young. However, it was still the size of a house, which meant it was much bigger than Justin and me.

The dragon was black, its scales mottled with stretches of red almost the color of the King's crest. Two horns grew out the top of its head that looked to be as big as I was. The wings were translucent, light filtering through.

They were a rarity in the world, and the sightings of them even rarer. They were intelligent, fierce creatures who killed and took for the sheer sake of doing so.

I'd thought them all named. I thought I knew them all, the ones that resided in Verania. Two lived in the north, a mated pair that lived high in the mountains where snow never melted. There was one to the west, a desert dragon that burrowed extensive tunnels underneath the sand. There were rumors of a fourth that lived in the Dark Woods, but it'd been at least a century since it'd been seen. That dragon had been old and white, and the woods were deep. It was possible it'd died years before, its bones resting where no man had stood for decades.

But this. This one was new.

And I knew the moment it spotted us, dark eyes glittering.

Justin must have felt it too, because he said, "Oh *shit*."

And all I could say was "*Faster*."

The weapons shed. It wasn't ideal, but maybe I could—

The dragon roared behind us.

And if that wasn't a sound to make you shit yourself, I didn't know what was.

I hazarded a look over my shoulder.

The dragon was *right there*.

And it was rearing back and I could smell the gases from the flammable liquid filling its throat from a gland near the back of its tongue.

Fire.

I most certainly didn't want to die right now.

Especially not with Justin.

We weren't going to make it to the shed.

I grabbed him by the arm.

I thought *ies* and *clo*, twisting my right hand in a circle over my head. The air around us froze in a snap as the moisture solidified downward, cocooning Justin and I in a circle of thick ice. I grabbed him and pulled him, covering him with myself.

And it came then. The fire. There was a low *mmmmm* that turned into a blast of hot air and orange-red light. It shone through the fractals of ice, and if we weren't mere inches away from getting burned to nothing, it would have been beautiful. But being that close to death really takes away from pretty fire-ice lights.

The fire died.

Justin said, "*Oh.*"

I gathered my magic.

The ice shattered around us with a swipe of the dragon's claws. Like giants, they were magical creatures in their own right and could counter most types of magic.

Which sucked.

Because that was just *lame*.

And it became even worse when the dragon lowered its massive head toward me and said in a loud, rumbling voice, "I really hate wizards."

I blinked. Because dragons weren't supposed to talk. "Um. What?"

"Cocky shits," he said. "With your whizbangs and pretty sparkles. Too bad too. I'd really have liked to wined you, dined you, then fucked you stupid."

"*What?*"

And then it brought a massive arm back, and before I could move, it brought it forward, and I managed to think *This is going to hurt* before I was flying through the air. I smashed into the side of the weapons shed, my breath knocked from my chest as I crashed through the wood. My head struck something metal and I saw *stars*, more than I'd ever seen before in my life. I landed awkwardly under a shelf in the far corner as the shed collapsed around me. As darkness started to fall, I heard Justin shouting.

"Get the fuck away from me!"

"You on the other hand," the dragon said. "You are *darling*. I think I'd like to hoard *you*."

"*Hoard?* You can't—"

Then Justin yelled again, but honestly, I couldn't be bothered because the stars were growing brighter and brighter until they were all I could see. And as I heard the snap of those great wings taking flight, I followed the stars into the dark.

CHAPTER 9
You Mad, Bro?

I WOKE up in the labs. "Ow," I said. "Motherfucking *ow*."

"Yeah, that's what happens when a building falls down on top of you."

I opened my eyes. Morgan, Gary, Mom, Dad, Tiggy, Ryan, and the King all stared down at me.

"Were you all staring at me while I was passed out?"

They all nodded slowly.

"You're so creepy."

"Your beautiful face," Gary said, sniffing, big eyes wet with tears. "It's *gone*. The *burns*. All the *burns*."

"What?" I yelped, sitting up. "*What*?" I was not vain by any means but it was my *face*, and I was *so fucking vain because it was my* face. "I'll never be a *model*—"

"Just kidding," Gary said, eyes suddenly dry. "Now you know how I felt when Knight Delicious Face pulled your unconscious body from a *pile of rubble, you arrogant bastard*!"

And then he started wailing and put his head on my shoulder. I rolled my eyes but hugged him anyways because I could. And also because I still had my face.

"Knight Delicious Face?" Ryan asked. "What's he talking—?"

"How long was I out?" I interrupted. Because now was not the time to discuss nicknames that should never be discussed. Even if they were true.

"A few hours," Mom said with a frown. "You've got a bump on your head and some bruising on your back and face. You were very lucky."

"Luck is my middle name," I said.

"Your middle name is—" Dad said.

"Of no real importance," I said with a glare because it was a family name and it was *awful*. So many *X*s and *Q*s and it *still* sounded feminine.

"What's his middle name?" the King asked.

"I'll tell you later," Morgan said.

"Bastards," I muttered. "All of you."

"Dark wizards and dragons," Morgan reminded me. "All in the space of two weeks. You are becoming a pain in my ass."

I rolled my eyes as I stretched. I had aches and pains all over, but nothing felt broken or split. My right hand was red hot from where I'd held up the ice spell, but it hadn't blistered. It was a good thing Justin—

Ah. Crap.

I looked to the King and felt like shit. "I'm sorry," I said miserably. "I should have done more to save him."

He reached out and put his hand on the back of my neck, bringing our foreheads together. "The knights were returning to the sparring fields when the dragon came. Did you know that?"

I shook my head. I'd been too busy running from a giant lizard that wanted to set me on fire.

"They were. They were too far away to do anything about it, but they were running. Do you know what they saw?"

"Two guys screaming hysterically as they ran for their lives? I'll admit. I was a screamer."

He sighed. "They saw the dragon pulling itself back to breathe fire. They saw you raise your hand in the air. They saw a blinding flash of blue light as you covered Justin with your body. They saw your magic, Sam. They saw your magic as you protected my son. You did everything in your power to save him. I couldn't ask for anything more from you, Sam of Wilds. And I am so very happy that you are okay."

And I hugged him then, because even though his son was a jerk that I was extraordinarily jealous of, the King was my friend, and I didn't like to see him upset.

"We'll get him back," I said.

"How's that now?" Gary asked. "And what's this *we* stuff?"

The King pulled away and stared at me.

"Dragons," I said. "They're hoarders. They keep the things they think are pretty. Gold and jewels. In this case, Justin. To each his own, I guess."

Morgan smacked me upside the head. Because that felt good with all the other grievous injuries I'd sustained. "Speak," he said. "Now."

"Before I lost consciousness, I heard the dragon say Justin was something he wanted to hoard."

"You heard the dragon speak to Justin," Morgan said slowly.

"Yeah. He also spoke to me, but he was really rude. Told me that he wanted to have sex with me, but since I was a wizard, he couldn't because wizards were gross or something. I mean, what was *that* about? Should I be insulted or flattered?"

The staring thing happened again.

Then:

Morgan said, "Of course you can also understand dragons."

The King said, "Don't take it personally, Sam. Justin takes after his mother. She was beautiful. I didn't know you were into dragons."

Gary said, "What would your babies look like? Little dragon Sam babies? I bet they would be cute. Or really ugly. Yeah. Probably ugly. You shouldn't have a tail. You can't pull it off like I can. Truth."

Tiggy said, "We gonna go smash dragons? I smash dragons."

Mom said, "He didn't want to sleep with you so he knocked you through a building? That's rude. He could have just moved on."

Dad said, "You can do better than the dragon. You are awesome and you dress nice and I like your hair and your jokes."

Ryan said, "What the hell? Does *everything* want to have sex with you?"

Everyone slowly turned to look at him. He refused to meet anyone's gaze.

Whatever the fuck *that* was supposed to mean.

So I focused on the first thing. "I thought it was weird too," I told Morgan. "I didn't think dragons could talk."

"They can't," he said. "Or at least I've never heard of one speaking before."

"So it's like a magic thing?" I said, wiggling my fingers, and I swore I heard Ryan make that *ungh* sound again. I reminded myself to ask him later if he was okay. "But that doesn't make sense. Justin's not magic and I'm pretty sure he understood what the dragon was saying."

Morgan frowned. "I honestly have no idea, then. We'll have to move quickly. The dragon was seen headed north. Dragons are fiercely territorial, but I don't have any record of this one having been spotted before. It's possible he was looking for a new territory to inhabit after having come a great distance."

"So call out the knights and have them start tracking," I said. "They can storm wherever he's being kept and rescue him." I just wanted to sleep and forget about this ridiculous day.

The King said, "Tactically, that's not a good plan. The dragon could easily wipe out a large portion of the knights in a single blast of fire. It's better to go covert. Only a handful of people. And I know just the handful." He smiled. I didn't like that smile.

And Morgan must have gotten the same thing from it, because he said, "Your Majesty, I don't think—"

"Ah," the King said. "But I do."

"No," I said. "No."

"Yes," the King said.

I glared at him.

"What's going on?" Mom asked.

"To be honest, I haven't understood a single thing being said here," Dad told her. "But that's nothing unusual."

"I just keep you around for your looks," Mom said. "Not your brains."

"Romance," Dad sighed.

"It's almost romantic," the King said wistfully. "Like the stories I heard as a child. The princess being rescued from the dragon's keep by her one true love. The hero rides in and slays the beast and everyone lives happily ever after."

Ryan's eyes went wide.

"Or, in the real-world version, they get set on fire and eaten," I said.

"Semantics," the King said with a wave of his hand. "Besides, you'll be there to protect him, won't you?"

"Everyone out," I said as I grit my teeth together. "I need to have a word with the King. Morgan, you stay too."

For once, everyone listened to me, though Ryan looked as if it was the last thing he wanted to do. His eyes were on me as he backed through the doorway, pulling the door closed.

I took a breath, trying to calm down. It almost didn't work.

The King said, "Why were you out in the fields?"

"Because Justin took me there."

"For what purpose?"

"To spar."

The King frowned. "But you're not sword trained."

"That's what I said."

"And yet...."

Gods, this sucked. "He thought. He *thinks*."

The King waited.

"Ryan and I are friends," I said.

"As you should be."

"Justin thinks it's more than that."

"Ah," the King said. "And is it?"

"No."

"But?"

"But nothing. It's not."

"Sam," Morgan said. "Everything."

Godsdamn him. "I'm leaving," I told the King. "For a while."

"So Morgan said. But he never said for how long or why."

I looked at the King because he deserved my respect. He wasn't angry. But he was tired. And confused. I reminded myself that his only son had been taken from him. "Do you know what a cornerstone is? To a wizard?"

The King's gaze darted to Morgan before turning back to me. "Yes, Sam. I never had the pleasure of meeting Morgan's. She was long gone from this world before he and I ever met. I don't see what this has to do with—"

"I think Ryan is mine," I blurted out, trying to get this over with as quickly as possible.

And the King said, "Oh. Sam. If I'd known.... Gods, I'm sorry."

I shook my head. "It's nothing you did. I didn't even realize it until that night at the restaurant when we were attacked. And I need to get out of here. But it's not just that, okay? Please don't think it is. There's something... different. About me. My magic. I'm not like other wizards."

"He's powerful, Anthony," Morgan said quietly. "More than me. Probably more than anyone else. And he needs to learn control before he can't any longer."

"Ryan allows you this control?" the King asked.

I shrugged. Like an asshole. "I think so. But it's never been tested."

"So you're running," the King said.

And *there* was the flare of anger. "I'm removing myself from the equation," I said. "Because your *son* seems to think I'm trying to steal Ryan away from him. Your *son* took me out to the sparring fields to try and in his words, 'Teach me a lesson.' I'm leaving because Morgan thinks it's right, and I never question him."

"You question me all the time," Morgan said lightly.

"That's because some of the things you say are questionable," I said.

"Just so we're clear," Morgan said.

"This is your *home*, Sam," the King said, sounding upset. "You should never feel like you've been forced from your home. Not to mention that what Justin did was wrong on so many levels. Castle Lockes belongs to you as much as him. You shouldn't have to feel the need to leave because of him."

"And I don't," I told him. "Not really. This is more me." And it was. Mostly. Enough that it didn't feel like a complete lie when I said it. But I knew that look in his eye. I'd known him for years. I knew what he was going to say even before he said it.

"I'm going to ask you this favor," he said. "Because regardless of what happened or what *will* happen, the fact remains that my son was taken by a dragon. He will be your King, and you must help him."

I sighed. "Crap. You would use the puppy eyes. You jerk."

"I'll go," Morgan said. "Sam doesn't need to do this. He'll head north, and I'll go with Ryan. We'll get Justin back."

"Sam?" the King asked.

Motherfucker. The King knew *exactly* how to play this. "It can't be you, Morgan," I replied. "You know that as well as I do. Because we need to show that we can work together if we're going to be in charge of Verania one day. You shouldn't have to worry about my magic. Ryan will be there until we find Justin and that will be enough. After that, I'll go to Randall."

"It's not your magic I'm worried about," Morgan said. "It's your heart."

Gods, that hurt. I laughed weakly. "It's stronger than you think. Consider it a penance. I should have done more to protect Justin. I should have never let the dragon take him. If it'd been you and the King out there, you would have never let that happen. I have to get him back because I allowed him to be taken in the first place."

"No one blames you," the King said, touching my hand.

"Maybe not," I said, looking away. "But I do."

THEY LEFT me, then. Per my request. I needed time to clear my head.

So of course, only a few minutes later, there was a knock on the door.

I knew who it was. I didn't know how, but I did.

"Yeah," I said.

Ryan came in, face stony. The King had promised to keep the cornerstone thing to himself, so at the very least, he couldn't be pissed off at me for that.

So that left the fact that I had somehow managed to let Justin get taken by the dragon. His fiancé was somewhere in Verania with a sexually aggressive dragon (which I was still offended about, by the way), and Ryan was stuck here with a malfunctioning wizard apprentice who secretly pined after him.

My life was a tragic farce of epic proportions.

He closed the door behind him and leaned against it.

I thought of at least a billion things to say, each one more ridiculous than the last (*You mad, bro? You look mad*), so I decided on keeping it simple. "Sorry."

He arched a pissed-off eyebrow at me. Before that moment, I didn't think eyebrows *could* be pissed off. I now knew otherwise. "For what?" he asked, voice hard. "Going out unescorted with the Prince? Facing off with a dragon? Almost getting yourself killed yet again? Which one, Sam? Hurry up and pick. I can't wait to hear how you explain it away."

Huh. That… wasn't what I expected. "You mad, bro?" I asked and immediately winced.

"Am I mad," he said flatly. "Am I mad? No, Sam. I'm not mad. I only came around the corner of the castle in time to see a fucking dragon rearing back to blow fire at you and Justin. I could only stand there when you turned the air around you to ice and the fire descended on you. I could only scream your name when he struck you and *knocked you thirty feet into the side of a building*. I could only run much too late when the dragon grabbed Justin and took off. Do you know what happened then? Do you, Sam? The pressure from its wings coming down collapsed the building on top of you. I sat there, watching it fly away as a building fell on top of you. So no. I'm not mad. *I'm fucking furious.*"

I didn't do well with anger, especially when it was directed toward me. Especially when directed by Ryan. His lips were curved in a snarl and his eyes were flashing, and all I could think was *Back off back off back off.*

Flippant, I was. "It wasn't a building," I said. "Just a shed."

He laughed bitterly. "Sure. Just a shed. Exactly what I told myself when I pulled your unconscious body out from underneath the rubble. I thought you were— we thought you had—" He rubbed a hand over his flushed face, the words seemingly stuck in his throat.

So I said, "I'm sorry," in a small voice.

"Sorry," he said. "You're *sorry*." Because apparently he thought repeating my sorry-ass words back to me was making this conversation easier.

"What do you want me to say? I didn't *ask* to be attacked by a fucking dragon!"

"You shouldn't have been out there in the first place!" he shouted at me. "What the hell were you thinking, taking Justin out to the sparring fields? Without an escort? How could you ever think that was a good idea?"

"You think I took him out there?" I snapped. "That's what you think."

"Why else would he be out there? Just because *you* have no regard for your own life, doesn't mean you get to endanger others."

"Right," I said. "Exactly. That's exactly what happened. Glad you have all of the facts and made a logical conclusion. And you're right! I *love* danger. It's what I do." I shook my head. "You know, for a moment, it sounded like you were worried about me. Fuck knows why I thought that. After all, I haven't seen you in what… twelve days? Avoidance much?"

He reeled back as if I'd slapped him. "Sam," he said hoarsely. "You… I…."

"Don't bother," I said, pushing past him. "The King has ordered me to help you find Justin. I'll do it, because I owe him everything. Not you. Not Justin. The King. Once I do and everything is back to normal in your perfect little life, I'll be gone."

I stormed out of the labs, slamming the door behind me.

"OH MY gods, you *diva*," Gary said the next morning. "You *didn't*."

I scowled at him and rolled my eyes, shoving another spare tunic into the bundle spread out on my bed.

"You went full-on bitchy and made a dramatic exit?" He sounded way too gleeful over my histrionics. "I have taught you well, my young apprentice."

"He was being an asshole," I said. "He deserved it. What a dick knocker. Fucking candy-ass bitch whore."

"The angrier you are, the less your insults make sense," Gary observed. "It's adorable."

I glared at him. "Go eat a moderately small child and choke on his bones."

"See? That didn't even make sense. Why would I eat a child? They're sticky."

"I will murder everything you love," I growled at him.

"That would be suicide," he said solemnly. "Because I love you."

I gaped at him.

He laughed at me.

"Cheating," I muttered.

"Eh, what can you do?"

"I smash him," Tiggy said from his spot on the floor.

"Tig," Gary said. "We discussed this. You can't smash everything."

"Yes you can," I said. "You can smash all you want. Smash Gary, then Ryan."

"I love Gary," he said. "No Gary smash. And Ryan take your flower. No Ryan smash."

"He didn't take my flower! And stop calling it that!"

"Don't yell at him because you haven't been penetrated," Gary said.

I wrinkled my nose. "Okay, time out on the fighting thing. Can we all agree that none of us should ever use the word penetration in that context again?"

"Yeah," Gary said with a grimace. "I don't even know why I said that."

"It gross," Tiggy said.

"Okay, rule four hundred twenty-seven of the Sam/Gary/Tiggy friendship has been agreed upon. No saying penetration when referring to boning."

"Aye," Tiggy and Gary said.

"Okay, time in. I can yell at whoever I want!"

"You really can't," Gary said. "It's unattractive on you. Some people pull off the angry look. You're not one of them."

"I am sexy angry. Watch." I turned the full extent of my wrath on Gary and Tiggy.

They laughed at me.

"Son of a bitch," I muttered. "Not even a little sexy tingle?"

"No," Tiggy said. "Not even."

"You looked like a constipated otter," Gary said.

"I don't know how I have any self-esteem left with you two by my side," I moaned. "It's why I can never have nice things."

"I suppose Ryan is a nice thing," Gary said.

And we were back to the anger. "That fucking princess rock flipper."

"Yes, dear, he *is* a princess rock flipper, which is why he was absolutely *terrified* when he carried you back into the castle. And why he wouldn't leave your side."

Terrified? That should not make me feel good. At all. But then, "Well, of course he was. His fiancé had just been kidnapped by a dragon. He was waiting for me to wake up so he could question me. Or, rather, yell at me. Because he's a cock-sucking roasted pork."

Gary stared at me.

"What?" For some reason, I put my hands over my chest like he was using unicorn vision to scope out my nipples.

"There is no hope for you," he finally said. "Like none. My vision is darkening like your overwrought soul. Hey, Tiggy?"

"Gary," Tiggy said.

"If Sam were a tree, you know what kind of tree he'd be?"

"What kind?"

"A pine. Because of all the *pining*."

"Unicorns should never tell jokes," I told them. They didn't hear me because Tiggy was laughing too loud.

"Gary funny," Tiggy said, wiping the tears from his eyes with his big hand. "Gary so funny."

"Whatever. You all need to get out. I need to finish packing before I go to my meeting this afternoon. We leave tomorrow."

"Hmm," Gary said. "Yes. Your *meeting*. Your *secret* meeting that you never tell anyone about or where it is or why you go. *That* meeting."

"I'm a wizard," I said. "I'm supposed to have secrets."

"Apprentice," Gary reminded me. "And I know everything about you."

"Lie. And rude. You do not. I am mysterious."

"Yeah, okay. You're mysterious just like you get sexy angry."

"Sometimes, I wonder why I put up with the both of you."

"Because you love us," Gary said.

"And we love you," Tiggy said.

So I said, "Goddammit," and hugged it out with the both of them, because *feelings*.

"You sure you want to go out?" Gary said before he left my chambers. "You took a beating. Maybe you should just stay in. It's not every day you get attacked by a dragon and then get thrown across a field."

I shrugged. "I'm sore, but it's not too bad. If I stay here, I'll just be brooding. It's best for me to get out. It'll be my last chance to see the City of Lockes for a while. I just want to say good-bye."

"We'll be back, you know. It's not good-bye so much as it's so long. You'll see."

I just nodded and closed the door. I didn't have the heart to tell him how apt I thought the *good-bye* had been.

CHAPTER 10
Are You a Foxy Lady or a Sam Girl?

I DIDN'T even *want* to go to the stupid meeting.

Stupid Ryan Fucking Foxheart.

He was such an asshole.

But I had to go.

Because it was my turn to bring muffins.

And I would *never* hear the end of it if I didn't show when it was my turn to bring the muffins.

I stopped by the kitchen and picked up the basket Cook had prepared as I'd requested in secret. He never asked what it was for because at least *he* thought I was mysterious. I'm sure he thought I took the muffins to the Dark Woods and crumbled them over goat's blood as I cast a spell that invited demons to suckle on my soul.

Or, he just didn't care and made me food because he was Cook and that was his job.

Whatever.

So I mysteriously took the basket of poppy seed muffins and absconded from the castle. Once I was outside the gates, I pushed my way through the crowds into a narrow alleyway, looking back to make sure I wasn't followed. The coast was clear.

I set down the basket and opened my rucksack. I pulled out a floppy brown wig and pulled it over my hair. The wig covered my forehead and ears, the hair curling out at the tips. There was a matching beard that covered most of my face and came down to the middle of my chest. And finally, a pair of thick-rimmed glasses.

Mervin had returned.

Yes, I could have probably easily altered my looks with magic. But I'd made a promise to Morgan early on not to use it for such frivolous things. And shaping magic could be dangerous. Addictive. Alterations here and there until you completely forgot what your original shape looked like. I never wanted to forget.

I went out of the alley at the opposite end and crossed three more blocks until I reached a café on the corner.

Look. I'd faced some pretty terrible things in my life. The Dark wizards. Fire geckos. An elf who had somehow thought we were meant to be and wanted to go through the elven rite of passage where during the act of consummation, he'd need to eat one of my fingers (*No, Svenel, I* don't *want to make love to you while you eat my thumb, you fucking asshole!*). I'd been cursed, burned, stabbed, hexed, kicked, punched, and on one memorable occasion, had somehow ended up tied to a table while an ogre whipped my bare ass and grunted how pretty my reddened skin was (I *knew* I wasn't a prude. Suck it, Gary!). Hell, just yesterday, *I'd faced down a dragon.*

But no matter where I'd been, no matter everything I'd seen, there was one opponent that rose above all others. An adversary so devious and cunning and bloodthirsty that she put all the others to shame.

Her eyes fell upon me from her seat at the head of the table outside the shop. The rest of the club was spread out around her like she was a queen and they were her subjects. Except she was more of a tyrant than anything else. One who had no scruples nor a kind bone in her body.

Her gaze grew calculating.

My hackles raised and I prepared for battle.

Lady Tina DeSilva.

The president of the Ryan Foxheart Fan Club Castle Lockes Chapter.

And my most mortal of enemies.

"Oh look, everyone. Mervin has arrived and he brought the muffins. If past experiences have any prescience as to what we can expect, then they're sure to be as dry as his conversational skills."

She was also sixteen years old.

And *evil.*

"Hello, Lady Tina," I said. Mervin's voice was lower than my own. I sounded ridiculous. "My, you're looking... alive today. The color of your dress really brings out the extraordinary paleness of your skin tone. Are you unwell? Dying, perhaps?"

She tittered. "No, dear heart. I am actually quite well. I would ask the same of you, because you seem to have some bruises on your face and are holding yourself rather stiffly. Did someone take offense to one of your ever-present asinine meanderings? I should send them some flowers for doing what I've thought of for months."

I laughed as I sat down at the opposite end of the table. "Ah, my sweet. Merely an accident of an inconsequential nature. Unlike, apparently, your makeup. Was it dark this morning when you applied it? Surely, that's the only explanation, unless you've somehow obtained employment as a jester. But then, you'd actually need to have a sense of humor for that. Perhaps you're applying to a brothel, then? I do hope your interview goes well. I'm sure you'll do wonders on your back."

The others (of which there were fourteen, ranging in ages from ten to fifty-two) looked back and forth between us with each verbal blow. They were used to it by now. This was, after all, the twenty-sixth meeting I had attended. It was almost *mandatory* that we cut each other to ribbons. If I was straight and Tina not the bitch from hell, one would assume we were almost flirting. But I was gay and Tina was the bitch from hell. We were not flirting.

She fluttered a silk folding fan across her face. "Oh, Mervin. The feelings I experience upon seeing your countenance is akin to what I understand dysentery to be like. Explosively so."

I cocked my head at her. "I'm sorry. Were you just speaking to me? I apologize most profusely. I was distracted by the size of the sweat stains under your arms. Are you overly warm today? It seems unlikely given the cold, dead heart that surely beats in your chest."

Her eyes narrowed. "You're an asshole, Mervin."

I snarled at her. "Bitch, I'll cut you, bitch."

We both smiled darkly at each other.

She fanned herself again.

I passed around the muffins. And fuck her. They weren't *dry*.

She said, "And now that Mervin has finally stopped talking, the meeting of the Ryan Foxheart Fan Club Castle Lockes Chapter can commence. Deidre, if you could please read a summation of the last meeting. And be quick about it."

A mousy girl of twelve years stood up and looked down at a piece of parchment paper in her hand. "Opening minutes," she said. "President Tina noted that Mervin looked more flush than usual and wondered aloud if he'd just gotten fellated by a street whore in the back alley. Mervin responded that at least he would, and I quote, 'be getting some' unlike Tina who couldn't even find a streetwalker to take her money. President Tina then stated she wouldn't be surprised when Mervin came to the next meeting with mouth sores and an itching rash in the most private of places. Mervin replied that if that happened, he would just come to her for a solution since she obviously knew so much about itching rashes in private places. President Tina called him a ridiculous cockhound and Mervin said he had never hit a girl before, but that there was always a first time. Delores then handed out the blueberry muffins to which Mervin said he was allergic and President Tina tried to force-feed him three of them. The minutes of the previous meeting were read and then for the next four hours, there was a discussion on Ryan Foxheart's biceps."

Deidre sat back down.

"Obviously," Tina said, "much has happened in the few weeks since we held the last meeting. First and foremost, our dearly beloved Knight Foxheart was promoted to Knight Commander Ryan Foxheart."

We all sighed dreamily.

"And, of course, since my parents are in the King's Court," she continued, "I was in attendance, and ladies, let me tell you, he. Was. *Glorious*."

I didn't know she'd been there. I thought I would have been able to smell the stench of putrid death. My nose must have been getting weaker. And I was *not* a lady. Yes, everyone else was, but I obviously *wasn't*.

"Was he as dashing and immaculate as the papers claimed?" an older lady named Wanda asked.

"More," Tina said. "His armor shone like moonbeams and his hair was parted to the right. You know what that means."

"He was feeling *romantic*," a girl named Crissy said. "He always parts his hair on the right when he's feeling *romantic*."

"Actually," I said, "his hair was slicked back for the ceremony."

They all stared at me.

Well, except for Tina. She glared.

I shrugged. "What? You were wrong. I was just pointing that out. How wrong you were."

"What does slicked-back hair mean?" a woman named Nicole asked tearfully. "We've never discussed what it means when it's *slicked back. What does it mean?*"

Tina got a wicked gleam in her eye. "Obviously, it was his marriage hair," she said, and I almost threw my muffin at her face. "He must have known Prince Justin had asked for his hand in marriage before the ceremony."

"That wasn't marriage hair," I argued. "That was his 'I'm in command now' hair."

Tina rolled her eyes. "Please, Ryan was all about Prince Justin. Rystin forever. He couldn't take his eyes off of him when the King made the announcement."

"I don't know," the oldest woman of the group said. Her name was Mary, and I thought she was awesome because she was a self-proclaimed Sam Girl. Well, she was awesome for other things too, but the Sam Girl thing made her even more awesome. "I was there too. Ryan didn't seem as pleased as one should with a marriage announcement. And he was staring at Sam for most of the night."

"Oh, here we go again," Tina muttered.

"He was?" I said, somewhat startled.

Mary smiled at me. "He was. The look on his face when the King proclaimed the ball to follow was to find Sam a suitor almost broke my heart. It was like he had lost the only thing that mattered to him. He's totally crushing on Sam. HaveHeart forever."

I said, "What."

Tina said, "He's *not* crushing on *Sam*. I don't know why you continue to insist on such a ridiculous pairing when there is *obviously* no chemistry between them. Ryan is now engaged to his beloved and will marry him and they'll have babies and dinner and gaze into each other's eyes. Epic poetry will be written about their love and hundreds of years from now, people will still speak of the wonder that is Rystin."

"I don't know," a girl named Courtney said. "I think Sam and Ryan stare at each other when the other's not looking. There's always this indefinable *something* there. It's almost like lightning crackling between them."

I said, "What."

"And did you hear?" Mary said, sounding gleeful. "They danced for *three straight songs*. No one dances for that many songs. He didn't even dance with Justin that many times. Not in a row. It was like they were in their own little world and nothing could bother them." She sighed, eyes fluttering.

"He's a *wizard*," Tina said, scandalized. "Justin is a *prince*. Why in the name of the gods would he want to take so many steps backward?"

"Sam is *so* mysterious, though," Nicole said, and I *knew* it! I *knew* I was mysterious. I took a bite of a muffin in victory. It was a bit dry. Dammit. "He's always got this look on his face like he's working out the secrets of the universe. And when he looks at Ryan? It's like he *is* the universe. And he wants nothing more than to solve Ryan's riddle."

"I *bet* he wants to solve Ryan's riddle," Mary said. "And then he probably wants to riddle his Ryan."

I choked on the muffin.

"You okay?" Mary asked me.

I coughed. "Yes. Sorry. The muffin was just far too moist. I wasn't expecting it."

"That look isn't about secrets," Tina said. "He probably just has gas. Intestinal gas."

"It's not gas," I snapped at her. "Er. Not that I would know. But it's probably not. And it's probably not anything to do with Ryan. I'm pretty sure Sam doesn't even really care about Ryan at all."

Mary laughed. "Oh, that's not true. Sam wants to eat him for breakfast. There is something there that doesn't exist between Ryan and Justin. And what about the date Sam went on? Ryan was obviously jealous the whole time."

"I was there!" a woman named Griselda exclaimed.

Everyone turned to look at her and said, "Oooh."

"Tell us *everything*," Nicole demanded.

"It was just... I just.... Oh my *gods*, you guys. So there I was, eating my meal with my husband, minding my own business when in walks *Sam and Ryan*. And that guy Sam was on a date with."

"Todd," I supplied. "He has epic ears."

"Yes, Todd," she said dismissively. "I couldn't hear what they were saying, but Ryan was standing *so* close to Sam, like he didn't want to let him out of his sight."

"He was *chaperoning*," Tina said. "It was his *job* to watch Sam."

Gross. I just agreed internally with something Tina said. I reminded myself to run tests when I got home to make sure I hadn't just been possessed by a demon.

"You weren't *there*," Griselda said. "It was *more*. When those Dark wizards came in? He pulled out his big, long sword and tried to protect Sam. And even when the wizards were standing *right there*, Sam and Ryan were in their own little world, bantering back and forth and the *tension*. You guys, the *tension was ridiculous*."

"He tried to protect Sam?" I said. "Please. He just stood there and Sam was all badass and trapped all the Darks by himself. Ryan was posing like he normally did. Dashing and immaculate my ass. More like—"

They stared at me again.

"Or so I read," I said. "In the paper. Nothing else. I wasn't there. I was on the other side of the city doing... stuff."

"But it was obviously Sam's fault that Justin has been taken by the dragon," Tina said nastily. "He was the one that kidnapped Justin and forced him out to the sparring fields. He probably had a deal with the dragon to take Justin away so he could steal Ryan. Sam of Wilds *hates* Rystin and it's just so unfair!"

"No one can control dragons," I said. "Hello. They're *dragons*. That's not how magic works."

"Yeah," Tina said. "Because *you* would know how magic works. If you did, you could magic yourself some less ridiculous facial hair."

"I could say the same about you," I said and she was *livid*.

"You guys," Courtney said.

"You know what, Mervin? I'm getting sick of your—"

"You *guys*," Courtney said.

"Oh please, Tina. Your personality is like a—"

"*You guys*," Courtney said.

"*My* personality? You are the absolute *worst*—"

"You guys!" Courtney shouted.

We all looked at her.

She had gone completely pale. She lifted a trembling finger. She said, "It's. *Him*."

We all looked where she was pointing.

And yeah. Fuck my life.

Knight Commander Ryan Foxheart stood on the other side of the street, talking with a small group of people.

We all screamed. Me for entirely different reasons than the others.

He looked up, startled.

The entire fan club was waving maniacally at him.

Except for me. I was sinking down in my seat.

Ryan waved back and held up a finger.

"Does that mean he's coming over here?" Nicole said weakly. "Oh dear gods. I think my underwear just fell off."

"*Nicole*," Tina hissed. "Keep your comments to yourself! Be a respectable fucking lady, for fuck's sake!"

"Mine did too," Mary said, patting Nicole's arm.

"Mervin, where are you going?" Griselda asked, and *damn* her for noticing me trying to flee quietly into the crowd.

"Uh. Nowhere? I mean, somewhere. I just remembered I have an important business meeting. For business. To discuss my business."

Mary grabbed my arm and pulled me back to my seat. "Don't be so shy, Mervin. That can wait. Who knows when we'll ever get this chance again? It's not as if—*oh my gods, he's coming over*."

Well shit.

I looked over and yep. There he was. Walking across the street like he didn't have a care in the world. To the outsider, he held himself tall and proud and looked every bit the knight commander that he was.

But I knew him. I'd been watching him (like a creep) for a long time. I saw the fake set of his smile. The slight purple lines under his eyes. The stiff hold of his shoulders. He was stressed and tired and confused.

"Ladies," he said, glancing over the table. "And gentleman." He smiled at me. They all giggled.

I didn't because I was too busy wondering if anyone would notice if I made myself invisible. It was almost worth the risk.

Tina, the awful person that she was, stood and posed, sticking her chest out as far as it could go. She looked like the back end of a horse. "Knight Commander," she all but purred. "How very kind of you to take time out of your busy schedule to come and mingle with the ladies."

"Hate you too, bitch," I mumbled under my breath.

"Are you some kind of social group?" he asked.

Tina *preened*. Like a *peacock*. "Not just *any* social group," she said. "This is the Ryan Foxheart Fan Club Castle Lockes Chapter. We are the largest Foxheart Fan Club in all of the City of Lockes. We're the Foxy Ladies."

"Well," Mary said, patting my hand. "The Foxy People. We don't discriminate."

"Fan Club?" Ryan asked, sounding adorably shocked. Then I remembered he was an asshole and I was pissed off at him, so he wasn't adorably anything. "Oh wow. He wasn't kidding when he said that."

"Who?" Tina demanded.

"Sam. He's a... friend of mine." There was a tightening around his eyes and I wanted to shout that we sure as shit didn't seem like friends yesterday, you motherfucker. I kept that bit to myself. Barely.

And almost all the ladies *sighed*. "Sam of Wilds?" Mary said. "He *knows* about us?"

Deidre burst into tears. "He's... just... standing... so... *close*."

"Can you sign something?" Nicole demanded. "This paper? This napkin? My chest? My inner thighs or my wildest dreams? Whatever you want."

"Heh," Ryan said. "Whoa."

"*Nicole*," Tina barked. "Rein your slut back in!"

"I can't believe Sam knows about us," Griselda said in awe.

"How?" Courtney cried. "How does he know? I want answers! I want him here. I changed my mind. I'm no longer about Rystin. HaveHeart forever!"

"HaveHeart is where pairings go to die," Tina growled. "Long live Rystin!"

"I... just... want... to... touch... him," Deidre sobbed.

"Whaaaaat is even happening right now?" Ryan said.

"Rystin is Justin and Ryan," Mary explained.

"And HaveHeart is Sam Haversford and Ryan Foxheart," Griselda said.

"Rystin and HaveHeart?" he said faintly. "I don't even...."

"I'm a Sam Girl," Mary told him. "Because of how he looks in tight pants. Edible. Edible is how he looks in tight pants."

"Oh my gods," I whispered feverishly. "This is happening right in front of me."

"And I'm a Foxy Lady," Tina said. "Because of reasons." She stared at his chest. Everyone understood her reasons. Even me.

He looked back at me. "So, you a Foxy Lady too? Or a Sam Girl?"

"What," I said, dropping my voice as low as it could go. "No. Not even. Shut your mouth."

He frowned. "Do I know you from somewhere? You seem familiar."

And with that, *everyone* at the table turned slowly to stare at me.

"Nope," I said. "I don't know you. I'm just here to do business. For my business."

"And what business is that?" he asked.

And because I couldn't help it, I said, "None of your."

And he *laughed*. And *my* underwear almost fell off.

"Sweet molasses," I said weakly.

"Are you sure we've never met?" he asked. "You remind me of someone."

"I have that kind of face," I said.

"I wouldn't know. I can't see it. Behind all that hair."

"It's a *beard*."

"I can see that," he said. "It's very long."

And so I leered, "Yeah it is," because my *life*. Then I coughed horribly and oh my *gods*. "I mean thank you! I'm proud of its length. And girth. Holy crap. Shut up, S—Mervin."

"What's a Smervin?" he asked.

"Sure," I said. "Oh no! Would you look at the time? I have another business meeting I really must attend to. For business."

"It's Mervin," Mary said. "And forgive him. He's just nervous right now. He has a little bit of a crush on you."

"Mary!" I shouted. "You traitor. I do not! I am *not* a Foxy Lady."

"So you're a Sam Girl," he said, sounding amused. Like an *asshole*.

"Yes," I said. "Total Sam Girl. The Sammiest Girl who has ever lived."

"So, HaveHeart, then?"

"I think Sam does just fine on his own." Ha! Flora Bora *Slam*, motherfucker!

"I'll be sure to let him know," he said, cocking his head at me.

That pissed me off. "You do that. I'm sure he just can't *wait* to talk to you."

And boy did he flinch at *that* one.

"We're so sorry to hear about Justin," Tina said, commandeering the conversation. And, just because she could, her eyes filled with tears and she sniffed. "You must be so devastated."

"Yes," he said tightly. "It's been rough. But we're going to get him back."

"And then you'll be married!" she said, clapping her hands, tears drying instantly. "It'll be the wedding of the century with flowers and tears and cake and *I love you*s and duck as the main course with greens, and there will be balloons and fairy lights and vows where you say he will be yours forever, and you will look into his eyes and *sigh*."

"That's... a lot of words," Ryan said. "You remind me a bit of Sam."

"I will murder everything you love," I snarled at him.

"What?" he asked.

Shit. "That guy behind you. He was kicking a puppy. But no need to turn around and look! He ran away and so did the puppy and that is the end of that story."

"Probably no duck, though," Ryan said, turning back to Tina. "Some people might be allergic. That wouldn't be fair."

"Oh, come on!" I said loudly.

"Excuse me?" Ryan said, looking confused.

"Puppy kicker came back. But he ran away again. Man, that guy is so fast."

"Mervin," Tina said, grinding her teeth. "Would you at least *try* and act like a normal person?"

"Only if you *try* and find a way to disappear and never return."

She turned back to Ryan. "I must apologize for Mervin," she said. "He's not as... cultured... as the rest of us are used to."

"I'll show *you* cultured," I said, and Ryan laughed again, quickly covering it up with a cough as Tina frowned.

"You'll see," she said. "You'll get Justin back, slay the dragon, and then you'll be married."

"I guess," he said. He smiled at her, but it was forced now. They couldn't see it because he was good at hiding. But I saw right through it. I almost felt bad for our fight earlier. The weight of Justin's kidnapping was weighing hard on him.

He graciously agreed to sign autographs before he left, saying he needed to finish preparing for his trip. When he got to me, I just sat there and stared at him. The girls were too busy gushing to each other over what Ryan had written to listen to us.

"Do you need me to sign anything?" he asked.

"This must be fun for you," I said.

"It's not bad," he said. He shook his head. "I'm sorry. I just... I *swear* I know you from somewhere. Where did you say you were from again?"

"I didn't," I said. I was starting to feel really sweaty because he was studying me way too closely and knowing my luck, my beard would fall off, followed by my underwear.

"Oh, where are you from, then?" he asked.

"I grew up in the slums," I said, voice harsh. "You wouldn't know anything about that."

He looked surprised. "You did? How old are you?"

"Eighty-seven."

"Right. So, early twenties?"

"Why?"

He shrugged, suddenly looking uncomfortable. "Maybe that's where I would have known you—" He cut himself off.

My jaw dropped. "You grew up in the slums?" How had I not known that? How had I not known *him*?

"Look, do you want me to sign anything for you?" He was starting to fidget.

"Here," Mary said, sliding a piece of paper in front of me. "Mervin is so forgetful sometimes. And I know he'd be furious if you didn't give him your autograph."

"I wouldn't be furious," I assured him. "There would be no level of fury."

"Good to know," he muttered. He reached down and took the pen from Mary and wrote something on the page and slid it over to me. He quickly said his good-byes and, with one last look at me, headed back into the crowd.

"What did you *do*?" Tina growled at me. "You *chased* him away? How dare you! I have half a mind to ban you for life, Mervin!"

Normally, I would have swooped back in and crushed her verbally. Normally, I would have tripped her with my words until she was stumbling and yelling. That's how the meetings always ended.

But not this time.

Because this time, I had looked down at the autograph Ryan had signed for me.

And all powers of speech fled as if I'd never had them at all.

> *To Mervin:*
> *Don't worry.*
> *I'm a Sam Girl too.*
> *Our secret?*
> *Ryan Foxheart*

CHAPTER 11
And the Adventure Begins!

I DIDN'T have time to do any amount of research when I got back to the castle. I thought for sure I could sneak back in and try to find out anything I could about Ryan Foxheart before he came to Castle Lockes. I knew he'd been conscripted into the Knights of Verania after serving in the King's Army, but before that, I really didn't know much.

But as soon as I crossed back into the castle, Morgan grabbed me by the arm and pulled me back down into the labs despite my protests.

"How did your secret meeting go?" he asked as he shut the door behind us.

"Secretly," I said.

"You still won't tell me what it's for?"

"Not even if you held a sword to my neck."

"That bad?"

"Worse," I said. "But why even ask? You could easily find out. All you'd have to do is follow and I'd never know it."

"I could," he agreed. "I wouldn't, though."

"Why?"

"Because you deserve your secrets," he said. "Much like I deserve mine."

"You have secrets?"

"So many."

"Tell me," I demanded. "We're friends. Bros, even. Bros don't keep secrets from each other."

"What was your meeting about today?"

"Bros can totally keep secrets," I decided.

"Wow, that bad? Should I be concerned?"

"Possibly. Probably. It's certainly not healthy."

"Underground cock fighting?"

I was horrified. "I would never do that to roosters," I said.

He winked at me. "I wasn't talking about roosters."

I threw up a little in my mouth. "I just learned something new. I never want to hear the word cock come out of your mouth again."

"Because you'd rather just have cock come in your mouth instead?"

"Wow," I whispered reverently. "That.... Morgan. That was a thing of beauty. And so disgusting, coming from you. What the hell. Thank you for subjecting me to that. And I hate you."

"I've got to keep you on your toes," he said. Then he sobered. "Are you sure about this, Sam?"

Dammit. Serious time. "The King asked," I said. "And he has a point. Justin will be my King. Ryan will be the King Consort. One day, I will be sworn to protect them like you do for the King and did for the Queen. It's our duty, Morgan."

He watched me for a moment before replying. I knew he was trying to gauge my sincerity. And I thought myself sincere. For the most part. "You've grown," he finally said. "Once, you were this gawky, loud little boy who turned a gang of miscreants to stone. And now you stand before me a man. Making choices as a man. I thought…." He shook his head. "I'm proud of you, Sam Haversford. Sam of Wilds. I am so proud to have you as my apprentice."

"I'm about to hug the crap out of you," I warned him. "Like, full-on feelings hug where it goes on for a bit too long and becomes slightly awkward and we both clear our throats and shuffle our feet when it's over."

"Must we?" He sighed.

"You're proud of me," I reminded him. "You think I'm awesome. You love me. Yes. We must. Open your arms, Morgan. I'm about to bring it in."

He opened his arms sarcastically. I didn't know that was possible for a person to do that. But he did. "Hugs, hugs, hugs," I mumbled as I pulled him in. His arms circled my back and I held on as tightly as I could because without him, I would not have the home I did. Without him, I would not be where I was. Sometimes, things could be hard. Things could be unfair. But Morgan was my friend. More than that, he was someone I could look up to. He would never steer me wrong. I didn't know how much I needed someone like him until the day he took my hand and led me out of that alleyway, listening to me babble incessantly about pink shoes and the tears of a succubus.

I sighed happily into his neck.

"Sam? I think it's gone on long enough."

"Shh," I said, reaching up to pet his face blindly. "Not awkward yet."

"No? I would have thought otherwise."

"You make me have feelings," I told him seriously. "Like you're my brother uncle dad."

"There's the awkward."

"It's not awkward when it's true. Am I your brother nephew son?"

He groaned. "Will that make you let me go?"

"Try it and see."

"Yes."

"Yes what?"

"Yes, Sam. You're like my brother nephew son."

"Good."

"You're not letting go, are you."

"No. That was a lie. You smell good. Like berries and sunshine. What lotion do you use? Is it called Berry Sunshine? You're *my* berry sunshine, Morgan."

He shoved me away as I laughed.

"You're going to miss me," I said. "Admit it."

"I am regretting every decision I ever made about you," he retorted.

"Lie. Don't front. I make your world brighter."

"Please, please, *please* don't say anything like this to Randall," he said. "And whatever you do, do *not* try to awkward hug him. That will not go over well."

"Yeah, he doesn't strike me as the hugging type. But then, he didn't strike me as the dick nose type and look how *that* worked out."

"This is going to end in disaster," Morgan said.

"Have a little faith, huh?" I said. "I've got this. I just have to get through the whole traveling up close and personal with Ryan while going to rescue his fiancé thing and then we'll be just peachy."

"Can you do it?"

Probably not, but I chose the path of false bravado. It was easier. "I'm Sam of Wilds," I said with a rakish grin. "I can do anything."

He wasn't fooled one bit. "Sam."

"I get it, okay? I know what I'm doing. Okay. Most of the time. Well. Sometimes. But this time, I totally do. I got this, okay? It's going to suck, sure. But it's not *about* me. It's about rescuing Justin and making sure he gets back home safe and sound. That is my priority. And I can do this."

"I know you can," he said quietly. "And the fact that you're even doing it in the first place says much about your character."

I scrubbed my hands over my face. "Enough with all the feelings. If we keep this up, I'm going to want to braid flowers into your beard. And I'm very good at braiding. Just ask Gary."

"Enough feelings," he said. "I've got something for you."

"Presents? Gimme, gimme, gimme. It better be expensive. And engraved."

"It's priceless and not engraved at all."

"Oooh," I said. "I am very okay with this."

"Wizarding secret," he said. He pulled open a cabinet and pulled out a black box. He turned and placed the box on the table next to my Grimoire. "Open it."

The box itself was made of stone, intricate carvings on the lid and sides. I recognized some of the runes. Sun. Earth. Clarity. Foresight. The box was old. Probably ancient. Runes like this weren't used in the every day. This was elder magic, from when the world was young and magic was a more visceral thing. I felt my own magic shiver as I traced the clarity rune with my fingers.

I lifted the lid. It was heavier than I thought it'd be.

There was a white cloth inside. Soft and smooth. I pulled it apart.

In the cloth lay a red crystal about the length of my finger. It was thin and cut with precision.

And I had absolutely no idea what it was. I touched it gently and smiled when a bright spark shot off in the crystal.

"It's a summoning crystal," Morgan said.

"A summoning what now?"

"You're given one once you pass the Trials," he said. "It allows a wizard to contact other wizards who have touched the stone. This one was specifically made for you by Randall. Only he and I have touched it, so you can only contact the two of us."

"Contact?" I asked. "How?"

"It won't be corporeal," he said. "I'll be able to hear you through the stone, and you'll be able to hear me. You think of me when holding it in your hand and I'll feel the pull of it through my own stone." He reached into an inner pocket of his robe and pulled out a blue stone, much the same cut and size as mine. "Use it sparingly, Sam. It's not a toy."

"I'm so going to use it as a toy," I told him. "I'm going to use it at three in the morning just to tell you I miss the sound of your voice. Do you think Randall will recognize me if I try to prank summon him?"

"And this is why apprentices aren't given these stones," he said. "Because of shenanigans."

"My shenanigans are awesome," I said. "But why give this to me now? I'm not going through the Trials with Randall. That's still years off."

"Randall suggested it."

"He what? He *hates* me. Why would he want me to have something this precious when I haven't earned it?"

Morgan shrugged. "I didn't question it. If Randall wanted you to have it, he has his reasons. It could be something as simple as the distance you're traveling is great and it's better for you to have a lifeline."

"Nothing with Randall is ever simple," I reminded him. "You know that as well as I do. He's plotting something."

"Probably. I'm sure you'll find out soon enough."

"And he knows I'll be delayed?"

"Yes. He's aware. He's using his own resources to help track the Prince. For now, head north to Meridian City. There are rumors the dragon was spotted near a village on the outskirts of the city called Old Clearing."

"I've been through there," I said. "Once. It's all sheep and farming."

"Food source," Morgan said. "Three people have disappeared from the village in the last month alone and scorch marks were found on the ground."

"It has to be getting desperate if it's eating people," I said. "The other dragons don't do that."

"That we're aware of," Morgan said. "Randall can speak for the mated pair in the north, but the desert dragon isn't as closely monitored. The Great White Dragon hasn't been seen in years, but I never heard of it eating any humans either."

"You realize that I'll have to go through the Dark Woods."

Morgan stiffened as his eyes flashed. "You'll do no such thing," he said. "Take the Old Road."

"*Around?*" I said incredulously. "That'll take weeks!"

"I don't care, Sam. You have had enough dealings with the Darks to last a lifetime. The last thing we need is for you to stumble on more of them."

"I could do that anywhere," I said. "They use the Old Road like everyone else."

"I'm aware," he snapped at me. "But it's one thing to stumble upon them there as opposed to finding them where they live. You mind me on this, Sam. Stay out of the Dark Woods."

"But—"

"You have a job to do. Assist Knight Commander Foxheart in rescuing the Prince. They'll return to the castle. You'll go to Randall. You'll learn from him that which I cannot teach you, and then you will come home. That is all you need to be concerned with. Do you understand?"

"Morgan—"

"*Do you understand*?"

I narrowed my eyes. "Yes. But I swear to the gods that if you're holding back from me and I find out what it is, I am going to rescind that awesome hug I just gave you and there will be none to follow for a very long time."

"The world weeps at such a thought." But his lips quirked up, the anger fading from his eyes.

"It should. I give great hugs."

"No Dark Woods," Morgan said.

"Fine," I sighed. "No Dark Woods."

FUCK THAT. We were totally going through the Dark Woods.

THE NEXT morning, we met in the lobby of the throne room before sunrise.

Mom cried and told me I needed to think about her every day. I told her then that nothing would change because I did that already.

Dad was gruff, but I could see the way his hands shook, and he told me that he would hold down the fort until I got home. I told him I expected nothing less and had to blink the burn away when he placed a rough kiss on my cheek.

Morgan had said what he needed to the day before. I had the summoning crystal stowed away next to my Grimoire in a rucksack that Gary wore attached to his back. He merely put a hand to my shoulder and told me he would see me soon. I told him not to let the castle run to ruins since I wasn't there to hold everything together. He assured me they would find a way.

The King brought in a High Priest to bless our journey. The High Priest asked if he should also bless the horses we would be using.

"We're not riding horses," I said.

"We're not?" Ryan asked, scowling prettily. Like a jerk. "But—"

"It's racist," I said.

"It's what?"

Gary was glaring at him.

"But he's not a horse," Ryan said.

The glare slightly lessened.

"No, but it's still demeaning to him. We don't ride anywhere we go. It's how we roll. You can always stay here if that's a problem."

"Maybe those legs are just for show," Gary whispered loudly. "Maybe he doesn't really know how to use them. The racist."

"I don't think you're using the word racist right," he said.

"Unicorns are a race," Gary snarled at him. "Is Gary gonna have to—"

"Here come angry glitter," Tiggy said. "I smash Knight Delicious Face?"

"Yes, Tiggy! Smash him! Smash the racist!"

"No smashing," I said, stepping in between Ryan and Tiggy. "Not yet. At least wait until we actually start The Epic Adventure of Sam, Gary, and Tiggy."

"You capitalized that, didn't you," Morgan sighed.

"I did," I said. "That's how you know it's epic."

Gary's rage glitter subsided. "The most epic there could be."

"And Ryan," Ryan said.

We all looked at him.

"The Epic Adventures of Sam, Gary, Tiggy, and Ryan," he said. "If we're doing this, I'm getting in on the capitalization."

"Fine," I grumbled. "If you must. Though the name now sounds ridiculous."

"Because it didn't before?"

"Because it didn't before," I mocked him.

"And again, why Knight Delicious Face?"

"Anyway," I said loudly. "Are we good? Did the Priest give us enough hoodoo so we can get the fu—fudge out? Sorry, Father."

"It's okay," the priest assured me. "I'm pretty sure your soul is already doomed."

"There's the idolatry I know and avoid."

"Sam, Ryan, a word if you would," the King said.

We followed him through the Great Doors into the throne room. He dismissed the two castle guards in the room, telling them to wait outside. They closed the doors behind them.

Ryan stood at attention like a good knight. I slouched. I was okay with that.

The King looked down at his hands for a long time before he spoke. Finally, he said, "Justin's mother… she. Well. She was a lovely woman. She was a Queen and not just in name and title. She was strong. She was kind. And she loved this kingdom with every fiber of her being. She laughed at me the first time I asked her for her name. She said a prince had the means to find out such things and she wasn't going to make it easy on me. And she didn't. At every turn, she seemed to be almost out of reach, always pushing me and pulling away. It was difficult. Many times I thought about stopping my pursuit and focusing my attention elsewhere. Many times I told myself it was the *last* time. Finally, one day, she stopped. She turned to look at me and her eyes were *soft* and she told me that she loved me and that I had better ask her to marry me, otherwise she was going to kick me in the shins. So I did.

"She died giving birth to Justin. There was so much joy, but it was drenched in misery. I had a son. I had lost my wife. Verania had a future king. Verania had just lost its Queen. My soul felt dark. But there was this little light. This little bundle of light that wrapped his tiny hand around my finger and held on tightly, as if reminding me that he was still there. That she was gone but he was not and he needed me now. Because he had lost her too.

"So I held on. I have made mistakes. I was not a perfect father. I could never claim to be. Justin is not a perfect son. He can be cold and calculating and manipulative. He often thinks only for himself and not of the bigger picture as a king must do. He is young and brash and full of an undeserved sense of accomplishment. But he still grabbed my finger and held on, and I will always hold on to him."

The King looked up at us for the first time since we'd followed him into the throne room. "I consider both of you my family. The other sons the Queen could not give me. I am asking you to save your brother and bring him home so that I may remind him of the time he held on to me because I was the only thing in his world. I ask that you bring him home so I can make him a better man. To be the King I know he can be."

Ryan stood up straight and balled his right hand into a fist, bringing it up and across his chest, pressing it over his heart. "On my honor," he said. "I will bring him home."

Kiss-ass.

They both looked at me.

I narrowed my eyes at the King. "You can't go around telling emotional stories like that and calling me your other son the moment before we leave! I need to stay here now and make you cookies and have you tell me you're proud of me and call you Dad Number Two and then let me paint a portrait of you standing in a field of flowers!"

"You can't paint," he reminded me. "The one time you tried, the subject of your painting looked more like a kraken then a human."

I scowled at him. "Artistic impression. Beauty is in the eye of the beholder. Philistine. And maybe the subject had krakenish qualities."

"She was an eighty-year-old grandmother named Matilda."

"It wasn't that bad!"

"The curator of the City of Lockes art museum demanded it be burned because it was an assault to all five senses," the King reminded me.

"All five?" Ryan asked. "How is that even—?"

"He used tomato paste when he ran out of red," the King told him. "And then he left it out in the sun for two weeks."

"It had to *dry*," I said. "And I was fourteen! I was still discovering my hidden talents."

"Some talents should remain hidden," the King said wisely.

"*You* should remain hidden," I said. "Just for that, I am not even going to stay and make you cookies and paint a portrait of you. We are leaving immediately and you'll never get to experience the wonder that is a Sam of Wilds original. Serves you right."

"He showed it to the woman he'd painted," the King said to Ryan. "Matilda called for a priest to exorcise it and then she fainted."

"That wasn't my fault," I said. "She overreacted. Who knew eighty-year-old women could be freaking drama queens?"

"You ate part of it in front of her."

"It was *performance* art!"

"You can still call me Dad Number Two," he said.

I rolled my eyes. "That's certainly up in the air. Gods. You tell me sad stories as if I don't already feel guilty enough and now I just want to do everything you ask of me to make you happy. This is so lame."

He pulled me into a hug.

"Cheater," I mumbled and I hugged him back.

"There's no guilt here," he said quietly. "You did nothing wrong."

I snorted. "That's certainly not true."

"It is to me," he said and gods*damn* him and his awesomely devastating sentimentality. It made me want to make promises I didn't know I could keep.

But I said them anyway. "We'll get him back."

He pulled away and smiled at me. "I know you will. And when you come home, you'll be here to stay, okay? I have half a mind to lock you up in a tower as it is to keep you safe."

"I'm not a princess."

He shrugged. "Close enough."

I loved my King very much.

WE STOOD at the castle gates, a large crowd of well-wishers gathered around us.

The sun was shining overhead. Fat clouds dotted the sky. There was excitement in the air. We felt young and alive and things were *happening*.

Pete said, "Don't die."

"Thanks, Pete. I can now go with my head held high."

"No, but, like, for real. Don't die. I would be sad."

"Your sincerity is heartwarming."

"It's what I'm here for. You better be strolling triumphantly back here as soon as you can, you got me?"

"I got you." I glanced back at my merry little band of travelers. A hornless gay unicorn. A half-giant. A knight who was a jerk but that I wanted to have for breakfast.

"And let the adventure begin!" I crowed and the crowd cheered. Streamers fell and flags flew and people shouted our names.

"Wait," Gary said, and the crowd stopped cheering. "Sorry, sorry. I forgot to pack my scarves. We can't leave yet."

"Why do you need scarves?" I asked.

Gary glared at me. "You know how my mane looks when it gets windy. I refuse to have a bad mane day just because you can't hold your horses."

"Oh my gods."

"Was that racist?" Ryan asked. "Hold your horses. That was racist. Am I right?" He elbowed Morgan. "Right. Racist."

We all slowly looked at him.

"What?" he said, sounding defensive. "Whatever. I don't know how the whole horse racism thing works!"

"That much is obvious," Gary said, voice dripping with disdain. "And I bet you would be just *fine* with me having wind-rape hair!"

"Wind-rape hair?" Ryan asked my parents.

"It's a thing," Dad said.

"Gary's very sensitive about it," Mom said.

"Pete, can you go get his damn scarves?" I said. "He'll never let me hear the end of it if you don't. I can only imagine how the next six months will go."

"Yes, Pete, be a dear would you?" Gary asked. "I *surely* wouldn't want to be a bother to *Sam*. I'm only carrying his possessions *on my back*. I'd like the one with the star pattern, the silk one we got in Forakesh, and maybe the Hydanic one. But heavens, that one *is* more of a fall scarf, and we certainly wouldn't want me to wear fall in the *spring*—"

"Gary!"

"Okay, fine! Pete. Just… grab them all. I'll make decisions as we go. Though no one should ever have to make scarf decisions on the fly. That's just preposterous."

Pete went back inside.

Ten minutes later.

"AND THE adventure begins!" I said again. The crowd clapped. It wasn't as jubilant as before. Fuck them.

We made it two steps.

"Did you pack the hoof pick?" Gary asked.

The crowd sighed.

"No," I ground out. "I don't *have* hooves. Ergo, it's not my responsibility."

"Well, *I* certainly didn't think of it," Gary retorted. "I was too busy doing lunges to make sure I was strong enough to carry *all of your shit* on my back like some common pack mule! And you *know* how my hooves get. I may be a strong, independent unicorn, but I have delicate hooves that must be properly taken care of lest they begin to hurt. And you *know* how I am with hurt hooves."

"Trust me, I know. The bitching never stops."

"Then why are you still *talking* about it?"

I ran my hand over my face. "Pete."

"Yes, Sam."

"Could you please get Gary's hoof pick?"

"Yes, Sam. Sam?"

"Yes, Pete."

"You should probably stop grinding your teeth. That's not healthy."

"Thank you, Pete. I wouldn't have known otherwise."

He walked away, muttering something about snarky apprentices.

Five minutes later.

"AND THE adventure begins," I muttered. A few people clapped. Most just stared.

We made it three steps.

"Tiggy," Gary called. "Oh, *Tiggy*. Did you remember to pack your pajamas? You know you can't sleep without your pajamas."

Tiggy's shoulders slumped. "I forgot," he said.

"Pete."

"Yes, Sam."

"Tiggy's pajamas."

"Yes, Sam."

Seven minutes later.

"AND THE adventure begins," I snarled. No one clapped this time.

I took a step.

Nothing.

And then another.

Nothing.

And then another.

Still nothing. I breathed a sigh of relief. I held my head up and looked north.

"Oh shoot," Gary said. "I forgot my—"

"*Gary!*" I shouted at him.

"Kidding, kidding. Jeez, Sam. Maybe calm down a little bit, huh? You're looking a little stressed out. Maybe we should play a traveling game. Like 'I Spy' or something."

"Gary, you don't know how to play I Spy. Every time, you mess it up and say exactly what it is you are looking at."

"I do *not*. Watch. I Spy with my little eye something that is the castle."

"Gary."

"Sam has a guess, everyone! The joy I feel is rapturous!"

"Is it the castle?"

"Yes," he said beaming. "You are so good at thi—Wait. *Dammit.*"

"This is going to be a long trip," I mumbled as I led the way to the gates of the City of Lockes.

"I'll go again. I Spy with my little eye something that is that chair. You'll never guess. *Dammit!*"

CHAPTER 12
Six-Inch-Tall Angry Naked Men with Wings

FOUR DAYS later, Gary still hadn't figured out how to play I Spy.

Ryan tried to explain the concept, but it was pointless. I didn't tell him that because it kept him occupied and his attention off me. I still wasn't sure if I was mad at him, even if he *was* a self-proclaimed Sam Girl. (I pretended that note meant absolutely nothing to me, even though I looked at it every night before I fell asleep— shut up.) I could feel him looking at me every now and then, but I stared resolutely forward, watching and waving to everyone that passed us on the Old Road. Many had already heard of the dragon taking Justin, but none had actually seen the dragon itself.

The first night we stayed at an inn in a little hamlet outside of the City of Lockes. Ryan was swarmed as soon as we got inside, people clamoring to meet him. Gary, Tiggy, and I ditched him immediately and made our way up to the room. Ryan stumbled in hours later, going for the empty bed, since Tiggy, Gary, and I were curled up on the other one, Tiggy's legs off the end as he held us against his chest. I cracked open an eye and Ryan had a frown on his face as he glanced over at us. I didn't know what that frown meant, but I took it as extraordinary judging that he was not allowed on the Cool Kids Bed and therefore was feeling sad and alone and wishing he had been invited.

That probably wasn't it at all, but it sure as shit made me feel better.

The third night we camped under the stars. Gary tried to tell a ghost story but got distracted by fireflies and chased them. Ryan smiled quietly after him and I wanted to throw my jar of beans at his face.

The fourth day, we came to the fork in the road where the River Hermed (which bisected Verania from the tributaries in the north until it reached the sea) met up with the Old Road. The river itself flowed through the Dark Woods. If we followed it north, we'd hit Meridian City and therefore Old Clearing within ten days. If we took the long way around via the Old Road, it would be three weeks.

The others stopped behind me.

"Oh my gods, are we finally there?" Gary asked. "We've been walking for *weeks*."

I rolled my eyes. "It's the fourth day."

"Tell that to my thighs," he said.

"I don't want to tell your thighs anything."

"Rude. Ryan would talk to my thighs."

"Not even involved," Ryan said.

"Can we kick him out of the adventure yet?" Gary asked.

"I smash him?" Tiggy asked.

"No smashing," Ryan said.

"Maybe later," I said, distracted. "Time for a course change, boys."

"Nope," Ryan said, following my gaze along the river. "Not going to happen."

I glared at him. "I'm sorry. I didn't know you were in charge here."

"Funny," he said. "I didn't know *you* were."

"Oooh," Gary and Tiggy said.

"I'm the wizard here," I said.

"Apprentice," Gary whispered.

"And I'm the Knight Commander," Ryan said.

"Of the Eighth Battalion," I reminded him. "Which is the Castle Guard. We are not in the castle. Therefore, you are in charge of *nothing*."

"Oh snap," Tiggy said.

"I taught him to say that," Gary said fondly.

"Morgan said to stay on the main road," Ryan said, "for your safety."

"I can handle myself."

"Yeah, I've seen how you handle yourself," he muttered. "Works out real well, doesn't it?" He winced. "Dammit. I'm sorry. That's not—"

"Go whatever way you want," I said coolly. "We're going along the river."

I turned and walked away. Tiggy and Gary followed. I didn't look back.

SO OF course it was fairies.

I *hated* fairies.

One minute I'm cursing Ryan in my head even as he was following us with a kicked puppy look on his face that was *not* affecting me in the slightest, and the next I felt the whisper of magic that wasn't my own.

I said, "Oh shit."

Ryan said, "What?"

Gary said, "Yeah, we're screwed."

Tiggy said, "I don't like this."

Magic is cool, okay? It's fucking *awesome*. I can do shit that people could only *dream* about. Morgan opened up my eyes to a wide world of things I never thought possible. *I can make things out of nothing.*

But you know what *sucks* about magic?

How easy it is to bind it. To confine it.

To trap it.

Vermilion root. Countermagic. Antimagic. The feathers of a phoenix. The blood of a dragon. Binding potions.

And fairies.

I *hated* fucking fairies.

Because they hated me. Well, one in particular.

And I could already feel my magic starting to dampen.

Gary and Tiggy could feel it because they were magical creatures. Tiggy's blood wasn't as potent as a full-on giant, but it still was more powerful than a human. Same with Gary. Since his horn had been taken from him, he didn't have the strength he used to. But they were both magic in their own right so they could feel that same thrum that sizzled across my skin.

"We should probably run," I said.

"That's probably a good idea," Gary agreed.

"Fast," Tiggy said.

"What?" Ryan asked. "What's going on?"

"Nothing," I said, moving behind him and pushing him to get him moving. The shield he wore strapped to his back felt hot under my fingers. "Nothing at all. This is just the time in the adventure that we practice how fast we can run for no apparent reason whatsoever. It's called the Super Fun Run. Everybody loves it. Now do it."

He snorted and looked over his shoulder. "This is going to be the part where I'll get to tell you I told you so about leaving the Old Road, isn't it? It's literally only been thirty minutes. *Literally*."

"Nope. There will be no I told you so. None whatsoever. I am just worried about your cardiovascular health. We need to get your blood moving. Keep you nice and limber."

Fucker was just pressing back against my hands. "And why do you need me limber, Sam?" he asked, sounding almost amused.

And of course my mouth went dry and I thought of sexy things like getting fucked up against a wall and telling him his smile would look even better if I was sitting on it. Somehow, I was able to restrain myself and instead made an inarticulate noise that came out somewhere between a growl and a moan. "I don't. Just. Shut your mouth. And your face."

"Sam," Gary snapped. "Stop touching Ryan and start running."

"I will punch your legs and leave you here for the fairies," I threatened him, pulling my hands away from Ryan as if he'd burned me.

"*Fairies?*" Ryan asked incredulously.

"No," I said. "No fairies. Just running."

Tiggy was already taking off down the road, kicking up large plumes of dust. Gary followed him, the packs on his back rattling and bouncing.

"Fairies, Sam," Ryan said.

I was too busy running to even think of something to say, but have no fear, it would have been witty and triumphant and he would have bowed at the word play.

That and the fact that I was still stuck on *limber*.

Like, how bendy was he?

Could he touch the ground with his hands without bending his knees?

That was an image that wasn't going to leave my head.

It showed the true depths of my talent that I was able to multitask in such a way to be running from certain imprisonment while also fantasizing about Ryan saying things like "I've always wanted to try and do the splits. On your cock."

Running with a boner is no fun. Trust me on that.

Fortunately for me, I didn't have to do it very long.

Because I stepped into a fairy ring.

Like a *douchebag*.

"Goddammit," I muttered, rubbing my forehead where I'd struck a seemingly invisible wall. I looked down and saw a circle of purple mushrooms surrounding me.

I looked farther down the path. Gary and Tiggy were stuck in their own fairy rings.

Ryan, on the other hand, had a large tree bending toward him, wrapping its limbs around his arms, holding them above his head. It'd happened so fast, he hadn't been able to even reach for his sword.

"So," he said.

"Don't."

"This is what it feels like to be captured with Sam of Wilds."

"Shut it."

"No, seriously. I wondered how quickly this would happen. I honestly expected it to at *least* take a full day."

"I hope you get splinters in your wrist," I told him. "Like big ones that get right under the skin and are a bitch to get out."

"No, but does *everyone* want to imprison you?" he asked. "Because it sure seems like everyone wants to imprison you."

"Yes," Gary called back from farther down the road. "Everyone does. Sam has a tendency to piss people off when he talks. Or breathes. Or exists."

"Hey! *No.* That is not even remotely true. I am *adored.* Maybe not universally. But by some people."

"Like your parents," Gary said.

"And me," Tiggy said.

"*Thank* you, Tiggy," I said. "You are a true friend and the feeling is mutual. Unlike, say, the feelings I have for the other two people on our adventure team."

"Really?" Gary said. "Enlighten me, Sam. Just what kind of feelings do you have for Ryan?" A pause, a hesitation, the longest fucking three seconds in the history of time. "And me?"

"There are at least thirteen ways I could see your life ending in the next four minutes," I told him. "Three of them involve lava."

"The youth of today," he said, shaking his head. "With your bows and arrows and magic fingers and attitude. I worry about the future, especially if you're all going to be so indifferently bloodthirsty."

"Uh, guys?" Ryan said.

"Bloodthirsty?" I said to Gary. "If I'm that way, it's only because *you* made me that way."

"Seriously. Guys?"

"*Me?*" Gary said. "If anything, I am the sunlight in your otherwise darkened world. I bring you the light to chase away the maelstrom that is your soul."

"Pretty sure the tree is taking me away."

"Sunlight?" I laughed. "Please. You're so lucky you have me. I tell you sex puns, which everyone knows are the highest form—"

"Uh, newsflash, Sam. *No one* thinks they are the highest form of humor."

"Yes, the tree is definitely taking me into the forest. Don't know why. It would be nice if someone acknowledged me. Is this wind-rape? I feel like this is going to be like wind-rape."

"Hi, Ryan!" Tiggy called out.

"You *lied* to me?" I screeched at Gary. "All this time I thought I was being humorously sophisticated and you were *lying*?"

"Tiggy! Thank the gods. This tree is trying to pull me into the Dark Woods. I can't get loose. Tell Sam to pay attention."

"Hi, Ryan!" Tiggy waved.

"You should see your face right now," Gary said to me. "You look like a tomato with a hole in it. Because that hole is your mouth. And it's open. And you're red. Okay, that wasn't the best analogy, but it was the best I could come up with and the tree is kidnapping Ryan." He looked over my shoulder with wide eyes.

"What?" I turned around. Sure enough, the tree was pulling Ryan into the Dark Woods. "What are you doing?" I shouted after him. "Why didn't you say anything?"

"Seriously?" he snapped. "I'm getting molested by trees and you're *yelling* at me?"

"Hmm," I said with a sniff. "No need to be all sensitive about it. It was just a question."

"Hey, Sam?" Gary said. "I'm pretty sure the mushrooms around Tiggy and me are moving."

"They're what?" I asked. "Are you sure you didn't just eat them? Gary, I told you that you can't go around eating whatever mushrooms you see. That's what happened last time and you were tripping balls for a week. You got into a fight with an imaginary duck named Hector who you said was homophobic."

"He kept calling me a *fruitcake*!"

"He wasn't *real* and now my mushrooms are moving." And they were. The fairy ring around my feet was shifting. The mushrooms had uprooted themselves and were *hopping* toward the forest, keeping the circle perfectly intact. I felt the edge of the circle at my back and tried to press against it to keep the mushrooms in place, but the magic in them (*earth* and *forest* and *green green green*) was overriding my own, pushing it farther and farther down. I pushed my back against the invisible wall behind me. My feet skidded in the dirt. There was no give. The circle never faltered. The mushrooms kept moving into the woods.

"Well, shit," I said. "I am truly annoyed now."

"Yeah," Ryan called from farther in the woods. "So sorry for you. I'm pretty sure this tree is passing me off to another tree that is not as discerning about personal space. I don't know that I've ever been groped by a forest before."

What made that *truly* bothersome was the sharp little curl of jealousy I felt at that. Yes, I can freely admit that I was jealous of a tree bad-touching Knight Commander Ryan Foxheart.

Gary said, "Doesn't that happen pretty much wherever you go?"

"I don't ask for it," he said back. "People just... touch."

"Maybe you should ask it to buy you dinner first," I sniped.

Gary knew me well enough. "Sam, it's just a *tree*."

"Shut up, Gary!"

"No, tree!" Ryan suddenly shouted. "You *don't* get to touch that!"

The blood rushed in my ears. I wanted to touch that.

"Thank the gods we got nonsexual mushrooms," Gary said.

"No bad-touch," Tiggy said, frowning down at his fairy circle.

"Okay, the next tree isn't touching my junk yet," Ryan said.

"We don't need a play by play," I said hoarsely.

"You okay, Sam?" Gary asked evilly. "You sound out of breath."

I tried to call upon my magic to light Gary on fire, but the fairy circle was too strong. Maybe if I was as old as Morgan or had more control than I did, I'd be able to do something about it.

And, of course, that traitorous little voice in my head said that maybe if I had my *cornerstone* well in place, this wouldn't be an issue. That was a thought I banished to the farthest recesses of my mind.

"What *is* this?" Ryan said, sounding closer than he had before. I looked over and could see him through the forest, arms still above his head, tree limbs groaning as they moved him slowly forward.

"Dimitri," Gary sighed.

"Who is Dimitri?"

"Ha-ha," I said weakly. "So, funny story. There are fairies? In the Dark Woods. And I *might* have pissed off their king."

There was silence. Then, "Of course you did."

I scowled at him even though he couldn't see me. "It wasn't my fault! He wanted to marry me and I told him I didn't see him like that and he got mad!"

"Yeah," Gary muttered. "Because *that's* the whole story."

"Close enough!"

"Everything wants to have sex with you," Ryan said in disbelief. "Literally *everything*."

"That tree didn't," I reminded him. "That was all you. Way to go. You got wood."

"Ha!" Tiggy said. "Puns."

"Not funny," Ryan said. "I'm still traumatized. There were… *leaves*. Near my… *you know*."

"Your cock?" Gary asked. "Dick? Your dong? Man tube? Baby maker? Your balls and chain?"

"Gary!" I said as I stepped over a fallen tree.

"Sorry. Your *penis*. Jeez. Prude."

"Just how mad is this Dimitri?" Ryan asked.

Oh. That. "Um. Very? Like, I might have led him on in hopes of escaping? And then left him at the altar?"

"What?" Ryan said.

"Fairy weddings work very fast," I said. "One minute I was minding my own business doing absolutely nothing in the Dark Woods and the next I was wearing flowers in my hair while a fairy named Harry was asking me to recite my vows."

"Your vows," Ryan said and *great*. We were back to that *repeating* thing again.

"I forgot about those," Gary said with a snort. It came out as purple this time, but was muted because of the fairy ring. "You made them up off the top of your head while trying to figure out how we were going to get away."

"It lovely," Tiggy said. "Pretty words."

"So, let me get this straight," Ryan said. "You entered into the Dark Woods again, knowing that Morgan told you to avoid them. You've been attacked by Dark wizards in said woods and now you are telling me you almost got gay fairy married to a fairy named Dimitri by a fairy named Harry. And you still go into them. *All the time.*"

"Yes. But, to be *fair*, all those other things happened way on the other side of the Dark Woods, so you really can't fault me for thinking they wouldn't happen here."

"I'm coming under the impression that these things happen no matter where you go."

"That's... pretty much true," Gary said.

"Shut up, Gary," I growled.

"Mean. Just for that, I'm going to recite your wedding vows."

"Oh my gods."

"Dearest Dimitri. I've known you but for three minutes, but my heart beats in my chest just for you."

"Gary, I swear to the gods, stop talking."

"Gary, please continue," Ryan said, and I *despised* him.

"You are a fairy and I am a man. A wizard, but a man nonetheless. Our worlds couldn't be more different, but please believe me when I say I love you just as much as I love standing here against my will."

Ryan choked out a laugh, and I wished a tree would bad-touch him again.

"All my life I've searched for someone like you. Only you're better. Because you have wings. That are shiny. So. Good job on that. Your parents must be proud. Oh? What's that? Your parents are dead? And they died horribly just three months ago? Oh. My bad. Dude. Seriously. So my bad. That was not cool. Can we go back to the love part?"

I buried my face in my hands. How he remembered this word for word, I'll never know. And why did *everyone* who did impressions of me do my voice so shrill? It was *insulting*.

"The love part. Here we are. Together. You and I. And we're getting dude-hitched. To each other. Because this is my life. And I couldn't run away. Even if I wanted to. So I guess this will be a thing. Forever. Lucky me. I'm not stalling, I just have so many words to say to you. Like, you are fun. For someone who took me prisoner and is now forcing me to marry him. So fun. I have to wrap it up? Rude. Okay. In conclusion, I'm super happy about this. And you are awesome. And I'm so glad Gary is laughing at me. The bastard. Tiggy, you are my only favorite. The end."

"Gary?"

"Yes, Sam?"

"Your death will not come easy. There will be pain as I choke the life out of you."

"Kinky. I'm down."

"How did you get away?" Ryan asked.

I shrugged. "Gary got free and kicked some fairies, and we ran."

He gaped at me.

"It was daring," I said.

"I don't even know what to say to that," Ryan said. "I don't even know what to say to any of this. You and I have been talking, *actually talking*, for a little over three weeks. And in those three weeks, we've been attacked twice, a dragon came to the city and knocked you through a building, and now we're going to meet your ex to whom you almost gay fairy married. How are you even a real person?"

"Hey," I growled. "He's not my *ex*. And you didn't talk to me for like two of those three weeks, so you can shut your mouth. And it wasn't a *building*. It was a *shed*."

"I was *busy*." The trees were bringing him closer to me. He was scowling. It was unfair how hot his scowl was. When I scowled, I looked constipated.

"Yeah, that *must* be it. Busy like a *champ*."

"That doesn't even make sense!"

"*You* don't even make sense!"

"I hate it when Mommy and Daddy fight," Gary said to Tiggy.

The trees stopped moving Ryan when he was three feet away from me.

"Who Mommy?" Tiggy asked, eyeing us both.

Gary rolls his eyes. "Duh. Ryan. Obviously."

"Ha!" I crowed. "You're the mother!"

"Whatever," he muttered. "I'd be a great mom. I'd mom like a champ. Wait. What the hell? *How do you get me involved in these conversations?*"

"Uh, easy? You open your mouth and respond. Not a hard concept. Even for a meathead knight like yourself."

"You just wait until this tree lets me go. I'm so gonna—"

And I never really got to find out how he was going to finish that sentence. In my deep and disturbing fantasies, he was so gonna fuck me into next week and we would have babies and buy a farm in the country, and I'd get to wear a really big sunhat while I plucked vine-ripened tomatoes from the garden.

But he never got to finish that sentence because we were surrounded by fairies.

"Balls," I muttered, watching my dreams of a sunhat disappear in front of me.

"Sam?"

"Yes, Ryan?"

"Why is there a six-inch-tall angry naked man with wings flying in front of your face? And why are we surrounded by even more tiny fluttering naked men?"

I sighed. "Because this is what my life has become. Ryan, meet Dimitri, king of the Dark Woods fairies. Dimitri, this is Knight Commander Ryan Foxheart."

Ryan's eyes bulged. "*This* is your ex?"

"He's *not* my ex," I grumbled. I looked up at Dimitri. He really was tiny. And naked. It was so very awkward. His wings fluttered rapidly, and his creamy skin was flushed with anger. He had a shaved head and the tiniest mustache in the world. He would have been delightful if not for the fact that I was pretty sure he wanted to murder me. "Heeeeey, Dimitri. Long time no see. How you been, buddy?"

"Sam," he said stiffly, and I'd forgotten just how high-pitched his voice was. It sounded like he was squeaking. I tried to keep my lips from quirking because he was angry and it sounded hysterical. "How nice it is to see you again. And you are so my ex."

"Oh my gods," Ryan gasped, like he was trying not to laugh. "This is amazing. I am having such a good time right now. Huzzah. Huzzahs all around."

Dimitri and I both glared at him.

He didn't look repentant in the slightest.

"What brings you to these parts?" Dimitri asked me.

"Your magic mushrooms," I told him. "They sort of forced us here. Except for Ryan. Ryan was flirting with the trees."

"I was *not*—"

"Is he always this loud?" Dimitri asked, frowning at Ryan. "He seems loud, even for a human."

The other fairies grumbled their agreement.

"He's usually pretty loud," I agreed. "He has to be. He's a knight commander. It's dashing and immaculate."

"Oh?" Dimitri asked. "So *he's* the reason you couldn't get married."

And what the fuck? "That is so not even close to being a real thing."

But Dimitri ignored me. He flew up to Ryan and hovered near his face. Ryan arched an eyebrow at him.

"I've heard of you," Dimitri said, poking Ryan in the cheek. "You are supposed to be some big to-do. I'll be honest. I'm a little disappointed."

"Trust me," Ryan said. "The feeling is not mutual. When Sam told me about you, I was expecting something completely different. This is so much better."

"He talked about me, did he?" Dimitri turned and leered at me.

"Oh gross," I muttered.

"I could see why," Dimitri said, looking back at Ryan. "Especially if you're the competition."

"No competition," I said loudly. "None. There is no competing."

"See?" Dimitri said. "You've already lost."

Ryan snorted. "Yeah, I don't think so. My cock is bigger than your whole entire being."

And. Just. *What.*

The fairies started tittering loudly.

Dimitri scowled. "It's not the size. It's what you do with it."

"And I can do many things with it," Ryan said wickedly. "Many, many things."

"Please, can I have some, please," I whispered, though no one heard me.

Dimitri poked Ryan's nose. "Listen, *human.* Just because you're jealous of the love Sam and I share—"

"Love?" I squeaked, sounding like Dimitri. "There is no love."

The fairies all turned to me.

Oh shit. "Uh. There may be a mutual appreciation of each other's willingness to avoid maiming or death?" I said.

"This is going so well," Gary said.

"It is?" Tiggy asked.

"No," Gary said. "Tiggy, the next thing we are going to work on is sarcasm. You've gone far too long without knowing how to use it. It shall be remedied and you will be the most sarcastic half-giant in all of Verania and it will be glorious."

"Pretty Gary," Tiggy said fondly. He tried to reach out and pet Gary, but his hand knocked into the invisible wall that rose around him from the fairy ring. His brow furrowed and I knew it was only a matter of time before Tiggy got pissed off. No one got between him and Gary when he wanted to pet the unicorn.

"There's love," Dimitri insisted. "You just don't know about it yet."

"Ah," Gary said. "*That* kind of love. Because that makes sense."

Dimitri sighed like Gary was the most annoying thing that had ever existed. "If your kind wasn't considered sacred, I'd let my people eat you."

Gary preened. "Sam. *Sam.* I'm *sacred.*"

"Thanks for that," I told Dimitri. "I will never, ever hear the end of it."

Dimitri ignored me as he flew back to Ryan and started poking his face again. "I will fight you for him. A duel to win the heart of the wizard."

"Apprentice," Gary whispered.

Ryan rolled his eyes at Dimitri. "It would be more intimidating if your penis wasn't pressing against my cheek."

"So much sass," I told Gary and Tiggy. "He uses it like he invented it. Which, to be fair, I think he might have."

"He's not *that* sassy," Gary grumbled.

Another fairy flew up and whispered in Dimitri's ear. Dimitri's eyes narrowed with whatever the fairy was telling him.

"You're engaged," Dimitri finally said. "To the Grand Prince of Verania."

And there went all my fun fantasies again for the day.

"I am," Ryan allowed. He glanced at me like there was supposed to be a reaction. I kept my face blank.

"So you have no claim over Sam of Wilds," Dimitri said, sounding triumphant.

Ryan cocked his head. "More so than you do."

The mask slipped. "Hey!" I snapped. "I'm standing right *here*. I'm not a prize to be won." I winced. "Oh my gods, that sounded awful to say out loud." I looked at Gary, who was openly laughing at me. "For fuck's sake."

"I'm not a prize to be won," he gasped out. "That was so awesome. You go, girl. Get down with your bad self and *preach*. We don't need no *mens*. We are *fierce* and hear Sam of Wilds *roar*." He puffed out his chest and pranced in place in his fairy ring.

"You're a tool," I said, feeling my face turn red.

"You just told everyone you're not a prize to be won," he pointed out. "You win the tool award. In fact, you *are* the tool award."

"You can be my prize," Dimitri said, slinking through the air back over to me. He made sure not to cross into the fairy ring because he knew full well I'd crush him like a bug.

"That's not doing for me what you think it's doing for me," I told him. "Probably quite the opposite in fact. Dimitri, you know you and I wouldn't work. You're a fairy who lives in the Dark Woods, and I like not being in the Dark Woods. Or gay fairy married."

"That's a lie, and you know it," Ryan said.

"I will keep you satisfied," Dimitri said with a leer. "I may be small, but there are things I can do with my tongue that you wouldn't believe." He flew a little bit closer. "*Sexual* things."

"That's a kind offer," I said, trying not to insult him by grimacing. "Really. But I'm okay."

"Perhaps," he said, waggling his eyebrows, "a little demonstration?"

"No thank you," I said. "I'm all about true love. And not having sex with you."

"If we could just—"

"He said no," Ryan growled. "Back off."

Dimitri looked over at Ryan, who was glowering at the king of fairies. He brought up a hand to stroke his tiny mustache (and I had to bite back *aww*ing in his general direction because it was just so *little*) and said, "Oh. This makes much more sense now."

"What does?" I asked.

"This," he said, motioning between Ryan and me. "You know. The *thing*."

I was bewildered. "What thing?"

Dimitri looked at Gary. "Is he serious?"

"Unfortunately," Gary said. "It's so awkward. It makes you wonder about the future of Verania."

"I am so lost," I said to Ryan, who was refusing to meet my gaze.

"Me too," Ryan said.

Tiggy snorted and said, "Oh, Knight Delicious Face."

Another fairy flew up, carrying a spear and wearing a helmet and not much else. I thought about asking why he had armor on his head and not his balls, but I didn't think that was proper etiquette while being held prisoner by the Dark Woods fairies. "What shall we do with them, my lord?" he asked Dimitri. "Should we kill them?"

"No killing," I said. "No killing would be amazing." Because fairies could be vicious little things. They looked humanish, but they were filled with forest magic, and once the façade dropped, they were all teeth and claws and would swarm until there was nothing left but bits of shiny bone. "Come on, Dimitri. For old time's sake. Buddy. Pal of mine. You owe me."

"And how do you figure that?" he asked, eyes flashing purple.

"The whole kidnapping me and trying to make me your fairy bride? That's a good place to start."

"You said vows before your unicorn kicked twenty of my people in the face!"

"That might have not been my best move," I admitted. "But, to be *fair*, you didn't leave me with much of a choice. Hey. Hey. Look at me. What's going on? Huh? Little guy? Why don't you marry one of these fine-looking fairies?" I pointed out the hundred or so naked men fluttering nearby.

"It's just not the same," he said with a sigh. "I have a size kink."

I coughed. "You have a *what* now?"

He shrugged. "I like them big."

I grinned at Gary. "You hear that? I'm *big*."

"Pretty sure he was talking about your actual size and not your dick, honeybunch," Gary said, sounding bored. "Tone it down. I'm embarrassed for you."

"I'm huge," I told Dimitri. "Gargantuan."

"Average," Gary said. "I've seen it."

"A little support would be awesome," I said through gritted teeth.

"Oh my goodness," Gary said, voice sugary sweet. "He's *ginormous*. The first time I saw it, I was, like, is that your third leg? Are you some kind of three-legged human monstrosity?"

"Don't listen to him," I told Dimitri. "He's an ass. You can keep him if you want. He has to weigh at least a thousand pounds."

"*Sam!*" Gary shrieked at me. "How *dare* you!"

Dimitri flew over to Gary and started looking him up and down. "He's got a point. We should totally get married. You could be my fairy queen."

Gary's ears perked up. "A queen, you say? Well. You never said anything about being a *queen*."

"No, Gary," Tiggy said sternly. "You no fairy queen. You Sam and Tiggy's queen."

Ah gods, my heart. "I really want to hug you right now," I told Tiggy. "Dimitri, drop the damn fairy rings. I need to hug Tiggy because of feelings."

Dimitri sighed and snapped his fingers. The mushrooms grew dim and I felt my magic come roaring back. Gary and I crashed into Tiggy at the same time, and his big hands came up to the backs of our heads and held us close.

"I can't *believe* you said my weight out loud," Gary hissed at me.

"I can't *believe* you said my penis was average," I hissed right back.

"If the penis shoe fits," he said.

"What? That doesn't even... penis shoe? Like a shoe. For your penis."

"Shut up," he grumbled, rubbing his forehead against Tiggy's chest. "I have had a very trying and emotional last seventeen minutes and I can't be bothered to be my usual witty and wonderful self."

"How do you explain the rest of the time, then?"

"As touching as this is," Dimitri said from behind us, "I would rather get this over with."

I let go of Tiggy and turned back toward the fairies. Ryan still had his arms held up by the tree. I tried not to notice the flex of his arms or how totally awesome it would be to have him tied up like that so I could do whatever I wanted and—

"Stop thinking sex thoughts," Gary whispered.

"I wasn't," I whispered back.

"Liar. You had your sex face going on."

"I don't even want to know what that looks like."

"Like your jaw came unhinged and you might start to drool."

"So... attractive, right?"

"That's not the word I would have used."

"Get what over with?" I said to Dimitri.

"The reason why you're here," he said, "in the Dark Woods. They don't seem to be a safe place for you anymore."

I cocked my head at him, picking and choosing my next words carefully. There was something here that I was missing. The air seemed to have shifted. It felt cooler now. "We're here because it's a shorter route to get to Meridian City."

Dimitri's eyes flashed again. They were almost violet. "And what business have you there?"

"You know, don't you," I said. "Something."

Dimitri flew up closer to my face. He smiled, and it was a dark thing. "I know many things. I am the king of this forest. Nothing happens here without me knowing."

"Then tell me," I said, "what you know."

He shook his head. "That's not how this works, apprentice. You know that as well as I do."

"Oh, we're back to apprentice now?" I asked lightly. "No more Sam?"

"There are whispers," he said. "In the trees. In the darkest part of the forests."

Something prickled across my skin, almost like I was chilled. "And what do they whisper?"

"The Darks seem to have an unhealthy fascination with you," he said, ignoring my question. "Do you know why that is?"

"One of their own took us to a cave," I said. "In the eastern Dark Woods. All of us went in. He never walked out."

"We heard," Dimitri said. "Those that die in the Dark Woods tend to leave a bit of themselves behind. He echoed. He darkled. He was nothing but blood and bones when they found him."

"Tiggy tends to get overzealous when his friends are threatened," I said coolly.

"So you say. But you just don't know, do you?" He looked back over his shoulder and said something in the tongue of the fairies. It came out low and guttural, almost like grunts. The cadence was stilted and staccato. As soon as he fell silent, the other fairies spread their wings, alighting from the trees and bushes and flowers. They spun in a leisurely circle around us. I felt something crawl along my magic. I felt soft. Dully muted. Tiggy growled low in his throat and tensed behind me. Gary came to my side, eyelids heavy. Ryan didn't seem to be affected, worry darting along his face.

"What is this?" I asked, sounding slow and quiet.

"To keep our palaver secret," he said. "You can't be too careful these days. The trees hear everything."

"But you're their guardians," I said. "Why would they betray you?"

He grinned. His teeth were sharp. "Who said anything about betrayal?"

I said nothing.

"You look for the Grand Prince," he said. "He was taken, was he not?"

"You sound as if you already know," I said. "Why ask?"

"Formalities," he said.

"Games," I corrected.

His smile widened. "Are you sure you won't rethink that proposal? The conversation alone is *stimulating*."

I shook my head, trying to ignore just how stimulated he seemed to be. It's never okay to have a tiny man flying around with his erection near your face. "You deserve someone who can give you all you need. I can't do that."

The bravado faltered a bit. "I knew you were different," he said. "The first time you came into the woods. I could have taken you then. You were just a boy. I could have taken you away from the human world and raised you how I wanted you to be. Molded you to be something more than you are."

"I'm thinking you need to back up," Ryan said, voice hard. "Right now."

Dimitri paid him no mind. "But I let you grow. In the world of men. Where they are cold and careless and plot the most calculating plots they can to ensure their survival. They think only for themselves and not about the suffering of others. You see, Sam, it's only about *power*."

I thought back to Morgan and the way he'd evaded my questions. "What is it?" I asked, curious.

"Your Prince was taken by a dragon, yes?"

This wasn't guarded information. It was all the City of Lockes could speak of in the days before we'd set out. "He was," I said.

"And now you journey to bring him back," Dimitri said. "His knight and his would-be wizard."

"That's the plan."

"Don't you wonder, though?"

Games, games, games. "About what?"

"About *where* it came from. Why now?"

I wanted to play his game too. "You would have experience with dragons, wouldn't you?"

He looked agitated. "Careful, apprentice."

"The Great White. I've heard the stories. Tell me. When did you last see him?"

"He is not your concern," Dimitri said. "Gods have little time for mortal men."

"But he's not a god," I said. "His clock ticks just like yours and mine. It may tick slower and longer, but it still ticks."

"He's not—"

"You haven't seen him, have you?" I said.

Dimitri was silent.

"Is he dead? Is that why this new dragon is here?"

"No one understands the minds and wills of dragons," Dimitri said.

"Including you."

Dimitri's smile returned. "The Dark Woods are deep. I can see far."

"How far?"

"Your human mind could never understand."

Dealing with fairies was an exercise in frustration. Everything went in misshapen circles. "Specifics."

"I *am* specific. You're just choosing not to listen."

"And you're choosing to speak in vague riddles."

"The dragon is north," he said. There was a bitter set to his jaw. "Where the Dark Woods end before the mountains rise. In the hills there is a keep, long forgotten. The road from Meridian City will lead you there. When you reach the village of Tarker Mills, head toward the mountains. There is a valley. You shall find your keep there."

I narrowed my eyes. "Why would you help us?"

"You demand answers and when I give them, you question me?" he asked.

"You never do anything without a price, Dimitri."

He laughed. "This is true. A bit of advice."

I waited.

"Stay out of the Dark Woods. There are things far worse than myself."

"I'm not afraid. Of you or anything else. I have proven time and time again that I am more than capable of handling myself." I turned to glare at Gary and Tiggy lest they decide to speak and make me a liar. They both just stared blankly back at me.

Dimitri flew up close. He reached out and put his hands against my cheek. "Chaos always rises from complacency. I like you, Sam. You are not like the others. I've always been able to see that. There is something inside of you that burns differently than anyone who has come before you. I thought to harness it for myself, but I won't be the one to force it. But remember. The Dark Woods are known to you now. And you are known to them."

He flew up above us into the swirling mass of the other fairies. They shimmered brightly in the afternoon sun. The tree holding Ryan released him, and the fairies disappeared into the woods, almost faster than the eye could follow.

We were left in the silence of the forest, and I felt the gold and green all around me.

I looked over at Tiggy and Gary. "What the fuck is going on?"

Gary looked into the forest. "I suppose there is a bright side. You didn't have to get gay fairy married."

CHAPTER 13
I've Got Wood and I'm Ready to Masticate

WE MADE our way back to the main road before I thought to use the summoning crystal. I pulled it from the pack on Gary's back, the others standing around me. Ryan's eyes looked pinched and I wondered if we were friends again. I didn't think I was mad, but I didn't want to admit that it took a tiny naked man to help me get over it. I didn't say that out loud because it sounded all kinds of wrong.

It didn't help that there were too many questions I had for him. Why he seemed so keen on defending my honor. Why had he intimated he'd grown up in the slums. Why he was the way he was (meaning why, out of all the people in the world, was *he* my cornerstone). Granted, these were questions I was never going to ask, knowing full well my expectations would make the reality that much more crushing.

I told myself we were friends. Anger can turn to bitterness, and we couldn't have that between us. Not when we needed to trust each other to stage a rescue from a dragon.

"Not a word from any of you about being in the Dark Woods," I warned them. "Morgan can be a bit... touchy."

Gary snorted. It was green this time. "Touchy. Right."

"Maybe because you can't take two steps inside before something bad happens?" Ryan said.

"I'm so glad you're with us," I told him. "Because of the way you point out things."

There was a small smile on his face that my heart absolutely did not trip all over.

I held the crystal in the palm of my hand in front of me. I thought of Morgan and felt something *pull* in my head, like a hook had lodged itself in my brain and tugged. It was borderline unpleasant and I felt itchy all over.

The crystal flashed in my hand, a dull pulse as it grew warmer.

Then it was almost as if Morgan was standing right next to us, his voice loud and clear. "Sam?"

I opened my mouth to say how awesome it was, that this crystal was the coolest thing ever, to assure Morgan we were okay and most definitely traveling on the Old Road like he instructed us to. Instead I said, "We went into the Dark Woods and I almost had to get gay fairy married again and now I feel really bad and Ryan got bad-touched by trees and Fairy King Dimitri was cryptic and annoying and apparently has a size kink."

Silence. Gary, Tiggy, and Ryan stared at me with wide eyes.

Morgan sighed.

"I feel better," I told everyone. "Do you all feel better? I do. Honesty is like a balm to my beleaguered soul."

"I don't even know why I tell you what to do," Morgan said.

"Because it makes you feel special?" I guessed. "Because you are."

"You think I'm special," he said flatly.

"Yes."

He sighed again.

So I said, "How's the castle?"

"You've been gone four days."

"Things can happen in four days. Like… stuff."

"Stuff?"

"Sure. You know. Things."

"I'm still going to yell at you, Sam."

"Dammit," I said. "Are you sure? Because you don't sound sure."

"I tried to tell him no," Ryan said. "But you know how he gets."

"Do I ever," Morgan said.

"Ha, ha," I said with a scowl. "Are you guys finished? I would like you to be finished."

"What were you thinking?" Morgan said, sounding slightly pissed.

And that made me angry. "I was thinking that I'm twenty years old and more than capable of handling myself," I retorted. "I was thinking of the fact that it's been days since Justin was taken. I was thinking that the quicker we moved, the quicker this would be over and everything could go back to normal."

"But at what cost?" he asked. "I don't even want to know how you got away from Dimitri this time. Last time was a fluke. What did you promise him?"

I blanked on that. "Nothing," I said. "He let us go."

"What? Why?"

"I asked him to," I said. "And he did. And then he did his whole cryptic wood fairy thing."

"You asked the fairy king to let you go and he did," Morgan said.

"Yeah. He still wanted to marry me, but I convinced him I wasn't right for him."

"I don't even know what to do with you anymore," he said faintly. "Every time I think I've got you figured out or I'm even beginning to scratch the surface, you do something else that just contradicts everything I know."

"You sound like that's a good thing," I said.

"Most of the time," he agreed. "I don't know if now is one of those times. I asked you to stay out of the Dark Woods, Sam. I wouldn't have done so if I didn't have explicit reasons."

"Then explicitly explain them."

"I didn't think I had to. You killed a Dark wizard. They will want revenge."

"And that's it. That's all it was."

"Isn't that enough?" He sounded annoyed.

"You're not telling me everything," I said. "And I don't know why."

"Even if I wasn't, it'd be for good reason," he said. "Not to mention the fact that you have other priorities right now. Not everything concerns you, Sam. You need to focus on the Prince and then getting to Randall. Nothing else. Are we clear?"

"Crystal," I said. "We're going to have a long talk later, you and I, about keeping secrets."

"Are we?" he said. "I look forward to it."

I debated keeping the whereabouts of Justin from him just for spite, but I wasn't that type of person. Well. Not completely. "Dimitri told us where Justin is."

"Of course he did," Morgan muttered. "And he just volunteered up this information without asking for anything in return."

"To be fair," I said, "he probably felt bad about the tree molesting Ryan."

"Everyone should feel bad about that," Ryan said.

"I don't," Gary said.

"I don't," Tiggy said.

"I sort of do," I said. "But not really."

"I'm going to leave them here," Ryan said, leaning over and speaking into the crystal. I tried not to even think about his breath on my hands.

"I don't blame you," Morgan said. "I've thought about it countless times. Where is he?"

"In a keep to the north. The fairy said it was forgotten. It's in a valley outside of a village. Tarker Mills. I've never been there before. I don't think I've even heard of it. And if they were having problems with a dragon, why has nobody spoken of it before? Surely they would have seen it coming and going."

"That's near the mountains," Morgan said. "They grow corn. And no, you can't sell them on the firework corn."

"I wasn't even thinking about it," I said, even though I really was. A hamlet whose main crop is corn? It was *destiny*.

"I'll see what I can find out about a keep," he said. "I'm assuming there was a structure there at some point. A tower. A church. Something. Head to Meridian City. Check in at Old Clearing to make sure it was the dragon attacking the sheep and burning the earth. I want you out of those woods as soon as possible, Sam."

"Because of your secret reasons," I said. "Friends don't keep secrets, Morgan."

"Wizards do," he said. "Stay safe. I'll tell your parents you are alive and as foolish as ever. I'm sure they will be pleased."

"Love you, boo," I said.

He groaned before the crystal went dark.

I looked up at the rest of them. "Well, I think that went well, don't you?"

"Morgan's going to murder you when we get back," Gary said.

I shrugged as I put the crystal back in the pack. "We won't be back home for six months," I said. "He'll calm down by then."

"He remembers long time," Tiggy said ominously. "He remembers *everything*."

"Nah," I said. "We'll just buy him some chocolates from that shop he likes or I can just alter his memories. Either way, we'll be fine."

"Candy or memory alteration," Gary said. "Those aren't extremes."

"*You're* extreme," I said.

"Thank you."

"Shut it. Let's beat feet before it gets any later." We started walking down the road. I only made it four steps before I realized we weren't being followed. I glanced over my shoulder as Gary and Tiggy continued on.

Ryan stood where we'd left him, hands curled into fists at his sides.

"You cool?" I asked him as I walked back up to him.

"Six months," he said, staring off over my shoulder.

"What?"

"You said you were going to be gone for six months."

"Well, yeah. You knew this. I told you. And then you acted like a chump and didn't speak to me for two weeks."

"You never said how long. You said it would be for a while."

"That *is* a while."

"Why?" he asked, finally looking at me. There was something in his eyes I couldn't quite figure out. The closest thing I could make it to be was anger, but that didn't seem right.

"Why what?"

"Why do you have to go? What are you leaving for? Where are you going?"

I hesitated. This was dangerous ground. He knew nothing of cornerstones, much less the fact that he *was* one. I couldn't tell him that he was a big part of the reason I was leaving, because the longer I stayed, the more difficult it would be as he didn't belong to me.

"Away," I said. "I'm going away because I have to. To learn better control of my magic."

"Morgan's your mentor," he said, like he was trying to argue with me. "He can teach you."

I shook my head slowly. "Not everything. Not this."

He took a step toward me and his eyes were so green, like the trees in summer, and all I wanted to do was to tell him this. To tell him that when I stood by his side, I felt right. I felt even. My head was clear and my heart was clean.

He said, "What is *this*?"

A question that could be taken so many ways.

I took the easy way out. "It's a wizard thing," I said. "You wouldn't understand."

"Where?" he said.

I looked away. "It doesn't matter."

"Randall," he said.

I turned to walk away. And made it three steps.

"Sam."

I didn't turn back around, but I stopped.

"The King told me," he said.

I said nothing.

"About what happened. About how you ended up at the sparring fields."

"Ah," I said.

"Is it true?"

"No," I said. "I lied to the King because I could."

"Don't do that. Just... don't. You deflect. You always deflect."

"And you always jump to conclusions without having all the facts."

"I didn't mean—it just... he's my—"

"I know," I said, trying to put him out of his misery. "He's yours."

Silence. For longer than there should have been.

Then, "I'm sorry. I should have never—"

"I know," I said and walked away.

Eventually, he followed.

DUSK WAS falling as Gary and I gathered firewood along the edges of the Dark Woods. Tiggy and Ryan were back at the river's edge at the camp. Ryan said he wanted to bathe, and there was no way in hell I could be in the same vicinity as Ryan Foxheart with soap-slicked skin, so I immediately squawked and volunteered to get the firewood. Or, rather, that's what I meant to say. Gary assured me as we walked away that it just sounded like I was barking.

We were slowly trudging our way back to camp when Gary said, "You and Knight Delicious Face okay?"

I opened my mouth to respond and everything came to a screeching halt when I realized that Gary had no fucking idea what Ryan was to me. I had never told him. I had never sat him down (as much as a unicorn can sit down) and said, "Oh, by the way, Ryan is my cornerstone and I can't have him so we're running away under the guise of needing to learn more control. Even though that's sort of true because I can do things no other wizard can."

Gary would be pissed at me for neglecting to share such important information. A pissed-off unicorn was something I didn't want to deal with right then (or ever), and I reminded myself it didn't matter in the long run anyway. Only Morgan and the King knew of what he was to me, and I was going to keep it that way. Either we'd go our separate ways eventually and Ryan would get married, or we'd get eaten by a dragon and the whole point would be moot. Funny how okay I was with impending death rather than telling my best friend I wanted to magically bond all over Ryan's face. Or whatever.

"We're fine," I said. "I think. He was being an ass. I was being an ass. He apologized and I said okay and now we're here."

"Cool story, bro," Gary said. "Now tell me the real version."

I sighed. "He thought I took Justin out to the sparring fields, not the other way around. He accused me of being reckless and not giving a shit, and I overreacted because that's what I do. He found out otherwise from the King, felt super bad, said sorry, and now we're here."

"What a dick," Gary muttered and I immediately felt better, because that's what best friends do. "Maybe we should have left him with Dimitri."

"Right? And then I think he was mad when he found out how long we were leaving for. He acted weird after he heard me tell you it was going to be six months before we got back."

Gary sighed. "I'm not even going to touch that one."

"What?" I asked. "You think he's mad we're going to miss the wedding? I'll be honest, I'm pretty sure I don't want to be there. Even though I should be."

"Yes," Gary said. "That's exactly why he's pissed. Good job."

"Whatever," I groused. "I don't even care."

"Obviously. The level with which you do not care is astounding. It almost eclipses your awareness."

"I don't even know what you're talking about!"

"Shocking."

"You are a terrible best friend."

"Bullshit. I am your everything."

"How sad is that?" I sighed.

"Shush. Do you have enough wood?"

I leered at him. "I *never* have enough—"

"Gross," he said. "Don't do that. It's rapey. How are you ever going to land a man if you're rapey?"

"I can just marry Dimitri," I said, starting to lead us back toward camp. "He has a size kink for me. And remember, apparently he has a tongue that I just wouldn't believe."

"Can you imagine? He'd have to be full-body hugging your penis just to jack you off."

"I really wish you hadn't said that. Now I can't stop thinking about it."

"Don't marry Dimitri," he said. "You're not meant to be a fairy queen. Not in the literal sense, anyway."

"I don't think that's going to be a problem. I have a size kink too. Human size."

"Ryan size," he corrected.

"Remember when he would come within thirty feet of me and I would run away? Those were the good old days. Now I'm chasing dragons and getting blue balls."

"Aww," Gary said. "Do you need to go masturbate in the woods?"

"No."

"I'll cover for you. Go masturbate in the woods."

"Gary."

"Just a little. Just pull on it a little bit."

"*Gary.*"

He sighed. "Chin up, kitten. We'll get through this just like everyone else does. You're not the first one to be stuck in a crapshoot. Pretty soon, you'll look back on all this and wonder what all the fuss was about and say Ryan who? And then you'll—*holy mother of crap cakes in a shit storm, you will never get over him because of the sheer magnitude of all his perfections.*"

I was feeling good about myself up until that last part. I turned to scowl at Gary, but his eyes were wide and staring over toward the river. I followed his gaze.

And.

Just.

Stopped.

There are moments in your life so profound, so extraordinarily crystal clear that even the remembrance of them is enough to feel like you're being consumed by fire. Moments that might not mean much to anyone else, but mean the world to you.

I had these moments.

I was five and my mother was dancing to a song only she could hear.

I was seven and my father put his arm around my shoulders while we watched the sunset and waited for the stars to come out.

I was nine and I wished for something more.

I was eleven and Morgan held my hand for the first time.

I was fourteen when I stumbled upon a hornless unicorn and a crying half-giant.

I was fifteen when Pete whispered that his name was Ryan and he was to be a knight.

I was seventeen when I brought a bird back to life and I never told anyone about it.

I was eighteen when my mother cried and said I would always be her little boy.

I was twenty when Ryan stood at my side and my magic said *finally*.

And now. *Now.*

Now was Knight Commander Ryan Foxheart climbing slowly out of the river, water cascading down his body, dripping over miles and miles of muscle. He wore nothing but a thin, white undergarment that stuck and clung to his groin and thighs. He reached down, the muscles in his back flexing as he scooped up water in his hands and brought it up and over his head. His nipples were pebbled. His chest was covered in a smattering of wet hair. He was lines and corded muscle, definition and carved from stone. If I had let my eyes linger, I would have sworn I could see the outline of his cock through the wet fabric. My skin felt tight and flushed and I *wanted*. There was green and gold, and it was so fucking bright that I almost had to shut my eyes from the weight of it.

"I swear he's doing this on purpose," Gary whispered hotly.

"I swear I want to do him on purpose," I breathed.

Gary choked and I didn't care.

I would never have him. I knew this. It wasn't meant to be.

But that didn't mean I couldn't be creepy and have this *one fucking moment* where I could pretend and wish and hope and dream and yes, now I had an erection and it was fucking *awful*.

"Do you see his *stomach*?" Gary murmured.

Of course I had. The thin line of hair that disappeared to his groin. The cut of the abdominals. Which were wet. Very, very wet. "I want to be the river," I told Gary, sounding slightly hysterical. "I want to be the river right at this very moment."

"Why is the sun setting so perfectly behind him?"

"Because the gods want to grace his shoulders with the fading light."

"I want to grace his shoulders with my—"

I'll never know what dirty thing Gary wanted to grace Ryan's shoulders with. And I was totally okay with that. I was *not* okay with why I would never know.

"What you guys doing?" Tiggy said. Very, very loudly.

And the creepy voyeuristic bathing fantasy came to a grinding halt.

Ryan looked up.

Gary and I froze.

Tiggy cocked his head and waved.

"You okay, Sam?" Ryan asked, and his voice was *husky*.

So I blurted out, "I've got wood."

Gary turned his head slowly to gape at me.

"Oh dear gods," I muttered. Then louder, "Wood. I brought the wood. I've got so much wood. Wood. Fuck. *Firewood.* I've got *firewood*. For the fire. Because it's going to get nipples out tonight. *Cold.* It's going to get *cold* out tonight. Sweet molasses." I bent down to pick up the firewood and stumbled, almost falling flat on my face. "Ha, ha!" I cried. "Whoops. I'm okay. Don't mind me. Just feeling a bit weak in the knees. But not because of anything that's happening right in front of me like thighs! No, sir. I've just got bad knees. But you don't, do you? You've got… knees. Like. *Knees.* And I've got firewood. For the fire." I bent down to pick up the wood, willing myself to just *shut up, shut up*! "Well. This has been erotic. *Enlightening.* Gods, this is *enlightening*. Like eye-opening. Nothing else!" I stood up, holding the firewood to my chest like it was supposed to block me from the glory that was Ryan Foxheart. "Oh my gods," I whispered fervently. "I'm a Foxy Lady."

"You're a *what*?" Gary screeched.

"Nothing!" I shouted at him. "Nothing! No funny stuff. I am bringing *wood* for the *fire* and now you're getting out of the river and why are you walking in slow motion? That's… that's just swell. *Hell.* That's *hell* on, on, on your *feet*. Because of the *river* rocks." And Ryan was *smiling* at me. Like I was *amusing*. "You're so wet," I told him unnecessarily.

He nodded as he stood on the riverbank. Then, never taking his eyes from me, he clasped his hands above his head and *stretched* his back. I immediately turned to Gary and whispered that I had a newfound fetish for *armpits* that I was just discovering and was quite unsure what to do with. Gary in turn said that they were obviously made for licking and I dropped the firewood again.

"Water feels good," Ryan said. "Not too cold."

"That's wonderful," I told him. "Just wonderful. I am so glad we're both here and talking like we are right now."

He grinned at me before turning around and bending over to pick up his discarded clothes.

"Dat. *Ass*," Gary and I said at the same time.

Because it was a nice ass. Better than nice. It was a splendid ass. Superb, even.

"Bite it," Gary whispered, pushing his head against my back. "For fuck's sake, go *bite it*."

"My mouth is not worthy," I said.

"What was that?" Ryan asked, standing back up and looking over his shoulder. His awesome, awesome shoulder.

Gary said, "Sam wants to bite—"

"Some food," I said, cutting in quickly. "I want to bite some *food* because I'm so hungry right now. And you should put on clothes."

He looked down at himself, then back up at me. "Why? It's just us out here."

"And no one can hear you scream," Gary supplied helpfully.

"We having naked time?" Tiggy asked as he started reaching for the ties on his pants.

"No!" I said. "No naked time. There is absolutely no need for naked time. In fact, we should put on all the clothes that we brought to be the opposite of naked."

"I'm always naked," Gary purred to Ryan. "And you'll have to forgive Sam. He's a little bit… frustrated. I told him he should just go into the woods and mastur—"

"*Masticate*," I exclaimed. "He wanted me to go and chew food in the woods, but I said, 'Why? Why do that? We can just *masticate* here. At the camp. With ourselves. Because that's what normal people do.'"

"Riiiight," Gary said. "Maybe you and Ryan can masticate together?"

"Or not," I said as I ground my teeth. "I like to masticate by *myself*."

"And you're so good at it," Gary said. "The up and down motions of your… jaw. And then, upon completion, you swallow. Right, Sam? You swallow, don't you?"

"Of course I do," I said, confused. What the hell were we talking about now? "I always swallow when I finish. What am I supposed to do? Spit it back out?"

Ryan tripped and fell back into the river.

We all stared at him.

He sputtered as he came out of the water. "Tripped." He coughed. "On a rock."

"Or something that rhymes with rock," Gary said.

"You tripped on your sock?" I asked him.

Gary said, "I just don't even know why I bother anymore. Tiggy, darling. Let's let the mens take care of dinner. You and I can have naked time and frolic in the river now. Lose the britches. It's time to make the humans feel inadequate."

Tiggy crowed his pleasure as he dropped his pants.

I looked down and whispered to my penis, "It's okay. I don't think you're inadequate. You're special in your own way. Except when you betray me. Like right now." Because Ryan was climbing out of the water again and I hated everyone and everything.

Sighing, I picked up the firewood and turned away.

CHAPTER 14
The Ballad of Sam, Gary, and Tiggy

I LAY on my back looking up at the stars, listening to Gary and Tiggy snore. Gary would adamantly deny this, saying a lady of his stature would *never* snore, but he was a liar and a fat mouth and his snoring sounded like an orgy involving otters and bears.

The fire was getting low, but the night was warm and the sky was clear and so I wished for things in my secret heart, waiting for sleep to take me away.

"You watch the stars a lot," Ryan said from somewhere off to my left. He was on first watch but hadn't spoken in a while.

"I guess," I said.

"Why?"

"They don't change," I said, even though I hadn't meant to. "Everything else around me can change, but they won't ever. And it doesn't matter where I am in the world, I can look up and see the same sky."

"Everything always changes," he said quietly. "And you wake up one day and don't recognize the life you had before you went to sleep."

I didn't know quite what to say to that, so I said nothing at all.

Nothing happened for a few moments, but then he was up and moving from the other side of the fire, dragging his bedroll closer to me. I didn't say anything as he spread it perpendicular to me, his head near mine. He lay back down and I tried to remember how to breathe.

"I can protect you easier if I'm closer," he said.

"Because I need you to protect me. Obviously." I refused to look over at him and instead looked back up at the night sky.

"I didn't mean to avoid you."

I rolled my eyes. "So you admit to the avoiding."

"Possibly."

"Were you aware of it?"

"Yes."

"Then you meant to do it."

I could hear the scowl in his voice. "Not specifically."

"So, no specific avoidance, but a vague avoidance."

"Talking to you is impossible sometimes."

"I'm a wizard."

"You say that a lot."

"It's a fact."

"It sounds like an excuse sometimes."

"Says the Knight Commander."

Gary chose at that moment to snort in his sleep quite loudly, shooting a puff of green and lavender sparkles out his nose. He resumed snoring annoyingly like the princess unicorn he was. Tiggy tugged him tighter against his chest in his sleep.

"How did you meet them?" Ryan asked. "There are at least thirty different versions of the story."

"What?"

He shrugged. The fire popped. An owl called out from the Dark Woods. "People talk about you."

"Why?"

"Because you're you."

"That's… succinct. And frightening."

"It's a reason," he said. "Trust me on that."

"Okay, then."

"So?"

I sighed. "Gary tells it better. Certainly with more… flair. He calls it the 'Ballad of Sam, Gary, and Tiggy.' There's singing involved. And rhyming. Possibly a choreographed dance, depending on his mood. It's really quite the production. And now that I think about it, that's probably why there are thirty different versions of the story. He tends to change things up upon repeat performances. Doesn't want to let down his fans." Gods, I loved that fucking unicorn.

"I'd rather hear the Sam version," Ryan said and I couldn't take it anymore. I looked over at him and found him watching me, head turned back at an almost awkward angle. The firelight danced across his face and I thought I'd never seen anything more beautiful. My magic felt so settled in my skin that I thought that I could do anything.

So I said, "Okay. Okay. There was once a strange and somewhat lonely boy…."

THERE WAS once a strange and somewhat lonely boy. He had wished upon the stars above and found them listening because one day, a man came to the slums and took him away to a castle. His parents came too, and they were amazed and awed at what life would be like for them.

And he worked. The strange and somewhat lonely boy worked as hard as he could, because Morgan expected great things from him. The boy wanted nothing more than to make Morgan happy and make his parents proud.

That left little time for anything else. Between schooling and magic and lessons in proper etiquette, the boy wasn't able to make many friends. True, he didn't have friends in the slums to begin with (because he was odd and mouthy and fiery and that combination made him an outcast), but he'd hoped things would be different.

There was a prince for whom he would one day serve, and while he was only a few years older, the Prince had little time for the peculiarity from the slums.

And the boy was okay with that. Mostly.

He was fourteen when the wizard Morgan of Shadows came to him with a great task.

He said, "You must go into the wilds of the Dark Woods and within three days bring back something unexpected."

"Unexpected?" the boy asked with wide eyes. "Is this a test?"

And the great wizard said with a smile, "Yes, little one. It is a test. And I have great faith in you."

That made the little boy feel warm and more than a little happy, because not many people had had faith in him. His parents, yes, but who else? He had no friends to miss him in the slums, no people to mourn his departure. But here! *Here* he had a man who was almost a legend telling him about *faith*, and the boy thought that if it were possible, he would bring the man the sun and the moon just to show how much his words meant.

It was also the first time he would be going out on his own. It showed that the wizard had trust in his apprentice, trust that he could perform the task set before him. Was he scared? Sure. He was fourteen years old. He was scrawny. His voice still tended to crack. He was confused why sometimes a handsome boy smiling meant something more than a pretty girl.

But he was more than his fears. He was an *apprentice*, and one day, he would be the King's Wizard, and people would remember his name and they would be *happy* to see him, *happy* to be his friend.

And so the boy packed a bag, hugged his parents (who were only the tiniest bit teary, especially the father), and walked out of the castle, out of the City, and into the Dark Woods.

And promptly got lost.

He didn't mean for it to happen.

One minute he was marching determinedly into the Dark Woods, and the next (after being distracted by *this* and *that*), he was in unfamiliar territory, unsure of where to go next. He knew magic, of course, but Morgan had warned him to use it sparingly so as to not attract unwanted attention. Especially if he was traveling by himself. He could protect himself, if it came down to it (which were among the first lessons Morgan had taught him: defensive spells and wards and counterattacks), but he often had trouble with the little things, like directions and staying on point. It wasn't his fault, not completely. His brain worked a little differently and it was easier for him to become sidetracked. His mother said it was a quirk. His father said it was a talent. Morgan said it was an issue to be worked through.

But none of them were with him in the Dark Woods and he was, and now he was lost and still needed to find something unexpected.

There was a large spider with a web six feet across.

It was unexpected, sure. But it was also gross.

There was the skull of a large elk, sixteen points upon its head.

It was unexpected, definitely. But it had died in the forest it had lived in, and the boy knew that's where it should stay.

There was a flower that blossomed only when touched by human hands.

It was unexpected, no doubt about it. But it smelled awful and caused the boy to sneeze.

That first night he huddled up against a tree. The canopy overhead was thick, but if he angled his head just right, he could see the stars.

Now, this boy had done his fair share of wishing upon these stars. Sometimes, the wishes came true. Most of the time, they did not. It never stopped him, though. Because the stars were always there, no matter where he was.

And so, like most nights, aside from that stretch of time when he first moved into the castle, he looked up at the sky and found the Fox and the Dragon and the Old Fish, friends that never left him, and on the outside of his vision, he saw the *green* of his magic. It was there, like the stars, his constant.

I wish to find the unexpected, he thought. *So that I may show Morgan that he was right to place his faith in me.*

He slept, then. Under the tree. Under the stars. In the Dark Woods.

When he opened his eyes again, the sun was barely rising and he heard a deep, choked sob that came from deeper in the woods.

Whoever it was sounded so sad and hurt that it clawed at the boy's heart, even as it made him wary. He knew there were tricksters in the forest, shape-shifters and fairies and selkies who could lure even the most hardened of men with promises of sex or love or the need for comfort until they were too close to see the flash of claws, the snarl of teeth.

He was a kind boy, a loving boy. But he was not a stupid boy.

He remembered words that Morgan had taught him, words that could cause rocks to float and be hurled. His was an earthy magic, with words like *ris* and *thri* and *par*. They were weaker words, but they would do in a pinch if he needed them.

He hoped he wouldn't need them.

He took light steps through the woods, avoiding the leaves that scattered the forest floor. Most knew him by his mouth, the never-ending babble that would pour out talking about anything and everything. They didn't know that this strange and somewhat lonely boy could be as silent as shadow when called upon to do so. That he could close his mouth and narrow his mind with a razor-sharp focus. He could move with the softest of steps, like he was not there at all.

The sounds of sadness grew louder and he almost hoped it *was* a trap, because the sobs were filled with such pain that it caused the boy's heart to shatter. A trap meant that nothing bad had happened to whomever was crying like their soul had been torn in two.

There was a clearing ahead.

He moved among the trees.

He heard a quiet murmur moving in tandem with the sobs.

He took a breath and peered around an old tree, the bark rubbing against his hands.

In the clearing sat a giant of a man, head bowed, face in hands, shoulders shaking as he cried. He had long black hair that hung around large fingers. He wore only trousers, torn and dirty. Across the long expanse of his back, scars stretched in sharp, white relief from the tanned skin. It took the boy a moment to see them for what they were.

Whip marks. The giant of a man had been whipped. Repeatedly.

Some of the scars were old. Some looked newer.

He moved his hand from his face, and his chin wobbled, and he let out another sound of anguish, his dark eyes welling and spilling over onto his already wet and reddened cheeks. He looked so *young*.

"It's okay," another voice said. "We've got away. We won't have to go back, I promise. We'll find somewhere to go and I'll build you a house and we can live there and have food and beds and good dreams and nothing will hurt us ever again."

The boy looked away from the giant and saw another wonder that took his breath away.

A beautiful white horse, tall and elegant and… talking.

The horse was talking.

It wasn't until the horse looked off into the trees that the boy saw the nub of bone on the horse's forehead that he realized it wasn't a horse at all.

It was a unicorn.

"So awesome," the boy breathed.

Quite loudly.

The unicorn immediately looked over at where the boy was hiding behind the tree. It glared, eyes flashing brightly and only then could the boy feel its magic, reaching out for his own. It wasn't as strong as a unicorn's should be, but its horn was gone so the boy didn't expect it to be.

He heard the giant of a man rumble loudly as he pulled himself to his feet and the boy thought briefly how he couldn't be a full giant, as they were twenty feet tall, but that his mother must have been a giantess, and his father a man. He had so many questions to ask but he first needed to make sure they weren't going to rip him limb from limb.

"Who's there?" the unicorn shouted.

"I smash," the half-giant growled.

"Tiggy will smash you," the unicorn agreed.

"Very hard," the half-giant said.

The boy most certainly didn't want to be smashed, but he needed them to know he wasn't a threat. A unicorn couldn't be evil, because their hearts were too pure, and if it was traveling with a half-giant, then the half-giant couldn't be all bad either. And they sounded scared and sad and all the boy wanted to do was make them smile and laugh and be happy.

This strange and somewhat lonely boy knew he had found something *unexpected*.

So he took a breath and pulled his shoulders back and held himself high as he stepped away from the tree and into the clearing.

The unicorn and half-giant stared at him.

The boy stuck out his chest proudly.

The unicorn snorted. It came out pink. "Well," it said. "That's not quite what I expected. Who knew the forest was infested with twinks."

The boy furrowed his brow. "What's a twink?"

"You'll learn one day, chicken," the unicorn said. "Around the time your cherry gets popped. Now go away. We're busy."

The boy gaped at him. "You can't speak to me that way! I'm a *wizard*."

"Sure, kid. And I'm the Queen of Verania."

"Smashing?" the half-giant asked.

"No, Tiggy," the unicorn said. "No smashing. We don't smash little twinks. We let them grow up so they can provide a valuable service by having sex with mens."

"Tiggy," the boy said.

They both looked over

"I like your name," the boy said. "And I haven't decided if I want to have sex with men or women yet. I'm only fourteen. I still have time to decide."

"Honey bear," the unicorn said. "You are the gayest thing I've seen since I last saw my own reflection."

"Oh," the boy said. "That's… eye-opening."

"I like your face, tiny human," Tiggy said as he took a step toward the boy.

The boy looked up at him in awe. "So tall," he whispered.

"Tiggy," the unicorn said in warning.

"His face," Tiggy insisted as he took another step and another. The boy felt the ground shake beneath.

"It's not a bad face," the unicorn said. Then he narrowed his eyes. "Who sent you here? Why are you by yourself? What do you want?"

"I'm on a quest," the boy said proudly, puffing out his chest again. "I must find something unexpected and bring it back to my mentor."

"Uh-huh," the unicorn said. "Fascinating. Super fun. Are you here to capture us and take us back to Koklanaris?"

The boy scrunched up his face. "Kokla what?"

"His face," Tiggy said again. His eyes were red rimmed, but the tears had stopped falling. He stood above the boy and leaned down until they were eye level.

"Whoa," the boy said. "Your eyes are huge, dude. Like as big as my hand."

"Dude," Tiggy rumbled. "Huge dude."

The boy smiled widely. "Dude."

And then he squawked loudly as the giant picked him up and held him against his chest before turning back to the unicorn.

"I keep him," Tiggy said. "He's mine."

"You can't keep him," the unicorn said. "He's a *human*. Do you know how much upkeep they require? They eat and poop *all the time*."

"Not all the time," the boy said. "I feel I eat and poop the regular amount of time. Maybe even a little less."

"He's mine," Tiggy said again. "I call him Steve."

"Uhhh," the boy said.

"Steve," the unicorn said flatly. "That's… okay. He looks like a Steve. I guess."

"I'm not a Steve," the boy said. "I'm a Sam."

"Steve," Tiggy said. "You're Steve. My Steve. I love you, tiny Steve."

Sam twisted in the half-giant's arms until he could get level with his face. He reached out and squished Tiggy's cheeks in his hand, making the half-giant pucker his lips. "Saaaaaam," the boy said slowly. "Saaaaaaam."

"Steeeeeeve," Tiggy said.

"Oh my gods," the unicorn muttered.

"You can keep me if you call me Sam," the boy said.

Tiggy pouted.

"Aww," Sam said. "That *face*."

"Sam," Tiggy said and Sam grinned. Tiggy sat down and held the boy in his lap. "I keep Sam," he told the unicorn.

The unicorn leaned forward and snuffled along Sam's face and neck and the boy laughed and laughed. The unicorn finished and stepped back. "You smell like magic," he said finally.

"I'm a wizard."

The unicorn waited.

"Okay. Not *quite* a wizard. An apprentice."

"To who?"

"Morgan of Shadows," Sam said proudly.

The unicorn looked suitably impressed. "You're an apprentice to the King's Wizard?"

"Yep. What's your name? How old are you? Do you like cheese? I once ate a whole block of cheese by myself and threw up for six hours."

The unicorn stared at him. Then, "Gary."

"Your name is Gary," Sam said.

"Yes."

"Ah. That's… not very unicorn-like."

Gary scowled. "And what is unicorn-like?"

Sam shrugged. "I don't know. Like Princess Moon Cloud or Ethereal Tear or Star Shine."

"You think a normal unicorn name is Princess Moon Cloud or Ethereal Tear or Star Shine."

"Yes."

Gary looked up at Tiggy. "Yes. We can keep him."

Tiggy held him tighter.

They stayed in the clearing and Gary and Tiggy told him how they'd escaped from a traveling carnival where they'd both been held prisoner by a man named Koklanaris. He'd kept them in cages for months, charging humans to come in and gawk at them, calling them unnatural wonders of the mysterious world. One night, not long before they'd met Sam in the clearing, Koklanaris had gotten drunk and hadn't properly redone the wards and dark charms that kept them in the cages. They'd escaped and run as far as they could until their legs grew tired and they could run no more.

Sam heard this story and felt a heavy weight on his heart. He reached out and touched Gary's face, running his hands gently along his snout. "Did he take your horn?" he asked quietly.

Gary shuddered and shook his head. "That happened. Before."

"You're very pretty," the boy said. "With or without it, you're very pretty."

And the unicorn said, "Thank you, little twink," pressing his face against the boy's.

They stayed the night in the clearing and the boy shared his food. They slept curled around each other until there came an angry snarl from the woods.

They woke instantly and the unicorn and the half-giant began to tremble.

Men stood in the clearing. Four of them, holding ropes and chains. There was one who seemed to lead the others. He stood in front of them, eyes shrewd and calculating. He was tall and imposing, looking as if he'd been carved cruelly from a mountain. His head was shaved and as Sam watched, he unfurled a whip in his hand.

"Those are my property, boy," the man said. His voice was like gravel and it grated on the boy's ears.

The boy shook his head. "They're no one's property. You can't own what belongs to the world."

Koklanaris (for there was no doubt in the boy's mind who he was) said, "Is that so? And who are you to stand in my way?"

"Sam," the boy said. "And these are my friends."

"Monsters don't have friends," Koklanaris said. "They exist to make me money and nothing more. Step aside and let the adults handle this."

"I am the apprentice to the King's Wizard," Sam said, standing tall. "You answer to the Crown, and I am an extension of that Crown."

The men laughed. Koklanaris said, "Boy, I don't give two shits who you are. Step aside before I kill you." He cracked the whip, and Tiggy whined quietly in fear.

Sam had had enough.

There was an anger in him, then. That the hearts of men could be so dark that they could not see the beauty of the creatures before them. This Sam was not the same Sam who turned the boys to stone in that alley years before. This Sam was practiced. This Sam was controlled. This Sam had friends, finally had friends that he would do anything to protect.

This Sam said, "Leave. I'll give you one chance."

Koklanaris raised his whip, and Sam raised his hands. Words came to him, words he'd never used before like *gre* and *san* and his fingers moved and twitched as the whip came down. Before the leather could crack against his skin, the green of the forest filled Sam's eyes and instead of pain, Sam felt the flutter of wings.

He opened his eyes and saw the whip had turned into dozens of butterflies, and they fluttered in the moonlight, swirling around Sam and Koklanaris. Tiggy and Gary gasped behind him and the men behind Koklanaris took a step back.

Koklanaris grew angry. He raised his hand back to slap the boy, but the boy said, "I could kill you," and Koklanaris hesitated.

"I really could," the boy said pleasantly. "I could kill you with the smallest of thoughts."

Koklanaris slapped him. The boy's head rocked back.

Tiggy roared. Gary growled.

And Sam (who was not the boy in the alley anymore) said, "You shouldn't have done that," while raising his hands again.

The men in the clearing ran.

Koklanaris said, "You don't scare me."

"I do," Sam said. "You're sweating."

"I smash," Tiggy said in a low voice. "I smash so good."

And the carnival man's eyes widened in fear and he too left the clearing. He looked back only once but then he was gone.

They waited until the fleeing men could no longer be heard before they each let out the breaths they'd been holding.

"You okay?" Sam asked his friends.

And Tiggy picked him up again and held him close. He said, "Tiny Sam. Tiny Sam. Tiny Sam."

They left when morning came.

As they reached the gates to the City of Lockes, people began to stare. They whispered about the boy from the slums who came back to the city from a wizard's quest with a half-giant and a hornless unicorn.

Morgan waited for him at the castle gates with his mother and father. The King was there too, and he had a small smile on his face as he watched them approach. The Prince was not there, but Sam didn't think too much on that.

Morgan said, "And what have you brought me?"

"Something unexpected," Sam said proudly.

"You return from the wilds with a half-giant and a unicorn," Morgan said. "That is *very* unexpected."

But the boy shook his head. "That's not the unexpected part."

Morgan, in his infinite wisdom, said, "Oh?"

"I went into the wilds alone, and I returned with friends," Sam said. "I've never had a friend on my own before. And now I have two. Unexpectedly."

And the great wizard looked away and took a stuttering breath. When he looked back at the boy, his eyes were bright and he said, "I think the most unexpected thing of all is you, little one. Because no one could ever hope to fathom the wilds of your heart. You were sent out on a quest and returned with more than I could have ever believed. I will give you your name now. Because you've earned it."

And the boy smiled so wide that it felt like his face would split. His parents cried, though his father would never admit to it. Even the King wiped away a tear, and Sam would make fun of him for years after because of it.

But he looked up at his mentor and said, "Yes, please. And thank you."

Morgan of Shadows smiled and said that until the day of the Trials when he would become a full-fledged wizard, Sam Haversford, the strange and somewhat lonely boy from the slums, would be known as Sam of Wilds.

Gary said, "This has been the weirdest twenty-four hours ever."

THE FIRE was almost out by the time I'd finished. My voice fell away and I looked over at my friends, still snoring and curled against each other.

"You love them," Ryan said, the first time he'd spoken since I started the story.

"Very much," I agreed. "I wouldn't be who I am without them. We might fight with each other and piss each other off, but I would die for them. And they would die for me."

"I don't want you to die at all," Ryan said quietly.

I looked over at him. He was staring up at the stars. "No one is dying," I said.

"Sam."

"What?"

"I...."

I waited.

"I knew you," he said in a rush. "From before."

I sat up quickly. "You did? How?"

He pushed himself up too, chewing on the inside of his cheek like he was *nervous* about something. He shook his head, steeling himself for *something*, and then did the most ridiculous thing. He covered his chest with his hands and said, "Please don't make my nipples explode!"

I said, "What?"

He blushed and dropped his hands. He looked away again, then back at me, eyes searching for something. "You ever been turned to stone, Sam? It's an interesting experience to say the least."

"No. Fucking. *Way*," I breathed. "*Nox? You're* Nox?"

He shrugged. "In the flesh. Go by Ryan now, in case you didn't notice."

"But... but... you were such a *dick*," I said, my voice going high. "What in the name of fuck?"

"I *was* a dick," he corrected me. "Things change."

"Um. No. Sometimes, you're still a dick."

He scowled at me. "Thanks."

"How the hell did I not know this?" I asked. I was pretty sure my world felt completely altered.

"I grew up," he said. "Worked out. Gained muscle. Joined the King's Army. Got recruited into the knights. Came to the castle after that."

"And you didn't think to tell me?" I asked. "At any point?"

He looked a little hurt. "Would you have even given me a chance if you'd known?"

"A chance for *what*?"

And *that* seemed to fluster him. "For... just... oh my gods. Sam. I don't... friendship, okay? Like... or whatever."

"Or whatever," I echoed. "So, instead of telling me that you were the guy that stole Mrs. Kirkpatrick's cloth, you decided to be dashing and immaculate."

"Maybe?" he said with a wince.

I just stared at him, too many things running through my head, so many things I wanted to say to him. So, of course, I said the thing that mattered the least. "Why did you steal her cloth?"

He rolled his eyes. "I was a teenage asshole from the slums. I stole everything."

And it hit me. Why my magic had manifested then. Why I'd been able to turn them to stone when I did. Why I'd done magic so complex without ever having done it before. Ryan had been there from the very first. He was my cornerstone, even then. He was the reason I was able to do what I did.

"Holy fucking shit," I whispered.

"What?" he asked.

"I... don't...." I shook my head. "I'm just... surprised. Of all the things you could have said, that's probably the thing I expected the least."

"Yeah, I figured as much. I don't think I've ever seen your eyebrows go that high before."

"It was very shocking," I assured him. "The most shocking of all. Why now?"

"Why tell you now?"

I nodded.

He looked down at his hands. "I don't know. You were telling me about Tiggy and Gary and it was personal and sweet, and I just couldn't take the thought anymore of you not knowing who I was. You said you didn't have friends before and there were times when we were kids that I wanted you to be my friend, but I didn't know how to ask."

"So you were a jerk instead," I said. "Makes sense."

"Teenagers usually do," he said. And then he blurted, "I did it because of you." He winced. "Ah shit."

"Did what?"

He groaned. "Gods, forget I said that, okay?"

"Yeah, because when have I ever done that? Remember who you're talking to here."

"Sam."

"*Nox.*"

"I am never going to hear the end of this, am I?"

"Not ever," I agreed. "You have decades of this to look forward to. It probably would've been in your best interest to not have said anything at all. I will lord this over you until my dying breath, and at no point will I feel badly at doing so."

For some reason, he didn't look too upset at the prospect. In fact, his mouth curved gently upward. "Everyone talked about you. Even before the alleyway happened. 'Little Sam,' they said. 'Little Sam who is going to do great things.' They talked about you like you were this sight to behold, and when I saw you for the first time, I thought there'd been a mistake. I thought that this kid, this tiny little kid whose mouth never closed, couldn't possibly be who they meant."

He reached and stoked the fire with a stick I'd used before, the tip blackened and charred. The flame flared briefly, little sparks rising with the smoke. "But then, one day, you knocked me down and took a bag of cloth from my hand. Do you remember what you said to me?"

I shook my head. "I remember you glaring and me thinking I was going to die a painful death. That's about it."

He chuckled. "You looked down at me and said, 'Don't be a jerk, dude. You don't have the right to take away something that makes other people happy.' And then you grinned at me and started running."

I winced. "Yeah, that sounds like something I would have said. It's easier to be unabashedly sanctimonious when you're eleven years old. The cynicism hadn't quite set in."

Ryan glanced over at me then back at the fire. "I don't know. You're still smug a lot of the time."

"Ass. I am the definition of humble. But enough about me. Surely you started chasing after me because you wanted to tell me just how right I was and apologize for everything you'd ever done. Be absolved of your sins to lead a righteous life."

"No," Ryan said. "I wanted to kick the shit out of you."

I couldn't stop the bark of laughter that came out at that. "That's... I don't know what that is."

He shrugged. "The truth. You made me mad."

"I tend to do that."

"You turned that corner down the alley and I *knew* you were caught."

"I saw the wall and thought I was fucked."

"That's because you were," he said. "And yet you still turned and faced us. You looked me in the eyes and then the next thing I knew, the alley was filled with people and your mom and dad and Morgan were threatening me, and I was *positive* that Morgan was going to make my nipples explode."

"Still one of my better rumors." I grinned up at him. "People *still* think he can do that. I would say I'm sorry for turning you to stone, but honestly, I'm really not."

He smiled again. I thought I saw a flash of teeth. "Didn't think you would be."

"In fact, I should probably thank you."

"For?"

"If you hadn't chased me that day, I'd have never turned you to stone and Morgan wouldn't have found me. If you think about it, you're sort of responsible for everything that happened afterward."

"That's... one way of looking at it."

I beamed at him. "Thanks for being a teenage dick bag, Ryan."

"Exactly what I was aiming for," he said, dry as dust.

"Then you succeeded admirably." I laid my head back down on my pack and looked back up at the stars. "What happened then?"

He was quiet for a moment. Then, "You left."

"To the castle."

"Yeah. It was all anyone could talk about. 'Little Sam and his magic.' 'Little Sam would be a wizard.' 'Little Sam ascended from the slums into Castle Locke.'" It was said without a hint of bitterness. In fact, if I had to put a name to the tone in his voice, I would have thought it was something like pride. "Before then. You'd never done anything like that?"

"No," I said. "Not once. Morgan thought it might have been a combination of being close to puberty and a survival instinct. It manifested itself then because I needed it to. You know. Because you were an asshole."

"You're welcome," he said.

I narrowed my eyes. "Why are you dashing and immaculate now?" I demanded. "People like Nox don't grow up to be people like you. You should be overweight and balding and have no teeth and awful body odor to go with your surly attitude. But no! You're all muscular and gorgeous and sassy and awesome and holy fucking shit I am not talking right now." Because what the fuck was I thinking? Why could I never keep my mouth shut?

And his smile was *blinding*.

"Oh crap. That's not what I meant to say. At all. Oh, look over there. There's a tree that looks like a dragon. That's surely a sign."

"Right. A sign that you needed a distraction and have failed miserably at finding one."

"Says you. It was a perfect distraction. We're talking about it, aren't we?"

"Uh-huh. Muscular *and* gorgeous, you say?"

"From a purely clinical standpoint," I assured him. "Absolutely nothing more."

"Absolutely nothing more."

I *despised* when he repeated my own words back to me and made them sound absolutely ridiculous. "At least some things don't change. You were a bastard then and you're a bastard now. Sometimes."

"Sometimes," he said, the grin never wavering. "Is that right?"

I scowled at him. "I take it back. All of the time."

"You really don't know, do you?"

"Know what?"

"The effect you have on people."

That... was odd. I had never really thought about it, to be honest. I didn't go through life wanting to affect other people. I wanted to learn magic and become a wizard. I wanted Morgan to be proud of me and confident in my abilities. I wanted my mom to smile every day and my dad to be able to put his feet up at the end of the day and not worry about what tomorrow would bring. I wanted Gary and Tiggy to never again know the sting of a whip or the confines of a cage. I wanted Ryan. I wanted Ryan to be happy and alive and to smile all the time. I wanted more, but since that couldn't happen, I would take what I could get.

"The King said you didn't smile," I blurted out.

Ryan looked startled. "What?"

"At your ceremony. He said he never sees you smile anymore. And I thought that was weird because I see you smile all the time."

"Do you?"

"Well, yeah. Like right now."

"You just... you have no...."

I cocked my head at him. "What?"

He sighed. "After you were taken to the castle, people began to realize the lives they were given in the slums were not always the lives they had to take. They thought if one of their own could grow to be someone so important, that they could change the shape of their destinies too. You inspired them, Sam."

"I didn't know that," I said honestly. "Not really. I go back. To the slums. Every chance I get. It's not as much as I used to, but I still try."

"I know. And that's what makes it all the more important. Your actions. And that's why I taught myself to read. It's why I taught myself to write. It's why I changed my name. It's why I joined up with the King's Army. It's why I kept my head down and worked until my back ached and my fingers bled. It's why I was recruited into the knights. It's why I was promoted to Knight Commander."

I shook my head. "No. That was you. That was only you. I didn't—"

"But it was because of you that I did it." He looked down at his hands. "Not directly, but it might as well have been. I thought that if you could change your future, to make it into something more, then maybe I could too. That I could do enough to take my mom out of the slums and give her the life she deserved after putting up with a son like me." He took a breath and let it out slowly. "I made it, Sam. Mostly. I changed my future. But she died before I could change hers. I made a promise to her. Before. That I would do everything in my power to become greater than what I was born into, be more than what my station allowed. And I... I needed... *need* to keep that promise to her."

I felt cold. "I'm sorry," I said, inadequate as it was. "I didn't know." And there were questions that I wanted (*needed*) to ask: how, when, where, why. But they all stuck in my throat and I said nothing more. I'd never known the loss of a parent. I couldn't even begin to understand.

"Most don't," he murmured. "They don't know me as Nox. They only know Ryan Foxheart."

I reached over and took his hand in mine, letting it rest in his lap. Our fingers intertwined, and he stared down at them. I didn't like it when he hurt, even if my act of comfort hurt me more. "I know you," I said quietly. "I know how you were. And how you are now." I hesitated, but pushed through it. "Do the others know? About where you came from?" Meaning did Justin know. And I thought I knew the answer, but I still needed to hear it from him, no matter how crushing it would be.

He shook his head.

I sighed and withdrew my hand. I was disappointed, though I didn't know if it was my place to be. It was none of my business what he told people about himself. I needed to remember that. Just because I was proud of where I'd come from didn't mean that others would feel the same. The slums were awful, sure, but they'd been my home for the first half of my life, and I knew happiness there. I didn't see the need to hide where I'd come from because others might look down upon it. Granted, most already knew I was from the slums. But, if anything, that just made the hurt a bit worse, that Ryan could see how most didn't give a shit about me, yet he still chose to hide it about himself. And maybe, for the briefest of moments, I entertained a dark thought: Just how easy would it be to let it slip to Justin that his fiancé was born in the slums? Would Justin still be as keen to marry Ryan? It would be so easy. Then Ryan would be free and I could—

No.

No. That's not who I was. That's not who I am. I could never do that to him, no matter how I felt about him. It wasn't my secret to tell.

"It's not like that," he said, and he almost sounded like he was pleading. "I'm not ashamed about being from the slums. It's just... I can't...."

"I didn't say you were," I said, trying to put him out of his misery. "You have to do what you have to do, you know? You don't need to justify yourself. Especially to me. I'm proud of how far you've come. And flattered that you think that I helped in whatever way I did, though I don't think I deserve that. I promise your secret is safe with me."

"It's not meant to be a secret," he said. "You have to believe me about that."

"I do," I said, even though it felt like a lie.

"Can we just—?"

"It's late," I said, because I could see this brewing into something more damning. "I should get some sleep. You good for the first watch still?"

He nodded. He opened his mouth to say something else, but closed it a moment later. Maybe he understood that it was time we stopped before we couldn't stop anymore.

"Give me a couple of hours and I'll take over," I told him.

He looked away.

I turned over on my side away from him and tried to take calm, even breaths. To shut my mind down so I could at least sleep for a little while.

Of course it wasn't that easy. It never had been and all I could think of now was *RyanRyanRyan* and *NoxNoxNox*. About how I could be so stupid to think I could get to know him better without there being consequences. Without allowing him to get even further under my skin. That was proving to be difficult.

After what felt like ages, he said, "Sam?"

I thought about ignoring him. Feigning sleep. Instead, I said, "Yeah." My voice was rough.

"What happened to him?"

"Who?"

"Koklanaris."

I smiled, though he couldn't see it. Most never thought to ask that question, so of course he did. "The day after I brought Tiggy and Gary to the castle, he was arrested and charged with abuse and cruelty to magical creatures. They're protected, you know. As long as they haven't hurt anyone else, they're protected by law. His entire carnival was dismantled, and he's in a jail in the desert. He'll be there for a very long time."

"Because of you," he said.

"I couldn't let him get away with what he did. It wasn't fair, and I wouldn't allow that to happen to anyone else." I thought to stop there, but truth for a truth, right? That's how the game is played. "I almost killed him in that clearing. It was very close. I sent him to jail so I would never have to. If he's lucky, that's where he'll stay. Because if I ever see him again, he won't be walking away."

He said, "*Sam*" like I had achieved something wonderful. Like I had revealed to him a great secret that only he and I would ever know.

And I suppose I did.

So I slept and dreamed of running through the streets of the slums, my heart beating rapidly, my lungs burning. And I laughed because even though I was chased into a blind alley, my cornerstone was there and he'd never let anything hurt me. Because only *he* could do that, and there, in a world that did not exist, he never would.

RYAN WOKE me a couple of hours before dawn.

He crawled under his blanket as I sat up.

His head was near my knee. Just inches away, really.

He looked up at me. I looked down at him.

Eventually, he closed his eyes.

I wondered at this complex man, this knight from the slums who wanted nothing more than to become something more. I thought it possible that he looked up at the stars and had wished for the same things I did. How funny that our paths crossed as they had. Then and now. And how every time was not the right time, no matter how much I could wish it to be so.

And I told myself we needed to find Justin soon, because I couldn't have him like this. I couldn't have him within reach. Not when I would just have to let him go once we got the Prince back. He was in love. And I was not the type of man to ever try and come between something like that. We would get Justin back and they would go back to Castle Lockes and I would go north. There would be a wedding, and I'd send my condolences at missing the ceremony and my congratulations at such a joyous union. I would learn what I needed to learn under Randall. I would come back to the City of Lockes under control and everything would be fine. Everything would be wonderful. Ryan would be happy, and I would be happy for him. This silly crush I'd fostered would be nothing more than a distant memory, and one day I'd find another person meant to be my cornerstone, and any time I passed Ryan in the halls or stood near him in the throne room, I'd smile and he'd smile back. We'd think fleetingly on this little adventure we'd had back in the early days.

And then we'd move on.

Because that is the only thing we *could* do.

Still.

I had to stop myself from running my fingers through his hair.

I knew now why Morgan had said he feared for my heart.

I did too.

CHAPTER 15
Mama's

THE CITY of Lockes was the capital of Verania. The King resided in Castle Lockes. For the most part, it was beautiful. The ports were far enough away that the air was clear and fresh. The roads, especially around the castle, were well maintained and landscaped. It was often said the only blight upon the City of Lockes was the slums, that area that stretched along the eastern edge of the city. But for the most part, the City of Lockes was bright and vibrant, a beacon of surety and the Veranian Dream.

Meridian City was the exact opposite.

It was dirt and grime, sex and debauchery. Not one single person in Meridian City could cast a stone, because all were bathed in sin. These were the thieves and the murderers. These were the liars and the cheats. These were the ones who slunk in the dark, just as likely to steal your wallet as to stab you in the kidneys. If you needed to hide from the law, you went to Meridian City. If you wanted to drink and get high and sleep with strangers (usually all in the same place), you went to Meridian City.

The air stank of smoke. There was garbage in the streets. People wandered drunkenly, laughing and screaming. Men fucked whores in alleyways. Women fucked whores in doorways. Madams and pimps prowled the corners, making sure their girls and boys presented themselves as they walked the streets.

It was everything the City of Lockes was not.

And I loved it.

It was rage and base desires. It was anger and sadness and despair and desperation, but it was *honest*. It beat with a corrupted, diseased heart, but it wore it on its sleeve and made no excuses for what it was. Meridian City was *wrong* and it *knew* it.

And there was a time I could have gotten away with entering the city without having to hide my face. But the older I'd gotten, the more my name had been spread and the more recognizable I'd gotten. I didn't mind, not really, but with the events of the last few weeks, and especially with Ryan at my side, it was going to make it difficult to go see who we needed to see before we went to Old Clearing. I needed information and there was only one person in Meridian City I could get it from.

"You two need to stay out of the city," I told Gary and Tiggy the afternoon we arrived to the outskirts of the city. I could hear groups of travelers on the Old Road through the trees of the Dark Woods. "It'll be too difficult for all of us to get in without getting recognized. I don't think it's going to take that long."

"But I want to see Mama," Tiggy rumbled.

"I know," I said. "But this isn't that kind of visit. We can't stay. And you two aren't exactly inconspicuous."

"I resent that remark," Gary said. "I am as inconspicuous as they come."

"Me too," Tiggy said.

"Says the hornless gay unicorn and half-giant. You draw too much attention. Because you're so amazing."

They both preened. Like I knew they would.

"Who's Mama?" Ryan asked.

"You didn't tell him?" Gary demanded. "He's going to meet Mama for the first time and I won't get to be there to *watch*? I don't even need to tell you how unfair that is!"

I rolled my eyes. "And yet you're telling anyway."

"This is going to be something I'm not going to like, isn't it," Ryan said. "I feel like that has happened a lot on this trip already."

"Adventure," I corrected him. "Not a trip. Adventure. Trips imply vacation. Adventure implies awesomeness. And no, I haven't told him about Mama. It hasn't exactly come up yet."

"But," Gary whined, "it's going to be hysterical and disturbing and wonderful and you're going to make me miss it. What have I ever done to you? Name one thing. Wait. Don't answer that. I just thought of forty things."

"At least," I said.

"So are you going to tell me who Mama is?" Ryan asked as I handed him a hooded robe from the pack Gary carried. I pulled out a similar one, muted and gray, and tied it over my shoulders, pulling the hood up and over my face.

"She runs the Tilted Cross among other things," Gary said with barely contained glee. "The only gay brothel and tavern in Meridian City. And she is Sam's fairy drag mother."

MERIDIAN CITY was run by a council with an elected figurehead to make the pretty speeches and faulty promises. They touted reform, plans to clean up the streets, to make the city more hospitable, less of a sinkhole.

The problem was, if you lived in or visited Meridian City on a regular basis, chances were you didn't give two shits about making the world a better place.

So the old people were voted out and the new people were voted in, all saying the same things over and over again. It was a circle, and one that had sustained itself for decades.

But everyone knew the real truth.

If you needed weapons, you went to Feng, a barrel of a man with half his teeth.

If you needed drugs, you went to Letnia, a beautiful older woman with an eye patch and a taste for cigars.

If you wanted anything else, you went to Mama.

And I needed information.

I pulled my hood tighter around my face as we pushed through the crowds. I thought I saw an orgy going on through an open doorway. A woman on a corner told me she was born with six fingers and that made hand jobs that much more intense. A man tried to sell me rotted fish. A girl not that much younger than me told me with glazed eyes that she'd dreamed of me the night before. A boy who had to be just into his teens asked if I wanted a blow job. "I'm cheap," he said with a bit of pride.

I pulled Ryan on.

His eyes were wide, darting all around. His face was flushed and he looked horrified and aroused all at the same time. It was a good look on him.

"You never been here before?" I asked, seeing the sign for the Tilted Cross in the distance. "Figured you army boys spent your leave here."

He shook his head. "Most did. I never saw the point. I don't need anything that's offered here."

I laughed darkly. "Now that certainly can't be true. You can get *anything* here."

"That so, Sam? Is that what you do?" His voice was harsh, almost as if he were judging me.

I flashed him a smile that didn't quite reach my eyes. "You need to listen to me. Okay? When we get there, you let me do the talking. You don't speak to Mama until she speaks to you. You don't ask her questions. You don't threaten her or try to intimidate her. You don't even look at her funny. She can and will destroy you and I won't be able to do anything to stop her."

"You sound scared of her," he said.

I shook my head. "Oh no. I'm not scared of her. Never have been. I've never given her reason to make me fear her. But that doesn't mean I don't respect her. She doesn't peddle children. She doesn't allow the harder drugs at her businesses. And she takes care of her boys and girls. They are there because they want to be, not because she forces them. They aren't walking the streets. They're courtesans and they are free to come and go as they please. As long as they follow her rules, she keeps them safe."

"A whore is still a whore no matter how you dress him up," Ryan said.

"Let's keep that opinion to ourselves," I said. "You'll thank me later."

"You should have let me bring my sword. I can't protect you if—"

"No weapons," I said. "I was clear on that. And I don't need you to protect me. I have my magic, and if something happens, then I'll be the one protecting you."

To that, he had no retort.

As I pulled him through the crowd, I felt the heat of his skin under my fingers.

This place drove me nuts.

It made my skin itch.

We reached the main doors to the Tilted Cross. A large man stood there that I'd never seen before. I hadn't been here in months, so I wasn't surprised that there was new staff. He was huge, bigger than Ryan even, and he held his arms across his chest in such a way that told anyone and everyone to fuck off.

So I grinned at him. "I have business here."

He glared down at me. "That so? You looking to get fucked?"

"Probably not today," I said, and Ryan made a choking noise behind me. "I need to see Mama."

"Is that so?"

"Yes, so can you let me in?"

1

63

"Bounce, baby boy. Unless you're a paying customer, get the fuck outta my sight. Mama don't have time for you."

I chuckled. "I'm not leaving. You're going to let me in."

"Am I? Or am I going to break your face?"

"You must be new here," I said, and that *pissed* him off.

"Sam," Ryan hissed. "Don't make the extremely large man angry." He grabbed at and bunched up my robe, and I knew he was getting ready to pull me back and insert himself between the two of us. It was almost sweet.

"A little too late for that," the doorman said, pushing himself off the wall. He rocked his neck side to side, cracking the joints. His hands were the size of my face. They would probably hurt. Fists that big usually do.

I reached into the pocket of my trousers and pulled out a small, flat disc. It was carved from black stone and inlaid with lines of gold. It was heavy and there was no mistaking what it was. I held my palm open so the doorman could see it. He stuttered to a stop and his eyes went wide. He looked flustered and I almost felt like a bit of an ass for antagonizing him as I had.

Almost.

"Forgive me," he said. "You go right in, sir. She's in her office. Moishe will show you up."

"Thank you," I said. "You do a good job. I was actually a little bit intimidated."

He opened the door and smiled shyly at me.

I'll admit, I melted a little. "Oh my gods, you're *adorable* and—"

Ryan pulled me in through the door, his grip tight on my arm. The door closed behind us, the long windowless hallway dark in front of us. Mama said it was for ambience. I chose to believe her.

"What the hell was that?" Ryan demanded.

I showed him the disc. "Mama's medallion. Very rare. I think only three or four people have one. It means I can come and go whenever I please."

"You can come and go to a whorehouse whenever you please," he said flatly.

I waggled my eyebrows at him. "Well, maybe not *that* kind of coming and going."

He groaned. "I walked right into that one."

"With no hesitation," I agreed. "But no. I'm not one to partake in the services offered. Mama and I have an understanding."

"And what would that be?"

I shrugged. "She met me when I was seventeen. She wanted me to come work for her when I was eighteen. I told her I wanted to wait to have sex until I was with someone I loved. She told me that was foolish. I told her she was an old jaded cow for thinking so. Then we laughed and got drunk and she made me meatloaf and I brought her wigs and now I have her medallion."

He stared at me.

"What? It's the truth!"

"I know," he said. "I no longer question the things that happen to you. It makes everything easier."

I grinned at him. "That's the best way to go through life. Believing everything I say and not questioning it at all. If Gary tells you otherwise, it's because he's jealous and a liar, so ignore him."

"So you're a virgin, then?"

"Uh. What?"

"You said you're not having sex until you're in love. You're a virgin."

"Who says I haven't been in love?" My voice was level, almost cool, but the back of my neck felt sweaty and I really didn't want to be having this conversation with him.

He frowned. "Have you?"

"Let's pretend this conversation isn't happening," I said quickly. "That would be awesome."

His frown deepened.

I went to put the medallion back in my pocket only to see he was still holding on to my arm and didn't seem inclined to let it go. I rolled my eyes at him and led us from the hallway into the Tilted Cross.

The tavern itself had another entrance on the west end of the building, and the thunder of voices and music bled through closed doors to our left, even though it was the middle of the day in the middle of the week.

Directly in front of us was a grand staircase with a gaudy chandelier hanging over it, the crystals hanging from it large and uncut. The carpet was red and the staircase a deep, darkened hardwood from the middle of the Dark Woods. Couches lined the walls. There were doors on either side of the branching hallways. Some were closed. Others were empty, revealing rooms with made-up beds and vanities. These rooms were the vanilla rooms, I knew. You had to go down to the basement if you wanted flogs and plugs. Mama made sure I stayed out of the basement, given my propensity for wanting to see and feel everything. She'd told me she didn't want me to be corrupted so quickly. I told her I was just fine with corruption. Then she showed me a thin wooden device that was meant to be inserted into a penis and I advised her that I was in complete agreement to avoid any and all corruption for as long as humanly possible. She had just laughed and laughed and laughed.

And all the boys! And the men! They prowled around, some in suits, some in absolutely nothing at all. They were young and old, skinny and fat, and cut and everything in between because Mama knew that tastes were varied. Some wanted a hairy daddy. Others wanted a smooth boy. Still others wanted both at the same time. "I give people happiness," she'd told me. "Even if it's just for an hour. Because there is happiness in release."

And they watched us with interested eyes. Calculating. Planning. Wondering who we'd come here for. Who we'd pick. If we were a couple that needed a third or if we'd go into separate rooms.

Moishe stood at the front desk. He was a tall, wispy man with almost colorless skin. He was achingly beautiful, his yellow hair falling down around his shoulders. I was convinced that he wasn't completely human, that he had to have some elf in there somewhere, but neither he nor Mama would ever say.

"Sam," he said, his voice light and musical. I should have known the hood wouldn't fool him. "How wonderful it is to see you again. Have you returned to take me up on my offer?"

Yeah, Moishe wanted to fuck me. He'd made that much clear repeatedly. He wouldn't even charge me, though he really didn't do that anymore. Only on special occasions for the most esteemed clients. But for me, he just wanted to taste my skin.

I pulled back my hood and Ryan did the same. I saw eyes go wide around us and the whispers started. They knew who we were. Some might not have known why we were here, but that didn't matter. Moishe's eyes flickered over to Ryan with faint disinterest before turning back to me. They were the brightest green I'd ever seen on a person. Almost shockingly so.

"Moishe," I said in greeting. "You're looking lovely as always."

He cocked his head at me, lips in a thin line, bloodless and almost clear. "Flattery gets you everywhere with me, Sam of Wilds. You know that. I have a room set aside. Should I have it opened up? I suppose I could entertain the idea of a third if you insist." He glanced back at Ryan again, then back to me. "But I'd really rather it be you alone. Did you know that magic has a taste? Like lightning. Like burning. I'm sure I could find that tang on your skin."

Ryan's grip on my arm tightened exponentially. I tried to tug it loose, but his fingers bit into my skin. Moishe, of course, missed none of it. "Does the Knight Commander need a boy?" he asked. "I understand how... frustrating it must be, being betrothed to a prince. Personal experience, you could say." His eyes went back to me. "Never able to just... *take* what it is you want."

"Nobody is taking anything," Ryan growled, and if *that* didn't make my heart stutter, I don't know what did. Too bad it was misplaced. I was no more in danger here than I would be back home in the castle. Moishe would never hurt me. And even if he wanted to, Mama wouldn't allow it. Ryan just didn't know how these things worked.

I said, "You know how it is for me, Moishe."

His lip curled. "Yes. *Love*. What a petty emotion."

"But lust isn't?"

He showed his teeth. "Lust is in us all. You don't need love to have it."

Old games, this. I had a fleeting thought of introducing him to Dimitri. That was a scary thought. "I need to see Mama."

He was looking back at Ryan, annoyance splayed clearly on his face. "She's busy."

"Moishe."

"Your little Prince was taken by a dragon," he said to Ryan. "Pity. He was quite exquisite. There was a certain taciturnity about him that I couldn't but help admire." Then his voice changed, just the slightest bit, from cold to frost. "You should let go of Sam now. Before there's a problem."

"*Moishe.*"

They both ignored me.

"You already have a problem," Ryan said hotly. "You're not gonna touch him."

Moishe smiled. "Maybe not today. But soon. I wasn't kidding when I said magic had a taste. I want his storm on my tongue."

"Oh for fuck's sake," I said.

"Sam, we're leaving," Ryan said, trying to pull me back toward the door.

"Knock it off," I snapped at him, jerking my arm away. "This isn't anything I'm not used to. If something is pissing you off, then go wait outside." He flinched as I turned back to Moishe. "And *you*. Take us up to Mama or I'll go myself. I don't have time for your shit today, Moishe. Either move or get the fuck out of my way."

He watched me with those cool eyes. His lips twitched once, like he thought I was precious, and he nodded. "But of course, Sam. I'm sure Mama is no longer busy now. You're different than you were before. Harder." His gaze crawled down my body, then back up. "In so many, many different ways."

And then he turned toward the staircase and walked away.

"Fucking Moishe," I muttered, knowing he could hear me. I looked back at Ryan. "You coming?"

He scowled at me. "I'm not leaving you alone in here."

"For the love of—Look. Just remember what I said about Mama. You can't lash out, Ryan. It's not how things are done here. She will just as soon kill you as look at you."

"I wonder sometimes about the company you keep," he said.

I looked at him and wondered that too. Maybe I was a masochist. That certainly would explain a lot. "I have my reasons. Do we have an understanding?"

He grumbled something under his breath that I couldn't quite understand. I chose to believe it was enthusiastic consent for everything I'd told him. It would have to be good enough. I was in Mama's good graces, but that would only get me so far.

I felt the eyes of the boys and men track us as we walked across the room toward the staircase. The air smelled of flowers and sweat and sex. It was a heady scent, pungent enough to get slightly drunk off of if you breathed it in too much. Mama said it was all the pheromones that the flowers and humans released. I thought it was more than that, that she'd had the drug lord Letnia engineer a concoction that circulated the room via the ceiling fans that spun lazily above, lowering inhibitions, raising the heat. She'd smiled her enigmatic Mama smile when I'd told her as much, calling me a silly boy, planting a sticky kiss on my cheek.

Ryan crowded me closely from behind, and for all my annoyance at his intimations that I couldn't handle myself, that I was a young, foolish boy with no experience to how the world worked, I found his insistence at protecting me from perceived threats oddly endearing. Part of me wanted to snap my teeth at him, to remind him that I'd survived twenty years without him. That I could handle myself. And I thought he knew that. I thought he knew I was more than capable of dealing with any threats against my person, but for some reason, he still felt the need to attempt to defend me from the big, wide world.

It would be comforting, if I allowed it.

But I couldn't. I wasn't supposed to feel safe with him. Not like that.

We followed Moishe up the stairs, all eyes in the room on us as we ascended. I ignored them. Ryan growled at them. Whatever.

We were led down a long hallway, and the sounds of sex and fucking echoed around us behind closed doors. Someone asked if Daddy liked that. Another begged in a broken voice. Still another just groaned. I had learned to disregard the sounds of the brothel, but Ryan's eyes were wide and he reached out and grabbed my arm again, fingers biting into my skin. I thought to pull myself away again but didn't.

A large ornate door stood at the end of the hallway. *MAMA* was burned into the wood, surrounded by carved leaves and trees made to look like dicks. She loved nature and cock, she'd told me once, so why not combine the two? I had had no argument to the contrary over such a thing. I rarely did with Mama.

Moishe knocked twice, waited a beat, then opened the door.

The office was circular, the walls covered in paintings of her favorite courtesans, all in various risqué positions, some more obscene than others. There was a large bookshelf on one side filled with everything from ancient philosophy to hardcore porn. Mama was brilliant and ruthless, but she was also smutty and knew more about the world than almost anyone else I knew. She had spent her younger years traveling across Verania and beyond its borders. She'd told me many stories of the lands to the east, where people spoke in a language that sounded like dogs barking. Once, she'd gotten lost there and somehow ended up in a three-way with two men who had ten-inch dicks while a volcano rumbled threateningly in the background. She'd said they couldn't understand each other at all, but one didn't need to understand when one could allow the body to do the talking.

Sometimes, I think Mama is full of shit.

But I wouldn't put it past her to have been spit-roasted with lava nearby. She's just that type of person.

And here she was, sitting behind her massive desk, regal and proud and intimidating as all fuck. Well, to most people, I guess. Not to me. Mostly.

She wore a blonde wig, cut short and severe around her face. The pale skin of her face was immaculately covered with makeup, the rouge dark on her cheeks, her eyes smoky, lips red and shiny. A tight black corset pushed up her chest, the illusion of breasts so well done that it was impossible to see that they were fake. I never asked her how she did it, how she made everything look so real, because she'd told me that a lady, like a wizard, never revealed her secrets. I never asked her for her real name and she never told me. She would always be Mama until she said otherwise.

And she towered over most men. She called herself the tallest woman in captivity. I'd told her she seemed freer than anyone else I'd ever known. She'd been sad then, for a moment. But like most real emotions from her, it passed in an instant, replaced by a salacious smile, a bawdy innuendo.

She was large, callous, loudmouthed, and brash—and absolutely wonderful.

Moishe stood by the door as I walked past him. Ryan dropped his grip from my arm. My fairy drag mother pressed a long fingernail to her lip, the skin dimpling as her gaze locked onto me.

"Sam," she purred, voice deep and strong. "What a pleasant surprise this is."

"Mama," I said in greeting. I walked around the desk and took her hand in mine, kissing the back of it. "You're looking beautiful as always."

She chuckled. "Don't I? I woke up this morning and thought to myself how wonderful it is that I am able to grace others with my presence."

I kissed her hand again before letting it go. "Humble, that."

"I have no use for humble," she said. "Humble means weakness."

"I'm humble," I told her. "I'm not weak."

"You're not humble," she said. "Your magic won't allow you to be."

Oh how she and I danced. "Or maybe it affords me modesty." I moved back around the desk. Ryan looked between the two of us, eyes narrowed.

"You think so?" she asked. "How positively illuminating. In my experience, most wizards don't even know the meaning of modesty."

"I'm not most wizards."

"Oh, how I have missed you," Mama said, clapping her hands together. "It's been far too long, precious. I don't like it when you're gone from me for too long. Tell me. Are the rumors true?"

I almost didn't want to ask, but Mama expected me to. She would have her say with or without me prompting her. "And what rumors would those be?"

She glanced over at Ryan, the first time she'd acknowledged him since we'd come in the room, and I *knew*. She could play coy, but Mama had never met subtlety. They weren't even passing acquaintances. I didn't think you could be subtle *and* be a drag queen. It just wasn't possible. "A knight, then?" she asked innocently, though her eyes gave her away.

"Knight Commander Ryan Foxheart," I said, trying to keep my voice even. "Betrothed to Prince Justin. The future King Consort."

"Sir," he said. Then he coughed. Choked, maybe. "Er. Ma'am. Lady Mama. Your Majesty."

"Oh my gods," I groaned.

Mama's grin was full of teeth. "Your Majesty? I could get used to that." She held up her hand toward Ryan. He stared at it awkwardly until I kicked him in the shin. He took a step forward and grabbed the proffered hand, kissing it swiftly before backing away, standing so close our arms brushed together.

"Thank you for having me to your whorehouse." He winced. "I mean your home. Where people pay to have sex."

"Is he broken?" Mama asked me, looking coolly amused.

I frowned at Ryan. "I haven't quite figured that out."

"I've never been to a brothel," Ryan said quickly. "Or met a... lady. Of your caliber."

"You mean with a cock?" Mama asked.

Ryan coughed again. Definitely some choking involved. "Yes? Yes. There's that part too. I've heard of you... people."

Oh gods. Mama cocked her head at him. To most, it wouldn't have seemed like anything. But for those that knew her, Mama was coiling to strike. "What do you mean by *you people*?" she asked.

I had to stop the bloodshed before it could start. "He means—"

"Pimps," Ryan said. "Is that what you're called? Pimps? Brothel owner? Whoremaster? Queen of the Fuck Palace?"

"Queen of the Fuck Palace?" I repeated. "Seriously? *Seriously*?" Granted, he didn't say something derogatory against drag queens, which I was thankful for, but I couldn't tell if this was worse. If she was insulted, Mama would most likely cut off his dick and nail it to the wall.

"Moishe," Mama said.

"Yes, Mama."

"Please let it be known that from this day forward, my working title for the business is now Queen of the Fuck Palace."

"Yes, Mama."

"You may leave."

Moishe closed the door behind him, but not before he stared at my crotch with his cold eyes.

"I like him," Mama told me, waving dismissively at Ryan.

"What? *Why*? You don't like anyone!"

"Uh, hi," Ryan said. "Standing right here."

"I like *you*," she said to me.

"Well, yes," I said. "But I like to think I am a special case."

"You *are* a special case," she said sweetly.

"You just insulted me, didn't you?"

"I would never do such a thing," she said, folding her hands in front of her.

"But *Ryan*?" I said. "You hate the knights. And the government. And the King! You called them capitalist scum who harbor resentments against the proletariats even though they rely on them for industry."

"Still standing right here," Ryan said. "And I don't know what proletariats are. But I feel like someone is insulting me. Somehow."

Mama rolled her eyes. "I'm allowed to change my mind about people, Sam."

"You just think he's hot," I accused her, as if this was not a common consensus by everyone currently in the room.

"Yeah," Mama said. "He is. Like fire. I want him to burn me. All over my face."

"Feeling a little objectified now," Ryan said.

I scowled at Mama. "That's not gonna happen. You keep your perfectly beautiful grubby fingers off of him."

"Hmmm," Mama said.

"Hmmm? That's all you got? *Hmmm*?"

"Just realizing something," she said. "Have you had many of those lately, Sam? Realizations?"

"I'm realizing a few things right now," I told her. "And several of them involve you. Spoiler. It doesn't end well."

"And how are you?" Mama asked Ryan.

"Fine," he said, though he didn't sound fine at all.

"Long trip?"

"Not too bad."

"Traveled through the Dark Woods, did you?"

"For the last few days."

"Have you ever had sex for money?"

"Not in a long time," Ryan said. "I don't do that anymore." He blanched. "I didn't mean to say that out loud. How the hell…?"

So I said, "*What*?"

"Never mind," Ryan said, refusing to meet my eyes.

"I like him," Mama said. "And I don't say that about many people."

"You've said it to five people," I reminded her. "Me. Moishe. Tiggy and Gary. And now *Ryan*?"

"I think I'm being insulted," Ryan said.

"Where are Gary and Tiggy?" Mama asked me.

"Outside the city," I said. "We're trying to keep a low profile. Too many people know our faces right now."

"There's the ego," she said.

I rolled my eyes. "It's a loud unicorn and a half-giant. It's not about ego or subtlety. It's more practical."

"Especially when you're coming to see the Queen of the Fuck Palace," she said.

"I blame you for this," I told Ryan. "All of this is your fault."

"I don't even know what's happening right now," he said.

"You're being interviewed," Mama said. "For a job."

"He is not!"

"Tell me, Knight Commander," she said. "Are you up for a little questioning?"

"This can't possibly end well," I muttered. "And you've already questioned him."

"What?" Ryan asked. "What job?"

But Mama didn't even give him time to think. "Mead or cider?"

"Cider."

"Oceans or mountains?"

"Mountains."

"Brisket or lamb?"

"Brisket."

"Topping or bottoming?"

"Both," he said. Then, "Wait. What?"

"Sweet molasses," I whispered.

"Well, then," Mama said. "Versatile. My, oh my. My day just got far more interesting."

"How do you *do* that?" Ryan demanded.

"Get you to say things you don't want to say out loud?" she asked. "Simple. I'm Mama. I can do anything."

"I think I've forgotten why we came here," I said, staring at Ryan.

"You're hired," Mama told him. "Of course, you'll need to renounce your knighthood, your oath to the King, break your engagement with the Prince, and then tell your one true love you can't be with him anymore."

"Won't his one true love know when he breaks the engagement?" I asked. "That seems to be pretty telling if you ask me."

Mama stared at me.

"What?" I asked.

"Are you really that stupid?" she asked.

"Why does everyone keep asking me that?"

"Ryan," she said. "Would you care to—?"

"Nope," he said quickly. "I don't know what you're talking about."

She glared at the both of us. "Really? *Really?*"

I was so confused. "What are you mad at me for?"

"You're fired," she said to Ryan. "Pack up your shit and get out."

"What?" I shouted at her. "You *can't* fire him! He's the best whore you've—wait."

"Um. I don't have any shit here?" he said. Or asked. I wasn't sure which.

"Oh," Mama said. "Then it will be easier for you to leave."

"I've never been fired before," Ryan told me. "I feel strangely upset by this whole thing."

"Mama tends to do that to you," I said. "Strangely upset or uncomfortably aroused. It's almost the same thing."

"Are you going to put Moishe out of his misery?" she asked me.

"If by out of his misery you mean killing him, then maybe," I said. "I've honestly thought about it for years."

"You know what I mean."

"Then no. That would not put anyone out of their misery. In fact, there might be more misery. Like, tons of misery."

"Moishe wants to have sex with him," Mama told Ryan.

"He has a wizard kink," I muttered.

"No," Mama said. "He has a *you* kink."

I grimaced. "That's not helping."

"He's not having sex with Moishe," Ryan growled.

Mama's eyes gleamed. "And just *why* is that, Knight Commander?"

"Because."

"Great answer," Mama said. "I believed it. Right down to my toes."

"You don't own me," I reminded him. "Do we need to go through this again?"

"Again?" Mama asked.

"Fairies," I said, trying to remember what it was I needed to ask Mama. She tended to suck me into her circular conversations and I always left without remembering why I came to begin with.

"Dimitri?"

I nodded. "A few days ago." I started to tune them out so I could think. I needed something from Mama.

"*Everything* wants to have sex with him," Ryan said.

"Really?" Mama asked. "Everything. Imagine that."

"Dark wizards," Ryan said. "Tiny men with wings. Fan clubs. Dragons. Guys with weird ears because apparently that's *sooooo* cool and whatever, you know? We all have *ears*. Gods."

"Huh," Mama said. "And just how much do *you* want to fu—"

"I remembered!" I said quite loudly. I wasn't even sure what they were talking about, but I was sure it could wait. "Old Clearing."

Mama's eyes hardened and the room felt colder than it'd been before. "Old Clearing, you say?"

"There've been reports. People missing. Livestock taken. Scorch marks upon the earth."

She sat back in her chair. When she spoke next, I could hear the great care with which she chose her words. "And so, naturally, you thought of the dragon and the Prince."

"Naturally. Well. Morgan thought of it. We know where the Prince is now. We think. Dimitri told us of a keep in the north near the mountains."

"Where?"

"Tarker Mills."

She arched an eyebrow. "And you trust the fairy?"

"Trust might be too strong a word," I admitted. "But I don't see what reason he'd have to lie to me. Even *if* he's a fairy."

"He's your ex," Ryan muttered. "Of course he'd lie to you."

"He's *not* my ex."

"You were almost married!"

"That was *once*!"

"This is just fascinating," Mama said. "Please continue to waste my time."

I scoffed at her. "Don't lie. This is the most fun you've had since the last time I was here. I bring joy and wonderment to your life."

"That's not quite how I would describe it," she said, even though we both knew she was full of shit. "There was no dragon in Old Clearing. At least, not from what I've heard."

"And you hear everything," I said.

She nodded. "I do. It's one of the perks of being Mama. Shit don't stick and stories get told."

"Then tell me a story," I said.

She eyed me warily. She stood up and walked around the desk. She wore high heels, adding inches to her already considerable height. They clacked angrily on the wooden floor. She brought a single finger to her lips in warning as she moved around us to the carved door. She cracked it open briefly, peering out into the hallway. It was empty. She closed the door again.

She turned back to me. "Do you feel anything here?" she whispered. "Any magic that isn't your own?"

I shook my head. "Nothing." I would have noticed the moment we walked into the room.

She sighed. "Good."

"Problems?" Ryan asked.

"Sometimes the walls have ears," Mama said. "And sometimes the ears are attached to little heads that should not still be attached to their bodies."

"That's... ominous," I said. "And confusing. You are ominous and confusing."

She smiled at me. "Thank you, precious. I have spent a very long time cultivating such a demeanor."

"Spot-on, then."

She studied me for a moment. I didn't know what she was looking for, but she nodded and said, "Your dragon has never been here."

"Come again?"

"The dragon has never been to Meridian City. Or to Old Clearing. I doubt it's been within days of here."

"I don't understand."

"You wouldn't, precious," she said. "Because none of us do, really." She sat behind her desk and leaned back in her chair. "People have disappeared from villages around Meridian City. Men. Women. Children. Not in great numbers and only within the last two months, but they're gone and have never been seen again."

"Why couldn't it be the dragon, then?"

"One would think if a dragon was attacking a village that it would not have gone unnoticed."

I rolled my eyes. "I don't need the sarcasm, Mama."

"Then don't ask dumb questions, precious."

"Why has no one brought this up to the King? Surely someone would have mentioned it by now."

"They're scared," she said. "The City of Lockes is far away. It's only a few people at a time and spread out over great distances. Take your pick, Sam. Any reason will do."

"Is it just from the villages?"

Mama chuckled darkly. "People disappear every day, especially from Meridian City. Who knows how many others there might have been. There's no census here. Too many people coming and going. I had a customer come in the other day I hadn't heard from in nearly two decades. I thought him dead long ago. Turns out he was just married."

"And he's not anymore?" Ryan asked.

Mama grinned. "I didn't say that. And lose that judgmental face, darling. You are obviously in no position to criticize the choices of others, if your words have any weight to them. And besides, you're much too pretty to scowl like that. I changed my mind. You're rehired. You can start right now. Take off your pants so that I may see your cock and know just what a knight commander carries with him as his weapon."

And that bugged the shit out of me. I was used to Mama's innuendos and sexual advancements and had always brushed them off with a laugh in the past. It didn't matter who it was directed at (though, once, I might have considered throwing a punch when she'd met my father and decided to call him "dinner"), I would look past it.

But this.

This was different.

I stepped in between the two of them, like I could block Mama from even seeing him. There was a bit of green and gold that fluttered off to the side, and a little voice said, *Why not? Why not pull it in and turn it into something more?*

Because I could.

"No," I growled at her and she just *smiled*.

"Now, isn't *that* curious," she said.

I felt Ryan's hand come up to the middle of my back. He pressed his palm flat against me and said, "*Sam*," and there was no green. There was no gold. There wasn't the need to think *iov* and *twe* and freeze Mama's lungs in her chest. There was only calm and peace and I was settled in a way I hadn't felt in a very long time. It was warm and sweet and I never wanted to feel any other way ever again.

It was absolutely awful. Because it wasn't mine.

But didn't I press back into his hand, for just a moment?

Well. If I did, that would be my little secret.

"We don't have time for this," I said to Mama, voice rough. I stepped away from Ryan. His hand dropped back down to his side.

"And yet, here you are," she said. "A prince is held by a dragon in a keep far away from here, but you still bless us with your presence. How delightful, Sam. We've missed you, of course."

"I came because we needed answers. We thought it was the dragon."

"Now you know it wasn't," she said. "It's something else."

"We're done here," I told Ryan. "Mama, thank you. You're most... informative. I wouldn't expect anything less."

She bowed her head. "Of course."

I turned and pushed Ryan toward the door. I needed to get the both of us out of here before someone did something stupid. Most likely me.

"Sam," Mama said. "A minute of your time. Alone."

"Fuck," I muttered. I should have known it wouldn't be that easy.

Ryan looked over his shoulder at me, worry marring his handsome face. I shook my head once at him. "It's fine. I'll follow you downstairs. Won't be but a moment." I smiled at him, but it was forced and I think he knew it.

He closed the door behind him and I took a deep breath, letting it out slowly.

"So," Mama said.

"So." I turned back around and met her gaze, no matter how hard it was to do so.

"Really, Sam? That's what you're going with."

"I have absolutely no idea what you're talking about."

"None at all," she said.

"Nope."

"Let me tell you a story."

I sighed. "Seriously? A whole story?"

"Once upon a time, there was a little drag queen with big dreams."

"This sounds like it's based on someone I know," I said.

Her eyes narrowed.

I said, "And no commentary. Got it."

She tapped her fingernails on the desk. "This little drag queen met a man when she was nineteen. This man was the sweetest man and he did everything for the little drag queen. He adored her. He worshipped her. He was everything she could possibly imagine. But this little drag queen was ambitious and self-centered and didn't appreciate the man as she should have. Eventually, she drove the man away. She told herself it didn't matter. That she didn't need him. That he was holding her back. It took her a very long time to realize that he was only holding her up. And when it hit her, she did everything she could to get him back. But it was too late. The man had found another who loved him as he should have been loved and they were happy. The little drag queen left him to his happiness and regretted all her choices every day thereafter."

I watched in fascination as the mask that Mama wore slipped for just a brief moment, and I saw the man underneath and he was sweet and kind and scared. But then Mama came back and the nails stopped rapping on the desk.

I said, "Regrets are hard to live with."

"Especially when they're from chances lost," she said. "Do you understand?"

"I don't think I do," I admitted.

"You're a smart boy, Sam."

"Thank you?"

"But sometimes, you're an idiot."

"I take it back now."

"We hide," she said. "The two of us. Me behind Mama. You behind your words."

I took a step back.

"Ever since I saw you, you know what I wanted for you, precious?"

I shook my head.

She smiled, and it was warmer than any other smile I'd seen from her. "I wanted you to be happy. I wanted little Sam to find something big and wonderful in the world, a love as bright as he is. My old, shriveled heart just *pounded* with it. You and I are so very different, but not so different that I can't see myself in you."

"Self-centered and ambitious?" I asked quietly.

Her smile took on a melancholic curve. "Not quite. The ambition, maybe. I don't know that you have it in you to be selfish. But sometimes I wish you did. Because then you'd see what should be yours for the taking."

"I can't," I said, because I knew now what she was talking about.

"I know, precious. Because that's not who you are."

"It's not fair." *To Justin. To Ryan.*

To me.

"Such things never are," she said.

"It's not...."

She waited.

Instead, I said, "I have to go."

"Do you?"

"I'm not running away from you," I promised her. Even though I sort of was.

"As if you ever could," she said. "I'd be liable to chase you until your legs tired and then drag you back to my den and never let you leave."

"I'd like that," I said.

"Sam. You need to watch your back, okay? I don't know what's out there. I don't know what's coming. But you need to make sure that you're ready for it. If I find out you've gone and gotten yourself killed, I'll murder you. Are we clear?"

"Crystal."

She stood up from her desk and walked around it, never taking her eyes from me. She towered above me as she put her strong hands on my arms, squeezing them tightly. She bent over and kissed my forehead, a loud smack that itched. "Life is about chances. Unless you take them, you'll never know what they could bring."

I nodded, because it was the only way she'd let me leave. And I think she knew that.

"I'll be okay, Mama," I said. "You'll see."

She looked like she didn't believe me. "I hope so, Sam. For all our sakes. Watch yourself, precious. The world has teeth and wouldn't care if one such as yourself got bit."

I turned and left my fairy drag mother standing alone in her office.

RYAN WAS waiting for me at the bottom of the stairs. Moishe was glaring at him, and the other courtesans were watching him with thinly veiled lust and interest in their eyes. He didn't look at any of them, only at me.

I reached the bottom of the stairs and he said, "Sam, what I said in there—"

"It doesn't matter," I told him. "Whatever you did, it doesn't matter to me."

"I had to get out," he said, looking away. "Of the slums. It cost money I didn't have. Favors."

I kept my face blank at the stark admission. He'd whored himself out so he could leave the slums behind. My stomach felt sour at the thought of it. He'd told me that I'd been a big reason for him leaving the slums. So, of course, I took it now as I'd forced him into this. It hurt. It burned. Guilt weighed me down, and I wanted nothing more than to put my arms around him and hold him close. To tell him that it would be okay. That everything would be okay. That I didn't care what he'd done in the past because all we had to do now was look to the future.

But I didn't.

I was getting too close to something that wasn't mine to have.

So I said, "We all do what we have to." I patted his shoulder and moved around him. Every step I took hurt more than the one before it.

CHAPTER 16
Oops

THE SUMMONING crystal lit up three days later. We were on the road to Tarker Mills, and I felt we didn't know much more than we had when we'd started out. In fact, even knowing the possible location of the Prince only led to more questions, and if there was one thing I fucking hated more than *anything*, it was unanswered questions.

So I brooded.

Gary, Tiggy, and Ryan noticed, of course. I scowled at them and rolled my eyes any time they interrupted my thoughts. Gary told me I was acting like a little bitch. Tiggy said I was being rude. Ryan just looked at me with big eyes that made me want to hug him forever and not let anyone hurt him ever again.

Naturally, that pissed me off even more.

There were secrets between us all. Well. *I* had secrets, specifically the cornerstone business, and it was itching and crawling along my skin, a low-level irritation that was starting to build.

Life was hard and I felt like whining, so I kept my mouth shut and glared.

The problem was that I *never* kept anything from Gary and Tiggy. And Morgan. Mostly. But Gary and Tiggy? *Never*. And the fact that the one time I did was something as huge as finding my magical anchor was only going to lead to a shitstorm when it all inevitably came out. Which, it would. Of *course* it would. That's just how my life went.

And yet, I said nothing.

I felt it justified, though. We had a quest to complete. Justin needed to be saved, the dragon defeated, and then we'd head to Castle Freeze Your Ass Off. I could worry about the cornerstone later. And the whole doing-magic-with-my-mind thing. There were more pressing concerns.

I wasn't in the mood, then, when the crystal started pinging.

"Motherfucker," I muttered.

"Are you going to get that?" Gary asked. "Maybe it will help you come out of your I'm-trying-to-be-a-martyr-but-am-really-acting-like-an-asshole phase. The gods only know how much more I can take before I give serious consideration to ending our friendship and your life."

"No killing," Tiggy said. "Even if Sam being a jerk."

"Tiggy! You're supposed to be on *my* side!"

Tiggy rolled his eyes. "Always am. Except for right now."

I dug through my pack and pulled out the crystal. It warmed as soon as it hit my hands. "Hello."

Silence.

"Morgan?"

A low curse.

"Not Morgan."

"Hello!" a voice blared loudly.

I sighed because I'd recognize that voice anywhere. After all, I'd once turned his nose into a penis. It's hard to forget someone like that. "Randall."

"Hello!" he shouted again. "Can. You. Hear. Me?"

"Very well," Gary said. "Too well. Like, you're shrieking."

Tiggy covered his ears.

"Be nice," I whispered. "He's old. He probably doesn't know any better."

"Damn things never work right," Randall muttered to no one in particular. "Hello!"

"Randall, we can hear you just fine."

"I'm trying to reach Sam of Wilds!"

"It's me, Randall. You've got to speak into the—"

The crystal went dark. We all stared down at it.

"Did he just hang up on you?" Ryan asked.

"I don't even know," I said.

"Shouldn't he know how these things work?" Gary asked. "Didn't he invent them? Or something?"

"To be honest, I didn't ask questions," I said. "Morgan handed me a magic jewel and said use it and I said okay. I'm easy like that."

"And in other ways too," Gary muttered.

"*What*?"

"What?" he asked, batting his eyelashes. My heart instantly melted because a unicorn batting his eyelashes is *precious*.

"Gah," I said, unable to help myself. "Your *face*. I *love* it."

The crystal started pinging and glowing again.

"Randall?" I said.

A voice responded, but it came out muffled and intelligible.

"Randall, you've got to move your hand off the crystal," I said. "We can't hear you."

The muffled voice grew louder and angrier.

"How old is he?" Ryan whispered to Gary.

"No one knows," Gary whispered back. "They say he rose up when the world was created and was formed out of ash and rock and—"

"He's almost six hundred and seventy, and he was born in a village in the east," I said. "His parents were mill workers."

Gary scowled at me.

"Sam of Wilds!" Randall shouted through the crystal, voice clear and cracking.

"Randall."

"Are you there?"

"Yeah. Can you hear me?"

"Barely. These stupid things never work. You kids today with your toys and your crystals and your exploding corn. Back in *my* day, we didn't *need* summoning crystals. If we wanted to hear from someone, we wrote a *letter* and got a response in three months. *That* was considered fast. Now, everyone is all about now, now, now. Tell me, Sam. Why is everyone in such a rush?"

"Rhetorical," I muttered to the others. "Don't answer it. It'll never end."

"I heard that, Sam of Wilds!"

"Of course you did." I sighed. Leave it to him to be able to hear whispered sarcasm.

"Don't you get snarky with me, you baby wizard," he snapped. "I know how to turn your little pecker into a chicken and you will *never* be able to change it back."

We all gaped at the crystal.

"Randall?" Gary said.

"Yes? Who's this?"

"This is Gary, Sam's friend."

"Are you the giant or the unicorn?"

"The unicorn. I just have to say that you're my new hero. 'Baby wizard' is the greatest thing I've ever heard. And *please* teach me the chick-dick spell. I have to know it. Immediately."

"A unicorn tried to kill me once," Randall said, completely ignoring Gary. "Well, I'd just tried to kill it myself, but only because it'd come down with a case of Raging Hubris for which there was no cure. I thought I was doing it a favor, but instead, it saw it as an act of violence. Of course, this was back in my younger days when I was a bit more fit than I am now. I could run a three-minute mile and still have enough endurance left over to have relations with…"

"Nope," I said. "Nope, nope, nope. This is not going to be a thing."

"…the Drumond sisters," he said, completely overriding me. "Now, the Drumond sisters were lookers, and both of them seemed to be in love with me. And by lookers, I mean you looked at them and said, eh, why not? But given the size of my…"

"Oh gods no," I whispered.

"…heart, I could not choose between them. Needless to say, they were extraordinarily jealous of each other, but I made sure to spread my time equally between them so each of them could have a little bit of Randall. Now back in those days, it wasn't required that one be accompanied by a chaperone. It certainly made things easier when we wanted to…"

"It's like we aren't even here," Ryan said in awe.

"…go dancing. Now people are so concerned with *virtue* and *innocence* that they are *blinded* to the fact that when people get together, sex happens. We are held by societal standards that the body needs to be covered up and that we need to speak in prim and proper tones and words. Why, back in *my* day, clothing was optional! If you didn't want to wear trousers, you didn't have to! It was okay to go out and for everyone to see your…"

"My stomach hurts," Gary said.

"…dedication to freeing your spirit from the confines of rigid morals and ethics that had no bearing on who we were as individuals and as a whole. But, I digress. The *Drumond* sisters were more than willing to step out with me, knowing my position on clothing and they *never* had to worry about my…"

"I no wear pants now," Tiggy said, reaching for his waist.

"Sam, Randall had better be wearing pants when we're at Castle Freeze Your Ass Off," Gary warned. "I am not traveling across the country just to have to spend four months in an ice castle with an old naked wizard."

"Tiggy, put your pants back on!" I shouted as he ran around laughing, bits and bobs flopping around.

"No!"

"I feel like this is pretty much your lives all the time," Ryan said.

"We normally don't get naked this much," Gary said.

"You're naked all the time," I said to Gary. "You don't wear clothes. By definition, you're a nudist."

"Just because I have no body issues, *Sam.*"

"I don't have body issues!"

"Then take off your clothes!"

"Fine!" I handed Ryan the crystal and my hands went to the buttons on my trousers, unsnapping them quickly and efficiently. "I'll show *you* body issues."

"Whaaaat?" Ryan said, eyes wide.

I slid my pants down to my ankles to prove a point. "See! I don't give a shit."

"Holy shit," Gary said. "You've got a gigantic—"

"…personality to think I'd ever be okay with dating two women at once," Randall said, oblivious to everything else. "And so I told them that I—"

"This wasn't what I had in mind," I said, face flushing, but for the life of me, I couldn't figure out how to bend down and pull my trousers back up. I was frozen solid.

Gary said, "You certainly are… packing. My, my, my. Little Sam is all grown up, isn't he?"

"Whaaaaaat?" Ryan said, eyes glazing over.

"Are you hitting on me?" I squeaked.

"No!" Ryan said, flushing brightly.

"Uh. I was talking to Gary?" Weird. Why would Ryan think I was talking to him?

"No," Gary said. "I was merely extolling virtues that I didn't know you possessed. I could never hit on you. You're like my much older, less fortunate stepsister."

"*Step*sister?"

"Is it getting warm out here?" Ryan asked no one in particular. "It feels like I'm on fire."

"No pants!" Tiggy shouted. "Hi, people! No pants. Wear no pants!"

I looked over to see who he was talking to. There was a group of travelers on the road, three men and two women. All of them were staring at us with shock evident on their faces. I covered myself with my hands while Tiggy stopped and cocked his head.

We fell silent.

"...and that's how I managed to escape the unicorn suffering from Raging Hubris," Randall finished.

AFTER SCREAMING quite loudly and pulling up my trousers as quickly as I could, I apologized profusely to the travelers who had stumbled upon us. One of the women growled at me and called me her little minx before the other woman reined her back in.

"You pulled down your pants in the middle of the road?" Randall said through the stone after the travelers had departed. "Gods, Sam. Have you no *shame*? You represent Morgan and the King!"

"But... you just... you were naked all the time!"

"I am not a King's Wizard," he said. "Have a modicum of *tact*, Sam. You are on a quest to save the Prince of Verania from the clutches of a mighty dragon and you're taking off your pants in broad daylight out in public? I always knew you were going to be trouble. Even before you gave me a phallus for a nose."

Ryan said, "You did what?"

"You are never going to let me forget that, are you?" I sighed.

"I had to *officiate* a *wedding* the next day!"

Ryan said, "No, seriously. You did *what*?"

I shrugged. "The first time I met him, I accidentally turned his nose into a penis. I was young and thought about dick a lot."

Ryan almost fell down. For no apparent reason. He wasn't even *walking*.

I arched an eyebrow at him. "You okay?"

"I just...," Ryan started. "I don't.... *Sam*."

"That pretty much sums up how we all feel about Sam," Gary said. "Fond with strong overtures of horror."

I grinned at Ryan. "You're fond of me."

He started coughing violently.

"Fond," Gary said to Tiggy.

"*Fond*," Tiggy repeated.

"What?" I asked.

They both sighed.

"Randall," Gary said. "Isn't it a requirement for all wizards to be at least slightly self-aware?"

"One would hope so," Randall said. "A wizard must be familiar with his surroundings at all times and able to pick up on all the subtle nuances from the people and/or creatures he associates with."

"Subtle nuances," Gary said.

"*Subtle*," Tiggy said.

I scowled at the both of them. "You guys are being ridiculous."

"Why did you summon me?" Randall asked. "You know I'm very busy."

"Uh. You summoned us?"

"I did?"

"Yeah."

"Oh. Well, then. It must have been important. Where are you?"

"A few days outside of Meridian City," I said. "Headed for Tarker Mills."

"And what did you find in Old Clearing?"

I hesitated. Then, "Nothing pertaining to the dragon."

Randall was silent for a moment. Randall silences were not good silences in that they were calculating. I could hear the gears whirring in his head as he picked up on my evasiveness. But he surprised me when he said, "Well that's good news, at least. It means the dragon's territory isn't as far-reaching as we thought it would be."

Gary looked at me oddly, and I knew we'd be having words later.

"Good news," I echoed.

"And how long until you get to Tarker Mills?"

"Three weeks or so. A little less if we're lucky."

"Luck always seems to be around you, doesn't it?"

"It does?"

He chuckled, though he didn't sound amused. It was a dry, raspy thing that grated in my ears. "You're alive, aren't you? That's more than I would have thought when I first met you."

"That's... comforting," I said.

"Is it? Wasn't meant to be. Simple recitation of fact."

"Always a pleasure, Randall."

"I wouldn't go *that* far. I thought there was a good chance you would have blown yourself up by the time you turned fifteen."

"I almost did," I said. "Several times."

"I still remember the day when Morgan told me about you. It was the day I first got an ulcer."

"Do you still keep in touch with the couple you wedded?" I asked him innocently. "I bet they look back on their ceremony fondly. Or was that question too nosy?"

"Did you just make a pun about giving him a dick nose?" Ryan asked me, sounding amused.

"Gods," Gary muttered. "This is so gross to watch."

"What is?" Tiggy asked.

"Tell you later," Gary said.

"I do, in fact," Randall said stiffly. "It took years for them to be able to look upon me without horror, but we've managed. It helps that they think the person responsible was lashed with a whip thirty times and then dropped in the middle of the Dark Woods dressed only in undergarments and covered in honey."

"And why honey?" I asked, despite myself.

"To attract bears," he said.

"That's elaborate."

"Revenge fantasies typically are."

"You had fantasies about me? Randall. Control yourself. I was barely a teenager, you old minx."

"Knight Commander," Randall said.

"Yes?"

"I order you to draw your sword and stab Sam of Wilds. Anywhere will do, though I would prefer it in the face."

"You seem like the type to prefer it in the face," I muttered.

"What was that?" he asked sharply.

"Nothing." I glared at Ryan as he reached for his sword. "And just what do you think you're doing?"

He looked confused. "Sam. It's *Randall*. He's *legendary*."

"And so you're going to stab me?"

"No," he said, but what he really meant was *maybe*.

"If you try and stab me, I'll turn you to stone again," I said.

"Again?" Gary, Tiggy, and Randall all said.

"Long story," I said, eyeing Ryan until he dropped his hand from his sword.

"They have stories," Gary whispered to Tiggy.

"*Long* stories," Tiggy whispered back.

I was about to curse them both when Randall said, "Morgan thinks you're keeping something from him."

"Goddammit," I muttered.

"So you are."

"Wizards have secrets."

"You're not a wizard yet," he reminded me.

"Oooh," Tiggy and Gary said.

"People have secrets," I corrected myself.

"They do. But not apprentices. Especially not to their elders."

"No secrets," I said. *So many secrets.*

"Sam."

"Randall."

"You know I'll get it out of you once you get here, don't you?"

"You can sure as hell try."

He sighed and then proceeded to say the worst possible thing he could. "Look. If it has to do with this whole cornerstone business, I understand. I do. Probably more than you could ever know. It's hard when the person you want can't be the cornerstone you need."

Everything fired at once in my brain and I was left gaping at the crystal, trying to say something, *anything* to get him to shut up and not say another godsdamn word because *Ryan was standing right there*, looking at me like he had a *billion* questions and I didn't know how I was going to answer a *single* one. Then I remembered that neither Gary or Tiggy knew who my cornerstone was and thoughts *did* flood in, and they were all *fury* and *rage*, and how many ways I could turn Randall's nose back into a dick so I could castrate him twice.

So to make the situation better, I opened my mouth and said, "Uhhh," like a *boss*.

Gary narrowed his eyes at me.

Tiggy looked surprised.

Ryan was confused.

"Oops," Randall said, not sounding apologetic in the slightest.

"Your *what*?" Gary asked dangerously.

"You know?" Tiggy said.

"What the hell is a cornerstone?" Ryan asked.

"Oh no!" I said loudly. "It's getting late. We really should get moving. Long distance to travel. Princes to save. Dragons to vanquish. Much too late to waste time talking about nonsensical things that have no bearing on our current situation."

"Like that's ever stopped you," Randall said.

"You're not wearing a watch," Gary pointed out helpfully.

"I can tell by the sun," I said through gritted teeth.

"It not noon yet," Tiggy said.

"He's just feeling bashful," Randall said.

I was going to turn all his appendages into penises so I could castrate him multiple times. There would be so much castration, everyone who saw would be like, dude, that's probably a bit excessive with how much you're castrating him. And I would turn and say *it will* never *be enough.* "Wonderful, Randall," I said, even though it came out a bit more murderous than I had intended. In fact, everything about me seemed to scream murder right at that moment, if the looks on everyone's faces said anything about it. "This conversation has been most illuminating. I'll be sure to properly thank you upon my arrival to Castle Freesias."

"That sounded like a threat," Randall said. He didn't sound intimidated in the slightest.

"Why would I threaten you?" I asked. "I'm only an apprentice, after all."

"Would you look at that!" Randall said. "How did that tunnel get here that I have no choice but to walk into? I'm about to lose you on the summoning crystal. Very shoddy connection. It's… getting… harder… can't… hear…."

The crystal went dark.

"He just hung up on you again, didn't he?" Gary asked.

"Yes. Okay! Time to go. We have twenty minutes to make up. I think we should do sprints. Silent sprints with no talking because that would be difficult." I hated the words as soon as they came out of my mouth because I'd just voluntarily suggested running. Running was stupid and it did nothing to make a person healthier. It was boring and lame and I wanted to do so much running right now. As fast as I could.

"You hate running," Gary said.

And I hated unicorns, but I didn't say anything about *that* now, did I? "Turning over a new leaf."

"Oh? Was it laying on your leaf bed of *lies*?" he asked.

"That… that didn't even make sense."

"It sounded better in my head," he admitted. "Like, devastating, even. I honestly expected tears from all the devastation."

"I'm not devastated."

"I'll think of something later," he said. "You'll be gutted emotionally and you'll cry and I shall emerge victorious."

"The fact you are going to actively spend time thinking of ways to make me cry really concerns me."

"It's not that hard. You cry at everything."

"I do *not*."

"Puppies in the slums with no one to give them food," he said. "And they have really big eyes and all they want to do is go home with you but you can't carry them because you lost your arms in a factory accident when you were fifteen."

My eyes burned as I said, "You monster. And that was surprisingly detailed. The no-arms thing? Masterstroke."

"What the hell was Randall talking about?" Ryan asked, ignoring our obviously important conversation. "And why is everyone pissed off at Sam?"

"That's nothing new," I said. "People are usually pissed off at me. And Randall is a crazy old man who lost his mind decades ago. Just drones and drools, that's all he does. You can't believe a single word that comes out of his mouth."

"What's a cornerstone, then?" he asked.

"Babble and crazy talk," I said quickly before Tiggy and Gary could cut in. "It's an old wizarding legend. Has nothing to do with anything. I don't even know why he brought it up."

"What's the legend?"

I shrugged, trying to remain calm and cool and collected, but I almost hit myself in the face with my own shoulder. "Just a magical foundation thing. Like I said, it doesn't matter. We should go."

"No. Fucking. *Way*," Gary breathed.

Oh shit.

I glared at him, trying to relay the urgent message of *shut up! shut up!* with my eyebrows.

But he wasn't even looking at me. He was staring at Ryan with this newfound appreciation, like he was the most wonderful thing that had ever been created. It took Tiggy a moment to catch on, but then his big eyes got even bigger and he started breathing slightly funny.

"Uh, what?" Ryan asked, looking at them warily.

Gary leaned closer to him, stretching out his neck until his face was inches from Ryan's own. Their noses almost touched. Ryan, gods bless him, didn't jerk back. Gary started breathing heavily in Ryan's face and I had no fucking clue what was going on.

"I like you," Gary finally said in a low voice.

"Thank you? I thought you already did."

"No. Like, I *really* like you. Before, I was just pretending. I actually think I almost despised you. But now I don't."

"You almost despised me."

"Almost."

"And now you don't."

"Now I don't."

"Because...."

Gary breathed more on his face, nostrils flaring. Then (finally), "Unicorns are fickle creatures. I don't need a reason to change my mind. It's been done and you should just accept it and be thankful I no longer plot to murder you in your sleep."

"Testify," Tiggy said.

"So now you have affection for me," Ryan said, "and you—"

"I didn't say affection. I said I liked you, not that I'm ready to pick out curtains. Gods. Calm the fuck down. You're engaged to be married. I will not be your dirty little secret. I am a strong, independent unicorn, and I will not take your shit."

"—and you came to this sudden realization after listening to what are supposed to be the ranting and ravings of an ancient wizard. Not to mention things were discussed in said ranting and ravings that have made all of you strangely cagey—well, more than normal—and less than willing to answer a simple question."

Gary inched even closer. Their noses pressed together. Ryan was going slightly cross-eyed trying to keep his gaze locked with Gary's. "That sounds about right," Gary said, never blinking.

Ryan flinched and pulled away as Gary let out a particularly loud breath of air.

"I win!" Gary crowed. "Unicorn one, supposed Knight Commander zero!"

Tiggy held out his fist. Gary bumped it with his hoof.

"Are you guys done?" I asked.

"Sam?" Ryan asked.

I averted my eyes, finding something interesting to stare at on the horizon. "What?"

"What's a cornerstone? Why is it important?"

Tiggy and Gary looked at me and waited.

So I looked at Ryan and said the only thing I could. "We're running out of time to get Justin back. We need to keep moving."

I turned and started walking down the road, trying to calm my racing heart.

I didn't look back.

Eventually, the others started following me.

CHAPTER 17
Gary Is an Asshole and Other Stories

"SAM."

I ignored him.

"Sam."

I marched resolutely forward.

"Sam. Sam. Sam."

It was such a nice day outside.

"Sam."

Not too warm. The breeze felt good.

"Sam. SamSamSamSam*Sam*."

"*What?*" I snarled at Gary.

"Hey, buddy," he said. "Hi. You got something you want to talk about?"

"No." I made sure not to glance back where Ryan and Tiggy were walking a bit behind us. We were halfway to Tarker Mills and this was the first time Gary had managed to get me reasonably alone ever since Randall opened his fucking mouth. I'd plotted at least fifty-seven ways that I could kill him, each more violent and gory than the last. I was almost scared how bloodthirsty I seemed to be. But then I reminded myself what Randall had spilled and I really didn't give a fuck.

"So, you don't have anything to say at all."

"Not a word."

"No... *stone* unturned?"

"Nope." I was able to stop myself before I punched him in the face. Barely.

"When I was little, you know what I wanted to be when I grew up?"

"I don't care."

"A stonemason."

"Oh my gods."

"When I was a wee slip of a unicorn. I went through a rebellious stage. Got stoned a lot."

"Gary."

"Sometimes when you get angry, your face gets stony."

"*Gary.*"

"My mother once gave me a piece of advice. She said a rolling stone gathers no moss."

"Are you done?"

"Yes. No. Wait. Did you hear I was sick last week? I had kidney stones. Okay. Now I'm done."

I glared at him. He smiled back at me.

We walked on.

"So," he said less than ten seconds later because he couldn't drop *anything. Ever*. "We gonna talk about it?"

"Nope."

"Like, not at all."

"Not at all."

"We gonna talk about how you didn't tell me?"

"Nope."

"Huh," he said. Then, "Well, *I'm* going to talk about it."

"I would really rather you didn't."

"Of course you would. Because you're about to feel my wrath."

"Gross."

"Not like that! Stop making it weird."

"I'm talking to a hornless unicorn named Gary. It's already pretty weird."

"Point. Now. First things first. When are you going to sink your ass down on his cock?"

I tripped and almost fell.

"Hmm," Gary said with a frown. "Maybe I should have gone with a different approach."

"Are you out of your fucking *mind*?" I hissed at him. "You can't just *say* stuff like that. He might hear you!"

Gary rolled his eyes. "Oh please. Tiggy is keeping him distracted for me."

"You *planned* this?"

"You always have to have a plan when you are going into battle."

"I'm not going to talk to you anymore."

"Sam. Sam. Sam. *Sam. SamSamSamSam—*"

A WEEK later, I was awakened in the middle of the night by a cold nose pressing against my face. I groaned and cracked an eye open.

Big unicorn nostrils right in my face. I could hear Ryan's and Tiggy's snores from the other side of the fire. Gary had been on watch.

"What?" I croaked.

"What are you doing?" His breath smelled of cinnamon and apples. Apparently it was a unicorn thing to have delightful odors.

"Sleeping."

"Oh."

"Yeah."

"So."

"So?"

"I thought of another one."

"Another what?"

"Did you hear about what happened to the murderers in Falquist?"

"What? What are you talking about? What murderers?"

He leaned closer and whispered in my ear, "They were stoned to death."

He never blinked.

"Oh my *gods*," I muttered, pushing his face as hard as I could. "Did you wake me up just so you could tell me that?"

"Yes. Obviously. Tell me."

"Fuck off." I rolled on my side and pulled the scratchy blanket over my head.

Right before I fell back asleep, I heard him whisper, "I'm never going to forget this. You will succumb to the power of the unicorn."

I WOKE up the next morning to a pile of stones next to my head.

Tiggy laughed.

Ryan's eyes narrowed.

Gary said, "Wow. How did that happen?"

GARY WASN'T getting what he wanted from me, so four days later he went a different direction.

"So, *Ryan*," he said quite loudly. "I feel like we don't talk very much."

I gritted my teeth but continued walking down the road. It was a beautiful day out and I was going to fucking enjoy it. Tiggy was chattering happily at my side about butterflies and bacon, and I was doing my best to pay attention to him.

"That's because we don't," Ryan said.

"Well. I feel like that's something to be rectified. Since, you know. We'll be seeing a lot of each other. For the rest of our lives."

My hands curled into fists.

"That right?" Ryan asked. "How do you figure?"

"Oh. Well. I'm sure we'll leave no *stone* unturned to find the Prince. One day soon, you'll turn a *corner* and he'll be there with the dragon. We'll defeat it and live happily ever after and Sam will be a great wizard and you'll be… wait. What are you supposed to be again?"

"King Consort," Ryan said. He sounded strained for some reason.

"*Riiiight*," Gary said. "That was it. I'd forgotten. Forgive me. So."

"So?"

"We need to become friends. Tell me everything about you. Your hopes. Your dreams." Gary's voice dropped. "Your fantasies."

Tiggy babbled on, "…and that bacon we had one time in castle. Good bacon. Good, good bacon. I…."

"My what now?" Ryan asked.

"Your fantasies, Ryan. We're having girl talk. If that's too much for you, I can go first."

"Please don't," Ryan said.

"Okay. We can wait until the campfire later to talk about that. I'll eat some grass, you can eat your old can of beans, and you can tell me how you like to get tied up and spanked or whatever knight commanders are into."

I choked and coughed.

"You okay up there, Sam?" Gary called.

"Just fine," I said without turning around.

THAT NIGHT, by the fire.

"How are those beans?" I heard Gary ask Ryan.

"Dry."

"Poor baby. So. You ready?"

"For what?"

"Girl talk."

"Uh."

"This one time, I got fisted by a large selkie named Honest Frank. His name was a bit of a misnomer because everyone knows selkies lie about everything. That being said, he didn't lie about punching my asshole."

"Oh my gods."

"Right? It was a most eye-opening experience. Your turn."

"Oh my gods."

"Ever been fisted by a selkie, Ryan?"

"No!"

"Oh. It's kind of like being with a merman, but less fishy."

"I've never been with a merman!"

"Seriously? What kind of mystical creatures *have* you been with?"

"Oh my gods. *None.*"

"Really?" Gary puffed out his chest. "I could change that. If you feel the need."

"Gary!" I snapped.

He looked at me, fluttering his eyelashes. It looked amazing. Fucking unicorns. "Yes, Sam?"

"Cut it out."

"Cut what out, Sam?"

"You know what."

"I'm just trying to get to know the Knight Commander. After all, he's going to be living only a stone's throw away from us for the rest of our lives."

"*Gary.*"

"Ha," Tiggy said. "Stone."

"I feel like something's going over my head," Ryan said.

"Do you feel like that a lot?" Gary asked. "Because you look like you feel that way a lot. Missing things. That are right in front of you. I know too many people like that."

I rolled my eyes. "You don't know that many people."

"Exactly," he said.

I frowned. "I get the feeling you're being a dick."

"Oh? You think so?"

"Quite possibly."

Gary looked back at Ryan. "You've been working out, right? You seem bigger than you did a year ago."

He shrugged. "I guess. Gained a stone or two of muscle."

"A stone or two of muscle," Gary said, slowly turning his head toward me. "How. About. That."

I threw my jar of beans at his head.

WE WERE four days outside of Tarker Mills when we stopped in the hamlet of Arvin's Crossing and treated ourselves to staying at an actual inn with a bed rather than another night on the cold, hard ground.

There was a tavern in the inn that served strange-smelling fish that made me wish for the beans again. The customers at the bar were in awe of Gary and Tiggy and kept touching them. I kept an eye on them as I poked the fish with a stunted metal fork. I swear to the gods it blinked at me.

"I can't tell if this is fresh or has been dead a really long time," I muttered.

Ryan made a face. "Either way, I don't think I can eat it." He pressed his fork against the fish on his plate and some viscous liquid shot up into the air. He turned a little green as he pushed the plate away. "I would send it back, but I think the cook only had one eye and a dirty mustache. You can't send food back to a man with one eye and a dirty mustache."

Against my better judgment, my curiosity was piqued. "And why is that?"

He shrugged. "One-eyed dirty mustache men are more likely to murder you."

"Is that so? Done an official study on it, have you?"

"Past experience."

"I don't know what that says about you as a person that you've had enough experiences with one-eyed men with dirty mustaches in order for you to be able to say that most if not all are murderers."

"Gay fairy married," he said, voice deadpan. "Dark wizards. Fairy drag mothers. Dragons. Magic mushrooms. Penis noses. Pseudo-elves that want to take your virginity. *Everyone* that wants to take your virginity."

"It is a precious thing," I agreed. "I can't wait to give it away."

He scowled at me. "Just hand it off, will you?"

I rolled my eyes. "It becomes a burden to carry after a while. Why are we even talking about this? We were making fun of you."

He eyed me for a moment. Then, "Before we left, I ran into one of those fan clubs you were talking about."

"Oh?" I managed to say, as if I hadn't just started sweating like a motherfucker. "That right?"

Ryan nodded. "Yeah. Strangest thing, I'll admit. There was a woman there… well, a girl really. She seemed to be in charge of the group."

"She wishes," I muttered. "That bitch."

"What?"

Oh shit. "I said, no more fishes because they make me itch." I made a show of pushing the dinner plate away. "So how was it meeting your adoring fans?" My voice was tinged with what I hoped to be the perfect amount of sarcasm. In reality, it came out slightly strained.

"Intense. Very… intense. They wanted me to sign stuff. Like papers and thighs."

"You poor dear. It must have been so hard to have everyone fawning over you."

He shrugged. "They were sweet. Well, most of them were. There was a guy there."

"Oh?" I said. I wondered if it was considered okay if I set something on fire to cause a distraction. Like a chair. Or Gary.

"Named Martin? No. Wait. *Mervin*."

"Sounds foreign," I said. "Must not be from around here. You'll probably never see him again. You should probably forget all about him. Forever. Are you tired? I'm tired and—"

"Said he was a Sam Girl."

"A what now?" I smiled to show that I thought it was amusing, but it came out as a grimace because I was freaking out.

"Sam Girl," he repeated. "Apparently it's a thing. Like Foxy Ladies."

"I'll be honest," I said. "The fact that you just said Foxy Ladies really made my day. Say it again."

"Foxy Ladies."

"Yeah. Didn't have the same effect that time. Maybe not say it so growly."

"Mervin wasn't very happy to see me," Ryan said, leaning back in his chair. "Said he wasn't a fan."

"Can't win them all, am I right?" I forced a hearty laugh to show this was just between us bros and that I understood completely. "Bros before hoes," I said and immediately cringed internally.

"What?"

Shit. "Uh… never mind. Thinking about something else. Like hoes. And bros."

"What about them?"

"I have no idea," I said honestly.

He squinted at me. "You're odd sometimes."

"Pretty much all the time. Let's talk about—"

"So, *Mervin* was a Sam Girl. Not a Foxy Lady at all."

"Oh, we're still going to talk about that," I said. "That's super."

"Did you know about that? Sam Girls?"

Of course I did. I had invented the term. "Nope. I had no idea."

"Apparently it's a big thing."

"As it should be. I'm awesome." I shouldn't have said that.

"True. You don't seem very surprised."

"That I'm awesome?"

"Sam."

"I *am* awesome."

"HaveHeart is apparently a thing too," he said, not once taking his eyes away from me.

So I said, "It's always nice to have a heart."

"No, that's not what it means. It means you and me."

"There is no you and me," I said.

Something flickered across his face. Something I couldn't quite make out. It almost seemed like *hurt* and *pain*, but it was gone behind the mask he usually wore, stoic and strangely charming. "True. Rystin was the other one. You know. For me and Justin."

"Very fitting," I said. Rystin sounded like a contagious genital disease. "It suits you two." I chose that moment to glance over at Tiggy and Gary so Ryan wouldn't see through my bullshit. They were off in some corner, whispering to some stranger, looking back over at us and then whispering some more. Gary was plotting. This wasn't going to end well.

"I just thought it was fascinating," Ryan said. "People pairing us up like that. I wonder what that was about?"

"I don't know," I said. *We belong together!* "Must be something they see that we don't." *Put your dick in me!* "Absolutely no idea." *All the ideas! I have* all *the ideas!*

"Anyway," he said, "I signed some autographs. The leader or whatever. She was very adamant. Tiffany, I think her name was."

"Tina," I said.

His eyes widened slightly.

I blanched. "Teee naaa," I said like a moron. "Tina. Go. Tinago Fall. Is a waterfall. In the Luri Desert. And that is your fun fact for the day. Because geography is knowledge and knowledge is power." I gave him an enthusiastic thumbs-up. I probably looked a little manic.

"Knowledge is power," he repeated. "You okay there, Sam?"

"Now that you mention it, I'm kind of—"

"So, as I was saying, you were right about the fan clubs."

"Of course I was," I said. "I'm right about most things. And the things I'm *not* right about are frivolous and have no bearing on anything anywhere. Ever." I looked back at Gary and Tiggy in time to see Tiggy slipping some money to the man they were talking to. That was definitely not good.

Ryan leaned forward, putting his hands on the table, spreading out his fingers. They were very nice-looking fingers, which of course led to thoughts of what those fingers could be used for. I had half an erection hidden underneath the table. Penises are seriously inconvenient sometimes. "You ever been to one of those meetings?" he asked casually.

And before I could even begin to think of a way to lie myself out of that one, Gary saved the day by coming back over to the table and saying, "You bitches talking about stuff?"

"Talkin' 'bout," Tiggy said as he followed Gary.

"What were you doing over there?" I asked him.

"Nothing," Gary said, when he really meant *something*.

"Gary."

"Sam," he mocked.

I wasn't going to take his shit. I went for the easy way out. "Tiggy. Buddy. Love. My sweet, sweet giant of man."

"Pretty Sam," he said, running a big hand over my head. "Sweet Sam."

"What were you guys talking about over there?"

He put a finger on my lips and squashed my nose. "Shh, Sam," he said. "Shh, shh, shh."

"Mmmph! Mhmmmph!"

"You two looked cozy," Gary said, looking between me and Ryan. "We interrupting something?"

"I was just telling Sam about the fan club meeting I ran into midafternoon the day before we left the castle."

"Fan club," Gary said flatly. "Midafternoon."

Ryan had the decency to blush. "Apparently I have fans? And they meet?"

"At meetings," Gary said, eyes burning into me as Tiggy still shushed me. "The day before we left the castle. Now, isn't that just *interesting*."

My eyes went wide. He *knew*. Gods*damn* perceptive unicorns!

"Sam," Gary said, because he was *evil*. "Weren't you at a meeting the day before we left the castle? A secret meeting that none of us know anything about? That you often attend? By yourself?"

"Mmmmph! *MMMPH*!"

"Tiggy, dear," Gary said. "Let Sam breathe. I'm sure whatever he's about to say will be most enlightening. Wouldn't want him to die by getting fingered to death or whatever it is you're doing."

"I no finger Sam," Tiggy said, insulted. "I no finger him to death." He pulled his hand away, and I pulled in a great, gasping breath.

"Stop… saying… *fingering*," I panted.

Gary's nose wrinkled. "Well, when you say it like *that*, it does sound unappealing. But back to the topic at hand. Sam. Love. Sweet pea. Meat muffin. Did you hear that you and Ryan attended meetings on the same day at around the same time?"

"Gosh!" I exclaimed. "What an amazing coincidence! No two people have *ever* had meetings at the same time before!"

"Hmmm," Gary said. "I'm surprised you two didn't *corner* each other."

"Zing," Tiggy said. "So much zing."

"And here's the conversation I don't understand again," Ryan sighed.

"I don't understand it either," I said. "Or anything Gary is saying. You shouldn't want to. I don't."

"Ladies and gentleman!" a voice called out from behind us. "Can I have your attention please?"

I turned and looked over my shoulder. There stood a man in the middle of the tavern, on a small stage. He smiled as the noise of the crowd died down. In his hands, he carried a small lute, the strings taut, the baseboard made of oak. He ran his hands over the strings once and a melodious sound fell from them, bright and cheery.

The blood drained from my face.

It was the man Tiggy and Gary had been talking to.

And he was the bard o' the tavern.

Meaning he sang songs.

Many times by request.

Many times made up on the spot.

I turned slowly to Tiggy and Gary, my heart thundering in my chest.

They were grinning at me, wide and toothy.

"You… *didn't*."

"Oh, Sam," Gary said. "You should never underestimate a unicorn and a giant."

"What's going on?" Ryan asked.

"We're leaving," I said. "Now."

Gary sat on me.

"Oh… *shit*," I managed to wheeze as my chair creaked underneath us.

"You're not going anywhere," Gary said, wiggling a bit.

"Can't… breathe…."

"Are you calling me *fat*?" he said, looking back at me.

"Seriously…. Gary… for the love of gods." His tail flicked once into my face. "Your asshole… is right *there*."

"Good thing I poop rainbows and cookie smells," he reminded me. As if that was supposed to make this any less awkward.

"I do hope you're enjoying your evening here in Arvin's Crossing," the bard said, completely oblivious that I was technically getting to third base with a unicorn while Tiggy and Ryan watched. I thought maybe I'd had a dream like that once. It was not sexy. "But, chances are, since you're in Arvin's Crossing, you're not having any fun at all."

The others in the tavern laughed uproariously. I was too busy getting squished by a gigantic ass. Plus, it wasn't that funny. Maybe it was a more of a regional humor kind of thing. Not like puns. Puns are universal. And awesome.

"But!" the bard said when the laughter died down. "We are truly in the presence of greatness tonight, folks. Guests of honor so astounding that the floor will tremble beneath your very feet. But first! A brief word from our sponsors who help keep me, your host, Zal the Magnificent, in business." He bowed and took a step off the stage.

A thin man with a receding hairline stood up and took his place. When he spoke, it was in monotone as he read from a dirty piece of parchment in his hands. "Do you have gout? Is your love life suffering because you're inadequately proportioned? Do you lie awake at night and dream about setting people on fire and bathing in their boiling blood? If you answered yes to any of those questions, then hold on to your hats, because I have a solution for you. Dr. Troy's Amazing Elixir of Rejuvenation, Revitalization, and Repression. Just one sip and your joints will be limber, you'll have a giant member, and you won't feel the need to conflagrate and dismember. Dr. Troy's Amazing Elixir of Rejuvenation, Revitalization, and Repression. Buy it today." He took a breath and then muttered quickly and quietly, "Dr. Troy is under royal decree to disclose that he is not a real doctor, has never been to medical school, and makes the elixir in his shack in the woods. It should not be consumed by anyone in their right mind or who wants to continue to live in a remotely healthy way. Do not feed it to animals or children or they will die a horribly painful death when their insides melt and leave the body in a most effervescent manner through every orifice available."

The man stepped off the stage.

"Gary, if you don't get off me, I'm going to magic you to death," I whisper-shouted.

"Shhh," Gary said. "It's rude to try and interrupt an artist about to perform."

"Bards are *not* artists." Because they *weren't*. They were jerks.

"Art is subjective," Ryan said.

"Your *face* is subjective," I muttered as I prepared for one of my ribs to collapse.

"You really need new insults," Gary said.

"I'm going to get some of that elixir and force-feed it to you."

"Maybe you should consider using some of it yourself," he said, wiggling his ass. "Little Sam feels like he could use a growth hormone right about now."

"Murder," I hissed.

"Shhhhh," Tiggy said. "Song man going to sing song."

Zal the Magnificent stepped back up, a cynical smile curving on his lips. That didn't bode well. "Thank you, Jerome," he said to the balding man, "for that ever-resplendent rendition. Your joy and humor are like sparkles of light in my darkened life."

The balding man flipped him off.

"Now," Zal said jovially. "You may have noticed a rather interesting group of travelers have found their way to our little tavern. Ladies and gentleman—though most of you are nowhere near gentle, and I use the term 'ladies' rather loosely, because if the shoe fits!—all the way from the City of Lockes, it's a really tall guy, a gorgeous and beautiful creature with eyes like jewels that sparkle in firelight, that other one, Gary, and the future sticky wicket for the Prince!"

Everyone turned to us.

"Wait," Gary said. "Did you mean *Sam* is the gorgeous and beautiful creature with eyes like jewels that sparkle in firelight? And *I'm* 'the other one'?" He sounded outraged.

"I tall guy." Tiggy was pleased. It didn't take much.

"What the hell is a sticky wicket?" Ryan asked, brow furrowed. "And is he flirting with Sam? Seriously. *Everyone*."

"Still can't breathe," I managed to say. "Vision getting fuzzy around the edges."

"Drama queen," Gary muttered.

The bard ignored us all. "They are on an epic quest," he said, sounding excited and amazed and slightly mocking all at once. "To save the Prince of Verania from the evil dragon that stole him to keep Justin as his own. Through fire and danger and certain death, they have traveled from the City of Lockes to seek the return of the one true love of the Knight Commander."

Most of the ladies (who were actually probably whores) and even some of the men (who were actually probably whores) sighed, as if the notion of the romance between Ryan and Justin was so wonderful it necessitated a starstruck exhalation.

"Yay, Rystin!" someone shouted on the other side of the tavern. I couldn't see who it was so I was unfortunately unable to mark them for death. It was disappointing. "Whoo! Rystin!"

"Rystin, indeed," Zal said, eyes alight with mischief. "We have a saying in Arvin's Crossing, don't we, my dears?"

"Yeah!" the crowd roared back.

"And what is that saying?"

"We travel far, we travel long, stories told through ale and song!"

"That was really lame," I said, shoving at Gary. He didn't budge.

"I think it's adorable," Gary said. "So backwoods and rustic."

"So!" Zal said. "We have a future King's Wizard. A knight commander. A giant. And a unicorn. And the lovely Tiggy and Gary have requested we sing for them!"

"You motherfucker," I said to Gary. "You too, Tiggy."

Tiggy pouted. "Song man said it be good."

"Don't listen to him," Gary told him. "Sam's just bitchy because he's not getting away."

"I feel like I'm in a waking fever dream," Ryan said to no one in particular. "Like, these past weeks are the product of extraordinary illness and I'm actually in bed hallucinating all of this."

"Do you often hallucinate about Sam while you're in bed?" Gary asked.

Ryan blushed terribly.

I told myself that the fact I couldn't breathe right then was the product of having a unicorn sitting on me. Nothing else.

"Now, we know my skills with the lute are divine." Zal ran his hands over the strings and a pretty chord echoed in the tavern. "My voice has been called melodious and sublime. Now I'll sing you a verse or six. Ladies and gentleman, guests of esteemed honor, I give you… 'Cheesy Dicks and Candlesticks.'"

"What," I said.

"What?" Ryan said.

"This is gonna be *goooood*," Gary breathed.

Tiggy grinned.

And Zal the Magnificent began to sing.

There once was a princely man,
Who had jewels for eyes and hair most fair.
Set, he was, to rule this land,
Undoubtedly down with panache and flair.

But plans have changed, due to nefarious deeds,
As a dragon came and stole the Prince away.
And Verania waits for him to be freed!
So he can return and be wed in a ceremony most gay.

Ohhhhhh!

Cheesy dicks and candlesticks!
And everything you need!
Listen as I sing a verse or six
Here in this land of sloth and greed!

"Whaaaaat the hell?" Ryan said.
"This is so much better than my dreams," Gary said reverently.

But fear not, my lads and lasses,
For there are heroes to be told!
A wizardly man and a knight who sasses,
A unicorn, a giant, all who're brave and bold!

They travel the lands on a desperate quest,
To save a love that's bright and true,
With the sword of knight and the wizard's best.
Sing with me now, you know what to do!

Ryan and I didn't sing.
Everyone else did.
Including Tiggy and Gary. Those bastards.

Cheesy dicks and candlesticks!
And everything you need!
Listen as I sing a verse or six,
Here in this land of sloth and greed!

Our heroes have traveled far and wide.
The wizard was almost gay fairy married.
He'd have been the most beautiful forced bride,
But thankfully, he was saved by Gary.

"You fat sack of crap," I growled at Gary. "That's not even close to what happened!"

"Please," Gary sniffed. "I was there. I have *eyes*. You would have been lost without me."

They learned the secret of the dragon's keep
Hidden deep in valley and made of stone.
And the knight turned a corner, and all maidens weep!
Because what feelings are these that have surely grown?

The tavern erupted into the chorus again while I glared at Gary with the strength of a thousand suns.

"Corners and stones again," Ryan said. "Sure would be nice if someone would explain to me what's going on."

"Yes, Sam," Gary said. "Wouldn't that be nice? If someone explained? What was going on?"

"I'm trying to listen to the song," I insisted.

From there they went to Mama's den,
And behind closed doors, met with she.
In a house of whores and men,
No one is more fucked than me!

There in the house lives an elf,
A noble creature graced with dignity,
Who has set a goal for his own self
To relieve our wizard of his virginity!

More chorus.

"Gary," I bit out. "You better hope you can run really fast, because I am going to light your whole body on fire."

"I'm already flaming enough," he said, rolling his eyes.

"At least they're not singing about Todd and his damn ears," Ryan muttered.

"Cheesy dicks!" Tiggy said. "Cheesy *dicks*."

And alas, like most stories do,
We now approach the end.
Will our heroes return with something new?
Tales of a prince they chose to defend?

Of battles fought and dragon's skin they did part.
Perhaps they'll return with badges made of scars.
Or will they discover the war in their hearts,
As it is surely written upon these stars.

My skin buzzed.
Ryan said, "Sam," in such a quiet voice.
Noise erupted around us.

Ohhhhhh!

Cheesy dicks and candlesticks!
And everything you need!
Listen as I sing a verse or six
Here in this land of sloth and greed!

The song ended to thunderous applause.

I STOOD at the bar, nursing a mug of ale, crisp and tart. A piano played a jaunty tune, people laughing and dancing into the night. I didn't know where the others were. Probably around somewhere. I felt I was justified in ignoring them for a bit. Especially Gary. Mostly Gary. Pretty much all Gary.

If we weren't best friends and he weren't protected by law since he was a magical creature, I would have skinned him alive and made him into a nice area rug.

So, of course, he found me first and said, "You mad? You look mad."

"Volcanic in my fury," I replied evenly.

He sighed. "Well, maybe it wasn't the best idea, but I think we can all agree that it was a good show."

My hand tightened on the wooden mug. It cracked audibly.

"Yikes," Gary said. "Definitely mad."

"If I were a unicorn," I told him, "there would be glitter *pouring* off me right now."

"Unicorn rage," he whispered, eyes wide.

"So much unicorn rage. Like, the ragiest unicorn rage ever."

"Is that why you are getting drunk by yourself and glaring at the wall?"

"I am *not* getting drunk by myself and glaring—oh. Wait. I am. Yes. That is why."

"Oh." He put his nose against my ear and snuffled loudly. I grimaced. "I love you," he said, his lips rubbing against my jaw.

"Gross. Stop it."

"Can't. Love you. Love you, boo. Love you so much. You my girl. Bitches before snitches."

"Except you snitched to Zal the Magnificent."

"I paid him for a performance piece. There's a big difference."

"You're going to need stitches by the time I'm done with you."

He snorted in my ear. "You're adorable when you threaten me. Seriously."

I snarled at him.

"Oops. I meant, oh no! Please, Sam! Don't cut me! I'm so frightened. You're sooo scary!"

"Damn right," I said, knocking back more ale. Like a *man*.

"It *was* a pretty good song, though," Gary said. He just couldn't help himself.

"I'm going to invent a spell for penis rot and give it to you and you're going to be all like, no, why did I do this to Sam? Why was I so mean? I should have been nicer and now my penis looks like an old-growth forest."

"That was… descriptive." He snuffled my face again.

"Go away."

"And leave you to pout all by yourself? Never."

"Don't be a cunt, Gary." I winced. "Okay, time out from the fighting. Can we all agree never to use that word? It's awful and disrespectful and I don't even know why I said it. I apologize profusely and beg your forgiveness."

"Agreed," Gary said. "I'll speak for Tiggy, who is currently trying to get Knight Delicious Face to dance. And of course I forgive you."

"Good. Rule four hundred ninety-eight of the Sam/Gary/Tiggy friendship is now in effect. No one can say… that word. Time in." I huffed out an angry breath and looked back down at the bar. "Go the fuck away, Gary. You're dead to me."

"Whiny little git," he mumbled, but he didn't move. "Why the hell didn't you say anything? We're friends, Sam."

"Not right now we're not."

"Shut up. I'm being serious right now."

"Oh, as long as you're *serious*."

He reared his head back and narrowed his eyes. "You're acting like a child. Knock it off."

"You made a bard sing a song about Ryan and me called 'Cheesy Dicks and Candlesticks,'" I reminded him.

His lips twitched. "Yes. Well. To be fair, I didn't come up with the title. That was all on him."

"You say that like it makes it better!"

"Doesn't it? I certainly feel better."

And as if the moment couldn't get any worse, Zal stepped up to the bar, leaning on his elbows and cocking his head at Gary and me. Gary pulled away slightly and rested his chin on my shoulder. I thought about punching his mouth, but was able to hold back. Barely.

"You," Zal said to me, "are a conundrum."

"You," I said to him, "are a dick."

He grinned. "The things I do for money."

"That's what whores say. The only difference between you and them is they get fucked while you did the fucking."

Zal's gaze flickered to Gary. "Got a bit of a mouth on him, doesn't he?"

"Wait until he gets *really* mad and starts with his nonsensical insults. That's when you know you're in trouble."

"Hash brown snow packer," I growled at him.

"Like that." Gary sighed.

"I like the both of you," Zal said.

"Joy," I said. "Unbridled joy."

"No, really. I do." He laughed and shook his head. "When Gary came and told me what you're doing for love, I was moved. Honestly."

"For love?" I said, not squeaking at all. "What love? There's no love!"

Zal shrugged. "You know. For the Knight Commander. And the Prince."

Ow. My feelings. "Oh. Right. Yes. That love. So much love there. Like… buckets. Of love. And that's exactly why I'm doing this." Well, that was a lie. "For their love." Which was an abomination and a sin against the gods. "There's nothing I'd rather be doing." I would have rather been doing anything but. "Which is why I'm doing it." I was ordered to by the King.

"Yeah," Zal said. "That sounded… believable." He glanced back at Gary. "You weren't kidding, man."

"Right?" Gary said. "Try living with it."

"With what?" I asked. "Stop speaking in code. What are you talking about?"

"Grown-up things," Gary said. "Shh."

"I'll show *you* grown-up." I winced. "Okay, so that may not have been the best way to prove my point."

"At least you're pretty," Gary said.

I blushed. "Oh hush, you." Then, "Wait. *Hey.*"

"You've certainly got your work cut out for you," Zal said to Gary.

"You should see them together," Gary said. "It's painful to watch."

"Kid, can I give you some advice?" Zal asked.

"You just sang a song called 'Cheesy Dicks and Candlesticks,'" I said. "I don't know that you're qualified to dispense advice to anyone."

He waved a hand dismissively. "I'm a bard. I'm supposed to make up shit like that to keep people entertained. It's sort of my job."

"I wasn't entertained. You should be fired."

"Liar," Zal said. "You're going to be singing that song on your deathbed. I made it up in ten minutes. The last stanzas were ad-libbed. You were so impressed."

Okay, I sort of was. But not that I had to tell him that.

"Cheesy dicks and candlesticks," Gary whispered in my ear. I shoved his face away as he laughed.

"Still doesn't explain *why*—"

"I don't know much about the ways of wizards," Zal said, looking down at his hands. "Or royalty or epic quests or magical beings and adventures to save princes from dragons. I know how to *tell* those stories, but I've never really lived them. I don't know that I want to. There are those of us that run headlong and feetfirst into danger like it's nothing. Then there's those of us that stay behind and document what happens. Or, as I like to think of it, the sane ones."

"Nothing difficult was ever won while staying sane," I said.

He gave me a quiet smile. "Exactly."

"Uh."

"You know what I love?"

"I don't. But you're going to tell me, aren't you?"

"Love," he said.

"Gross."

He ignored me. Dammit. He'd already found my weakness. "Love is an amazing thing. It can move armies. It can destroy people. It can cause even the mightiest of us to fall to our knees in supplication. It's terrifying and wonderful, and if you let it, it can be the greatest thing in the world."

I was almost in awe. I had to stop myself from sighing dreamily. "You sound like you speak from experience."

He laughed. "Hardly. I fuck too many people to fall in love. Last night, I had an eleven-way with trapeze artists from a traveling circus. You wouldn't believe how bendy they were. I don't think I've ever seen that much jizz in the space of three hours in my life."

We stared at him.

He rolled his eyes. "Just because I don't fall in love doesn't mean I don't believe in it. I just happen to believe in it more for other people than myself."

"You're my new hero," Gary said. "I want to be you when I grow up."

"But, but," I sputtered. "You said things about love meaning being on your knees for armies!"

Zal arched an eyebrow. "Oh boy. I don't know if that's quite what I said."

"An *eleven*-way?" I said, sounding scandalized. "That's so many *arms*."

"I bet you couldn't even tell where one body ended and another began," Gary breathed on me.

"All those writhing bodies," Zal agreed.

"Nothing!" I said, because that made sense. "I just want a two-way!"

"Sam's a virgin," Gary said. "The only thing he's writhed with is his hand."

"Gary!"

"Truth in advertising," he retorted.

"I don't writhe," I told Zal. "There's no writhing. Where do everyone's *feet* go in an eleven-way? Is there orgy etiquette for feet? Why haven't I been told about this!"

"Some people like feet in their face," Zal said. "Nothing wrong with a little tongue to toe action."

"I don't want my feet sucked," I told Gary. "I am not into feet sucking."

"You don't even know," Gary said. "It's never happened to you yet."

I frowned down at my feet. I tried to imagine someone licking my toes and I cringed a bit. Then I thought of *Ryan* doing it and—

"Oh no," I whispered. "I have *kinks*."

"That's not a bad thing," Zal said. "Kinks are wonderful if they're carefully and consensually explored. Why, last night I discovered I had a kink for eleven-ways." He wiggled his fingers over our shoulders in a slinky wave. Gary and I turned around to see a group of men and women, all with long blond hair, pale skin, and bright eyes, drinking in a corner. They all waved back and half of them giggled.

"You know," Zal said, gaze lingering. "If you're not ready for love, we could make this a twelve-way tonight. They're only in town until tomorrow. You could invite us to come in."

"My room's not big enough," I said faintly.

He grinned. "I meant come in you."

"Oh gods," I wheezed, putting my head on the bar.

"He's slightly prudish," Gary said to Zal. "My sweet, innocent little boy."

"He's made for love," Zal said, as if he understood completely.

"Some people are hardwired that way," Gary said. "Some of us want to get married and have babies, and others of us want to be tied up by a centaur and spanked."

I thought about hyperventilating but decided against it.

"Are you okay?" Zal asked.

"Nothing!" I said, because it still made sense in my head.

"I don't even know how we got to this point," Gary said. "Again."

"You often have conversations about kinks and orgies?" Zal asked.

"You're making it worse," I moaned.

"Love!" Gary said. "That's what this was about. Love."

"Love," Zal agreed. "Kid, I'm going to lay it on the line for you."

"I can't take you seriously anymore," I told him honestly. "I don't know where your feet have been."

Zal pointed behind me back at the trapeze artists. "See the big guy sitting on the end? His name is Oyev. That's where they've been. Can I tell you about love now?"

"I don't think that helped like you think it did," I said.

"Why don't you just tell the Knight Commander how you feel?"

I glared at him. "He's affianced. To the *Prince*." Then, belatedly, "I don't feel anything. I don't even know what you're talking about. Because there's nothing to talk about."

"Really."

"Really."

"So he's just going to get married."

"Yes."

"And that's what he wants?"

"Why wouldn't it be? He's *doing* it, right?"

Zal smiled sadly. "Sometimes we do things for the greater good, even if it causes our hearts to break."

"You bother me," I said to him. "I'm not sure if I'm pleased that you exist."

"He watches you, you know," Zal said and *what*?

"No he doesn't," I said weakly.

"All night," Zal said, as if I hadn't spoken at all. "Since the moment you walked in together. He rarely takes his eyes off of you. You might not have been looking, but I was."

"It's always like that," Gary said.

"It is *not*."

Zal shrugged. "He's doing it right now."

I told myself not to look. I told myself that Zal was full of crap. I told myself that having hope for something so ridiculous was dangerous because it would crush me when nothing happened.

I looked anyway.

Of course I did.

Across the tavern, Tiggy and Ryan stood among a group of revelers vying for their attention. A man was talking to Ryan, a hand against his bicep.

But Ryan was looking directly at me.

And when he saw me looking back, his eyes widened slightly and he dropped his gaze.

"That doesn't mean anything," I said. Because it didn't. It couldn't.

"Stubborn, isn't he?" Zal said.

"Painfully so."

"The Prince is my duty," I said. "I'm sworn to protect him. That's all this is. That's all this ever was. I allowed him to be taken by the dragon. I should have been faster. Stronger. Better. If I'd done what I was supposed to do, none of this would have happened. Ryan needs me to get Justin back. That's all this is."

"Sometimes, I want to punch him in the mouth," Gary told Zal.

Zal stared at me. "He's like this *every day*? Maybe he just needs to get laid. Take the edge off. I can talk to Oyev and see if he can help out. Virginity is a sweet thing, but it's so much better to be destroyed and be sticky."

"No Oyev!" I said. "And selling sex as being 'destroyed and sticky' is *not* the best way to go about it."

Zal rolled his eyes. "Sorry. It's slow and gentle and he'll stare into your eyes and your souls will meld together and the only thing you'll taste is his sweet breath upon your lips. He'll whisper in your ear how you are his treasure and when his seed blooms within you, the flower of true love will begin to grow."

I didn't know what it said about me that I kinda got a boner from that. Maybe that I was awesome. Or very, very sad.

"I will be excellent at boning," I said. "When I'm ready for it." Now. Now would be good. I'd be fine with now.

Zal shook his head. "I think I understand why everyone adores you. You're a conundrum wrapped in an enigma in a package built of twink."

"That's... remarkably astute," Gary said.

"I am not a twink!"

"Shrieked the twink," Gary whispered.

"I think I'm pretty much done. With the both of you. Good day!" I turned from the bar and walked away.

"Regrets, kid," Zal called after me. "If you never try, then you'll only know regret."

I thought to avoid Ryan altogether, but he saw me and broke away from the guy who was *still* holding on to his bicep and met me halfway. People danced around us as the music swelled.

"Okay?" he asked.

"Fine," I snapped. "Ugh. Sorry."

"It's okay. Who do I need to kill?"

I tried not to grin. I failed. "No one. Everyone. I don't know."

"That clears it up. Good job."

"Sass master."

"I thought I was the God of Sass?" he asked. "It sounds like I was demoted."

It was easy, this. Banter. I could do banter. So, like a tool, I said, "I got invited to a twelve-way orgy with a team of trapeze artists and the guy that sang about cheesy dicks." *Shit.* "Wait. That wasn't banter. I meant for that to be banter."

He scowled, eyes darting over my shoulder where Gary and Zal still stood at the bar. "You're going to an *orgy*?"

"What? No! I don't want to be destroyed and sticky and have my feet sucked on!"

His nose wrinkled up. "You... what?"

"That's what happens at orgies," I explained, because it didn't sound like he knew. I felt overwhelmingly relieved at that. "You don't know where to put your feet, so they go into Oyev's mouth."

"Are you drunk again?" he asked.

"Only a little bit," I assured him. "And now I realize that I've been drunk a lot around you, but I promise I don't have a drinking problem. Mostly. And I'm not drunk enough to go to an orgy. Apparently I want someone's seed to bloom in me and make flowers turn into treasure. Or something. I don't know. I might be drunk. Let's banter."

"I don't think you have the capacity to do anything but have words fall out of your mouth right now," he said, a small smile on his face. Like he was *amused*. Like I *amused* him.

"I don't want to have regrets," I blurted out. I took a step back.

He took an answering step forward. "And what do you regret?"

"Ignore me. I didn't mean to say that."

"But you did."

I took another step back. "Wine loosens lips. Not that I need it."

Another step forward. "Maybe," he said. "But for all that you talk, it's superficial."

I scowled at him. "Nice word usage. You dick."

He shrugged. "I have a shield. It's made of metal."

"Fun."

"Yours is made of words."

"Oh. *Oh.* I see what you did there."

"Pretty cool, right?"

I narrowed my eyes at him. "Dude. Are you trying to psychoanalyze me?"

"I'm pretty sure it would take a group of people far more qualified than I years to even remotely come close to being able to analyze you. *Dude.*"

"That... sounded like you insulted me with a compliment."

"I feel like a lot of your life is insults through compliments."

"Why does no one else see this?" I asked without meaning to.

"What?"

"You. This. I don't understand. The King said you don't smile."

"So you've said."

"But here you are."

"Here I am."

"Smiling." And he *was*. And it was *wonderful*.

"Would you rather I not?" he asked as his knee bumped into mine and when exactly had he gotten so close?

"I don't get you." I frowned.

"Why?"

"Because."

"Succinct." There was laughter in his voice.

"You're a knight."

"You're observant."

Suddenly it felt very important that he understand this. "The King said you don't smile. You're a knight. People say you're stoic and ruthless and hardworking and brave. You're supposed to be. That's what a knight is. But you're also kind and ridiculous and a complete and utter dork and I see you smile *all the time*. I don't understand."

The music slowed around us into something surprisingly sweet. The cheerful voices and the raucous laughter died down as men and woman joined together and swayed along the dusty, wooden floor. I was suddenly very out of my depth and thought that running away was possibly the best idea I'd ever had.

And I almost made it. I really did.

But before I could turn completely, Ryan grabbed my hand and said, "We should dance."

"Should we?" There was more in that question than just those two words.

And of course he squeezed my hand and my magic rolled under my skin, and I swore I could almost hear it speaking. It was saying *yes* and *yes* and *yes*.

He said, "Sam, it's just a dance."

I wanted to argue with him. I wanted to tell him it would never be just a dance. What a cornerstone meant to a wizard and how it *could never be just a dance*. That all of this was a bad idea because out there somewhere was the man he loved being held by a creature that apparently only I could understand. His prince was gone. His hand was in mine. And we were here, far from home, away from most all the people we knew and loved and my magic said *yesyesyes*.

"Just a dance," I said.

And he pulled me close.

It wasn't like at the castle. There was no one else. I wasn't sniping at him. He wasn't snarking at me.

But his left hand was on my waist, and I felt every single touch.

And his right hand was in my own, fingers curled and dry and warm.

Our feet moved, more elegantly than I'd ever done before.

And his eyes never left mine.

This boy I'd known as Nox.

This man I knew as Ryan.

I thought for a moment, for a singular, shining moment that maybe I could have this. That maybe this could be mine. That maybe, maybe, maybe.

I knew it wasn't meant to be.

But I allowed myself to think such thoughts.

Because no one else could hear them. They were my own. Like a wish upon stars held in secret hearts.

We danced.

And we danced.

And we *danced*.

Chapter 18
Literally Everyone Eats Breakfast

We were only thirty minutes outside of Tarker Mills when we were attacked.

Again.

Thirty minutes.

Seriously.

Fucking fire geckos.

And Dark wizards.

Fuck everything that wanted to attack us.

Fuck them!

I was being weird toward Ryan, and I knew it. I didn't know how to *not* be weird toward him after we danced, because it'd felt like something *more*. Something substantial. So of course that freaked me out and I started acting *weird*. Well, weird*er*.

Example one:

"You okay, Sam?"

"Ha-ha, why wouldn't I be? Everything is peachy! I'm okay. I'm *better* than okay."

"Okay. I only ask because you haven't stopped staring at me for the last four hours."

"You lie with all your lies!"

Example two:

"Gary, why Sam sweating?"

"Well you see, my dear Tiggy. When a boy loves another boy very much, it makes him awkward and have feelings in his penis and *mmmphh*!"

"Sam, why you use magic and glue Gary's mouth shut?"

"Is *that* what that was? Gosh! I just thought I was singing to myself!"

"*MMMMPH!*"

Example three:

"Hey, Sam. Want to join me in the river? We can bathe before the sun sets and it gets too cold."

"*Sweet molasses.*"

"What?"

"Stay back, foul temptress!"

"What?"

"Er. Not you. Uh. I… sensed the presence of a succubus. Like, near here. Ooooh. So very near."

"You can do that?"

"Yes. Yes I can. Because I have magic. And my succubus-tracking abilities. It's a thing. A real thing. That I do all the time."

"Riiiight. Your magical succubus-tracking abilities."

"Shut *up*, Gary!"

And on and on it went.

To make matters worse, the road between Meridian City and Tarker Mills had had absolutely *nothing* on it. No people. No cities. There were villages here and there, but the flatlands here were mostly farmlands in service of the Crown, and they stretched on as far as the eye could see. Meaning no distractions. No chance for escape.

Just me and Ryan.

(And Gary and Tiggy, who were doing their *damnedest* to make things significantly more difficult. I told them both once while Ryan was relieving himself behind a tree that I would make sure they'd be pooping in buckets for the rest of their lives when we got back to Castle Lockes.

They, of course, had just smirked at me and implied certain acts of an obviously deviant nature that I might consider practicing on Ryan Foxheart. This had led me to blush furiously when Ryan came back to the road and I couldn't look him in the eye for two days.)

But we were almost there! Minutes away! My spirits were high! I hadn't said a *damn* thing embarrassing and/or remotely sexual in at last twenty-four hours. I hadn't even had any inappropriate thoughts about Ryan. Sure, there was a bit of pining going on (*Why won't you love me?*) but it was nothing I couldn't handle. I was an apprentice to the King's Wizard, for fuck's sake. I was on my way to slay (hopefully) a dragon. I was going to save the Prince and then when I got back to Castle Lockes after successfully training with Randall, there'd be a welcome home party and I would meet the (new) man of my dreams and his name would be Sloan Fontaine or Wesley York IV and we would dance until the early hours of the morning (much like I'd done with Ryan at the tavern, but whatever) and then he'd take me back to his estate and I would find out if I was a fan of rimming or not (spoiler: I was probably a fan of rimming).

I had *plans*.

Things were looking *up*.

"What are you so happy about?" Gary asked me suspiciously.

"Everything, my good man," I said. "I have *plans*."

"I don't want to know what they are if the manic smile on your face is indicative of anything."

"I'm probably into rimming," I told him, and Ryan tripped and almost fell down. Sometimes he was so graceless for a knight.

"That so?" Gary managed to say. "How do you figure?"

"Just seems like it, I guess."

"Plans, have you?"

"So many plans."

"Rimming plans."

"Why the fuck not?"

He sighed. "I remember when you were a prude. My little boy who got flustered even saying the word *sex* is now talking about rimming. Kids. You grow up so fast. Pretty soon you'll be getting fisted and I won't know where the time has gone."

"I was *never* a prude," I said. "I'm just not as sexually liberated as you. Especially with fisting. I can't honestly think of a time in my life where I'd find that to be a good idea."

"What rimming?" Tiggy asked.

"Butt stuff," Gary said.

"Seriously," Ryan groaned. "You guys."

"It is," Gary said. "Didn't you know that?"

And before I could start to think about Ryan and rimming, I said, "It doesn't even matter. It's a beautiful day. We are alive and healthy and not in any peril and we're on our way to save the day!"

"I think he's broken," Gary said to Tiggy. Then he looked over at Ryan. "You broke our best friend."

"*Me*? What did *I* do?"

"Everything," Tiggy rumbled. "Sam broken. I smash Knight Delicious Face?"

"Maybe," Gary said.

"No smashing," Ryan said. "And can we *please* talk about Knight Delicious Face? What the hell does that *mean*?"

"Don't even care about what's going on around me," I said, trying to maintain my cheer and most certainly *not* completely focusing on the alliteration that is really rimming Ryan. "Doesn't matter to me at all. Wesley York IV has a date with my asshole."

"Who the fuck is Wesley?" Ryan growled.

"Your *asshole*?" Gary choked. "You just made everything hurt."

"Smash so good," Tiggy said, curling his fists.

And, of course, that's when a tree at the edge of the Dark Woods burst into flames, the fire green and orange with shots of blue running through it.

We all froze.

"No," I muttered. "I am having a *good* day and this is *not* part of having a good day. Sloan Fontaine will bring me great ass pleasure and I won't even know what hit me."

"Are you a secret slut?" Gary asked. "Do you covertly have all the mens? Who is Sloan and why don't I know him?"

"Sloan Fontaine," Ryan scoffed. "Sounds weak. I bet I could take him in a fight. Probably doesn't even work out or anything. I work out. Like, *a lot*."

"*I* don't even work out," I said, trying to figure out why I was defending two people who were imaginary and most definitely not going to rim me.

"Smash smash smash," Tiggy muttered.

"Fire geckos?" Gary said.

"Fire geckos." I sighed. "I fucking *hate* fire geckos. Why do so many things in the Dark Woods want to see me dead?"

"Or gay fairy married." Ryan pulled out his sword and shield. "Can't forget about your ex."

"He's not my ex," I snapped at him. "I am having a *good* day and we're not talking about Dimitri."

"Oh no," Ryan snarked. "We'll just talk about Sloan Fontaine and Wesley York IV. Gods, could they have more douchebag-sounding names?"

"They're not *real*!"

"*You're* not real."

"That was weak sauce, dude."

"Yeah. I'll admit. That wasn't my best."

"As adorable as you two are being right now," Gary said, "there is the matter of *fire geckos* that we have to worry about."

"Fucking fire geckos," I muttered. I could already hear them snapping and snarling in the Dark Woods. It sounded like a shit ton of them. Mean little bastards, they were. The biggest would stand on its hind legs at about two feet tall. Their skin was mottled red and gray and orange. Their teeth were sharp, and that they could expel fire from their skin made them all the more vicious. That and the fact that they tended to swarm and had a penchant for fully cleaning their kill and leaving nothing but bits of glistening bones.

"Maybe we should—"

"There they are!" a voice cried out from behind us.

We all turned.

Coming out of the woods behind us were two Dark wizards.

"Mother*fuckers*," I groaned. "Are you *serious*?"

"At last!" one of them cried. "We have found you."

"At last," I mocked, my voice going high-pitched. "You have found us."

They appeared a bit taken aback by my sarcasm. Good. They deserved it. I was having a *fucking good day*.

"You would do well to bite your tongue, apprentice," the Dark said. His hands were twitching at his sides, and I could feel his magic building. He was stronger than the ones at the restaurant weeks before.

"So I've been told." I took a step back and felt Ryan at my side, shoulder to shoulder. Tiggy and Gary were behind us, looking back toward the Dark Woods and the approaching fire geckos, still hidden in the forest.

"Er," the other Dark said. "Why is that tree on fire?"

"Did you light the tree on fire?" the first Dark said. He sounded as if he were offended. "This is an old-growth forest. That tree is at least three hundred years old! Why would you murder it? They're not made to burn. They're made to hug and give us oxygen and shade on a hot summer day."

Great. Hippie Darks. Fantastic. "I didn't *murder* it," I said.

"Did you hug it before you sent it up in flames?" he demanded.

"How is this your life?" Ryan asked, staring at me.

"Why are you looking at me like this is *my* fault?" I asked.

"Because you're the common denominator in all the crazy," he said. "I thought that much was obvious."

I rolled my eyes as he flourished his sword, obviously trying to show off. It wasn't working. Sort of. My penis thought it was working. "Hey, remember the last time we went up against a bunch of Darks and you were dashing and immaculate. Oh. *Wait*. You weren't. Because you didn't do anything. I did."

"Oh gods," Gary muttered. "Not again."

Impressively, Ryan scowled at me while still keeping his eyes on the Darks. "Please. I so had the situation handled and then you stepped in unnecessarily."

"*Unnecessarily*? There were four Dark wizards and only *one* of you with your little sword!"

"It's *not* little."

"Eh. I've seen bigger." And I had. There were some that even the biggest of men had to hold with two hands to get a good grip on. They were heavy and thick and could never be fisted with a single hand alone.

"That's not what you were saying when it was poking you in the middle of your date," Ryan said. "You know. With *Todd*. Who has *ears*."

"Oh my *gods*," Gary moaned.

"Maybe you should have watched where you were sticking it when you were bending over in front of me," I snapped. "You can't just shove it wherever you want. It's not sanitary."

"Is this… is this what I think it is?" the first Dark said with a frown. "What is this?"

"I have no idea," the second Dark said. "I don't know if I'm being threatened or turned on. It's somewhat frightening that I can't tell the difference."

"Sanitary? I keep it clean!"

"Rubbing it off once a week does *not* count as sanitary."

Tiggy giggled. "That sounds like two things."

"I do it more than once a week," Ryan protested. "Two times a day. At *least*. When I get up and before I go to bed."

"Really? I've never seen you do that."

He rolled his eyes. "Usually, you're asleep when I start. I try to keep quiet so I don't wake you up. I'll make sure you're awake the next time I'm doing it so you can watch me."

Gary started coughing harshly.

"They have to be doing this on purpose," the first Dark said. "Right?"

"I can't tell," the second Dark said. "The UST is killing me, though. They're like Russ and Rochelle from that serial story you read in the newspaper."

"Oooh, you mean 'Companions'? I love that story. It's always will they or won't they and I just want to push their faces together and scream at them to kiss."

"Right? Sort of like now." The Darks both stared at me meaningfully. I glared back at them.

"What the hell is UST?" Ryan asked me. He was back on the defensive, eyeing the Darks in front of us. I could hear the fire geckos getting louder. I didn't know if the Darks had heard them yet. "Is that like a wizarding spell?"

I was sure my face was bright red. "Yes. That's exactly what it is. A wizarding spell. They're trying to hex us. With all their UST."

"Really," the Dark the First said flatly. "That's what you're going with."

"And it's not *our* UST," Dark the Second said.

"Don't even try it," Gary said. "You won't get anywhere. Trust me on that. It's like talking to emotionally constipated brick walls."

"Are we going to fight or is this another one of those times when I think there is going to be fighting but instead there's talking?" Ryan asked.

"How close?" I gritted out to Gary.

"A minute, maybe less."

"When I say run, you run."

"You have a plan?" Gary asked.

"Yes. Running. Running is my plan."

"Why are we running?" Ryan muttered. "We can take them. There's only two of them."

"And a shitload of fire geckos," I reminded him, "that want to set you on fire, then eat you."

"I'm not scared of little lizards," he scoffed.

"Then you can stay here," I said. "It's been nice knowing you. Tiggy, you know what to do. Sack of potatoes."

Tiggy grinned and popped his knuckles.

"Why don't you just do some magic?" Ryan asked, and for some reason, his pupils dilated and his voice went slightly hoarse. "You could... uh. You know. Do magic. All over them. Just. Get it out there and *do* it."

"*Oh my gods*," Gary said. "Seriously? *That's* what does it for you?"

"Does what?" I asked. "What the hell? And I just can't *do* magic *all over them*." Even though I probably could. I couldn't tell him I didn't want to take the chance of us getting swarmed by fire geckos and me unable to do anything to stop them from hurting him. Them. Stop the fire geckos from hurting *them*.

"What are they whispering about?" Dark the First asked.

"Gods only know," Dark the Second said. "Do you hear that? Sounds like... rumbling."

"Must be your stomach. You didn't eat breakfast. I *told* you to eat breakfast."

"You know I'm not a breakfast person."

"What does that even *mean*? *Everyone* eats breakfast. You don't hear people saying they're not a *lunch* person or not a *dinner* person."

"I just don't like chewing in the mornings," Dark the Second said. "There's something weird about walking up from sleeping for eight hours and then putting food in your mouth."

"How is that *weird*?" Dark the First asked incredulously. "Literally everyone does it. Literally."

"I really wish you'd stop saying literally," Dark the Second said. "I literally don't think you understand what that word means."

"We should probably try and put that tree fire out," Dark the First said. "It's *literally* hurting me to watch it burn."

"Stop," the second Dark moaned. "I'm begging you. Please stop."

"You're *literally* begging me."

"No I'm—wait. That one was right. I *was* literally begging you. Okay, maybe you get it now. Sort of. Just restrict your future uses as much as possible and we'll be fine and why are they running away?"

And we were. As soon as I gave the signal, Ryan squawked as Tiggy picked him up and threw him over his shoulder like a sack of potatoes, running in the opposite direction of the Darks. Gary quickly followed, little plumes of dust kicking up around his hooves, the packs on his back sliding left and right.

I took up the rear, looking back over my shoulder as the Darks shouted after us. The air around Dark the First began to shimmer and I knew. And even though he was too far away for me to hear him speak, I knew the words that were going to come out of his mouth, what his first attack would be. It was in the shift in the air. The flash of blue, cold and electric. The hairs on my arm stood on end as the smell of ozone filled my nose.

The fire geckos roared in the woods, already near the edge.

Dark the First muttered dark syllables.

His hands twitched and he began to conduct his symphony, thunder loud and lightning struck.

Electricity bolted from his hands, arcing toward me. I had the time to hear Ryan shout in warning, a cry filled with fear and anguish, and I felt my magic settle even further, another piece of the cornerstone locking into place, whether I wanted it to or not. It felt like ease and wonderment and coming home home *home*. I was bright and heartsore because it was a *taste* of what it could be like. A mere shadow of how great it could be.

But it was enough for this moment. For now. For good.

I didn't have to think or speak. There was something flitting along the edges of my vision and tongue, like memory or déjà vu. It rankled that it was so close, like a dream faded but not forgotten. Not completely.

The lighting struck the palm of my left hand that I'd raised in front of me. It coursed up my arm and everything was blue blue *blue*, and it tripped and stuttered over my heart as it crawled along my chest. For a moment, I thought to take it in, to take this wizard's magic and make it my own, to pull it inside and keep it there. It'd be so easy, especially with yet another piece of the cornerstone solidified in place. But there wasn't enough time. The fire geckos were at the edge of the forest, and I could hear their growls and snarls, the snap of their jaws and teeth, the scrape of their claws. A burst of fire erupted from the edge of the woods as the lightning crackled in me, wrapping itself around me, and I thought how *easy* it would be. Not to absorb it. To redirect it. To make it my own.

Only a few seconds had passed since the electricity first hit my hand. The last bit slunk in through my skin as the Dark's eyes widened. I raised my other hand and pointed it toward the Dark Woods, and there was no need for words, no need for complicated hand movements. One moment the lightning was circling my heart and the next it was flowing out of me as the first of the fire geckos breached the tree line, eyes blazing.

Everything felt *blue*.

And the lightning left me then. Just like I'd allowed it in. It curled down my arm, bits and pieces arcing out along my skin before shooting off toward the approaching geckos. They screamed as the ground erupted around them, bodies seizing and fire spitting.

And then it was silent.

"So," Dark the First said. "That was a thing that happened."

"Yeah," Dark the Second said, sounding like he was choking. "It did."

I took a deep breath and let it out slowly. A line of fire geckos lay charred and smoking along the side of the road. I could hear more in the woods. It must have been quite the pack of them.

"He's still coming with us," Dark the First said, steeling his resolve.

Dark the Second snorted. "Yeah. Okay. You go get him, then."

I said, "Come and get me." Like a *badass*.

Dark the First hesitated. "Or maybe we'll just let him go."

Dark the Second said, "That sounds like a better plan."

They ran one way.

I ran the other.

I took a moment to think of *syl* and *bre* and a sharp breeze blew back behind me, blowing my scent and the smell of burned gecko toward the Darks. When the remaining geckos burst from the tree line, they didn't even look in my direction. Their nostrils flared and they growled, skittering along the ground as they took off after the Darks.

I looked up ahead and the road curved around a shallow bend. I took the curve and skidded to a halt. Gary, Tiggy, and Ryan were stopped in the roadway, staring at me. Tiggy still had Ryan over his shoulder, but Ryan had moved almost to a sitting position, his hands in Tiggy's hair.

I didn't know I'd had an audience.

I really should have expected it.

Nosy bastards.

"Heeey," I said, waving a hand at them, going for nonchalant and failing miserably.

"What," Gary said.

"Sparklies," Tiggy said.

"Ungh," Ryan said.

Silence.

Then, "I don't suppose there's a chance you didn't see any of that."

"Saw everything," Gary said.

"Lizards get fried," Tiggy said.

"Ungh," Ryan said.

More silence.

"Well, then. So. Look. I'm a *wizard*. These things are *expected*."

"You redirected lightning that was shot at you by a Dark wizard and used it to take out half a pack of fire geckos," Gary said, sounding slightly hysterical. "What part of that is *expected*?"

"Magic Sam is powerful Sam," Tiggy said. "Fizz bang snapple crack."

"How do you *do* that?" Ryan asked, voice very, very hoarse.

"Uh," I said. "Magically?" Good argument.

"Gross," Gary muttered.

"You poking my ear," Tiggy said to Ryan. "Knight Delicious Face poking my ear."

Ryan flushed even further. "It's just my sword," he said stiffly.

"So gross," Gary said.

"Let's move on before they come back," I said, hoping that was the end of the conversation.

Of course it wouldn't be that easy.

I was walking away when Gary said, "Sam."

I stopped, curling my hands into fists at my sides. I didn't turn around.

"I've known wizards," he said, and I knew the others were listening with the same intent. "Met even more. There are limits. Hard limits as to what they can do. Magic is not the be-all, end-all. It's not infinite. I know, because my *own* magic is not infinite. Not even when I had my horn."

"And?" I said.

"You," he said, and I could hear the love and reverence in his voice. But it was covering up an awe that sounded almost like fear. "You can do things that I've never seen before. That no one has ever seen before. Sam. Look at me."

And I did. Because he was my friend. I turned and looked at Gary. At Tiggy. And at Ryan. I looked at Ryan and wondered just how afraid for my heart I was. We were so close now. Tarker Mills was visible in the distance. Beyond that on the horizon were the Northern Mountains, great peaks that rose high and disappeared into the clouds. Between those peaks lay a keep with a dragon and a prince. We were so close to what we'd come for, and my heart hurt at the thought of how, while this was just the beginning for Tiggy, Gary, and me, it was going to be the end of Ryan and me. We'd save the Prince and part ways. The next time I'd see him, he would be married to Justin and I would be the same, a wizard's apprentice without a cornerstone. The time apart would dull the sharp edges of the hurt, and with luck, any feelings would have started to fade. Maybe one day, I'd be able to look back on this adventure and think to myself that my first heartbreak made me stronger. Made me better.

"Sam," Gary said, "just how powerful are you?"

Because they never knew. Morgan, Randall made sure no one did. There were things that couldn't be discussed. This had been one of them. But they'd figure it out. Sooner rather than later, especially once we got to Castle Freesias.

So I said the only thing I could. "I don't think anyone really knows. Come on. We're almost to the end."

CHAPTER 19
Things Are About to Get Corny

MY SELF-REFLECTION and obviously extraordinarily valid man pain and angst came to a crashing halt only fifteen minutes later.

"So. Much. *Corn*," I breathed.

"Oh no," Gary said. "Sam—"

Because there *was*. It was still very early in the season, but fields upon *fields* stretched with tiny corn stalks, and all I could picture in my head was months down the road when they'd be taller than *I* was and how *everyone* was going to need Sam of Wilds's Amazing Fireworks Corn because *how else would they know when the corn was ready*? Sure, these people had probably been growing corn for hundreds of years, but they didn't know what I knew! And there was no person in existence that didn't like fireworks, which was why my idea was so brilliant to begin with.

Fuck Morgan and his insistence that it would never work.

In fact.

"Morgan!" I bellowed when he answered the summoning crystal. "You magnificent bastard. The corn! The *corn*."

"No," Morgan said. "No. Sam. *No*."

"You don't understand. There is *acres* of it. It goes on as far as I can see. And I *can see very far*."

"Sam."

"Morgan. Listen. I am giving you a once-in-a-lifetime opportunity here. You can be part of all of *this*." I waved the crystal around to show him.

He sighed. "Sam, you realize I can't actually see anything, right?"

"You have a very vivid imagination."

"Do I?" he said, dry as I'd ever heard him.

"Business partners!" I said, not willing to be deterred. "Sure, it'll take some time to build up the capital, and I'll probably need you to invest in the startup. Maybe half. Okay. I lied. All of it. I'm pretty sure I don't have any money. Well, I do, but you keep it in the banks and won't let me touch it."

"Because you want to make firework corn."

"To be fair," Gary said, "there is a lot of corn. And when it burns down the fields, it'll probably go quickly. I don't think anyone will suffer when they burn. Too much."

"I will leave you in the Dark Woods," I hissed at him.

"Sam, there will be no firework corn," Morgan said. "I think it might be time that you let that one go."

I glared at the crystal in my hands. "You know, Morgan, when you took me to the castle the first time, I wish you'd told me that your main job was to crush dreams."

"Because you would have done what, exactly?"

"Given you more hugs because your soul is obviously black and withered."

"Crisis averted," he said, and with that, I was filled with such an ache. It'd been weeks since I'd seen Morgan. He was my mentor, but more than that, he was my friend. Our magic was entwined, and not for the first time, I wondered if he could be my cornerstone. I'd never asked him if wizards could do that for each other. He calmed me, but it didn't necessarily settle my magic. But maybe I hadn't tried hard enough.

Deep down, I knew, though. Deep down, I thought it might only be Ryan. Even if Morgan had told me that there could be others, in my secret heart, in the place that wished to the stars, there was only Ryan.

"Uh-oh," Gary said.

"What?" Morgan asked.

"Sam is having an overabundance of feelings."

"I get hugs," Tiggy said. "Sam has feelings, Tiggy gets hugs."

"What brought this on?" Morgan sighed.

"I miss your face," I told the crystal. "I love you and you are my friend and I don't think I tell you enough that we should be friends forever. Because we should. Five hundred years from now, we should still be talking about firework corn. I will never leave you. Ever."

"Does he do this often?" Ryan whispered to Gary.

"Only when Morgan pretends that he doesn't love Sam even though it's obvious he thinks Sam is the greatest thing in the world," Gary whispered back.

My eyes were wide. "You think I'm the greatest thing in the world?" I said into the crystal.

"Notice how that was Gary saying that," Morgan said. "Not me."

"I wish I was a bard so I could write a song for you," I said, ignoring him completely. "It wouldn't be like 'Cheesy Dicks and Candlesticks.'"

Morgan coughed loudly. "I don't even want to know."

"I don't think most of us do know," Ryan said. "Or, at least, I don't. Is it normal to be in a constant state of what the fuck with these three? I feel like that's normal."

"Yes," Morgan said. "Every day. All the time. Some days, you even think you're getting used to it only to realize you're not."

"Don't say fuck!" I growled at Ryan. "Remember your place!"

He rolled his eyes and I did not find that attractive. At all. "Sorry," he said. "I meant to say mothercracker."

"Morgan!"

"Sam."

"You are so cool, you are so awesome," I sang. "You give me feelings that make my heart blossom."

They all stared at me. I'm pretty sure Morgan did too, even if he couldn't see me.

"What?" I asked. "It was good."

"Good being the operative word," Gary muttered.

"Hugs?" Tiggy asked. "I not have hugs yet."

"You shouldn't sing," Ryan said hastily. "It... burns."

"Morgan liked it," I said. "Didn't you, Morgan?"

"That is certainly something you would say," Morgan said.

"Guess what it was called?"

"Do I have to?"

"No. Because I'll just tell you."

"Sam—"

"It was called 'Dear Brother-Uncle-Father: An Ode to the Fiery Depths of My Feelings for Your Personage.'"

"You capitalized that, didn't you?"

"You bet your sweet ass I did," I said. "Now it's *official*."

"Sam."

"Morgan."

"No corn. Get to Tarker Mills. Find the keep. Rescue the Prince. Go to Randall. Are these instructions in any way unclear?"

"You know that song I just sang for you?" I asked him. "I take it back."

"I weep," Morgan said. "A word in private, if I may."

I looked up at the others. "Shoo. Secret wizarding business."

"Says the apprentice," Gary coughed.

"What?"

"Nothing," he said sweetly. "Ryan, Tiggy. Away with us. While we wait, I can regale you with the time that Sam was running from a mermaid and somehow ended up naked in a tree."

"You *promised*," I snapped at him.

"I lied," he said as he ushered Ryan and Tiggy away. "So it all started with this mermaid named Abigail who decided she wanted Sam to eat her flounder, if you know what I mean...."

When they were out of earshot, Morgan said, "Mermaid, Sam? Do I even want to know?"

"No. Definitely not. It was this whole... *thing* that turned into an *ordeal* and did you know getting splinters in your ass is not a fun way to spend a Tuesday?"

"I can't say that I do. Especially on Tuesdays."

"So what's up, mentor-mine? Everyone is gone now. You can tell me you miss me without embarrassment."

"You have enough embarrassment for the both of us," he said.

"Yeah, yeah. I hear the words you aren't saying. I love you too. No one believes me that you're secretly a big ball of sap."

"Lies," he said. "All of it."

"Uh-huh."

"Sam."

"Morgan."

"Crap," he said. "Now I *am* going to sound like a big ball of sap."

I grinned. "Go ahead. I won't tell everyone the moment we get done speaking. That would just be rude."

"How's the situation with Ryan?"

And, of course, my smile faded. "Right for the heart. Good aim."

"I find it's easier than dancing around words."

I glanced down the road to make sure the others were far enough away. Ryan's head was rocked back, his mouth open as he laughed, undoubtedly at Gary's story about my naked tree mermaid adventure. It was a good look on him.

Who was I kidding? All looks were good looks on him.

So I lied. "It's fine. I'm handling it."

But, of course, it was Morgan I was talking to. "Sam."

"We danced," I said suddenly. "In a tavern when the song was slow. He asked me to dance and I said yes."

"Why?"

"Because I could. Because I wanted to. Because I wanted to know what it was like to have something that I'll never actually have."

"I wish," he said and then stopped. He took a breath and let it out slowly. I could picture him, sitting in the labs, his face scrunched up in concentration. His forehead lined, eyes narrowed. The tip of his tongue sticking out between his teeth like he did when deep in thought. "I wish things could be different for you."

I laughed. It wasn't nearly as bitter as I thought it'd be. "I know. And that's why I love you."

"You're almost done."

"Am I?"

"With this part, yes. It's all about the journey, Sam. One day you'll get your ending, but until then, remember it's about the journey. The things you've learned. The future you'll have. I know it may not seem like it right now, and I know it might hurt, but you will be okay. You're my apprentice. I expect nothing less of you."

"I wish you were here," I admitted to him. "It might get tough."

"I wish I was too," he said. "But I also know you're stronger than anyone else I've ever met."

And who knows what we might have said then. How long we might have sat there, spewing our feelings at each other until we were drowning in sunshine and rainbows and Gary's cookie poop. When I have an abundance of feelings, I tend to go on for days. It's a proven fact.

And I tried to work up the courage to tell him about the lightning. About how I'd been able to redirect it through my body and hold it around my heart. How the ceiling to my magic just seemed further and further away, and maybe for the first time, I felt an inkling of fear that there was no ceiling, that it could eventually consume me until I was nothing but a collection of energy with no conduit for release.

I opened my mouth to say something. *Anything.*

But it was ceremoniously cut short when I saw a stranger talking to Gary, Tiggy, and Ryan. My hand tensed around the crystal as green and gold flickered around the edges of my vision.

Tiggy and Ryan looked relaxed. Carefree.

Gary, though. Gary looked slightly off. He was holding himself stiffly.

"Hey," I said to Morgan. "Gotta go. There's someone on the road."

"Okay. Just watch yourself. I don't know much about Tarker Mills, and I don't need you getting captured by Darks or fairies or mermaids or—"

"I get it," I said, cutting him off. "And it doesn't happen *that* often."

"—or selkies or pissed off traveling merchants or that one guy who pledged a blood vendetta against you—"

"That was *not* my fault." It was in my early days of learning to use magic and I'd accidentally set a guy's hair on fire. I'd put it out before it had caused any damage, but Evil Carl (as he had so named himself) didn't care. It was an affront to him and he swore vengeance against me and promised one day, I would rue the day I ever heard the name Evil Carl.

Naturally, unable to keep my mouth shut, I told him I was already ruing. That's when the blood vendetta came into play, blah, blah, blah, and I'd never heard from him again. I rarely thought about it. It was just one of those things that happened to me.

"I get into shenanigans," I told Morgan.

"So I've noticed. We still need to finish our conversation." I couldn't tell if that was a warning or a threat. "But it can wait. Find the keep and let me know what you see before you approach. Understood?"

"Yeah, love you, boo," I said and broke the connection before he could squawk righteously at me as he was wont to do. I stowed the crystal in an inner pocket in my tunic and walked down the Old Road toward Tarker Mills.

Gary, Tiggy, and Ryan looked back at me upon my approach.

"And this is Sam of Wilds," Gary said. His voice was even, but he still held himself stiffly. "The apprentice to the King's Wizard."

The stranger was an older woman. She wore a long flowing dress, green and orange and red. Her hair was gray and braided in a thick ponytail that rested over her shoulder and against her breast. There was a sash of sorts across her chest. No weapons that I could see. She looked sweet and kind, like a grandmother should. Tiggy and Ryan seemed charmed by her. Gary was not.

"It is an honor to meet you, Wizard," she said, ignoring the *apprentice* that Gary muttered under his breath. Her voice was calm and serene. I felt myself relaxing just by the few words she spoke. "I am Eloise, the mayor of Tarker Mills. I understand you have traveled far." She held out her hand and I took it briefly. Her skin was warm and smooth. She dropped my hand a moment later.

"Ma'am," I said politely. "You've got a lot of corn."

"That we do." She sounded amused. "We're the main supplier to the northern region of Verania. The mountains aren't conducive to such a crop. Tarker Mills has fed many people over the centuries. We're quite proud of what we do here."

I was closer to her now. I could see the lines around her eyes and mouth. The pattern on her dress. The intricate design on the sash across her chest, angles and planes that curved into purposed design.

Near the top of the sash, at her shoulder, was the pattern of a dragon stitched in great detail. Black with mottled wings.

Huh.

How about that.

I averted my eyes quickly.

But she was sly, that Eloise.

She said, "Word has spread about your quest."

"Has it? People tend to talk too much."

She smiled. "They do. But it is an epic undertaking, is it not? To rescue a stolen prince." She glanced over at Ryan. "My condolences for your loss."

"I haven't lost anything," he said. "Just temporarily misplaced. We'll get him back soon enough."

"Will you?" she asked, and I knew now why Gary was uneasy. "That's good to hear." She looked back at me. Her eyes were big and blue. "I was telling your companions how honored we were to have you come to our little village. We don't often get visitors of your caliber all the way out here. You must let us house you for the night before you continue on down the road."

"Sounds good," I said before anyone else could speak. "It will be nice to have a warm bed for a change."

She nodded before her eyes flicked over my shoulder. I looked back and saw black smoke rising above the tree line. Fucking fire geckos.

And redirected lightning that I had no idea how I did. Aside from the fact that I somehow *willed* it so.

"Uh," I said. "Yeah. About that. Fire geckos, man. Just… a bunch of fire geckos. Nothing else."

"Yes," she said, all calm and level and so fucking *tranquil.* "We do have a bit of a problem with them out here. Nasty creatures, those. I'll have some people from the village watch the fire to make sure it doesn't jump the road. It's the absolute worst thing to have any sort of flame near the corn. Why, only a madman would think otherwise."

"Ha," Tiggy said. "Firework corn. Poor Sam. Ideas all broken and sad."

I glared at him.

Eloise turned back toward Tarker Mills, and Ryan and Tiggy followed. Gary and I purposely fell behind.

"She's weird, right?" he whispered to me. "Gave me the heebie-jeebies."

"Maybe it's just that she seems so nice," I whispered back. "We don't know many nice people. We don't know *any* nice people."

"I'm nice."

"You're bitchy."

"Close enough."

"Look, just keep your eyes open, okay? No separating. Keep any questions and answers as vague as possible. Don't let anyone approach you from behind without you knowing it."

"You should let Ryan approach you from behind."

"*Gary.* Now is not the time."

He snorted. It came out periwinkle and mint. "It's always the time for you getting sexed up in the butt."

"I'm going to feed you to Eloise because I bet they turn out to be cannibals."

"Nah, they'll be witches in disguise that need your fingernails for a potion."

"Fuck."

"Yeah. That sounds about right."

TARKER MILLS was a small hamlet set against the backdrop of the Northern Mountains miles in distance. The buildings and house were built of wood and mud and brick. There were men and women in the fields working with the corn. People smiled at us as we entered the village, waving and saying hello and making us feel more welcome than any other place we'd been before.

It was all bullshit.

No one could ever be that nice.

It was eerie and off-putting.

Vaguely, I wondered if maybe I was just too cynical, but I pushed that away because no, I had a healthy amount of cynicism and Tarker Mills was creepy.

So I gave them my own creepy smile back, wide and welcoming.

And they smiled wider. I almost expected them to burst into song, to sing about how wonderful the world was and how perfect people were, and love and rainbows and butterflies and puppies. And, of course, cheesy dicks and candlesticks.

They didn't, but I'm sure it was close.

A feast! they said. *A feast for the travelers.*

Eloise smiled and decreed it so.

As we were paraded around Tarker Mills, long wooden tables were brought out to the center of town, covered in blue and green tablecloths. We were handed mugs of mead and wine and ushered toward the tables.

Great plates of food were brought out. Cornbread. Corn tortillas. Corn soup. Corn on the cob. Corn casseroles. Cream corn. Corn salad.

"You guys really like your corn," Ryan said.

"Oh, Knight Commander," a man laughed. "You're just being *corny*."

Everyone laughed except for us. Because it wasn't funny.

It was terrifying.

Sex puns I could understand.

Corn puns were beyond my realm of comprehension.

I smiled weakly and ate more corn.

Gary, Tiggy, and Ryan followed suit.

There were about fifty people altogether in Tarker Mills. There didn't seem to be any children, which I thought was odd. Everyone appeared to be my age or older, and from what I could see, Eloise was the oldest person in the village.

"What brings you this far north?" Eloise asked from her spot at the head of the table.

I looked up and found all eyes on me. I put down my fork slowly and rested my hands on the table. "Our quest," I said slowly. Because she'd been the one to bring it up first and now she was acting like she didn't know.

Eloise arched an eyebrow. "Oh? How exciting."

I smiled at her. "Very. That's an interesting sash you're wearing."

She reached up and touched it briefly. "Thank you. It was handmade here in Tarker Mills."

A clue! "The detail is very... detailed," I said. Then I tried to hold back the wince because holy fuck, that was not subtle.

Gary groaned, but he was too far away for me to try and kick him.

"It's all about the details, don't you think?" Eloise asked.

"Usually," I agreed. "Details are important."

"What is important to you, Sam?"

"I'm not sure I understand your question."

"You don't? I thought it very simple."

"Then why don't you go first."

"Unity," she said promptly. "Being united under a common purpose."

"Corn?" I asked.

She grinned. "Mostly."

"There are rumors," I said.

"Aren't there always?"

"Of a keep."

"A keep. How fascinating."

"I haven't even gotten to the most fascinating part yet," I said.

"Do continue," she said, leaning forward, elbows on the table. The rest of the town had stopped eating and listened intently.

"It's supposed to be right near here," I said. "In a valley near the mountains. We think the Prince is being held there." I tilted my head forward and whispered loudly, "By a *dragon*."

"Oooooh," the people of Tarker Mills breathed as one.

"Girl, preach it," Gary muttered through a mouthful of cornmeal.

"Pretty Gary," Tiggy said, running a hand over Gary's mane. "My face feel funny." He laughed loudly and I couldn't help but chuckle. I reached down and picked up the fork, scooping up more corn *something* and taking a huge bite. I was feeling a lot better about being here. I didn't know what I was so worried about. I gave Ryan what I hoped was a saucy wink and he grinned at me, bright and beautiful, and I opened my mouth to tell him as much when—

"A dragon, you say?" Eloise asked. "That sounds frightening. Are you frightened, Sam?"

"No," I said immediately. "Not about that."

"Oh. What frightens you, then?"

I opened my mouth to tell her that I didn't think this was the right time to discuss my fears (especially surrounded by strangers), but instead, I said, "Snakes. Failure. Not being able to live up to my potential. Letting my parents down. Letting Morgan down. Not being able to find Gary's horn. Not rescuing the Prince in time and having to face the King. Randall telling me that there's nothing he can do to help me. The extent of my magic. Ryan figuring out that he's my—*holy god, why am I still talking?*"

"Because we're all friends here," Eloise said. "Don't you want to be our friend?"

"No. Because I think you and this town are creepy as fuck and I'm highly suspicious of you because I think you're hiding something." I frowned. "And I didn't meant to say that out loud."

She frowned at me. "That wasn't very nice."

"I feel floaty," Tiggy said, corn still stuck to his chin. "Floaty Tiggy say good-bye."

"I would float away with you," Gary told him. "You, me, and Sam can float away and maybe Ryan because I think I might actually be starting to like him. But don't tell Ryan I said that, okay?"

"You like me?" Ryan asked, smiling bigger. "For sure now?"

"Tiggy," Gary hissed. "I told you not to tell him."

"Gary likes me," Ryan told me. "And that's good because I think I adore him. Whenever I see him, I want to smile."

I ground my teeth together as hard as I possibly could to keep from opening my mouth, but there was this *compulsion* I couldn't fight, so I blurted out, "I like you too! I like you *more* than Gary. There's no contest. My like for you is legendary."

"That's true," Gary said, eyes glazed just a tad. "I don't think there's anyone that likes you more than Sam. After all, you're his corner—"

"It's the truth," I said, trying to fight against the weight of my tongue, the need within to spill everything. I shook my head and squeezed my hands into fists. I glared up at Eloise. "What did you do to us?"

"Coercion," she said, the smile still on her face. "Truth. Mistletoe mixed with elven berries and fire from the geckos and the tongues from a chimera mixed into the corn. We only speak the truth here in Tarker Mills. We have no place for lies and deceit, Sam of Wilds. While you're here, you'll only speak in truth, and your magic won't be able to touch us."

The people of Tarker Mills nodded in agreement.

"You all take this?" I asked.

"Yes," a man across from me said. "Every day, Eloise allows us to eat the truth so we may speak it at all times."

"And let me guess," I said. "Eloise doesn't have to eat the truth herself."

"She doesn't have to," a woman said. "She *is* the truth."

I looked back at Eloise. "What are you?"

"What are *you*?" she asked.

"A wizard's apprentice," I said promptly and against my will. "Though I don't know if I'll ever become a full-fledged wizard. I don't know if I have the strength."

Shut up, shut up, shut up!

"And why is that?"

It was no use. "Because of what I am. Who I am supposed to be." It poured out from me, and try as I might, I could do nothing to stop it. I tried to call on my magic, but it seemed to be so far away that it was inconsequential.

"And that is?"

"The most powerful wizard in an age," I said, putting as much force behind my words as I could. It was rewarding to see Eloise's eyes widen slightly. "I can do things that others can only dream about."

"Ungh," Ryan said. "That shit is so hot."

Everyone turned to stare at him.

He was bright red. "I said that out loud, didn't I? Dammit."

"*What?*" I squeaked.

"When you do magic, it turns me on," Ryan said, shaking his head frantically. "Ah gods. I can't—stop. Just *stop*. Ahhh, I get erections when you cast spells. Oh *shit*."

"Sweet molasses," I managed to say.

"This… this is not what I thought was going to happen today," Gary said.

"What you think happen?" Tiggy asked.

"I thought Ryan and Sam would continue to ignore how much they want to bone each other and we would all be suffering in silence because Sam won't pull his head out of his ass to see that Ryan wants to eat said ass for dinner."

"I do," Ryan said through gritted teeth. "For breakfast, even. And lunch. And a midnight snack. Especially when you do magic."

"You have a *magic* kink?" I said, because that was the *only* thing I could focus on.

"Yes. But only for you. Your magic gets me hard," he said, looking like he wished he could be anywhere but where he was. "When you do anything, I get hard, really. Even your ridiculous sex puns. You remember when you wrapped those Dark wizards in stone at the restaurant?"

"Yeah," I managed to say.

"I wanted to tell you that you gave me an e-rock-tion." He bent over and banged his forehead against the table. "Why, why, *why* did I say that out loud? Please. Someone. Anyone. *Kill me*."

"Sex puns," I breathed. "Knight Delicious Face said a sex pun."

"There it is again!" he exclaimed. "Knight Delicious Face. What is that?"

"You're a knight," I said. "And your face is delicious."

"You think I'm delicious?" he said, suddenly shy.

"Oh my *gods*," Gary moaned. "This is so awkward I can't even stand it. I physically hurt from how awkward this is. I don't even care that we're apparently in mortal danger. I just don't want to listen to you two flirt anymore. Eloise? Yoo-hoo, Eloise? If you're going to kill us, can you please do it now? I can't take this anymore."

Tiggy was poking his face and giggling. "I love everyone," he said. "Except people who hurt Gary and Sam. I smash those people."

Everyone at the tables was staring at us but I couldn't care less because *Ryan fucking Foxheart got boners because of me.*

Just play it cool, Sam. You're under a truth spell, but you got this. Just play it cool.

So I opened my mouth and played it cool.

"I jerked off to the thought of you the day I first saw you," I said, cringing immediately. Not cool! *Not* cool!

"You were *fifteen*," he said, sounding scandalized. "Why did you... I can't even... I jerked off to the thought of you the day after that."

"I was *fifteen*," I said, eyes wide.

"I know," he said. "I felt guilty for three days and then I did it again. Your *mouth*."

"What's wrong with my mouth?"

"Nothing," Ryan said. "Except for the fact that it doesn't have my dick in it and holy *fuck*, this needs to *stop*." He looked horrified.

I was too. Except I also had a boner.

Horrified boners are horrifying.

As was the fact that all I could think about was telling him that he was my cornerstone. Cornerstone. Cornerstone. *Cornerstone. Corner*—"I'm Mervin!" I managed to say instead. It came out strangled, like I was choking.

"How much of this mixture did you give them?" Eloise asked with a frown.

The man across from me said, "Too much. I thought since they were magical, they'd need more. I gave them three times the normal dose." He looked over at me with a contrite look on his face. "I'm so sorry."

"I don't forgive you," I told him. "Like, at all. There is no forgiveness between you and me. In fact, I'm so far from forgiveness that it's a foreign concept to me and I shall never understand it with you. You dick."

The man pouted.

Good. That made me feel good.

"This is going to get worse before it gets better," Eloise said with a sigh.

"Mervin?" Gary asked.

"Mervin," Tiggy said. "No Mervin. You're Sam."

"Mervin?" Ryan said, furrowing his brow. Then he figured it out. "What?"

Don't say it. DON'T SAY IT. "I go to the Ryan Foxheart Fan Club meetings dressed up as a guy named Mervin because I secretly pine for you and your biceps. Also? My muffins were *not* dry and anyone that says otherwise is a lying bastard." I glared at the people of Tarker Mills, daring them to say anything about my muffins.

"I *knew* it," Gary whispered. "I fucking *knew* you were sort of creepy in a sweetly romantic way and did things that most people would consider ridiculous. *You went in disguise to a fan club for Ryan.* Who *does* that?"

"Lovey Sam is creepy Sam," Tiggy agreed.

"I'm also a Foxy Lady," I told everyone even though I wanted to do anything but. "And then Ryan gave me his autograph thinking I was Mervin and he said he was a Sam Girl and I went home that night and put it under my pillow. And I've been to at least thirty meetings and I wish I wasn't saying any of this out loud. So bad." I tried to close my mouth, but I couldn't help but add, "HaveHeart forever!"

"I think this is getting out of hand," Eloise said. "Why don't we—"

"I *knew* that was you," Ryan said. "Okay, well I didn't. But I *did*."

"That doesn't even make sense," I told him. "But that's okay. You don't need to make sense because I'll still lo—*no*." I looked back at Eloise. "You *don't* get to have that. You *don't* get to take that from me."

I tried to pull my magic toward me, and on the edges of my vision, the green and gold fluttered. I stood, pushing my chair back.

"Sit down," Eloise said.

I opened my mouth to tell her to fuck off and then torch this whole fucking village, but instead, I sat down.

"No magic," she said.

The green and gold flitted away as if they were never there at all.

"I seriously despise you," I said truthfully.

She didn't give a damn. "The scorch marks," she said. "Near the tree the fire geckos lit."

"Lightning from Dark wizards," I said. "I took their magic and made it my own."

I thought that would instill the fear of the gods in her, but it only made her cheeks flush and her breath short. "He will be so pleased," she murmured. "What we have brought to him."

"Who?"

"Our Great Father," she said and the people of Tarker Mills bowed their heads in supplication.

"The Great...." I trailed off, my gaze dropping to the sash. Particularly the beast etched near the top. It all clicked into place. "The dragon. You worship the *dragon*?"

"He descended from on high," she said as Tarker Mills quietly agreed with her. "He came to us and we knew we'd found our salvation."

I shook my head. "That doesn't make sense. The dragon hasn't been in Verania that long. How long have you known about it?"

"Fifty-seven glorious days," Eloise said.

"Fifty-seven days," I repeated.

"Yes."

"You turned your entire town into a cult in fifty-seven days."

"Not a cult," she snapped. "A *religion*."

"Fifty-seven *days*," I said. "You built an entire religion in less than two months!"

"You sound impressed."

"I *am* impressed," I admitted. "You must be a special kind of crazy if you can create that kind of idolatry in such a short amount of time."

She stood swiftly. "I'm *not* crazy."

"Kind of crazy," Gary said.

"A lot crazy," Tiggy said.

"Crazy and you force-fed your neighbors a compulsion mix," I said. "Come on. Let me use my magic. You're a lady and you look like a grandma, but I still want to hit you right now."

"Do some magic," Ryan whispered to me, right in my ear. "*Slowly*. So I can watch."

"When we get out of here, I'm going to do so much magic all over you," I told him. "You're going to be covered in it." At that moment, I really wished I'd been born mute and had never set eyes on Ryan Foxheart.

"Make it stop!" Gary wailed.

"Yeah. Cover me in your magic." Ryan was blushing so hard, I thought his face was about to explode. "I want to stop talking. You have no idea how much I want to stop talking." He leaned closer and I could feel his breath on my face. It smelled of corn and eroticism.

"Um," Eloise said. "Maybe you guys could—"

We ignored her completely. "I'm going to do so many spells," I said, because it seemed impossible for me to stop. "You won't even believe how many spells I can do. Flora Bora Slam, motherfucker." Our lips were inches apart.

"I want you to Flora Bora Slam *me*," Ryan said and I just *choked*.

"Therapy," Gary said. "I'm going to need so much therapy. It's like watching cows mating and it's wet and sticky and uncomfortable but I can't look away because I'm worried some of it is going to get on me."

"We're not *cows*," I growled at him.

"I'm not very good at metaphors," Gary said. "I try to be, but I'm not. It's something I wish I could be better at. I would also like to learn how to tap dance and make macramé art because I think I'm not worldly enough."

"You think macramé is worldly?"

Apropos of nothing, Tiggy said, "I love chicken. And turtles. And the sky. And shoes."

Gary narrowed his eyes at me. "Yes, *Sam*. I'm sorry if it's not up to your standards of wanting to cover Ryan with your magic."

"That sounds so awesome," Ryan breathed, and I was going to *kiss* him. I was going to fucking *kiss* him and—

"Except you have a fiancé," Gary said and that pretty much brought about the end of any thoughts about kissing I might have had.

Ouch.

I pulled my head away. "You love Justin," I said as my heart clenched. "You love him and want to marry him and have his babies and live in a castle and suck on his dick in the moonlight as he calls you things like babycakes and lovebone."

Lovebone? Eloise mouthed to herself.

He shook his head adamantly. "No, Sam. Listen. It's not like that. It's—"

"*Enough*," Eloise snarled. "No more talking."

We both fell silent. We had no other choice. Ryan looked stricken, like all he wanted to *do* was talk more, to finish his sentence, but the compulsion we were under was powerful and we could only do what Eloise told us.

"Now," she said, "where were we? Ah, yes. The offering."

And I just *knew* she was about to start monologuing, but I could do nothing to stop it. If looks could kill, though, her head would have been severed from her body the moment she opened her mouth.

But apparently Eloise wasn't in the mood to monologue and instead got right down to business. "The Great Father will be here soon enough. We mustn't keep him waiting. Michael, Frank. Would you be so kind as to escort the apprentice to the altar? He has a date with a god."

Two very large men stood up from farther down the table and started stalking toward me. I tried to do something, *anything* to stop them, but whatever mixture they'd overdosed us on was stronger. Gary, Tiggy, and Ryan were fighting against it too, and as the men grabbed me by the arms, my eyes met Ryan's. Sweat tricked down his brow as he tried to move. There was fear in his eyes, but it wasn't for himself. It was meant for me and I wondered, for just a moment, what things could have been like now that we were forced to be open to each other.

I wondered what would have happened.

Then I was struck upside the back of my head and all I knew was dark.

CHAPTER 20
The Sexually Aggressive Dragon

WHEN I came to, I was aware of three things:

First, I had a bitch of a headache.

Second, I hated corn and Tarker Mills with a passion.

Third, Ryan Foxheart wanted to sex me up.

I opened my eyes and became aware of two more things.

I was tied to a post in the middle of a valley on a stone altar with heavy chains wrapped around my chest, arms pinned to my sides.

And I was alone.

"Motherfucker," I muttered.

Maybe I did get captured too much.

I still felt sluggish and heavy, the compulsion elixir still running through me.

Which was just peachy.

I hadn't been out that long, though. The sun was still high in the sky. There were fat white clouds above and bright green grass below. A soft breeze blew through my hair. It smelled sweet. It would have been relaxing had I not been chained to a sacrificial altar and the fact that *I* did not smell sweet. Apparently, at some point during my unconsciousness, I'd been sprayed with what tasted like some kind of meat juice (what I *hoped* was some kind of meat juice and not the pheromones taken from the anal glands of a yak) that I'm sure was supposed to make me more appetizing to any large predators that wanted to eat me.

I wondered just how many people Eloise had done this to.

Or what they were going to do to Gary and Tiggy and Ryan.

I turned my head as far as I could, trying to look behind me. I couldn't see much as the post was very wide. Just the valley stretched out far.

The altar itself looked brand new, the stone smooth and shining in the sun, and I remembered that technically, there had only been a cult to use such an altar for fifty-seven days, and I gave serious thought to Ryan's comment that I really did seem to be the common denominator to Verania's what-the-fuckery.

But then I remembered one time that Morgan had accidentally become an amnesiac bearded lady in a carnival for six months and decided it was more of a wizard thing than a Sam thing.

I felt better after that.

For a couple of minutes at least.

Then I was just bored.

"I'd really like not to be chained in the middle of a field," I told no one in particular.

Ten minutes later.

"CHEESY DICKS and candlesticks! And everything you need! Listen as I sing a verse or six here in this land of sloth and greed!"

Ten minutes after that.

"HEH. RYAN wants to do me. Sweet."

Five minutes after that.

"OH MY *gods*. He wants to *do* me! *What the fuck am I going to do*? He's *engaged* to the *Prince*. Everyone is going to find out and I'll be a home wrecker and I'll be arrested and thrown in the dungeons and poop in buckets and I won't ever see the light of day again. All because I couldn't control my *feelings* and my *erection* and I..."

Thirty-four minutes after that.

"...AND WHAT if he gets married and tries to make me his thing on the *side*? I won't be a godsdamn dirty secret! I'm a fucking *wizard*, and I won't be a *strumpet*, a warm hole for him to dive into when the frigid Prince doesn't feel like getting it up. Fuck you, Ryan Foxheart! Fuck you and everything about you! I don't need this. I was perfectly *fine*..."

Twenty-six minutes after that.

"...AND YOU can sure as shit *bet* that if he makes *me* dress up in a garter belt, I'm going to make *him* wear one too. I'm not going to let his kinks rule over mine. I want to fuck him while he wears nothing but a—oh. That's better."

Because all of a sudden, that heavy, sodden feeling lifted as if it'd never been there at all. I could think clearly. My magic crawled along my skin. I still felt the little tickle at the back of my throat and neck that said *obey, obey, obey*, but it was starting to fade. It wouldn't last that much longer.

And now I was just cranky and pissed off.

The chains didn't appear magicked to bind me in place. There were some halfhearted runes carved into the altar, but they weren't complete and were done with a novice hand. Suddenly the missing people from around Old Clearing made much more sense. They had to have been taken by Eloise's cult and placed here as a sacrifice to the dragon. What a bitch.

My hands twitched at my sides as I pushed the green and gold through the metal around my chest and arms. I didn't even try to speak any ancient earth words. I didn't have to.

The chains collapsed around me.

I stretched and popped my neck.

Flexed my hands.

"You fucked with the wrong wizard," I growled, feeling smug with how badass that sounded.

I felt less smug when I took a step, tripped over my feet, and fell off the altar and belly-flopped onto the ground.

"Not okay," I wheezed, trying to get more air in my lungs as I rolled on my side and curled up into a ball. "I am not okay. Everything hurts. Everything hurts so bad. Just gonna stay here for a while and die. No need to worry about—"

A loud roar echoed across the valley.

"Well fuck me sideways," I said succinctly and looked north.

Sitting on the rim looking down into the valley was a familiar black dragon. It'd only been a few weeks since I'd seen it last, but I was absolutely positive it'd gotten bigger. And angrier. And maybe it had more teeth with which to eat me.

As I watched, it pushed out its wings, the span of them great and awe-inspiring. Well, it would have been awe-inspiring had I not been the subject of its rapt attention. Now it was just terrifying, and all the bravado I'd built up when the chains fell from me fled rather quickly.

My eyes bulged when it brought down its wings in a harsh push, the grass around its feet flailing in the forced wind. The wings went up and then down again, and the dragon lifted up and off the ground.

And I will admit, though it pains me to do so, that instead of having an awesome one-liner that people would quote for decades to come (*You think you can handle me? Fine! Come at me, bro!*), I squeaked, "Holy fucking balls of shit," and tried to stand.

Of course, I tripped again and hit my head against the stone altar and wondered where all those really bright flashing lights had come from.

The ground shook around me as I opened my eyes.

The dragon's massive head peered down at me. Its nostrils flared as it scented what I was now positive was yak anal gland pheromones because that's just how things went for me. Its tongue extended, a great forked thing that rubbed against my face, leaving a thick sticky trail in its wake.

"I'll admit," I said. "This is not one of the top-ten experiences of my life."

"Wizard," the dragon rumbled. "I despise wizards."

"Yes, yes," I said. "You don't like wizards because of my sparkles and my whizbangs."

The dragon reared its head back. "You can understand me?" he said, voice rough and deep.

I rolled my eyes. "Clearly."

He shot forward again, snapping his jaws near my face. His breath was hot and wet. Somehow, I managed to keep the squeaking to a minimum. "You're a pretty thing," he growled. "But I won't hesitate to eat you up. Little tasty boy cake you'd be. I'd let you rest on my tongue before I swallowed you whole."

"That doesn't sound like fun for anyone," I managed to say. "I'm all skin and bones. No meat. It'd be a waste of your time. Honestly."

"How is it you can understand me?" the dragon asked, scraping a giant claw near my side. The grass tore up from the earth, leaving a long dirt gash. "Your kind has never been able to do so before. Tell me, pretty. Tell me before I grow tired of you and start by eating your feet."

"I don't know," I said, and that must have been the wrong answer because his teeth scraped against my dusty boots. "No one knows! I'm just an apprentice."

"Apprentice," the dragon scoffed. "Weak little human."

"Stopped your fire, didn't I?"

The dragon's eyes narrowed. "*Now* I remember you. Your little ice sparkle. You thought yourself so clever. The last time I saw you, you were under a pile of rubble. How is it you survived?"

I shrugged. "It was a weak hit. Maybe don't forget leg day when you're working out."

The dragon hissed. "Shall we find out how weak the hits can be?"

"You think you can handle me?" I said. "Fine! Come at me, bro!"

And once I pulled off that magnificent line, I reached up and punched the dragon in the eye.

"Ow!" it cried as it pulled its head back. "What the *fuck* did you do that for?"

"Ha!" I crowed as I pushed myself to my feet. "Take that, motherfucker!"

"You punched me in the *eye*." It shook its head, blinking rapidly.

"Consider it—" I paused dramatically. "—an eye for an eye." I winced. "Okay, that sounded a lot cooler in my head."

"I don't think that would have sounded *cool* to anyone." It shook its head, apparently trying to clear its vision.

"Hey!"

"Seriously, though," it said. "Of all the places to punch, your first thought is to punch an *eye*. Who does that?"

"You were going to eat me!"

The dragon snorted and a little lick of flame curled out its nose. "I was not, though I'm giving very serious consideration to doing so *now*."

"You can't *threaten* someone with imminent death and not expect some kind of reaction," I retorted.

"It's called *posturing*," the dragon said. "It's what I *do*. You humans keep showing up in my valley, tying yourselves up for no apparent reason. I come down here, roar a little bit, then break the chains and let them leave. They always run. But *nooo*. You had to use your tiny little human hands and *punch me in the eye*."

"I don't have tiny hands," I said, trying to save face. "I'll have you know, I've got *big* hands. Everyone says so." No one said that, but he didn't need to know.

And then it leered at me. "You know what they say about big hands. You big, little wizard?"

"Oh my goodness," I whispered.

It curled up one of its massive paws into a fist and brought it down next to me. It was almost as tall as I was. "So big," I breathed.

"You know what they say," it said, "about big hands."

"Dude," I said. "What?" Then, "Oh *man*. Are you talking about your *dick*?"

"You seem flustered, wizard," the dragon said, leaning close and breathing me in. "You getting turned-on?"

I really, really wasn't. "You said you wanted to fuck me after you wined and dined me!"

"Is that what you want, pretty?" the dragon asked. "I'm a dragon, and maybe if you're lucky, I'll be dragon my balls across your face later."

So, that happened. "Um. That might have been too much."

"Or was it not enough?"

"No. Definitely too much." I started to back away slowly. But for every step I took, the dragon took an answering step and I was always stuck in his shadow.

"Are you adventurous, pretty?" the dragon asked. "And I mean sexually."

"No," I said honestly. "I think I might like rimming, but I've never done it. And also? I don't know if you're sexually adventurous. I think you meant to say sexually aggressive. There's a difference."

"Is that right? I wouldn't know."

"Ugh. That was kind of rapey."

The dragon's eyes narrowed. "I have never raped anything in my life," he said, sounding offended. "Everyone wants a piece of this."

"Because of the size of your… hand."

And then, just because my day apparently could use a bit more weird, the dragon actually smiled. It looked like he had thousands of teeth. "It's a big hand," he agreed, taking another step.

"You took something from the King," I said.

"Did I?" the dragon growled. "And what might that be?"

"You know."

"Say it."

"The Prince."

"Ah," the dragon said. "I'm sorry, but your prince is in another castle."

"What?" I was confused. What other castle?

It sighed. "You young people today. Never respecting the classics."

"Is he alive?" I asked, refusing to let the dragon distract me any further.

"Maybe I ate him," the dragon said.

That stopped me. "You wouldn't."

"How do you know? Expert on dragons, are you?"

"Hey! I can talk to you, can't I? How many other people can do that?"

"True," it said. "But I haven't yet decided if that's a revelation or an annoyance. It could go either way." It snapped its jaws at me again. I would have rolled my eyes, but I was too busy taking a step back in absolute terror. I was pretty sure it was justified. Big teeth are scary teeth.

"You said you let other people go who are tied up here," I said.

"Right. Well. Grr. Rawr. I'm a ferocious beast and all that. And speaking of, why *are* people always tied up here?"

"Seriously?"

It cocked its head at me and waited.

"Oh man," I said. "You're going to be *insufferable* when you find out."

"Find out what?"

"So, you know that village outside the valley?"

"Yes," it said. "I chase their sheep sometimes."

"To eat them?"

The dragon grimaced. "No, not to *eat* them. I just like the little noises they make when they run screaming from me. You sound just like them."

"I do *not* sound like frightened sheep!"

He jerked his head at me and I might have shrieked. Slightly.

The dragon chuckled. "Pretty little sheep wizard."

"You're a dick," I muttered.

"This has been said before. The village?"

I groaned. "They might have built a cult and made you their central deity and the people tied up out here are sacrifices made to you because they think you're a god or something. No big deal. One time, someone bought me a sandwich because I'm an apprentice to the King's Wizard. Same thing."

I didn't know much about dragons. But I will say that I never gave much thought to a dragon being able to look smug. But now I did because the fucker *preened*. "Is that right?" it said. "A god, you say? *Sacrifices*, you say? Well now. This certainly changes many, many things."

"We need to go back," I said. "The people there are awful and they eat too many corn-based foods. We have to stop them. They have my friends and—"

"Nope," the dragon said. "Not yet. There's something you have to do for me. As a god, I command you."

"Um. Go fuck yourself."

"Maybe later, pretty. I'd like to see what that mouth of yours can do, even if you are a wizard."

"You son of a—"

And before I could move, before I could even formulate a plan to defend myself against a creature that towered above me and blocked out the sun, I was in its claws, and those great wings rose up and down. The wind roared around me. And then we were up, up, *up*, and I screamed, "You fucking *asshole*!"

The dragon just grunted.

The ground fell away below me and I learned rather quickly that my body was not okay with heights. And flying. And that I had an extraordinary fear of falling from high places and so I might or might not have upchucked copious amounts of corn as we passed through a cloud.

"That's disgusting," the dragon said, turning its head to look back at me. I wanted to irrationally point out that I would rather it pay attention to where it was flying to and not stare at me. "I'd appreciate it if you didn't vomit on me anymore. I just took a bath."

"I'd *appreciate it* if you'd let me go!" I shouted back at it.

"Are you sure about that?"

"I've never been more sure of anything in my life!"

"Okay," the dragon said with a shrug.

And then he opened his claws and dropped me.

I decided right then and there that the dragon and I would never be friends.

The wind roared around my ears as I plummeted toward the earth. I told myself that I was a *wizard* for fuck's sake, that I could very easily think of a way out of this, but instead of *actually* thinking of a way out of this, I screamed quite loudly.

They say that moments before your death, life flashes before your eyes.

That's pretty much bullshit.

Because in those moments before your death, all you can focus on is *your impending death*. I thought about how much it was going to hurt. I thought about what it would look like when someone stumbled upon me. Would I be recognizable as a human being? Or would I just look like a big puddle of meat and blood and bone? My mom and dad would be sad, and Morgan would be too. Randall would probably be relieved that I couldn't turn his nose into a cock anymore. Gary and Tiggy would mourn me for life because of the best friend code and would most likely never recover because I was that awesome.

And Ryan. Well. At least Ryan wouldn't want to bone me anymore. Sucks, that. I really wanted to find out what that felt like. Ryan. And boning.

I opened my eyes to accept my immediate future like a man and saw the dragon falling in front of me, eyes amused as it watched me. Its wings were curled around its body, free falling in tandem with me.

"Having fun?" it shouted at me.

"*NO, I'M NOT HAVING FUN!*" I bellowed.

"Oh! That's too bad. I couldn't tell from all the screaming."

"*YOU FUCKER! SAVE ME!*"

"Ask me nicely," it said, somehow able to look *bored*.

I almost said I would rather die, but that would have been a lie and the ground was getting *really fucking close*. So I put on my big-boy pants and roared, "*PLEASE, YOU FUCKING DICKBAG TOAST WHORE!*"

"I don't even know what that meant," it said, but then its wings snapped open and those claws shot out and wrapped around my middle. The wings caught an updraft and the descent was slowed immediately, so much so that my back cracked from the force of it. The dragon pumped its wings, and we rose back up toward the sky.

"I'll be honest," I told it tiredly. "I believe I've shit myself."

"Gross," the dragon said. "Learn to live a little, drama queen."

"You drop me again and I'll turn you inside out."

"Oooh, so scary. Will you do that with your tiny little human arms?"

"I work out!"

It waited.

"Well. Okay. Not work out *per se*. I *think* about it. Sometimes. My arms aren't tiny!"

"Too right," it said. "You're going to do me a favor."

"Yeah. About that. No." I was still trying to figure out if I'd actually shit myself. I hoped not. There'd be more corn.

"Uh-oh," it said. "My grasp is slipping."

And his grip around me loosened.

I screamed bloody murder and held on to one of his claws.

"Gods," it said. "You're loud for having tiny arms."

"That doesn't even... you... are all dragons this fucking annoying?"

The dragon stiffened. Then, "I wouldn't know. Never really met another one."

And I really didn't know what to say to that so I said nothing at all. I closed my eyes and prayed that the flight would soon be over.

And that I hadn't actually shit myself.

CHAPTER 21
So, This Is Awkward

IT DIDN'T take long before we started to descend again near the base of the Northern Mountains. The dragon had kept silent through the remainder of the flight. I thought about drilling it with as many questions I could think of (because when was I ever going to get the chance to talk to a dragon again?), but I instead spent the majority of the time trying to keep my gorge from rising again.

So it was with immense relief when the ground came into view again. And when I saw a stone structure rising out of the middle of another valley, I knew we'd reached the keep that Dimitri had first spoken of weeks ago.

"Jesus," I said. "Dimitri was right."

"Who?" the dragon asked.

"Fairy king," I said. "Tried to get me to marry him. Don't ask. It was this whole thing that spiraled out of control. Like the time I was kidnapped by a dragon."

"I didn't *kidnap* you."

"Um. You took me against my will. That's, like, the definition of kidnapping, dude."

"Dude?" the dragon scoffed. "*Dude*? I'll never understand why the king of the fairies would want to marry you, *dude*. Unless you suck cock as good your lips indicate you should."

"Ugh," I groaned. "You are the absolute worst. For once I'd like to meet a celibate person and/or magical creature so I don't have to fear for my virginity. This is getting ridiculous."

"A *virgin*?" it asked, leering at me as we circled the keep. "Well, now. That certainly is unexpected. I suddenly feel the urge to despoil you completely. You know what they say, once you go dragon, all the rest is just laggin'."

"No one says that," I said. "Absolutely no one."

"Six people say it," he insisted. "I made sure of it."

"That's… isn't that bestiality?"

"We're all just animals," he said. "Wild, sexual, writhing animals."

"Yeah. No."

"You say that now. Just you wait."

"Gross."

He landed in front of the keep. The keep itself was a large stone tower that rose from the center of the valley. It looked ancient, and there was evidence of a larger structure that had once stood around it. Large chunks of stone lay strewn around the tower as if the building had been blown apart or collapsed. I couldn't tell what its purpose had been, be it church or a small castle, but I didn't think it mattered.

The keep itself was large, and the entrance at the base was tall enough to accommodate the dragon. It pushed against the massive doors with its nose and they creaked open, scraping against the stone floor, grating against my ears. I gave maybe a second of thought to run screaming in the opposite direction with my hands flailing above my head, but I was able to curb that back and follow the dragon into the keep.

It'd been a church. I was sure of it now. Long gone were any pews or religious icons hanging from the walls, but the raised dais at the end and the size of the bottom floor suggested a congregation had once gathered here.

Now, though, it was a dragon's nest.

And where it hoarded its treasure.

There was gold, of course. Massive amounts of gold in bricks and coins and nuggets. Shining jewels and goblets and scepters. That was expected.

What was *not* expected was the books.

Castle Lockes had a library that rivaled any in all of Verania. Scholars from all over the world came to the castle and could spend weeks getting lost in the stacks, finding scrolls and texts that hadn't been touched in centuries.

This was bigger.

Against a far wall, stacked from floor to vaulted ceiling that I couldn't even make out in the shadows, were books. More than I'd ever seen in my entire life. From what I could see, most were in good condition, though some looked to be in tatters or were burned.

"I thought dragons only hoarded beautiful things," I said. "Objects that shine and glisten."

The dragon followed my gaze to his book collection before he looked back at me. He cocked his head and for a moment, I wondered if I'd somehow committed a faux-pas, that it was insulting to discuss a dragon's possessions with said dragon. But then it said, "There is beauty in the written word," and I couldn't really think of anything to say after that.

And it wasn't until Grand Prince Justin of Verania came stomping down the stairs in the rear that I was able to find my voice again.

"Dragon," he snapped, and I jerked at the sound of his voice. "Why do I hear voices? Who have you brought with you? I thought we were going to finish reading the—"

And his eyes widened when he saw me.

He looked good. His hair was a bit longer (which, of course, made it curlier and more devastating; when *my* hair got too long, I looked homeless), and he was maybe a bit leaner, but he appeared to be in good health. He wore a simple tunic and trousers. He was barefoot, and for some reason, I found that oddly disarming. The whole thing felt surreal. Normally he was poised and pinched, and here he looked like anyone else.

"Sam?" he said, voice slightly choked.

And this was the Prince of Verania, *my* Prince, but for some reason, instead of addressing him as such, all I could think about was how his *fiancé* wanted to *do* me, so I said, "Heeeyyy, buddy. You doing good? You look good. For being kidnapped.

By a dragon. Like I just was. But I'm here to rescue you. I think. I really don't know. I might be confused as to why I'm here."

Justin stared at me.

"You're very strange, pretty," the dragon told me.

Justin's eyes bulged as he looked up at the dragon. "You can talk again?" he demanded.

The dragon said, "You can understand me now?"

And I said, "So, this is awkward."

"Why haven't you been talking this whole time!" Justin shouted.

"I *have* been," the dragon snapped. "You just couldn't understand me!"

"I understand you just fine now! What did you do differently?"

"*I* didn't do anything! I brought the wizard here to translate!"

"Oh, isn't that just perfect! I've been sitting here for *weeks* with you just *growling* at me, when we could actually have been having conversations this entire time!"

"I wasn't *growling*," the dragon growled. "I was actually *talking* to you, but you don't speak dragon so you didn't understand me!"

"Wait," Justin said. "Are we speaking dragon or Veranian?"

"I… have no idea," the dragon said.

They turned to look at me. So I said, "Heeeeyyy, buddy. You look alive. That's just super," all the while thinking guiltily of how Ryan's breath felt upon my cheek. I was an *awful* person and where the hell did I get off thinking about someone else's man? And maybe, just *maybe*, Justin had turned over a new leaf while being held captive by the dragon. Maybe he'd found in himself his heart and was able to see that the world was a wonderful and mysterious place and there was no reason to go around being a gigantic dick all the time.

Justin rolled his eyes. "Did you break him? He sounds broken. Well, more than usual."

Nope. Still a gigantic dick.

"I found him tied up to a pole not far from here." The dragon puffed out its chest. "Apparently there's a cult that made a *religion* because of me and they were sacrificing people to me because of it."

"I wasn't *tied* to the pole," I said. "By the time you'd gotten there, I'd already freed myself."

"Oh yeah," the dragon. "That's right. And then you tripped off the altar and landed facedown on the ground."

Justin snorted.

I glared at both of them. "I'm not a fan of either of you."

"Feeling is mutual," they both said at the same time.

"Great," I muttered. "Now there are two of them."

"Why are you here, Sam?" Justin asked.

"Um. I told you. To rescue you? I thought that much was obvious."

He laughed. "And this is your idea of a rescue? Seriously?"

"Hey! I was *fine* until the cult!" And the Darks and fire geckos and fairies and drag queens, but he didn't need to know any of that.

"The cult," the dragon whispered. "The cult that's for *me*."

Oh gods. He and Gary could never meet.

"I'm actually a little insulted," Justin sniffed. "My father sent just *you* to rescue me? I thought at the very least I'd warrant the knights."

"There's nothing wrong with me!"

"Well, that's certainly not true, Sam," Justin said. "I don't know why you try and convince yourself otherwise."

"Well," I said, feeling slightly vindictive. "It isn't just me. It's Gary. And Tiggy. And Ryan."

Justin's eyes narrowed. "Really," he said flatly. "You. And Gary. And Tiggy. And *Ryan*. That's who my father sent."

"It's supposed to be some sort of test, I think," I said. "To be honest, I'm not really clear. I think he said something about how it was romantic if Ryan rode up on a steed to slay the dragon and rescue the Prince, but then that turned racist because of Gary, so there *is* no steed and so I'm pretty sure the King's idea of romance is slightly whack. He did try to marry me off to Captain Bad-Touch, after all. He had rapey eyes. Kind of like someone else I know." I turned and looked at the dragon pointedly.

Of course it ignored me. "Slay the dragon?" it said. "How barbaric."

"You tried to set us on fire!"

"I tried to set *you* on fire," it said. "You're a wizard. You deserve to be on fire."

"Rude."

"No," it said. "Truth."

"*And* if I hadn't been a wizard, then Justin and I would have been flambé and you wouldn't have been able to hoard him like you did."

"With your whizbangs," the dragon said. "Ice sparklies."

"Exactly," I said. "You're welcome. The both of you."

They rolled their eyes.

"Where is the rest of the really sad rescue party?" Justin asked.

"Oh shit," I said. "They're still with the cult. I think. They fed us some kind of coercion and truth spell mixed with corn and we couldn't do shit about it."

Justin took a stuttering step back. He cleared his throat. His eyes darted over my shoulder then back at me. "Truth spell?" he said.

Godsdammit. "Uh. Yeah? Yes."

He coughed. "And... what sort of truths were there?"

"Wizarding truths?" That sounded believable.

"Wizarding truths."

"Yes. That's why they tried to sacrifice me first. They thought the dragon would be impressed by me."

"I'm not," the dragon said. "I might need to smite my subjects because they got it way wrong. You're pretty, but you stink of magic. And you threw up on me. That's not how I want to start a sexual relationship."

"You dropped me," I reminded him. "Uh. Not that I'm trying to argue about getting into a sexual relationship with you. You're not my type. I like my men more... not you."

The dragon huffed. "You don't know what you're missing."

"Thankfully so."

"Any other truths, then?"

Yes. A shitload of them. So many fucking truths that I couldn't even be sure if it had been a dream or not. So I said, "No. That was pretty much it."

"You never were a very good liar," he said.

"I do okay," I said.

"Tell me."

"What?"

"What did he say?"

"Ryan?"

"Sam."

"I'm not stalling."

He took a step toward me. "You're totally stalling."

I said, "A little," because how do you tell a prince that his Knight Commander of a fiancé has a magic kink and wants to do things to your butthole? It's hard.

(Sex pun.)

"Did he tell you about us?" Justin asked, eyes narrowed.

And. Wait. What? "What *about* you?"

"Uh. Never mind."

"Justin."

"I think I might love you," the dragon blurted out.

I prayed to the gods he wasn't talking to me.

And he wasn't. He was staring right at Justin.

"Heh," I said. "Awesome."

"What?" Justin said.

"Your face," the dragon said. "I want to do things to it."

"Heh," I said. "More awesome."

"Uh. I don't even know your name," Justin said, hedging.

The dragon pulled himself up to full height. His wings fluttered behind him. He looked proud. Regal. Terrifying.

I waited for it with bated breath. Because this was a big moment, maybe even historical. Dragons named themselves after they were born. After trial and experience. Their true names were supposed to be words of power that they rarely shared with others. The fact that the dragon was willing to share his true name with us was nothing short of a miracle. I reminded myself to write it down in my Grimoire, which I'd sorely been neglecting these past few weeks.

I knew, I just *knew* that he'd be named something majestic like Mountain Storm or Fire Eyes or HeartWing (granted, my track record for guessing the names of magical creatures was certainly not the best).

The dragon said, "I am from the Old Line; the blood that runs through me stretches back hundreds of thousands of years. I hail from the faraway jungles, in a land never before seen by man. I am fire and skin and wings. I am the dark dragon. I am the Beast from the East. I am…"

"*Ohmygods ohmygods ohmygods*," I muttered half-hysterically.

"…Kevin," the dragon finished triumphantly.

"*OHMYGODS OHMYGODS OHMY*—wait. What?"

"Kevin," the dragon repeated.

"Your name is Kevin."

"Yes," Kevin said, chest still puffed out proudly, eyes gazing off into the distance as if imagining dragony things us mere mortals could never understand.

"Kev-in," I said, trying to understand why it didn't sound like Fire Eyes when I said it. "Huh."

He glanced quickly at me before going back to being regal and staring at the horizon. "Kevin."

"Well," I said. "That's… a name. That you picked. For yourself."

"Yes," Kevin said. "I spent ten years ruminating on it before I picked it."

"I can see that," I said slowly. "And Kevin is… the best you could come up with? Obviously," I added quickly when Kevin stiffened. "It's fitting. For you. And your being. All your dragon-ness." I was making this so much worse.

"Isn't it?" Kevin said, though I could hear the word of warning in his voice.

Justin rolled his eyes. "A dragon named Kevin is in love with me. I just… I don't even. Gods."

"A dragon named Kevin wants to fuck me," I said without meaning to. And then I cringed.

"*What?*" Justin said, voice all low and dangerous.

"What what?" I asked.

"Baby," Kevin cooed to Justin. "I don't even. No, baby. Look at me. You're the only man for me. Hey. Hey. Look at me. Look at me, Bright Eyes. Hey. Who's my big strong Prince? Hmm? Hey. I don't. Not anymore. That was so long ago. Before I even met you. I was a different dragon back then."

"Um," I said. "That was, like, weeks ago. And you also said I had lips made for sucking cock when you kidnapped me. And you just said you wanted a sexual relationship with me. Like five minutes ago."

Kevin went down on his stomach and put his head near Justin, who stood with his arms crossed and his back to the dragon. "Hey. No. Listen. I didn't mean it. Baby. Look at me. Hey. You're the only one for me. I don't care if he's got cock-sucking lips."

I scrunched up my face in disgust. "Um. Ew. And also? Offensive."

Kevin bumped his nose into Justin. "Baby," he purred. "It's you. Even when we couldn't understand each other, we spoke the language of love."

"You had sex with Kevin?" I asked, my voice going high.

"What?" Justin said. "No. Gods, Sam. Do you ever think before you speak?"

"Yeah, Sam, gods," Kevin said. "It's not always about sex, even if you have those lips made for dick."

"He's very sexually aggressive," I told Justin. "I don't think you should sleep with him."

"Stop cockblocking me!" the dragon hissed.

"He's engaged," I reminded Kevin. "To a knight."

Kevin snorted, a lick of flame curling from his nose. "Easily remedied. I shall eat the knight and then he won't be engaged."

"You don't eat people, though," I said.

"You don't?" Justin asked. He uncrossed his arms and turned back toward the dragon.

Kevin glared at me before turning back to Justin. "No," he admitted. "Too boney. I try to stay healthy. I'm mostly a vegetarian. Every now and then, I'll treat myself to a cow on my cheat day, but that's about it."

"You're a vegetarian," I said.

"Mostly," he said.

"You're mostly a vegetarian."

"Yes."

"You're ruining dragons for me," I said. "Everything about you is ruining dragons for me."

"Oh?" Kevin said. "Is it because I'm your first?"

"Yes. My one and only and—"

He reached out with a claw and scraped it on the ground next to my feet. "How did it feel to have your dragon cherry popped?"

Justin coughed quite angrily. It was impressive.

Kevin quickly pulled his claws back and turned to Justin again. "No, baby," he said. "It was just a joke. Just joking around. Sam and his cock lips mean nothing to me. You're my one and only. You complete me. Without you, my six hearts are just forty-pound organs that beat dully and without cause. You're so special."

"Aww," I couldn't help but say.

"You'll see," Kevin said. "I'll make sure you have everything—"

His nostrils flared as he jerked his head toward the great doors. A low, rumbling growl started somewhere in his middle and crawled its way up his throat and out his mouth.

"What is it now?" I sighed because it was always going to be *something*.

"Something approaches," Kevin said. "Three heartbeats. Coming down the road, maybe ten minutes away."

"It's probably the cult," I said. "Bringing you corn. Don't eat it because you'll end up telling someone embarrassing things that you're not ready for, like how much you want to do them—"

Justin glared and took a step toward me.

"Do them no wrong," I finished hastily. "Because doing wrong things is bad and no one should do them. Especially to others."

"Stay in the keep," Kevin snapped and clambered out the front doors. He nudged them shut behind him, leaving Justin and I in relative darkness.

"So," I said. "This is awkward."

Justin sighed. "Come on. We can watch what's going on from up top."

Unable to think of anything else to do, I followed him as he turned toward the stairs.

CHAPTER 22
Cornerstone

THE STAIRS curved up around the interior edges of the keep. We passed by a landing or two that collapsed long ago, but other floors were still intact and cluttered with even more of Kevin's hoard. Books and treasure, paintings and dishes. He'd amassed quite a bit for having been in Verania for less than three months. Or maybe he'd brought it from the east, where rumors of thick, haunted jungles run rampant.

The last floor before the roof of the keep was different.

It was clean and sparse, and there was a large bed in the corner with pillows and blankets knocked askew. A dresser stood near the doorway with a bookshelf on the opposite wall. An open window near the back of the room let in light and a sweet spring breeze. This room was comforting. Almost like a home.

"This is where you've stayed, isn't it," I said.

Justin hesitated, then shrugged. "It's not that bad."

"It doesn't look like it, no."

"He's...."

"Kevin?"

"He's taken care of me," he said quickly, as if embarrassed. "Food and water. This room. He brought these things. For me. I don't know how he got them. I don't know why. But he did."

"Yeah," I said. "He sure seems real swell."

Justin scoffed. "It was better when I couldn't understand him."

"And that might be my fault. My magic... I don't know. It has to be a proximity thing. It reacts with the dragon and the dragon's magic reacts with mine. Okay. Honestly. I have no fucking idea."

Justin stood near the doorway. "I read to him. Sometimes. He likes books. Even if he couldn't understand them. Or me. He likes it when I read to him."

I didn't even know what to do with that. So I said, "Couldn't you have escaped? When he was gone?"

Justin shrugged. "He barricaded the tower."

"But—"

He walked out of the room.

I followed.

We went up the remaining set of stairs, which led to a hatch in the ceiling. Justin pushed up on the splintered wood and sunlight poured down onto the stairs. I blinked against it as I reached the top.

Kevin was sitting on the edge of the roof, like an overgrown stone gargoyle, tail curled out along the side of the keep. If it weren't for the fact that his name was

Kevin and that he wanted me to suck on his penis, I would have thought him an extraordinary beast. Unfortunately, he'd colored my perceptions and all I wanted to do was cover my mouth so no one could accuse me of having dick lips again.

"You will stay here, my Prince," Kevin said to Justin. "Do not come down and attempt to defend me."

"Okay," Justin said. "Wasn't planning on it."

"Even if it looks like I'm at death's door, you must stay hidden and safe."

"Sure." Justin sounded bored.

"Even if I'm screaming and my blood is pooling on the ground, do not under any circumstances rush down and cry over me, confessing your deepest love and begging me not to go."

"Right." Justin rubbed a smidge of dirt off one of his knuckles.

"And if I should go, I plead with you to not throw yourself off the top of the keep to your death because you think that you can't live without me and want to follow me through the Veil—"

"Oh my gods," I said because I couldn't take it anymore. "Seriously. Just... seriously. What is this even...? I don't. Gods."

"It's romantic," Kevin said.

"It's creepy," I said.

"I think it's all right," Justin said with a shrug.

Kevin preened.

"How are you going to explain your dragon lover to the King?" I asked, unable to think of anything else to say.

"Easy," Kevin said. "I'm young, hung, and have absolutely no refractory period."

"Dude," I said in awe. "Just. Dude."

"He's not my dragon lover," Justin said.

"Not yet," Kevin said.

"Weird," Justin said. "Maybe I liked it better when I couldn't understand you. Is that what you've been saying to me this whole time?"

"Not at first."

"Really? How long did it take?"

"Four minutes."

Justin sighed. "The whole time."

"Mostly," Kevin agreed.

"And then you see Sam and his lips and now you're pushing for a three-way?"

"What?" I said.

"No, baby," Kevin said, voice sweet. "No. You're the only one for me. Of course not. I would never. I wouldn't do that to you. Unless you wanted to. Do you want to? Gosh. I've never even considered it. Is that what you're thinking about? The three of us? Me lying on my back and you two climbing all over my junk? Is that what you want?"

"I'm the denominator," I whispered. "Oh my gods, *I'm the denominator.*"

Justin wrinkled his nose. "Not really a threesome-with-Sam kind of guy."

"Hey!" I said because someone needed to defend my honor. "I would be a *great* person to have a threesome with. I'd be all tender and caring and making sure both parties got equal attention from me. By the time I got done with both of you, you'd be so satisfied, you'd be ruined for all others."

Kevin and Justin stared at me.

Oh shit. "Uh. Not that that's an option. Because it's not. Seeds need to bloom in me and make treasure because I love being on my knees for armies. Crap. That's not what I meant to say."

"And how do you know him?" Kevin side-whispered to Justin.

"He's to be my wizard when I am king," Justin said. And if I'm being honest, he could have tried to sound a bit more thrilled at that.

"Yikes," Kevin said.

"I'm not going to rescue you," I told Justin.

"I won't have to eat you, then," Kevin said, snapping his jaws at me.

"You don't scare me anymore," I said, even though it wasn't completely true. "I'm not made of leaves and twigs, you wannabe carnivore."

"It's a healthier *life* choice!"

"Don't talk to Sam about life choices," Justin said. "All of his have been wrong."

"You're kind of a bitch," I said. "Your Highness."

Whatever retort Justin may have had was put on hold when Kevin tensed, the bony spines on his back going rigid. Justin and I looked over the edge of the keep down toward the entrance to the valley.

I choked at the sight that lay before us.

"Is that what I think it is?" Justin asked. He almost sounded amused.

If what he thought it was happened to be Ryan riding Gary full-out into the valley, sword and shield drawn, Tiggy running at their sides, hands balled into gigantic fists as they hurtled themselves toward the keep, then yes.

Gary looked majestic as fuck, mane flying back around his head where he wore a makeshift battle helmet that I'd never seen before, nostrils flaring, coat gleaming. I reminded myself to tell him later.

Tiggy looked scary as fuck, with the snarl on his face, the muscles bunching in his thighs.

Ryan looked hot as fuck with his sword and shield and hair flying in the wind, and I'm pretty sure I was on my way to a full erection by that point because that shit was fucking *erotic*.

"This feels like a sex dream," I breathed.

"This feels like a *what*?" Justin asked.

"Uhhhh. Nothing. I didn't say anything. Oh, look. Fascinating things are happening. Let's focus on those."

And as if waiting for me to say so, Kevin spread his wings and roared, the sound crawling along the valley. I saw Tiggy stumble slightly and even Gary faltered, but they pushed on. I'd never thought them more brave. Or more ridiculous.

And I couldn't even begin to comprehend Ryan riding atop Gary. I couldn't even find the time to think that Ryan was somehow a racist because of it.

Kevin launched himself off the top of the keep and spread his wings. He fell near silent, his wings catching him before he landed on the ground in front of the great doors.

"Don't kill them," Justin called after him. "Maybe just scare them a little bit."

I gaped at him.

"What?" he asked me. "We might as well enjoy it if we have to watch."

That... okay. I couldn't fault him for that. Because Gary was doing a great impression of a warrior princess with his battle screech as he charged up the road toward the keep. And Tiggy was trying to scream along with him, but he wasn't really understanding what they were doing so he was screaming, "*I'm yelling too!*" And Ryan might have been manly screaming, but I was distracted by the way the sun fell in his hair and I had to stop myself from sighing dreamily.

Of course, they all stopped screaming when Kevin landed in front of them, the dirt puffing up in clouds around his claws. Kevin hissed, his forked tongue curling out around his lips, the spines along his back quivering. If I hadn't known that he was a mostly vegetarian, sexually aggressive lizard, I would have been terrified. As it was, I rolled my eyes.

"Eep," Gary said.

"Whoa," Tiggy said.

"Prepare, dragon!" Ryan shouted. "For today, you will meet your end!"

Justin and I both snorted.

"I'm sure he didn't mean that to sound as douchey as it did," I said.

"No," Justin said. "He meant it all right. He does that sometimes."

"Tiggy," Gary hissed. "Take off this fucking helmet."

Ryan slid down from Gary and flourished his sword, eyes never leaving Kevin. Kevin snarled at him, dragging his claws along the ground, tail flicking dangerously from side to side. His muscles bunched in his legs, and it looked as if he were about to launch himself at Ryan. I wondered briefly if I should intervene.

Tiggy leaned over and lifted the helmet from Gary's head. Gary, ever the diva, shook his head daintily, his mane settling perfectly on the side of his head.

And the dragon. Just. *Stopped.*

"Um," Ryan said. "Hello? Dragon? Are we doing this or—"

"What great beauty is this?" Kevin breathed, sounding soul struck.

"Um. What?" Ryan asked, taking a step back. "Talking. It talks. Of course it does."

"Did you hear my battle scream?" Gary asked Tiggy, completely ignoring Kevin. "I was all like, *GRAAAHHH* and it sounded pretty awesome if I do say so myself."

"It very loud," Tiggy said. "Tiggy scream too. *GWAAAHHH!*"

"No," Gary said, shaking his head. "Not gwah. Grah. *GRAAAHH!*"

"*GWAAAAHHHH!*"

"Dragon," Ryan said, poking Kevin with his sword. "Hey. Dragon."

"*GRAAAHHHHHHH!*"

Kevin ignored Ryan, eyes only on Gary.

"Seriously?" Justin asked me. "*Seriously?*"

"Hey! You leave them—okay. Even I can't defend this. Oh my gods. What the hell."

"*GWAAAAHHHH!*"

"*GRAAAHHH*—never mind. We'll work on this later. Well, finish the dragon thing, find a tavern and scope out the mens."

"Scopin' out mens," Tiggy agreed. "And cake."

"Yes, dear heart. We can have cake. Now, where were we?" Gary looked back at Kevin, who was still staring at him. "Oh, right. Dragon. That'd probably be a good place to start. You there. Dragon! Hello! Yes, you!"

Kevin looked over his shoulder as if there was another dragon standing directly behind him that Gary could have been addressing. "Me?" he asked.

"Yes. You. Now. Have you seen a wizard? Well, apprentice, really. He's about six feet tall, skinny as all get out. I've told that boy he needs to eat more, but does he listen to me? Of course not. His nose is always buried in his Grimoire or in the labs or running for our lives. He's got black hair, or maybe it's better described as onyx. Onyx, Tiggy?"

"Onyx," Tiggy agreed. "Pretty Sam."

"Onyx, then," Gary said. "But you probably know him from his mouth. It never closes."

"Hey!" I snapped. "It closes all the time!"

"Only when you swallow, dear," Gary said and then, "Sam! Oh my gods!"

Tiggy, Gary, and Ryan all looked up.

Justin and I waved.

"Are you a prisoner of the dragon?" Gary asked. "What the hell am I saying? Of course you are. Gods, Sam. If you ever do that again, I swear I'll murder you. You gave me gray hairs! *Gray hairs*, Sam. At *my* age? You asshole!"

"Uh, it makes you look distinguished?" I tried.

His eyes narrowed. "Distinguished. That's what you're choosing to go with."

"Are you all right?" Ryan asked, tone weary and concerned. "When you were taken, I couldn't—"

"I'm fine," Justin and I both said at the same time.

"Er," I said. "The Prince is just fine."

"Because that's who you were asking about, right, Ryan?" Justin asked.

"Uhhh," Ryan said. "I should probably fight this dragon."

"Can we please ignore the awkwardness and go back to where Sam said I was an old cow?" Gary asked. "He should never be allowed to speak again. Ever."

"If you ask me, I'll tell you what *I* think," Kevin blurted out.

"Hmmm," Gary said. "Intrigued. Go ahead."

Kevin swallowed thickly, throat bobbing up and down. "Okay. So. Um. Come on, Kevin, you can do this. You got this. Just say it. *Say it.* Ahem. You are the most enchanting creature I have ever seen. I have not known true beauty until this day. Any beauty I thought I might have known before was an obvious lie because there is no comparison."

"Sucks for you," I told Justin, elbowing him in the side.

"He's dissing you too, asshole," Justin grumbled.

"Nah. I've just got dick lips."

"I don't think that's as good as you keep thinking it is."

"Five minutes ago, you were his one true love. Now, I bet he doesn't even remember your name."

"I don't suppose it matters," Justin said, lips curving dangerously. "I'm already engaged to be married. You know. To a knight."

And that round went to Prince Asshole.

"You took my breath away," Kevin continued, oblivious to the drama from above. "When you removed your warrior's helmet, I wondered if the gods had chosen to honor me this day for any world where you exist must truly be a blessing."

Gary stared at him. "Tiggy," he said, crooking his lips toward the half-giant. "Who is he talking to?"

"You," Tiggy said. "He wants to eat Gary flower."

"My flower was eaten a long time ago." He looked the dragon up and down and said, "I'll see where this goes. Continue."

"First, might I know your name?" Kevin asked. "I assume it is something so magical that the very utterance of it would cause rainbows to weep in glorious joy."

"Gary."

"*Gary*," the dragon whispered in awe, the name on his lips sounding almost like benediction. "Have two syllables ever sounded more beautiful together? Geh. Ree. The gods must have outdone themselves the day that word was born. They took the exquisiteness from the earth and rolled it together with a pinch of sunshine and love and gorgeousness and when it was finished, it was *Gary*."

"Wow," Gary said. "That was… words."

"This is getting uncomfortable," I told Justin.

"I might have gotten lucky that Gary showed up," he said.

"So," Ryan said, his sword now dragging in the dirt. He looked slightly put out. "Are we, like, gonna fight here? I'm not really sure of the protocol for something like this and—"

"Ryan," Gary said. "Shut up. I'm being wooed."

"But—"

"Ryan. *Shut. It.*"

"Gods," Ryan grumbled.

"I apologize for the Knight Commander," Gary said to Kevin. "He doesn't understand how love works."

"That's bullshit," Ryan said. "I know love. I've got so much love. You don't even know."

"He does?" I asked, heart beating traitorously in my chest.

"You do?" Justin asked.

"Hi, Sam!" Tiggy said, waving at me.

"Should I take him out for you, my sweet?" Kevin asked. "All you have to do is but ask and I will make sure his blood is spilled upon the ground. I'll roast his skin with my fire. I'll tear off his head. I stick my claws up his perky ass if his screams will make you happy."

"Whoa," Ryan said. "And thank you. It is rather perky."

"Hmmm," Gary said.

"Gary," Ryan said. "Buddy."

"Hmmm."

"*Gary*. You said we were friends! You said you *liked* me."

"I say that about a lot of things. Like people. And ham."

"Are you going to stop him?" Justin whispered to me.

"He's a grown unicorn," I said with a shrug. "He's got this." And I really didn't think that Gary would allow Kevin to murder Ryan. Not really. Gary wasn't *that* big of a jerk.

Kevin started rumbling deep in his chest.

Gary grinned.

I sighed. "Gary."

"What?" The perfect picture of unicorn innocence.

"You know what."

"Sam!" he exclaimed, eyes going wide as if he hadn't been aware I'd been standing above him this whole time. That asshole. "Lovely to see you alive and well. And with the Prince, no less. I'm sure you two have had some... interesting things to discuss."

"Gary," I warned.

"Ugh. Fine. Dragon."

The rumbles ceased instantly as Kevin turned back toward Gary. "Yes, my exquisiteness?"

"You don't need to kill the Knight Commander."

"As you wish."

"Maybe maim him a little."

"*Gary*."

"Fine," Gary muttered. "No maiming either. *Some* people just don't know how to take a joke."

"I do," Kevin said. "All of your jokes. I'll laugh at every single one because undoubtedly, your humor exceeds that of even court jesters. Might I fuck you later tonight?"

Gary coughed roughly. "That... um."

"I'll go slow," Kevin said, as if that were the only issue at hand. "I'll go so slow for you. Open you up until you're wet enough to sit on my—"

"Sam!" Gary cried. "Look at that. That's Sam. Our friend Sam. And the Prince! Hello, Prince! I am so glad to see your bright and shining face."

"You are?" Justin asked, coolly amused. "That's a first."

"Whaaaa? No. Ha-ha! You and I go way back."

"Do we?"

"We do."

"Huh."

"In fact, I think I should want to see both your faces up close. Tiggy, dear, won't you escort me to the top of the keep?"

Tiggy grinned. "Tiggy don't know what you just said. Sure."

"Lovely," Gary said. "Just lovely. And while we go up there, the dashing and immaculate Knight Commander here shall battle my fierce dragon to the death!"

"Your wish is my command," Kevin said, bowing his head.

"*Gary.*"

"Okay, okay. Gods, Sam. No need to bring out scary eyes. Kevin. Yoo-hoo, Kevin!"

Kevin had already started rushing at Ryan, who was scrambling back a step or two, sword at the ready. "Yes, light of my life?"

"No killing," Gary said, sounding as if he'd only known hardship his entire life.

"Or maiming," I said.

"Or maiming," Gary said, rolling his eyes. "Because Sam is a killjoy and we never get to have any fun at all. But if we're going that direction, then Ryan can't kill Kevin either."

"Um," Ryan said. "Then what's the point?"

"No killing," I told Ryan. "Kevin is nice. Sort of."

"Thank you, pretty," Kevin told me. "Though I wish you would use that mouth of yours less for talking and more for sucking my cock."

"*What?*" Ryan growled.

"That was probably the wrong thing to say," Gary said. "You mens have fun. Toodles!" He and Tiggy then took off at a brisk pace toward the keep, avoiding Kevin's tail as it snapped from side to side. I heard Gary grunt as he pressed against the great doors, the metal grating against the stone.

"Ooh." Gary's voice carried up the stairs. "Look at all this *stuff.* If I marry him, Tiggy, then all of this will be *mine.*"

"Gary getting married?" Tiggy asked.

"Possibly," Gary said. "I am a catch, after all. I've been proposed to on numerous occasions and—*oh my gods, look at the size of that emerald it's bigger than my face*—I might as well get around to accepting one of these days. You can't help when you fall in love with someone. It just hits you in the center of your chest and—*there is so much silk here that I just want to bathe in it forever and ever*—you can't fight it. It's not about how much stuff a person has, or how much gold he has to his name—*sixty-six sixty-seven sixty-eight oh my gods sixty-eight chests filled to the brim with gold*—it's about love. That feeling that blooms inside and makes you unable to breathe without them in your arms. And I'll tell you, Tiggy. I just might be in love. Is that a *diamond*? I thought that was a *chandelier.* Tiggy. I'm in love."

"You're judging me, aren't you," I asked Justin.

"Yes," he said. "So much. Those are your friends."

"No," I corrected. "Those are your rescuers. Who your father sent. Obviously, a reflection upon you."

Justin scowled.

Point for me.

Score: Justin, one. Sam, six billion.

Kevin and Ryan continued to circle each other below as Gary exclaimed over this and that as they slowly made their way up the staircase. I pretended not to want to glower at Justin and to keep from cheering at Ryan to slay the dragon like I belonged to his fan club or something.

And then I remembered I *did* belong to his fan club or something, and not only that, I had *admitted* to belonging to his fan club, only to have him say that he wanted to put his dick in my mouth and had fantasized about me since I was fifteen years old.

This, of course, led to thoughts unbecoming of someone in my current position. Namely, I was thinking about fucking Ryan Foxheart in the asshole while standing next to his fiancé while Ryan himself fought a dragon below us, all the while listening to Gary get closer and closer, talking about how true love was *real* it was a *tangible thing*, that he didn't think he'd *ever feel this way and oh my fucking gods look at how many diamonds that crown has at least six and how many carats is that*?

So when Gary poked his head up through the hatch and said, "*There* you are," I couldn't be held responsible when the first words out of my mouth were, "I am *not* thinking about fucking him, I swear to gods because that is just *wrong*, so don't even bring it up, okay, because shut up."

Cue awkward silence.

"Um," Gary said finally. "What?"

I said, "Oh. That was a quote. From a book I read."

And because Gary couldn't *not* be an asshole, he said, "Great, and what book was that?" even as Justin turned his full glare back on me because I was a lying liar who *lied*.

For the life of me, I couldn't think of a title of a single actual book ever written, so I said, "*The Manticore and the Butler*."

"Ah," Gary said as Tiggy pushed him up through the hatch gently. "*The Manticore and the Butler*. Sounds riveting. Who is it by?"

I made sure my eyebrows expressed just how displeased I was at him. "Mervin Sondheim," I said through gritted teeth.

"Mervin Sondheim," Gary said. "You sure know a lot of Mervins. So. Tell me. What is the book about?"

"It's a love story between a manticore and a butler. They love each other, but societal norms dictate they can't be together."

Gary's lips twitched. "A lion with wings and human face and a butler sure sounds like it would cause disruption. How does it end?"

"They both die. Painful deaths. Involving many bad things." I hoped it sounded like a threat.

"That doesn't sound like a happy ending," Justin said with a frown.

"It isn't," I told him. "But sometimes murder is inevitable. Right, *Gary*?"

He smiled sweetly at me. "If I was going to corner you and ask for you to write a review of *The Manticore and the Butler* and your words would be written in stone, how would you rate the book?"

"I'd give it five hearts," I muttered, wondering what his insides would look like if they were on his outside.

"Out of?"

"Five."

"Indeed. It sounds as if this novel left quite an impression on you. Tell me, what was that quote again?"

"Uh."

"You said it with such alacrity not five minutes ago," Gary said. "Surely it won't be that hard to repeat it. Since you rated it... what was your rating system again?"

"Hearts."

"That's right. Five hearts. Because of reasons. The quote?"

I hoped my eyebrows were now broadcasting his imminent death at my hands. "Um. It was. I am not gonna fuck him because shut up it's wrong. So. I love you, Nick the manticore."

"Nick the manticore!" Gary crowed gleefully. "Oh my gods, I can't believe you just *did* all that!"

"I don't read books," Tiggy said. "I like cats."

Justin said, "I think the dragon is just playing with Ryan."

We all looked over the edge of the keep.

Sure enough, Kevin kept circling Ryan, not allowing him to get a hit with his sword. He moved lightning quick for something his size, and I knew if this were a real fight, it'd be over rather quickly. For a moment, I thought that maybe I should do something to rescue him, but then I saw the way he ducked under a whip of Kevin's tail, and I figured he was okay to be dashing and immaculate, at least for a little while.

"Face me like a man!" Ryan snapped as Kevin danced away.

"I am not a man," Kevin reminded him. He flicked his claws against Ryan's breastplate, knocking him over. Kevin looked up at us and said, "Did you see that, Gary? I did that for you!"

"Super," Gary called back down. "You're so neat." Then, in a lower voice, "I'm going to have so many of your babies."

"Oh gods," I groaned. "Would you shut the fuck up?"

"It's true love," he insisted.

"If he hurt you, Tiggy gonna smash," Tiggy said, petting Gary's head.

"Of course you would, Tig," Gary said. "You're my big strong giant."

"I'll hurt him too," I said.

Gary rolled his eyes. "No you won't. Your magic won't work on him."

"And you can't do shit with a sword," Justin said.

I scowled at the both of them. Then, "Wait. How the fuck are you even here?"

"Tiggy," Gary said. "The coercion bullshit wore off of him quicker than they thought it would, I guess. One minute I am randomly telling them about getting tied up by Octavio while they tried to teach me the Dragon Psalm that had ninety-six verses, and the next Tiggy is smashing their faces in and now we are here."

"I feel like you're leaving out large portions of the story. Like starting with the fact that Ryan was riding you."

"Jealous?"

"Of Ryan," I said quickly. "Oh, totally. Yep. That is the only reason I'm jealous. Because of that."

"Riiight," Gary said and we all winced when Ryan was thrown into a tree. He got back up slowly, picking up his sword from the dirt.

"You doing okay there, buddy?" I called down.

"Fine," he said. "I'm a knight. I got this. You'll see. We'll have dragon meat for dinner."

"Gross," Gary said. "The only person who is going to be eating my future husband is me, and not in the way you're thinking."

"Nope," I said. "Not even going to listen to you."

Kevin, of course, puffed out his chest and attacked Ryan with gusto.

"What a weird day this has been," Justin muttered.

"The King misses you," I said quietly as Gary and Tiggy wandered away to inspect a chest of treasure on the opposite side of the keep.

Justin snorted. "I'm sure he does. Needs to have his successor in place."

"That's not it at all and you know it."

"Because you know so much about *my* relationship with *my* father."

"No," I said. "Because I know your father. I know what kind of man he is. I know the look on his face when I woke after you were taken. He was heartbroken, Justin."

His hands tightened into fists at his sides. "Only because you'd been hurt. It had nothing to do with me."

"How can you say that?" I asked. "You are his son. There isn't anything he wouldn't do for you. To make sure you got back safely. That's why he sent us."

Justin wouldn't look at me. "I get why he sent Ryan. I don't get why he sent you."

"I'm your wizard. Of course he was going to send me."

"My wizard," he repeated.

"Apprentice, sure, but yeah, dude. Your wizard."

"I distinctly remember you saying you weren't going to be my wizard at all."

I winced at that. "Yeah, well, you may have been coming at me with a sword and pissed me off. People say things when they're angry that they don't always mean."

Justin said nothing.

"Look I know you don't like me. I can't really say that I like you all that much, either. But in the end, that doesn't matter. We're responsible for something greater than ourselves. One day, an entire kingdom is going to be under our watch. You will lead it, and I will be there to help you. We're stuck together, okay? Family doesn't let each other go, even when things suck."

"You think we're family," he said flatly.

I tried to keep my anger in check. "Maybe like distant cousins."

He snorted. "You don't get it, do you?"

"Get what?"

"Gods, you're so fucking infuriating."

"So I've been told once or twice."

He turned toward me, mouth set in a thin line. I heard the angry yell from Ryan down somewhere below and Kevin's answering roar. But I never took my eyes off Justin. There was a flash of green just outside of my vision, but I had to tell myself *no, no, no*. Because I could collapse this keep around him if I wanted to. Just a few well-placed thoughts here and there and a twitch of my fingers and he'd be covered in stone.

He said, "It's always about *you*."

I arched an eyebrow at him. "How you figure?"

"I'm going to be the fucking king one day," he snarled at me. "I'm going to take my father's place and rule over all of Verania. It's why I was born. It's what I was raised for. It's why I took all those fucking lessons in etiquette and diplomacy. It was in the hundreds of hours of meetings I attended with councils and heads of state. With advisors and commanders, all telling me what I was supposed to do. How I was supposed to be. What I would become. And then *you*."

It was said with such venom that I almost took a step back. But I didn't because I didn't fear him. I was not scared of Justin. I would never hurt him, but that didn't mean I'd take his shit.

"*You* get taken from the slums," he said. "*You* are brought into my home. You who did nothing to deserve it. Nothing to earn it. All because of a fucking magic *trick* you did one day when you were sticking your nose where it didn't belong. And it only took *days* for it to be all about you. Oh Sam the sweet little wizard. Oh Sam the boy who came from nothing. Perfect, innocent Sam who came to the castle and who everyone loved. Morgan talked about you as if you were a prophecy fulfilled. The staff talked about you like you were royalty. Beloved and cherished. My friends, my fucking *friends*, thought you were smart and loyal. And my *father*. Well. Let's just say it wasn't long before he was speaking of you as if you were his second son."

"I didn't ask for any of this," I said quietly.

"You never had to!" he cried, and Gary and Tiggy jerked their heads up. Tiggy started toward us, a low growl rumbling from his chest. I held up a hand to ward him off, to placate him. He stopped, but he wasn't pleased. "You never had to ask for *anything* because it was always given to you! How do you think it made me feel when I would sit at my father's side, doing everything I could to get him to notice me, to say something about how well I was doing, how proud of me he was, only to hear him talk about *you*. About what *you* did. About what *you'd* become.

"And to make it worse, you could come and go as you pleased. You didn't have to stay in the fucking castle. You didn't have to follow rules and guidelines and codes. You could do whatever the fuck you wanted because you're fucking Sam of fucking Wilds. You fuck up and everyone laughs and shrugs. You got a Dark wizard *murdered* and nothing, absolutely *nothing* happened to you. *Nothing*. I make a mistake and the entire fucking *kingdom* will hear about it."

"That's not fair," I said, trying to keep from raising my voice. "I'm sorry if you felt that I've taken things from you, but I'm not sorry for my life. I won't ever apologize for who I am and I shouldn't have to. You can't ask that of me, Justin. And that Dark wizard that I *got murdered*? He was going to kill us. He was going to hurt Gary. And I will never let that happen. Gary is my friend and I will never let anyone hurt him. And Tiggy loves us. He loves us enough to protect us. Much like I tried to protect you."

He recoiled as if I'd slapped him. "You don't love me," he said hoarsely.

"No," I said. "I don't. But you are my Prince, and I would do anything to protect you."

"Fuck you, Sam. Gods, fuck you so much. You sanctimonious little bitch."

"Your father loves you. Your people love you. Ryan lo—"

"Don't you fucking talk to me about Ryan!" he shouted. "You don't know *shit* about that. You don't get to speak a godsdamn word about us." He took a step toward me.

I said, "Don't. Whatever you're thinking, don't."

Another step and the stone beneath my feet cracked. The *green* was so bright and I had to force it away. Dark syllables danced across my mind, but I stripped them of their intent. I couldn't do this. I couldn't hurt him. I couldn't. I wouldn't.

There was a large shadow flashing overhead and then Kevin was there, landing near Tiggy and Gary. Gary murmured something to him quietly, words I couldn't make out. Kevin gave an answering rumble but didn't move from his perch.

And that meant Ryan was coming. They must have heard Justin's voice.

Fuck this day so fucking much.

"He came here to save you," I said. "There was no stopping him."

"And I'm sure it didn't hurt that you were going too," Justin said, chuckling bitterly.

"Nothing happened." But wasn't that a lie? Because something *had* happened. *Everything* had happened.

"He was mine, you know," Justin said. "My father told me that a king needed a queen. When I told him I was gay, he said that a king needed a consort. He said that if I didn't find someone on my own by my twenty-fifth birthday, that he would arrange a marriage on my behalf. That he would find someone for me and I would be forced to marry them. Do you know what that feels like, Sam? To know that your future is put on a deadline and if that deadline isn't met, that you'll be matched with a stranger, someone who you've never met but will spend the rest of your life with."

I didn't say anything because I *didn't* know. I didn't know what it felt like to be forced to love someone, because I loved someone with so much force it hurt my heart to even think about it. Someone who didn't belong to me. No matter what was said, Ryan wasn't mine. It didn't stop the keep from starting to rumble, the stones vibrating underneath our feet. Gary called my name, told me to focus, to fucking *focus*, but I pushed his voice away.

"So I picked someone," Justin said, oblivious to my anger. "I picked Ryan. I made a godsdamn choice and even if I didn't love him, even if I didn't have feelings for him, I picked someone. I made my own choice. I wasn't forced by my father. And it was *fine*."

And, of course, that's when Ryan showed up, clambering through the hatch.

Justin, hearing his fiancé, smiled darkly at me and said, "I've fucked him, you know. Had him on his hands and knees and I fucked him. He begged for my cock and I gave it to him with all I could. There were bruises left by my fingers on his hips." The stone beneath his feet split and he took another step forward.

"Justin," Ryan barked. "What the fuck are you doing?"

"Teaching a lesson," Justin said, eyes never leaving mine. I kept my face a blank mask, not allowing him to see anything, be it hurt or jealousy. It was weakness and I wasn't going to allow him to see it. "He needs to learn his place."

"This isn't you," Ryan said, coming to stand beside him. He put his hand on Justin's shoulder. "You don't want to do this."

"He'll never be yours," Justin said, ignoring Ryan. "We made a deal. An oath. Did you know that, Sam? A knight's word is his honor. He wanted to make a name for himself. Wanted to rise up through the ranks. He agreed to be the King Consort to secure his place among the knights. It may not have been born of love, but it was still my choice. And his. Regardless of how we started, I care about him. And I know he cares about me."

"You know I do," Ryan said quietly, looking at Justin. "And I keep my oaths." He looked over at me with something akin to sadness.

And didn't that just sting. Even though I knew it, even though I knew there were feelings of a sort between them, hearing them spoken aloud hurt more than I thought it could. And I knew Ryan was a man of his word. Regardless of what he felt for me, however far it reached, he would keep his word to the Prince. Because he had to. He'd made an oath, and it was the strongest promise a knight could make.

I tried to pull the magic down then. Tried to contain it so nothing more would happen. I needed to leave. I needed to leave this all behind, separate myself from the others. Find an empty space far from anyone and then release it all at once. I didn't know what would happen, didn't know how powerful that release would be, but even I knew it'd been building for weeks. I'd just chosen to ignore it.

The stones began to shift underneath our feet.

I gritted my teeth together.

Gary shouted something I couldn't make out.

The hatch. I had to get to the hatch.

I couldn't allow them to get hurt. Not any of them. Not even Justin.

I took a step and the stones cracked again.

And then Ryan said, *"Sam,"* his hands coming up to my face, and everything just *stopped*.

The rumbling.

The shifting.

The flashes of green and gold.

The ache along my skin.

The buildup that thrummed within me, begging to be released.

It all just stopped.

I opened my eyes.

And there was Ryan, always Ryan. He cupped my face and his thumbs traced my cheeks. His eyes were so bright and he said, "Hey, Sam, you're with me, okay?" I just nodded, unable to look away, even though I *knew* I wasn't with him, not really. But it didn't matter because I felt soothed, his touch a balm, and I knew then I'd never find anyone like him again. There might be others out there who could anchor my magic, but they'd never be like him. He'd never have to know, but I would. I would know him forever.

And so, of course, that's when I understood I'd underestimated Justin yet again.

"You've got to be fucking kidding me," he said.

"Justin, why don't we—" Gary started, but was cut off almost immediately.

"Does he know?" Justin demanded. "Did you tell him?"

And he *knew*.

I took a step back out of Ryan's hands. I looked over his shoulder at Justin and said, "No. Don't do this. I didn't. I wouldn't. Don't do this. Please."

"What's going on?" Ryan asked, eyes narrowed as he looked between the two of us.

"Tell him," Justin said. "Or I will."

"Justin, I'll go, okay? I swear to the gods I'll go. I won't do anything. Please, just don't do this."

"Every wizard needs an anchor," he said to Ryan. "My father taught me that. Told me one day, Sam would find a person who would help him build his magic. Would help him to become a better wizard. Magic needs to be built upon a foundation, and a cornerstone *is* that foundation. It helps the wizard become more in control. More settled. Because magic, if unchecked, can grow and twist you into something off. Dark. And the cornerstone is usually someone with intent. *Romantic* intent. Isn't that right, Sam?"

"Sam?" Ryan asked. "What is he talking about?"

"I never wanted this," I said. "I promise. Both of you. I didn't ask for this to happen. I swear I didn't."

"You told me a cornerstone wasn't anything," Ryan said, voice hard. "You told me that it didn't matter."

"Did he?" Justin asked with a laugh. "That was a lie. It's *everything*."

"That's enough," Gary snapped. He moved swiftly, hooves clacking along the stone until he was by my side. He brushed up against me and I took strength from it. Everything felt too loud, too bright inside my head. He knew. "You're free to go. Ryan, take the Prince back to Castle Lockes. Forget this place and leave Sam the hell alone."

"I smash?" Tiggy growled, coming to stand on my other side. "I smash Prince and Knight Delicious Face?"

"Sam," Ryan said, taking a step toward us.

"Don't you get it, Ryan?" Justin said. "You're his fucking cornerstone. Because of *course* you are. The one time I make a choice for myself, the *one time I get to choose*, Sam of fucking Wilds tries to take that choice away. I won't let him. Not this time. You pledged yourself to me, and I will never let you go."

And there it was. Out there. Words that could never be taken back. I'd never wanted him to find out. Not like this. Not ever. It should have felt better, having all my cards on the table.

But gods, it didn't. It hurt.

"Is that true?" Ryan asked.

I said, "Don't—"

"*Is it true?*"

I took a breath. Let it out slowly.

And said, "Yes."

"You lied to me. I asked you and you *lied* to me." He was angry and hurt, just like I'd knew he'd be. "Were you ever going to tell me?"

"No."

"Why the fuck not?"

"Because," I said, "you have an oath. One I won't let you break. Your word is your bond and you are bound to Justin."

"How long?" he asked, sounding even angrier. "How the fuck long have you known?"

"The restaurant. With the Darks."

He took a step back. Away from me. Toward Justin. "Sam... that. That was *months* ago."

And because this had to end, I said, "And it doesn't matter anymore. We've got what we came here for. It's time to leave. It's time to say good-bye."

CHAPTER 23
Shit Just Got Real, Son

SO, THAT turned out to be a huge clusterfuck.

Because of course it did.

And I felt bad for Justin. I really did.

Still hated him with a fiery passion.

But I felt bad.

(And then I remembered the whole comment about having Ryan on his hands and knees and I didn't feel that bad anymore.)

I told the others I needed to speak to Morgan in private. "Wizarding things," I said, going for ominous and instead sounding slightly manic.

Tiggy looked pissed off.

Gary looked murderously at Justin.

Kevin stared at Gary.

Ryan stared at me.

Justin said, "I don't get why we have to wait. We're not even going with you."

Tiggy scowled.

Gary started sweating glitter.

Kevin stared at Gary.

Ryan stared at me.

Justin said, "Gods. Call Morgan. The sooner you're done, the sooner we can go."

"Yes, my lord," I managed to say without it coming out sounding like I was about to descend into Unicorn Rage. I didn't think it'd be practical for both Gary and I to be raining glitter. It didn't even cross my mind that I, in fact, could not descend into Unicorn Rage and was not made up of glitter and sunshine on my insides. My insides, at that moment, were a cold, dark thing where good feelings went to die horrible, painful deaths.

I couldn't see the keep by the time I felt I was a good distance away. I wondered briefly if they could no longer understand Kevin, as it most likely had to do with his proximity to me, but it was a passing thought. I had a feeling that the dragon would be following us to Castle Freesias whether we wanted him to or not, given how enamored he was of Gary. Hopefully, he'd meet another person to become infatuated with. Or a raccoon. Or a tree. Or a well-built barn. I didn't really think that Kevin was that discerning in his tastes. After all, he'd kidnapped Justin. That alone should speak volumes about the type of things he was attracted to.

And that sounded a lot less bitter in my head.

I pulled out the summoning crystal, vowing to not let Morgan know anything was wrong, to tell him we'd been able to rescue Justin, the quest went A-OK, and Ryan and the Prince would soon be returning to Castle Lockes while we continued north. I would be a man about this, having done my duty with a minimal amount of bloodshed. It was a proud day. Everyone would be thrilled.

"Sam?" Morgan said as the crystal lit up. "Are you—?"

"We rescued Justin," I said and thought *shut up shut up SHUT UP*, but, of course, it was no use. "We rescued Justin but not before we got captured by a cult who fed us corn of truth and made me confess that I'm creepy and go to Ryan Foxheart Fan Club meetings in disguise because I want to put my penis on his heart. But then the corn of truth made *him* tell *me* that he gets a boner every time I do magic or breathe or walk or exist and then I was sacrificed by the cult to a sexually aggressive dragon named Kevin who said I have lips made for sucking cock. He kidnapped me and took me back to his keep and Justin was there, and then Ryan rode Gary in to save us even though it was totally racist, it was *consensual* racism because Gary said that was okay for reasons I really don't understand yet. Then Ryan fought the dragon, but not really, because Kevin is in love with Gary and then Justin told me he's plowed Ryan like a field before he figured out that Ryan is my cornerstone and told him to his face, and Ryan is *pissed* off at me because I lied to him about it, but I didn't *mean* to. Oh, and we were attacked by Darks and fire geckos and somehow, the Darks shot me with lightning and I redirected it and took out the fire geckos and the Darks ran away. And also? I think I might be in love with him. No. Scratch that. I am. Pretty much an all-consuming, forever kind of love that is really gross for other people to witness because I want to stare lovingly in his eyes and call him boo and mini-muffin. It's awful to say that out loud. I know. But I don't give a fuck because I want him to be my mini-muffin. Is that so bad? I don't think that's bad. Well, maybe a little bad. Okay, it's awful, but you know what? I deserve to be awful. I want to be able to be the most awful thing ever seen. Wait. That doesn't sound right. What the hell were we talking about? I don't even know anymore. It's just this whole… *thing*, you know? Of course you do. You know everything. You always have. You probably knew I was going to call you like this. Because you're my berry sunshine. Gods. This fucking sucks. Stupid fucking Prince and stupid fucking Ryan. Fuck all this noise."

Silence.

"So," I said, remembering my manners. "How are you?"

"Um," Morgan said. "Good. And so is the King. And your mom. And your dad. Who are standing right next to me. And just heard every word you said."

"Well I'll be fucked," I said. "Okay. Uh. Ignore everything I just said. That was just… a test. To see… if you could… hear me. Rambling. About stuff. And obviously you all could, so the test is successful and I'll just be going—"

"He's your cornerstone?" my mother asked quietly, and it'd been so long since I'd heard her voice that I didn't know if I could trust myself to speak. "Oh, Sam."

"It's fine," I said roughly.

"It's *not* fine," Dad said. "You're not fine, and don't you pretend otherwise. How long have you known?"

"Awhile."

"Sam." His voice was flat.

"The night of the date with Todd."

"*Sam*," Mom said. "Why didn't you say anything? We would've—"

"I couldn't. Okay? I just couldn't. He's not mine. He will never be *mine*."

"You still should have told us," Dad said, and I knew he was trying to keep his anger in check. Knowing him, it wasn't toward me, but the situation. "We could have been there for you. Why'd you keep that to yourself?"

"He didn't," Morgan said, throwing himself on the fire along with me. "I knew."

"As did I," said the King. "And forgive an old man his selfishness. I wasn't thinking clearly. Justin had just been taken and I was concerned with his well-being. I never should have asked this of Sam."

"You're damn right you shouldn't have," my father snapped. "I'm sorry about your son, I really am. And I am overjoyed that Justin's safe. But this is *my* son we're talking about. Not only did you put him in danger, you did so knowing how he felt. Gods, Anthony, if you weren't the King and if I didn't respect the hell out of you, we'd be settling this with our fists. Spoiler: you would lose."

Ladies and gentlemen, my father.

"Dad," I admonished lightly. "You can't threaten the King. You'll be pooping in buckets by nightfall."

"I don't care," he retorted. "I'd poop in buckets for the rest of my life if it meant your heart was safe."

"Oh my gods."

"Okay," he said. "That didn't come out the way I wanted it to. But I stand by it."

"Oh my gods."

"Sam, I want you to listen to me, okay?" the King said. "I'm about to give you a direct order."

I stood a little taller without even thinking about it. He was my King, after all. "Yes, Your Highness."

"Come home."

"Of course. Anything you—wait. What?"

"I want you to come home. Back to Castle Lockes."

"I can't," I said, a small fissure of *want* bursting within me. Gods, I just wanted to go *home*. "I have to go to Randall at Castle Freesias. We talked about this."

"He can wait," the King said. "I think you need your family more than anything right now, and I'll be damned if I let a little thing like your magic keep you from them."

"But it's *not* a little thing," I said. "It's getting worse. I'm doing things that no wizard should be able to do. Morgan was right to send me to Randall. He's—"

"Morgan," the King interrupted. "Is it important?"

"Yes," Morgan said slowly. "I think it is."

"And do you agree with me that Sam should be surrounded by those that love him most?"

"Yes."

"Good," the King said. "Then make Randall come to Castle Lockes. He can just as easily evaluate you here as he can at Castle Freesias."

"I don't think—"

"Morgan. He'll need to be here, regardless," the King said quietly.

"Gods," Morgan muttered. "I didn't even...."

"What?" I asked. "Why would Randall come to Lockes without—"

And that's when it hit me.

The wedding.

Randall would need to be there to officiate the wedding between Justin and Ryan. The King wasn't on his way out and wouldn't be hopefully for years to come. But Ryan could just as easily be Prince Consort as he could be the King Consort. It was the wedding of the century, and of course the oldest and most notable wizard in existence would be there. And of course the same wizard was ordained to perform such ceremonies. He'd married the King to his Queen all those years before. And most likely a long line of royalty and notables before him.

Well that fucking sucked.

But I needed to man the fuck up. No more of this stupid bullshit. I needed to get up and get over this and be who I was supposed to be. I could do this.

"That's fine," I said briskly. "I'll come home. Most likely, Justin and Ryan will go on ahead. I'll take a few days and then start out. Just so you know, we'll probably be coming back with Kevin. I'm pretty sure he and Gary are dating. Or it's like Stockholm Syndrome. Either way, it's creepy and sweet and will most likely end up with me walking in on something that will scar me for life."

"Kevin," Morgan said. "You're bringing back the dragon named Kevin that you can talk to because he's in love with Gary."

"Oh, it's not just me. Everyone can talk to him. They just have to stand next to me because I think it's a proximity thing. Though, I'll be honest, most people probably won't want to stand near me and him at the same time because he tends to want to sleep with everything that has a pulse. And maybe a few things that don't."

"Just what kind of quests are you sending my son on?" Dad asked.

"This is not a normal thing," Morgan said quickly.

"Kind of normal," I said. "Seminormal."

"Not helping," Morgan said.

"Sam," Mom said. "Don't sleep with a dragon for your first time. If that's what you want to do down the road, I won't stop you. But I want your first time to not have scales and claws."

"And of course my mother knows I'm a virgin," I muttered.

"Well, yes," she said. "A mother's intuition. I know everything." I could hear the frown in her voice when she continued. "Well, I didn't know about Ryan being your cornerstone, so maybe not everything. I have failed you as a mother."

"Just one time," I told her. "Not all the other times."

"You should have told us," Dad said.

"What could you have done?"

"Something."

"Like?"

"Just... shut up. I would have punched someone. I still might. Now I know why Tiggy wants to smash everything."

"He looked at me when he said that," the King said. "It's okay. I pretty much deserve it."

"And Tiggy and Gary?" Mom asked. "They're okay?"

"Yeah. Aside from Gary being dragon-wooed and Tiggy possibly destroying a town filled with corn and cults with his fists."

"Sometimes," Dad said, "the sentences that come out of your mouth make me smile. That was one of them. I no longer want to hit something too badly."

"He *is* smiling," Mom said. Then, dropping her voice as if she thought I wouldn't hear her, "Should we talk about the fan-club thing?"

"I don't think he meant to say that," Dad whispered back. "He'll probably be too embarrassed to talk about it."

"It just makes so much more sense now, doesn't it? He's so like you."

"Yeah. He's a wizard's apprentice, but he also has a creepy sense of romance."

"Sam," Mom said, louder. "You get that from your father. Sometimes when I wake up at night, he's watching me sleep."

"It's true, son," Dad said. "We're kind of creepy. But we love with our whole creepy hearts."

I groaned. "If that was supposed to make me feel better, you failed."

"I followed your mother around for a week before I got the courage to go up and talk to her," Dad said. "I stayed in the shadows and tried not to breathe heavily."

"Of course," Mom said, a smile in her voice, "I knew he was there the whole time. The first time he approached, I wondered if he was finally going to murder me. So I knocked him flat on his ass and told him I would gut him if he tried anything."

"So badass," I whispered in awe.

"And then I gave her the flowers I'd brought for her," Dad said. "I'd accidentally squashed them, but she didn't mind."

"And then we had you," Mom said. "Okay, well, I skipped a bunch of steps there, but you get the idea. I don't think you want to hear about your parents having sexual inter—"

"Stop it," I said. "Stop it right now."

"He's just jealous because we're not virgins," Dad said. "Not even close to being virgins. And kind of virgin."

"Oh, you," Mom giggled.

"Oh my gods," I said, because I wanted this to be over.

"Feel better now?" Mom asked.

"Um. I think horrified is the word you're looking for. I feel horrified."

"We are good at this parent thing," Mom said.

"Pretty much the best," Dad agreed.

"I would marry the both of you if I could," the King said. "You are wonderful."

"Oh, come on!" I cried.

"He's just being polite, dear heart," Mom said.

"Politely wanting to get all up on this," Dad said.

"No," I said. "You are not allowed to be in the same room with each other ever again. There will be no parental three-ways. I command you."

They all laughed at me like jerks.

"Can I have a word alone with Sam?" Morgan asked quietly.

For a moment, Mom, Dad, and even the King sputtered, but then they stopped and I knew exactly the look on Morgan's face that brooked no further argument. It's all eyebrows and frown lines and narrowed eyes, and I almost ached at missing him. Missing them all. I knew I needed to go home. I needed them right now, and even if it meant having to face the one thing I didn't ever want to see, at least I'd have my whole family by my side.

Eventually their voices faded until I knew it was just Morgan and I. He let me breathe for a moment, knowing I needed it.

I wished I could see his face.

He said, "Sam, I'm so sorry."

"Yeah," I said hoarsely.

"I should have fought harder to go in your place."

"Nah," I said. "You know I would have found some way to get involved. I'm awesome like that."

"Awesome. Right."

"Morgan?"

"Yes, little one?"

"You were right."

"Oh?"

"To be worried about my heart."

A sigh. "I know."

"I just thought…." I took a breath. "I thought I'd control it better. It fucking hurts."

"You said he felt the same?"

"No," I said. "The coercion forced him to say he was attracted to me. Nothing more. And it's not like it matters. He swore an oath. To Justin."

"What? What kind of oath?"

"One that they both agreed to for mutual benefit. It's none of my business, anyway. Or any of ours. It's between them. You know what a knight's oath means. Especially when made in fealty to a king-in-waiting." It meant that only Justin could release Ryan from his oath. And that was never going to happen.

"This fucking sucks," Morgan said.

I couldn't help it. I laughed. "You sound way too much like me."

"Well, it does."

"Yeah."

"It's a good idea. Not traveling back with them."

"Sure," I said. "I have all the ideas."

"I'll get in touch with Randall."

"He's going to be pissed."

"He'll get over it. I want you to come straight home, Sam. No detours. No deviations."

"Yeah, I'll get right on that."

"Sam."

268TJ KLUNE

"Are we going to talk about the lightning thing?" I asked quickly. "Or...."

He sighed. "Lightning, Sam. Really?"

"Right? That's what I said. While I was running for my life."

"The Darks aren't going to forget."

"Eh. I can take them. Apparently."

"You really shouldn't."

"It's weird, though, right? They must be super pissed off if they keep following me. Was Lartin some kind of big to-do? I'd never heard of him before. Was he like their king or something? Can wizards *have* kings? Oh wait. Randall. Sort of. Oh gods. Did we kill the king of the Darks?"

Silence.

"Morgan!"

"Hush, I'm thinking about what to say."

"You mean you're trying to figure out what secret to keep."

"He was important to the Darks, Sam. No official ranking. I guess it's easiest to say that he was beloved, in his way. People had an affection for him, even if he was a bit out there."

That... sort of made sense. "You mean like that special uncle that everyone just loves but is still kind of creepy because his touches last just a bit too long but he's always really apologetic about it and then he brings you pie?"

Morgan sighed. "I don't even know why I bother anymore."

"You love me. Don't front. Essentially, we killed someone popular."

"Creepy popular. And not just killed. Obliterated."

"Tiggy tends to get... protective."

"Sam, the only way they could tell it was Lartin was because one of his fingers found embedded in the bedrock was wearing a ring with his signet on it. Let me repeat. Finger. Embedded. In rock."

"Very protective, then. Maybe we could have gone about it a bit differently, sure, but it's not like there is a bounty on my head or anything."

Silence.

"There's a bounty on my head, isn't there?"

"*Finger.* In the *rock.*"

I grinned. "Okay. I'll admit. This is a first. And I'm strangely thrilled by it. How much am I worth?"

"Yeah. About that. So. They're not really offering *any* coin for it. Or gold. It's more of a... for the sake of doing it. And the notoriety."

"What? I'm not worth *anything*?"

"I wouldn't say that," Morgan said. "You're worth plenty. To me. And your mom. And dad. And Gary and Tiggy. Just not to the people who want to kill you."

"Not helping," I growled. "Who gets a bounty on their head when there is no actual bounty?"

"You do, apparently. First I've ever heard of that happening. But then, you talk to dragons and get gay fairy married, so I try not to question things too much anymore."

"Those weren't my fault! First, I can't help it if I attract the weirdoes. Second, I'm about to be attacked by angry cult members who are carrying scythes and torches."

"You *are* a weirdo. And tell those angry cult members... wait. *What*?"

Farther down the road, cresting the hill into the valley, came the people of Tarker Mills, Eloise in the lead. She looked so badass with her hair billowing around her that I almost was able to admire her and forget the fact that most likely, she was coming to kill us all. For once, I'd like to have the wind blow just right and make my clothes billow around me and have someone say, "Dude. Look. That guy is so cool. I want to be him when I grow up."

"Uh," I said to Morgan. "I have to go."

"When you get back, I am *never* letting you out again, do you hear me?" he said. "A cult. Sam, only *you* would stumble upon a cult."

"You say that like it's insulting."

"It's certainly not a compliment."

"Well, if it makes you feel better, they've gotten me over Firework Corn. I never want to see corn ever again."

"Sam."

"Yeah."

"Stay safe." And the crystal went dark.

"Gods," I muttered. "I can't even get the exit line. I don't get the guy, my clothes don't billow when I crest hills, I don't even get the last word. What the fuck."

I thought about taking a stand right then and there. I didn't want to hurt any of them (except for maybe Eloise; I wanted to beat her in the face with corn) because they were under whatever "truth" they'd been fed that day. I didn't want to underestimate her either. After all, she'd built an entire cult up in fifty-some-odd days, and that takes real dedication. That and the fact that she was probably batshit crazy. I was also still pissed off at her that she'd made me eat her hair. That shit is *not* hygienic.

So I did the only thing I could think of.

I ran the opposite direction.

CHAPTER 24
Upon These Stars

THEY MUST have heard me running gracefully (read: not gracefully at all), because when I rounded the corner to the keep, Ryan, Gary, and Tiggy were already moving forward. Ryan had his sword drawn again, and Gary and Tiggy looked ready to lay down some righteous fury.

"What the hell is happening?" Ryan demanded.

And yeah. Apparently working out should become part of my regimen because I was seriously out of breath. I held up a finger at them as I bent over, trying to catch my breath.

"Sam," Gary said.

Gods, didn't he understand the point of the *finger*?

I glared at him.

He rolled his eyes.

"He breathes a lot through his mouth," Justin said, sounding disgusted. "I've noticed that."

I wanted to tell him that I was going to shove some magic up his ass, but I couldn't quite yet make the words come out.

"Why are you noticing his mouth?" Gary asked sweetly. "Aren't you getting enough at home?"

Ryan scowled like a champ. I couldn't even begin to guess who that scowl was meant for.

"Tiggy gonna smash some things," Tiggy said. "Tiggy angry."

"No, Tiggy," Gary said. "Not things. You want to smash princes."

Tiggy turned toward Justin, who had the decency to take a step back.

"Cult," I finally managed to say. "Coming... to murder... our faces."

"Well shit," Gary said. "I told you we should have killed them all. But Knight Sanctimonious Face over there was all, like, 'No, we can't. We're good and our hearts are pure and we must spare lives and watch as I pose with everything I do.'"

"I did not say that," Ryan said. "And I *don't* pose."

I gulped up another breath. "You're posing... right now."

And he was, standing there, sword drawn, shoulders squared, chin held high, eyes on the horizon. And gods, he looked so fucking hot doing so. Like a douche, yes. But a hot douche.

"I told you we should have killed them," Gary said.

"We can't just *kill* people," Ryan said.

"They were holding us prisoner."

"That doesn't make it right. Killing people never does."

"Oh?" Gary asked. "What about Moishe?"

"I'll kill him," Ryan snarled. Then, "Uh. I mean. No way. What. Who?"

"Do I even want to know?" Justin asked, edging away from Tiggy, who was frowning at him.

"Elven whore," Gary said. "Works for Sam's fairy drag mother. Long story."

"Funny," Justin said. "You all seem to have a lot of those now."

"I've got your long story right here," Kevin said, curling his tail around Gary's legs.

"Dude," I said. "So not cool. Like, at all."

"Hush," Gary said, leaning into the dragon. "I think it's endearing."

"You've known him for two hours. He can't yet be endearing."

"It's endearing," Gary insisted as Kevin's tail started to rub against his own. "And maybe slightly invasive."

"You're not getting to third base with my best friend while I'm watching," I told Kevin.

"Why not, pretty?" Kevin purred. "The more the merrier, I always say. We can just go back into the keep and drink some wine and take off our clothes and just go for it, you know? Just *do* it. It's just our bodies. Everyone's got one. Sweaty, naked bodies that—"

"I am so uncomfortable right now," Ryan said.

"Guys," I said. "Cult. Coming to murder our faces. Priorities."

"Why don't you just use your magic?" Justin asked. "It shouldn't be that hard."

"Ungh," Ryan said.

"It's harder than you think," Gary said, wide-eyed and innocent.

Justin grimaced at Ryan. "Did you just *drool*? Seriously, Ryan. I can't take you anywhere. What the hell?"

"What?" Ryan said, wiping his mouth. "No. Of course not. That'd be weird." His eyes were still glazed over as he looked down at my hands as if he expected me to cast a spell right in front of him. Instead, I was focusing on not getting an erection because apparently I had a kink for Ryan's kink for my magic.

"I didn't come this far to get murdered by a cult," Justin said.

"Wow," Gary said. "I didn't think you went far at all. I thought we were the ones that did all the work to rescue you. Funny, that."

"You're kind of a bitch, aren't you?" Justin said.

"*What* did you call me? Oh, Gary's gonna bring the *pain*—"

"Shut up," I snapped. "All of you. For fuck's sake."

Surprisingly, they all shut up.

"Wow," I said. "I didn't think that was going to work. Huh. I must be intimidating."

"Like a butterfly," Gary said.

I ignored him. "Kevin's going to stop them."

They all slowly turned to the dragon, who looked like he was trying to slip his nose under Gary's tail. "Er," he said. "What now?"

"You're a god to them, dude," I explained. "They built a cult around you. They'll listen to you. Tell them to fuck off so we can get the hell out of here."

"What's in it for me?"

"Gary," I said.

"I'll do it," he said promptly.

"Wait," Gary said. "*What?*"

I rolled my eyes. "Like he's going to not go with us now. You know he's going to follow us home."

"We're in love," Kevin announced quite loudly.

"No," Gary said. "We're in lust. There is a difference."

"It's love," Kevin said. "You make me burn. Without you, I am nothing. I want to fellate you until you cry."

Gary stared at him. "I might have gotten in over my head."

"I shall protect you, my love," Kevin said, pulling himself up to his full height. "You are the most important thing in the world to me, and since we will not be having an orgy with all your friends—wait. What was that?"

"I didn't say anything," Gary said.

"No?" Kevin said. "I swore I just heard you say you wanted to have an orgy with all your friends."

"I didn't say that."

"You sure?"

"Positive."

"Oh. Well, as I was saying. Since we will not be having an orgy... right? Anyone. No one. Seriously? Not a single one of you? Ugh. Fine. Since there will be no orgy, I shall instead defend your honor. Because you're my one and only."

"I don't believe you so much anymore," Gary said. "Because of the orgy."

"You have to act godlike," I said. "Make it believable. Really sell it."

Kevin cocked his head at me. "So, like I normally act?"

"What? No! The exact opposite of how you normally act. The furthest thing from how you normally act. Don't even act like you normally do and you'll be closer than you are right now."

"Got it," Kevin said. "Act like normal. Because I'm a god. Should I do an accent? That's normal. Normal people have accents. Thees ees yer god spakin. Bow down ter meh."

"We're doomed," I moaned.

"We really should do something about your pessimism," Gary said. "Have a little faith, huh? I mean, just look at us."

I looked at them. A hornless gay unicorn built out of rainbows and bitchiness. A half-giant who wanted to smash everything. A dragon who winked and flicked his tongue at me. A prince who I wanted to protect but also punch in the face. A knight I had a heart boner for.

"We're doomed," I moaned again. "Doooomed."

"Dragon," Gary said.

"Yes, light of my life?"

"I don't want to die today. Nor do I want any of my friends to die today. And by friends, I mean Sam and Tiggy."

"Hey," Ryan said, sounding put out. "I thought we were friends."

Gary turned to look at him with narrowed eyes. It was rather frightening. "You thought that, huh?"

"Gary," I said.

"Fine," he growled. "Justin and Ryan can't die either. But they're not my friends. Especially Justin. But mostly Ryan."

"Ow," Justin said flatly. "My heart."

Ryan actually looked hurt by it.

"I shall protect you all," Kevin said, puffing out his chest and raising his head. His eyes flashed and a lick of fire rolled out of his nose. "And then we should talk about that orgy."

So we stood in a line, our backs to the keep, waiting for Eloise and the creepy people of Tarker Mills to descend upon us. Somehow, Ryan ended up next to me and kept trying to inch his way in front of me.

"What are you doing?" I whispered.

"Nothing," he said and then tried to shove me behind him.

"Are you trying to protect me?" I asked, starting to get slightly pissed. "Dude. Knock it off. You're not my knight in shining armor. You're a dick in dented tin."

His jaw clenched. "Might as well be," he said. "After all, I'm your cornerstone. It's what I'm supposed to do."

Oh, that motherfucker. "You do *not* get to say that," I hissed at him. "You're not my *anything*. And I don't need you to protect me. I've been doing just fine without you and will continue to do so long into the future. Go be dashing and immaculate somewhere else."

"Get down with your bad self," Gary muttered. "We don't need no mens."

"Tiggy and Gary and Sam don't need no mens," Tiggy agreed.

"Maybe," Ryan said, "if you'd been *honest* with me, we wouldn't even *be* in this position in the first place!"

"Are you two seriously having this argument right now?" Justin asked.

I ignored him as I glared at the back of Ryan's head. "Bullshit," I said. "We're here because a dragon kidnapped your fiancé. Who you swore an *oath* to."

"I would like to be kept out of this," Kevin said. "I feel like there's a lot of misplaced anger going around. Bow down ter yer god, hoominz."

"The oath has nothing to do with you," Ryan said through gritted teeth.

"Just as anything having to do with a cornerstone has nothing to do with you," I said and he *recoiled*. I had the sense to feel slightly bad at the wounded look on his face. It didn't matter, though. I was pissed.

But before Ryan could retort with whatever was going on in that stupid head of his, Eloise and the cult rounded the final corner to the keep. Their eyes widened when they saw Kevin sitting regally next to us, tail and wings twitching.

"He… is… *glorious*," Eloise breathed.

I wished I could say the same for her, but she looked worse for wear. Her hair was a mess around her face, and I thought she was missing a tooth or two, which went well with the shiner she was sporting on her right eye and a bruise on her cheek suspiciously shaped like a hoofprint.

"Dude," I said reverently, not even trying to keep my voice down. "Did you kick her in the face?"

Gary preened. "That I did."

"I love you," I told him. "Seriously. I am in awe of you."

"I punched seventeen people," Tiggy said.

"And you're my favorite giant ever," I said. "They will tell stories of your bravery."

"I punched and kicked people too," Ryan said.

I ignored him.

"Awkward," Gary whispered to Tiggy.

"You're alive?" Eloise asked as she glared at me. "How is that possible?"

"Do god stuff," I muttered, elbowing Kevin. "Be all godly."

Kevin took a step forward, his claws digging into the earth. The crowd in front of us said, "Ooooh."

When he spoke, his voice was deep and rumbly. He sounded ridiculous. "You approacheth my keepeth, mere mortals. What sayeth you for spaketh to me? Eth."

"Oh my gods," I said. "Dude. Come on. You had one job."

"Forgive us, our lord dragon," Eloise said, curtsying deeply. "We are truly blessed to be in your presence. You humble us by allowing our audience. You are truly a creature of magnificence and beauty."

"Heh," Kevin said. "Wicked."

"My lord dragon, if I may," Eloise said, eyeing me again. "Why do you harbor the sacrifice? Was the wizard not up to your obviously high standards? I would've assumed you'd have eaten him by now."

"Hey," I said, offended. "I am, like, the *highest* of standards."

"Whatever helps you sleep at night," Justin said under his breath.

"Hmm?" Kevin said. "Oh. Well. I was... saving him. For. A snack. Later. I have irritable bowel syndrome and he looks to be a bit... stringy."

"*Stringy*? You listen here, motherfucker. I'll cut you—"

"And loud," Kevin said. "But those *lips*. I was waiting, I guess."

Eloise's eyes widened. "You wished to have us here to witness the sacrifice? Oh, my lord. What an honor." She turned back to her people and clapped her hands together giddily. "The great and venerable dragon god is going to eat the wizard right in front of us!"

"What?" Kevin said.

"What?" I said.

Ryan tensed and tried to push me behind him again. This did not go unnoticed by Justin, who scowled at us.

"He's not going to eat him," Ryan snapped.

"I'm not going to eat him," Kevin said.

"Why?" Eloise asked. Then she frowned. "Unless... you're... *not* the god we thought you were."

"What?" Kevin said. "Shut up. I am totally a god. So godlike. God of Dragons, they call me. Beast from the East. They all say so."

"Who calls you that?" Gary asked curiously.

"You know," Kevin said. "*Them.*"

"Well," Eloise said. "If you truly are a god, then you should eat the wizard. We are your loyal subjects and we have provided a sacrifice for you."

"Um," Kevin said.

"Don't you dare eat my best friend," Gary said. "You'll never know the pleasures of my supple body if you do."

"Supple, you say?" Kevin asked, his voice a purr.

Eloise grimaced. "Are you really going to listen to this... this *blasphemous* creature?"

"Honey," Gary said, "the only thing that's blasphemous up in here right now is your hair. That shit be tragic."

"Boom," Tiggy said and fist/hoof-bumped Gary.

"Dragon," Eloise snarled. "I command you to eat the wizard."

And that's when things screeched to a halt.

Kevin tensed dangerously, spikes along his back quivering.

"Oh, bitch, you gone and done it now," Gary muttered.

"What did you say?" Kevin asked, voice suddenly more dangerous than I'd ever heard it. He moved then, curling himself almost like a snake, his tail wrapping around all of us. "You *command* me? A *human?*"

"If you are truly our god," she said, "you will rejoice in our sacrifice to you."

His eyes narrowed. "No one *commands* me. Least of all you."

Something flickered in her eyes, almost like fear. The crowd behind her took a step back away from Eloise.

"Dragon," she tried.

"Tell me," Kevin growled. "Do you often make demands of your gods? Is that what you think they're there for? For humans like you to lay your burdens upon them, to do as you ask, and if they don't, you doubt them? Tell me, woman. Is that what you are asking? Of a *god?*"

Her eyes turned to slits, mouth a thin line. She straightened her shoulders. Her hands tightened around the handle of the axe she carried. She opened her mouth to undoubtedly give the order to attack, for the people behind her could not disobey an order to sacrifice themselves for her.

But she didn't get a single word out as the dragon struck quickly, neck stretching, jaws snapping closed. Eloise didn't even have a chance to make any sound as his neck worked when he swallowed her down. All that remained was the axe on the ground, the handle resting between her feet that jetted twin sprays of blood where they'd been severed at the ankles.

His throat worked as the muscles carried the woman down his esophagus, and when he looked forward again, he grimaced. Coughed once. Burped loudly, and I wondered if it tasted like Eloise. Then he said, "That's going to be a bitch to pass later."

"Holy fuck," I breathed.

Kevin grinned at me.

"You have some cult leader stuck in your teeth," I said faintly.

He looked at the crowd staring up at him in horror. He raised his head, glared down at them, and said, "Boo."

They all ran screaming.

THAT NIGHT, I lay on my back on the roof of the keep, watching the stars above, wondering just how in the hell my life had gotten to this point.

Then I realized it was mostly my fault, and that made me sort of depressed and happy all at the same time.

I told myself that it was because I was extraordinarily complex.

Mostly, though, I believed it was just because I was weird.

The stars were bright above me. Away from the lights of any city, they shone down like beacons in the dark. I had so many, many things I wanted to wish for, but I couldn't think of a single one. I was exhausted and sad. Tomorrow, Justin and Ryan would start on their way back to the City of Lockes. We would follow them in a few days.

At first, Ryan looked stunned that I was coming back to Castle Lockes instead of going to Castle Freesias. That lasted about two seconds before he started vehemently disagreeing with our plans, saying we should travel together, that it'd be safer.

I told him I was being followed by Darks and was traveling with a dragon. It was safer for the Prince if he was away from me.

Justin, of course, had immediately approved.

Ryan argued.

I told him it wasn't up for debate.

Ryan had refused to look at me for a long time after that.

Whatever.

I didn't need his shit.

(I needed his shit.)

(Gods, that sounded wrong.)

It didn't matter. It didn't. We'd get back to the city and I would work with Randall and Justin would marry Ryan, and eventually, everything would be okay again. Everything would be—

"I figured you'd be up here," he said, and I closed my eyes, because of *course* he would follow me up here. Of *course* he couldn't leave well enough alone.

"You figured right," I said, voice light and even.

I didn't look over at him as he hoisted himself up through the hatch. He closed the hatch behind him. He obviously wanted this to be private, but beyond that, I didn't know what else. Whether to try and change my mind about traveling separately or to chew me out for not telling him what a cornerstone was, it didn't matter. No good could have come from the conversation and I sure as shit wasn't going to give him the satisfaction. I was weak when it came to Ryan Foxheart, and I wouldn't let him make me weaker.

So when he said, "Mervin, huh?" I flushed furiously and refused to even dignify that with a response.

"Yeah," he said quietly. "Should have seen that one." He moved to stand at the edge of the keep, off to my left. I could see him out of the corner of my eye. I kept my gaze resolutely on the stars. "That one's on me."

I waited.

"You never would have told me, would you?"

I could have played dumb, but I was done with games. It wasn't just about this. It was about everything. "No," I said.

He nodded, as if that's the answer he expected. "Because of Justin."

"Partly."

"Oh? What were the other parts?"

"It doesn't matter."

"Of course it does."

"Why?"

"Because it matters to me."

"Why?"

"Gods," he said through gritted teeth. "You infuriate me."

I rolled my eyes.

"Sam."

"What?" I just wanted him to go the fuck away.

"I care about you, okay? I do. You have no idea how much or for how long."

"Stop it," I said, sitting up and finally looking at him. "Just stop it." I kept my voice from cracking as best I could. I pushed myself up from the ground. "You can't say anything like that. You can't."

"Why?" he said, taking a step toward me.

"Ryan," I said, and I was *pleading*. I was *begging* for him to shut up. To keep talking. To come closer. To go away.

"I wanted to talk to you," he said, taking another step, and I *willed* myself to move away. To run as fast as I could, but *nothing* happened. I was paralyzed in front of him, and I couldn't even find a fucking flare of magic because my godsdamn cornerstone was standing right in front of me, and I could do nothing that might end up hurting him. "For the longest time. I wanted to walk right up to you and say my name. That I was Ryan. That I was Nox. That I was here because of you, that I did this because I wanted to prove to you that I could. That I crawled out of the slums because of you."

"You don't owe me shit," I said. "You fucked your way to get where you were. You said you were a whore. That you slept with people, men, for money to get out of the slums. You said you wanted to get out of there because of me. If you did, then I made you do that… that *thing*. That no child should ever have to do. *I* did that to you. Stop making me out to be some kind of hero when I'm anything but."

"You can't blame yourself for the choices I made," he growled.

And so I swung the trap shut. "Then you can't blame me for the choices *I* made too."

He flinched, but didn't move away. I could have reached out and touched him, if I'd wanted to. And I wanted to very much. But I couldn't. "You should have told me," he said. "The moment you knew, you should have told me."

"You're with the Prince. You're getting married to *Justin*."

"I have a *right* to know."

I laughed bitterly. "No, you don't. You didn't even know what a cornerstone was before... this. This *everything*. It's not something for *you*. It's not something *you* need."

"It's *about* me," he snapped. "You can't tell me it's not. You were leaving to go to Randall because you couldn't control your magic. I fucking help you control your magic. How the hell can you say it's not for me? That it's not something I need?"

"It's not a one-time thing," I said. "It's not just you. There could be others. There *will* be others. Because you can't be what I need. You can't be the one to anchor it down. There will be others and I will find them and they will help me and I will show them why I was made for them. I will show them how great I can be, because I will *never* be anyone's second choice. I will *never* be second best to someone I love."

"No one else," he said hoarsely. "Sam. You can't. You can't."

"Why? I *have* to. I don't have a *choice*. If I don't, I am no better than the Darks. Except I am stronger than all of them put together. Do you know what would happen? Do you know what I could do? Ryan. I could destroy everything."

"No," he said. "There has to be another way. There will be. We'll find it. *I'll* find it."

"There is no other way!" I shouted at him.

"There's *always* another way," he snapped. "You can't just fucking give up."

"I have to," I said. "I have to give up on you. Because there is nothing left for me with you."

"Sam," he said, and gods, I hated how he said my name. Like I was everything to him. Like I was important. Like I was all he could ever want. "You can't believe that. You don't. Just... please. We can—"

"Then let's go," I said, taking a step toward him. Challenging him. Already knowing his answer. "Let's go right now. Leave this behind. Break your oath. Break it and come with me and we'll be everything together. Break it."

"Sam," he choked out, reaching for me in an aborted attempt. "You—I *can't*. My word is my *honor*. I am a Knight of Verania and that is *all* I am. It's all I have. I promised my mother that I would be something. And I *am*. She was all that I had for the longest time and I did this for her. I am *doing* this for her. She wouldn't want...I can't just—"

"*And what about me?*" I roared at him. "*Where the fuck do I fit in with your honor?*"

His fingers twitched and then he was cupping my face and saying *Sam* and *please* and *I want* in a fractured voice that I just could not handle. He said, "You don't have to do this, okay? I promise. I promise. Come back with us. With me. Just... come with me. I'm selfish. I am. I don't care. I'm sorry, but I don't. I want you to come back with me and just be there with me. You've—okay. I know. I know. It sucks. It's awful. But I'll make it work, okay? I can do this. We'll figure something out. Yes, there's Justin, okay? And I gave him my fealty. But we can be—"

"Can you even hear what you're saying?" I asked him, trying to pull my face away. "Can you even hear what you're asking me to do?"

His grip tightened on my face, not hurting, but not soft, either. "I don't know what else *to* do," he said, sounding more miserable than I'd ever heard him before.

"Why?" I asked again, my eyes never leaving his. It felt quiet, this moment. And huge. My skin was too tight, and I was breaking apart underneath it. I *ached* and even before he spoke, I knew his words would shatter everything but there was nothing I could do to stop him. "Why are you even pushing this? Why do you care? What the fuck do you want from me?"

And he said, "Can't you see? Sam. *Sam.* Gods. It's—there. It's *here.*" He grabbed my hand and held it over his chest. I could feel the rapid beat of his heart underneath my fingers. "It's here. Ever since I first saw you, you've been with me. I couldn't have forced you away if I tried. I'm sorry I made an oath. I did it because I thought it was the right thing to do. And I'm sorry that I can't break it. But you have to believe me that it's always been you. I promise. I promise." His voice cracked and my hands shook. "I promise, because when I look upon these stars, there is *nothing* I wish for more than you."

I can't be blamed, then.

I can't be blamed for kissing him.

Because everything broke within me, and I was hollowed-out and empty.

So I kissed him.

I surged forward, and he exhaled into my mouth, a rush stronger than a sigh. I took it in as my eyes fluttered closed and as a day's worth of his stubble scraped against my chin. I've kissed people before. A girl was my first, when I wasn't sure who I was. Her name was Claire. A boy named Dougie on a dare. A castle guard named Craig when I turned eighteen and got drunk on my birthday. They were kind and sweet, but they were never like this. The tug of my lip as he worried it between his teeth. The slide of his tongue against mine, slick and warm, my heart ratcheting up in my chest. His thumbs on my cheek as he pulled away briefly, lips red and wet. Then he was on me again, pulling us together, our bodies aligning perfectly. The heat of him wormed its way through my clothes, and I might have whimpered quietly. But he swallowed it down, never letting it escape, a secret between us here in the dark, the stars shining down upon us. His breath was hot as he kissed his way up my jaw, the swipe of his tongue against my ear. My fingers curled against his chest, and he was all muscle as I breathed him in, woodsmoke and sweat and blood and we had to stop this. We had to stop before we couldn't stop. I never wanted to. I never wanted it to end. Which is why it had to.

I said, "No," my voice like gravel.

He brought his lips again to mine, his tongue insistent as it brushed my lips.

He pulled away, but only just, pressing his forehead against mine. Our eyes were opened, and we panted at each other, holding on tight. His eyes were blown wide, the pupils dilated until there was only a hint of color. His cheeks were blotchy, and his lips were spit-slick, and I thought savagely, *I did that. I did that to him*, and how my magic *sang*. It *sang* because I'd given it what it wanted most, tasting him, having him. For a brief, shining moment, I thought myself capable of anything.

Everything. But it faded because I knew the truth. We'd carved out this little space just for him and me, but the moment we let go, the moment we stepped back, it would be over and we'd never have it again.

So I couldn't be blamed, then. For holding on for just a little bit longer. For thinking this could be real, that it was just this easy. For wishing—wishing harder than I'd ever wished for anything before—that this moment would never end because I'd found someone made for me and I wanted to show Ryan why I was made for him.

He croaked, "Sam."

"Yeah."

"My word is my bond," he said quietly. Desperately. Trying to get me to understand.

"I know." Because I did.

"I would break it for you. I—"

"Would you?" I asked him. "Would you really?"

And he hesitated.

That was all the answer I needed. I didn't blame him, not completely. I knew what oaths meant to knights. Especially when made to their kings and future kings. A knight who could not be trusted to honor his oath might as well not be a knight at all. I knew what was important to him. I didn't blame him. I'd made my own oaths. My own promises. I understood.

And so I let him go.

He tried to hold on, tried to keep me from stepping away, but in the end, he couldn't without hurting me. His hands trailed down my arms until he gripped my fingers and opened his mouth to say what, I don't know. Because he closed it again and shook his head, tugging on my hands, trying to pull me back.

"We danced," he said. "Three times the first time. If I'd known. If I could have known what—Sam. I don't...."

"We'll be okay," I said. "One day. One day, this will all have faded. Everything we feel right now."

"I don't *want* it to fade," he snapped at me.

"We don't have a choice. I won't be your secret. I won't let you be mine."

"It won't be. He'll understand. He'll—"

"Ryan. Let me go."

"No," he said, shaking his head. "No. I won't. You can't make me. You can't—"

"Ryan."

"Fuck," he said. "I wish—"

"I know."

I pulled my hands away. He let them go this time.

I took a step back. And another. And another.

He never looked away.

Once there was enough space between us so that neither of us could reach out and touch the other, I said, "You'll leave. In the morning. Take the Old Road back to the City of Lockes. Take what supplies you'll need. There's an extra rucksack. Don't stop. Don't delay. Don't wait for us. Go home and be happy. You are a knight commander. You worked hard for it. Be proud, Ryan. You've earned it. You deserve it. Marry Justin. He cares about you and you care about him. That will be enough. For your oath."

"What about you?" he asked, voice ragged.

I smiled, though I felt it tremble. "I'll be okay. You'll see. I'll be okay. I'm Sam of Wilds. I'll always be okay."

I thought he was going to say more, to wear me down until I was begging him not to leave, to kiss me just one more time. To never let it stop.

But instead, he nodded. Curled his hands into fists at his sides. Exhaled heavily. His shoulders were tense, but it mattered not. In the starlight, he looked beautiful, and I felt like that little boy again, that fifteen-year-old boy who saw him for the first time and who understood by the stumbling of his heart that nothing would ever be the same again.

"Go," I said. "Please. Go."

And he did.

I looked up at the night sky as the sounds of his footsteps faded down the stone steps.

The stars shone brightly.

CHAPTER 25
Stories from the Journey Home

THEY LEFT early the next morning.
I told them to be careful.
Justin scoffed and took Ryan's hand in his.
Ryan nodded but didn't look at me.
I wanted to tell him I didn't regret a single thing.
But I didn't.
I watched the road long after they'd disappeared.

"WHY DON'T we just fly home?" Gary asked. "It'd only take a few days."
"Humans don't ride upon my back," Kevin said. "It's racist."
Gary swooned.

"ARE YOU sure?" I asked Kevin that first night after Justin and Ryan had left. We were at the top of the keep again. Gary and Tiggy were below us, looking through the books to see if there was anything of value that we could take. Mostly, it was explicitly detailed pornography, describing sexual acts that made even Gary blush. (*"Triple* penetration? My gods, your asshole would be like a cave entrance after that.")
"About?" Kevin asked, tail twitching. His black scales looked luminous in the moonlight.
"Going with us."
"Are you questioning a god?" he asked. "Spake der truth, hoominz."
I rolled my eyes. "Yeah, that doesn't quite work on me."
"Had to make sure. It was nice while it lasted."
"And then you ate her."
He grimaced. "Not my finest moment. But she was a threat and now she's not, so I guess it worked out in the end. And eventually, she'll work her way out of my end. Ironic, don't you think?"
"Ugh," I said.
"Indeed."
"She was a threat to you?" I asked.
"Well, yes. And to you. And Gary. And Tiggy. Since we don't like Ryan and Justin, we won't count them."
"You defended us," I said, surprised.
"Why wouldn't I?" he asked.

"Why *would* you? I'm a wizard. You hate wizards. You don't even really *know* us."

"Are you a good person?"

"Uh. I think so? Most of the time."

"And Gary and Tiggy are good?"

"Yes. Better than me, for sure."

"There you go," he said, as if it were nothing.

"You're very strange," I said after a while.

"Dragons usually are," he said.

"But." I hesitated, unsure of my place. "You said that you'd never met any other dragons."

"We're giant lizards that fly and breathe fire," he said. "That's strange in itself. I'm just generalizing."

"There are others, you know."

"I know," he said quietly. "Maybe one day I'll meet them."

"But not today?"

"Not today, pretty."

It was nice, though my heart was breaking. It was nice sitting out in the spring night air where just twenty-four hours ago, I'd discovered what Ryan Foxheart tasted like, sweet and clean and warm. It was nice. All of this was nice.

"Why'd you come here?" I asked him.

"Because I could."

"Where did you come from?"

"Far away."

"What were you looking for?"

"A place to call my own."

"Dragons are frustrating," I said, because I could.

"Are they? You know many of them?"

"No. But if you're anything to go by, it's not that broad of a generalization."

"I've seen things," he said. "Many different things. There are lands far away from here that you couldn't even possibly dream of. I've seen cliffs of ice so tall they disappear into the clouds. I've seen flowers deep in jungles that eat everything that happens by them. I've seen the hearts of men, the darkness that lies within. I've been captured by wizards who wanted nothing more than to spill my blood to make their spells. I've seen people cower in fear at the mere sight of me. I've seen a city that floats in the clouds and the beings that live there have translucent skin and cannot speak for they have no mouths. I've seen a volcano erupt during a lightning storm, ash in the sky as the mountain explodes. I've seen many things, pretty."

"I don't understand," I said.

He sighed. "I've seen many things. Both good and evil. Majestic and destructive. Stars falling from the sky and a man whose tattoos moved across his skin as if they were alive before he tried to rip one of my hearts from my chest. I have seen many, many things. But I have never seen one look at another the way the knight looks at you."

I said, "Don't."

"Why?" he asked. "Because you don't believe it or you don't want to hear it?" I said, "Just. Don't."

He looked up at the night sky, scales glittering. "Everything is so vast. It's humbling to remember just how small we really are."

I followed his gaze skyward. The stars were so bright tonight.

He said, "I left to find a home. To find a place I could call my own. To feel safe for the first time in my life. I didn't think I would ever actually find it."

"And you have now?"

"You're not going to hurt me?"

"No, I would never hurt you." I paused, considering. "Unless you tried to get all up in my business again. Then I make no promises."

He laughed. It was low and gravelly, and I thought I could listen to it for a very long time. "If I get all up in your business again, it'll be because you invited me in."

"So never, then."

"Promises, promises."

"You feel safe with us," I said.

"Yes, pretty."

"Why?"

"Because of how you and Gary and Tiggy care about each other."

"They're dicks," I said.

"Oh?"

"But so am I. We fit. They're my friends."

"I noticed."

"You're a dick too," I said.

"Thank you, pretty," he said with a toothy smile.

"I'm sorry," I said.

"For what?"

I shrugged. "For whoever hurt you. It wasn't right. No one should ever have to go through that."

"You're an odd one, aren't you?"

"Yeah. Probably. Enough people tell me as much."

"That's not a bad thing."

"Most times."

"I'm sorry I tried to burn you and broke your ice spell and then knocked you through the side of a building."

"It was a shed."

"Still. I feel real bad about that."

"Do you?"

"Sort of. You have to admit I looked pretty badass doing it, though."

I groaned. "Yes. You crested the hill and your wings were billowing. I can't billow *anything*."

"You can billow me anytime you want," Kevin said.

"Um," I said. "Ew. And also, that didn't make sense. But ew. Because of that thing you do with your tongue."

"What thing?" he asked, flicking it at me again.

"Argh," I said. "My life."

He laughed and it faded into the night and we just sat there, the dragon and I, lost in our own thoughts. I tried not to think about Ryan, but it was an impossible task and one I wasn't quite ready yet to accept. I wondered how long it would hurt for. I wondered how long it would take my heart to heal.

I thought about wishing on the stars for the pain to go away, but I couldn't. Not yet.

"He doesn't deserve you," Kevin said fiercely, breaking the silence.

I closed my eyes. "Yeah."

"Gary told me. What a cornerstone was. He doesn't deserve the title and he doesn't deserve you." He sounded resolute. More so than I could ever be.

"One day I'll believe you," I said.

I felt him curl his tail around me. I waited for the moment it would become inappropriate, but it never came. He curled it around me and pulled me closer. His skin and scales were hot to the touch. It almost felt safe. "And one day," he said quietly, "maybe I could be there to tell you I told you so."

They were hesitant, his words. As if he feared rejection. So I said, "Yeah. I think you could be."

I could hear his smile. "Tell me about your city, then," he said. "Are there people there who will make a cult for me?"

And so I spoke into the night, telling him of the City of Lockes. Of the streets and alleyways. Of the markets and the slums. Of a Good King. Of my kind parents. Of my brother-uncle-father Morgan. I fell asleep in the middle of describing the way the sun hit the castle walls and I dreamed of home.

"I CAN'T leave *everything*," Kevin growled at me the next day. "This is all my *stuff*."

"We can't carry hundreds of pounds of gold and jewels," I reminded him. "Or thousands of books. Or your completely random collection of forty-seven push brooms that I don't even want to ask about. Kevin, I'll be honest with you. I think you've got a problem."

His eyes narrowed. "What problem?"

"You're a hoarder."

"Uh, no shit. I'm a dragon."

"No, but, like, you *really* hoard."

"I like shiny, pretty things!"

"Push brooms aren't shiny or pretty."

"You shut your whore mouth," Kevin snarled.

"Oh boy," Gary said. "This is going to get awkward."

"I like brooms," Tiggy said. "We take brooms?"

"No brooms," I said to Tiggy.

His shoulders slumped. "Tiggy never gets anything," he muttered.

"Oh my gods," I said. "You are like the saddest thing I've ever seen. Damn you, Tiggy. You can take one broom."

"Seven brooms," he said.

"Three."

"Two," he countered.

"I don't think you're doing it right," Gary said fondly.

"One," he shouted. "One broom!" He cackled and ran toward the brooms.

"See?" I said to Kevin. "Compromise."

"Okay," Kevin said. "Here is my compromise. I take all my stuff and I won't burn your face off."

"You can't compromise with violence."

"I'm a dragon," he said. "I can do pretty much anything I want."

"We can't carry all this with us," I said.

"I can make multiple trips," he said. "I'll fly back and forth while you guys walk back to the castle."

"Oh," I said, sighing more heavily than the situation required. "I guess this stuff *is* important, especially if you're willing to leave Gary unprotected all that way. With all the dangers. And the murderers."

"What?" Gary said.

"The murderers?" Kevin whispered.

"The murderers," I whispered back.

Kevin gasped and brought his front claws to his chest. "I would *never* leave him unprotected! Especially not from *murderers*. You, sir, are a villain for even suggesting as much! He is my fire, the reason for which my hearts beat, the…"

"I hate you so much, Sam," Gary muttered.

"…very *air* that fills my lungs, the sun rising in the morning, the moon rising at night, the reasons there are birds in the sky and flowers in the *fields*…"

"Shouldn't have left that pile of stones near my head, motherfucker," I whispered to Gary. "Payback, Wilds style."

"…the way the light refracts off a river's surface, the reason golden leaves fall from trees! He is responsible for the sweet breeze of spring and the lovely bite of winter…"

"Yeah," I said. "I don't think he's done any of that."

"All of it," Gary said. "I've done all of that. Biting winter and moon leaves or whatever. I'm pretty much amazing."

"So you can't leave him unprotected," I said. "Someone might steal him away and make him a dancer in a burlesque."

"Wait, wait," Gary said. "You never said there'd be a *burlesque* involved. Just how big are the production values? How much say would I get to have in the direction of the show?"

"Minimal," I said ominously. "To both."

Gary whirled on Kevin. "You *better* not even *consider* leaving me to get kidnapped into some cut-rate high school production of a sex show. I swear to you on all I have, you will *never* get to sample all of Gary's goods because the bakery will be closed, and girl, let me tell *you*. My muffin is *delicious*." He licked his lips obscenely.

"Scarred for life," I breathed. "This was a very bad idea."

"Muffin?" Kevin asked.

"Delicious," Gary purred.

"But... but...," Kevin sputtered. "My *stuff*."

"We come back for it," I said, trying to get the image of Gary as a large baked good out of my head. "Eventually."

"Or," Kevin said, "I can carry Gary with me and make return trips."

"Gary don't fly," Gary said, a shimmer of glitter around him. "Don't make Gary show you what's up."

"All my stuff," Kevin said mournfully, rubbing his claws over his treasures. "All my pretty, pretty things."

"We'll come back," I said, daring to reach out and touch his leg. "I promise."

"But what if someone *steals* it?"

"You mean like you did?" I asked.

"Yes," he said, completely oblivious. "*Exactly* like that."

"They won't," I said. "You're a god, remember? They wouldn't dare. You'd eat them."

"Because dis is yer god spakin—"

"Sure," I said. "Why not."

"Fine," he finally grumbled. "But if anyone even *thinks* of touching my hoard, I will find them and light them on fire and their children and their *children's* children..."

"This is going to go so well." I sighed.

"...and their *children's* children's children...."

I THOUGHT to leave the next day.

But I couldn't take the chance that we'd catch up to Ryan and Justin.

So I delayed.

I said I wasn't quite ready to leave yet.

I said that Kevin needed more time to say good-bye to his possessions.

I said Gary needed more time to rest his thighs.

I said that Tiggy needed more time to recover from laying waste to Tarker Mills.

They knew what I was doing.

But they didn't call me on it.

"Sure, Sam," they said.

"Okay, Sam," they said.

And so we waited.

AND ON the seventh morning after Ryan and Justin left, we stood in front of the keep: a dragon, a hornless unicorn, a half-giant, and a brokenhearted wizard's apprentice who was still kickass but super sad about stupid boys and their fucking faces.

"And let the adventure begin!" I said, trying to sound jubilant.

"Hurray," Gary said. He did not sound jubilant.

"So many brooms," Tiggy said, carrying one broom.

"This sucks," Kevin muttered, glancing back forlornly at his keep. "The things I do for love."

"Lust," Gary said.

And we started walking back to Castle Lockes and an uncertain future. Toward the unknown. Toward heartbreak and—

"Shit," Gary said. "I forgot my scarves."

"Gary," I said through gritted teeth.

"What?" he said, sounding defensive. "You know I can't go anywhere without my scarves. What of the wind-rape?"

"Why were your scarves even out?"

"Er."

"We were trying to see which ones could be used to tie him up," Kevin said. "For sexual things. Spoiler: it was all of them."

"Oh my gods," I gagged. "Stop it. Go get your fucking scarves."

"I'll go!" Kevin cried joyously, already turning around.

"You stay right where you are," I snapped. "You just want to go back and look at your treasures."

Kevin pouted and refused to look at me.

"Tiggy," I said, trying to keep my voice even. "Would you go get Gary's scarves? Please."

"Take my broom?"

"Yes. You can take your broom."

"Take my broom," he said.

Six minutes later.

"AND THE adventure begins," I said and took a step.

"Tiggy," Gary said. "Tiggy, dear. Did you repack your pajamas?"

Tiggy hung his head. "No. I forgot."

"For the love of *fuck*—"

"No need for that kind of language," Gary sniffed. "It's unbecoming on a lady of your station."

"Gaaaaah!"

"I'll get them!" Kevin said as he stomped toward the keep.

Three hours and forty-six minutes later.

"...BUT IT'S all my *stuff*. You don't *understand*!"

"I will leave your ass here," I threatened.

"Sam's just upset because he doesn't have—"

"Gary, you do *not* want to finish that sentence."

"—scarves or pajamas or brooms or piles of gold," Gary finished anyway. "What? I've told you. You're *not* intimidating. I've slept near you while you've had wet dreams. That sort of takes away any fear you might have engendered in me. Especially when it sounded like you were muttering about being spit-roasted."

"*Really*," Kevin said gleefully. "I'm sure we can work something out—"

"*AND THE ADVENTURE BEGINS*!" I roared.

They were quiet as we walked out of the valley. It felt good.

Then, "So, Kevin. Have you ever played I Spy?"

"No, my sweet lovedrop. But I assume we role-play spies, go on dangerous missions until we double-cross each other. Sexually."

This was going to be the longest trip of my life.

Fifth day on the road.

"WHAT DO you mean *everyone knew*?" I said incredulously.

"Exactly that," Gary said. "Everyone knew that you were in love with Ryan and Ryan was in love with you. Everyone, Sam. Literally everyone."

"That's not true! And he doesn't *love* me." It was easier to convince myself of that than know the truth.

"You two couldn't have been more obvious if you had made signs and hung them around your neck that said HaveHeart4Evah."

"Mom didn't know."

"Yes she did."

"Dad didn't."

"Uh. Yeah. He did."

"Kevin didn't."

"Yes I did. You sighed when he rode up on Gary. Like, full-on dreamy sigh."

"Sam," Gary said. "Everyone knew. Random strangers. Dark wizards. Gay fairies. Drag queens. Bards. Elves. Townspeople. Cults. *Everyone*."

"I'll be honest," I said. "That's rather embarrassing. And also? So many remarks make much more sense now. I really need to be more aware of my surroundings."

And then I walked into a large boulder.

"Oh, honey." Gary didn't miss a beat. "It was embarrassing for all of us."

The ninth night.

"I JUST didn' unnerstan, ya know?" I slurred. I reached down and knocked back the rest of my wine. The tavern was loud around us. "You wanna be with someone, so why not just *be* with them? I mean, seriously. Right? Come on. Just. Just *be*. Ya know? I mean, there's *ways* to be stuff. Together. I didn't even *know*, ya know? And then the corn told us the truth and I was like… just. *There*, man. I was just. *There*. I don't know. Refill, barkeep. Yeah, I'm talking to you. All right! Ha, ha! No, don't be stingy. Fill it alllll the way up. That's nice. Keep the tab *flowing*. Or open. Whatever. Words are hard. This wine is good. Wine! *Get in my mouth, wine!* Ha. I'm wining and whining. What was I saying? Oh. Right. Ya know? So he was all, like, *I love you, babe, but I promised my dick to the stupid fucking Prince.* And I was all, like, *Shoot, girl, I don't even need you. I got this. I'm my own man.* Ya know? And he was all, like, *But, babe. You make me feel so alive. I'm not dashing or immacular. Immaculen. Immaculy. But babe. I'm not dashing or awesome without you.* And I was all, like, *Shoot, girl. Shut up.* Ya know? I don't know. And now we're going to go back to the castle and they'll be wedding each other. And I'll have to *be there.* Who... who *does* that? Ya know? Like. Who *does* that? Jerks is who does that, that's who. *Jerks.* And I have to *be* in the wedding, ya know? They'll be all happy and stupid and I'll be—*holy crap I love this song.* Play it louder! *PLAY IT LOUDER!* Yeah. Whoo! Don't you feel like dancing? I do. Not like *waltz* dancing because that's just *stupid*. Even if it's *three times*, ya know? Waltzing for three times with a single person means *nothing*. I did it *twice* with Todd and he had these *ears* that were just. Ya know? And so *what* if I accidently gave him a hand job. So. *What.* I bet I'd give *good* hand jobs. *I* don't have any complaints about the hand jobs that I do to myself. In fact, I would so far as to say they're pretty darn good, ya know? The right amount of grip and everything. And when I'm done? You know what I do when I'm done? I *thank* myself because I am a considerate lover, okay? Ya know? I'm *nice* when I finish. I tell myself how *good* it was for me, didn't I think so? Barkeep! Bar. Keep. Fill me up. Just leave the bottle. It's easier. Where was I? Oh. Right. So I didn't even *want* to go to the Ryan Stupidheart Fucker Fan Fucking Club meeting to begin with, ya know? I went because I was just checking to make sure there were no spies or whatever. No one to *infiltrate the castle* or whatever. Tina, man. Tina would infiltrate the castle, ya know? Because she's just.... Gods. She thinks my muffins are dry as my conter... constant. As dry as my *consternation*. Or whatever. *My muffins aren't fucking dry, Tina.* Ya know? That's what I say to her and she's all like. Like. Like, *Mervin.* She said. She goes, *Mervin. You make me mad because you're all witty and awesome and so fucking cool and I'm not because I'm a teenage bitch who wants to play with Ryan's dong.* Or whatever. Ya know? I mean. Who does that? Right? Who *does* that? Sorry. Sorry. Man. Sorry. What's your name again?"

The elderly woman I was talking to stared at me. "Um. You just sat here and started talking and never asked me for my name."

"Oh. That's cool. Or whatever. Your name's not Ryan is it, because that *would fucking suck*."

"No. Um. My name is. Um. Betty?"

"Betty! Bet. Tee. Hey. Hey barkeep! Get my friend Betty here another drink, would you? She's. She's my *friend*, ya know?"

"Oh my goodness," Betty whispered.

"It's cool," I told her loudly. "They know me. I come here all the time." I leaned over to her and whispered, "I've never been here before. They have no idea who I am." And then I winked at her. "Gods," I said, trying to keep my eyes from crossing. "You're cute for a lady who is older and a lady. Like a sexy grandma. Do you. Like. Do you want to go? I don't know. Play cards or. Something. Like braid hair and shit. I don't know. Ya know?"

"No," Betty said. "No. I just want to eat my dinner, but you're leaning in it with your elbows."

"Oh no! Oh my gods. Betty. *Betty.* I'm so sorry. I'm so—are you eating pasta?"

"I was. Um. Trying to?"

"And my elbows were in it?"

"Um. Yes?"

"So. Would you say it's… elbow macaroni?"

"No. Um. It's… spaghetti? So. It'd be… elbow. Spaghetti?"

"That's not a thing," I told her. "Elbow spaghetti. What even. Gods, you're so weird. I'm going to go sleep. Thank you for inviting me to your birthday party. Bye."

And then I passed out.

The tenth morning.

"OH MY gods," I moaned as I dragged my feet down the road. "Kill me now. Or kill the sun. I don't care which."

"Someone learned a lesson last night," Gary said, sounding way too chipper while I was obviously dying.

"Was that before or after he woke up in a bowl of noodles?" Kevin asked. Like a jerk.

"Spaghetti face!" Tiggy cried. "Wizard Spaghetti Face."

"He capitalized it," Gary said. "Now it's forever."

"That's a stupid fucking rule," I grumbled.

The thirteenth night.

"SO," GARY said. "Kevin and I. Need to go into the forest. For. Food."

I stared at the both of them. "For food."

"Like. Berries. Or something."

"Berries," I repeated.

"Yes," Kevin said. "So we can have fruit for breakfast."

"Berries."

"Forest berries," Gary said. "From the forest."

"Fine," I said. "I'll take the first watch. Don't take long."

An hour later, things got gross.

I was lying by the fire listening to Tiggy snore next to me and watching the stars above when I heard it echoing through the trees.

At first, I thought it sounded like a ghost eating feral cats.

And then I thought it might have been monkeys fighting with peeled, wet oranges.

But then I heard, "OOOOH, KEVIN. OH. MY. FUCKING. *GODS.* HOW LONG IS YOUR *TONGUE?*"

And I said, "Nope. Nope, nope, nope."

"OH, MY LOVE, YOU TASTE LIKE THE FINEST AMBROSIA. I WANT TO DRINK YOU DOWN MY THROAT."

I threw up a little bit in my mouth.

"HOW CAN YOU EVEN *BEND* LIKE THAT?"

"GARY. GARY. YOU MAKE ME FEEL ALIVE AND I WANT TO DO THINGS TO YOUR ANUS."

"Please make this just be a nightmare," I whispered. "I'm begging you."

"YOU CAN DO *ANYTHING* TO MY ANUS."

"WHO'S BEEN A BAD UNICORN? HAVE *YOU* BEEN A BAD UNICORN?"

"Please say no," I said. "Please say no."

"YES. *YES*. I'VE BEEN SUCH A *BAD* UNICORN."

"Whyyyyy?" I moaned as I pulled my blanket over my head.

"BAD UNICORNS GET PUNISHED. DID YOU KNOW THAT?"

"YES! YES, I KNEW!"

"YES, WHAT?"

"HUH? YES, WHAT WHAT?"

"NO. YOU'RE SUPPOSED TO SAY YES, SIR."

"OH. WE'RE REALLY GOING THERE?"

"Don't go there," I muttered rocking back and forth. "Don't go there."

"WELL, YEAH. IF YOU'VE BEEN A BAD UNICORN. THAT'S KIND OF THE RULES."

"WHOSE RULES?"

"KEVIN'S RULES FOR A GOOD BOUT OF FUCKING."

"He shouldn't follow those rules," I told a sleeping Tiggy.

"OH. OKAY. I GUESS I CAN DO THAT. IT'S BEEN A WHILE. MY SAFEWORD IS MURIEL. MY WORD TO GIVE ME A MOMENT TO BREATHE IS FONDUE. MY WORD TO KEEP ON GOING BECAUSE EVERYTHING IS AMAZING IS SAM."

"Oh, *come on*!" I said into my hands.

Monkeys renewed their wet orange fight with feral-cat-eating ghosts.

"WHO IS MY BAD UNICORN?"

"I AM, SIR. I AM YOUR BAD UNICORN. SPANK ME WITH YOUR MOUTH."

"IS THIS OKAY? DOES THIS FEEL GOOD?"

"SAM. SAAAAAAAM. I AM SO SAM RIGHT NOW."

"This is not okay," I cried. "Nothing about this is okay."

Tiggy continued to snore.

"YOU NAUGHTY UNICORN. I'M GOING TO HAVE TO TEACH YOU A LESSON IN RESPECT."

"MAKE ME RESPECT YOU SO HARD. SAM, I AM. SAMSAMSAM*SAM*. I AM—WHAT IS THAT? IS THAT YOUR *PENIS*? HOLY MOTHER OF THE GODS, I DON'T KNOW IF THAT IS GOING TO FIT IN ME."

"Cheesy dicks and candlesticks and everything you need!" I tried to sing. It came out broken and sounding like I was dying. Because I was.

"OH, THANK YOU, MY HEART. IT'S ALWAYS AFFIRMING WHEN SOMEONE TELLS YOU YOUR COCK IS BIGGER THAN ANYTHING THEY'VE EVER SEEN."

"UM. I DIDN'T QUITE SAY IT LIKE THAT. SIR. OOOOOH. I DIDN'T EVEN KNOW YOU COULD *DO* THAT. I AM SO FUCKING SAM RIGHT NOW. I AM THE SAMMIEST I HAVE EVER BEEN. SAM ME ALL YOU WANT, YOU DIRTY BASTARD."

It went on for another four hours.

The fourteenth morning.

"BERRIES?" TIGGY asked as he looked down at his oatmeal.

"We couldn't find any," Gary said.

"We looked long and hard," Kevin said. "Very long. And very hard."

I let out a wail because *why did this have to happen to me*?

"Sam?" Gary asked. "You okay? You look… clammy."

"I've heard things," I whispered, clutching my hands at my chest. "I've *heard* things."

"What things?"

"*Things,*" I breathed.

"Oh," Gary said, sharing a fond look with Kevin. "I see what this is."

"Sam?" Kevin said. "We should talk about this, okay, buddy?"

"No," I said. "Never."

"Sam," Gary said gently. "You see, when a dragon loves a unicorn, they have a special hug they do in the forest."

"And sometimes," Kevin said, rubbing my back with his claws, "the dragon likes to lick the unicorn's asshole until he—"

I ran screaming down the road.

The nineteenth day.

"AND A *further* thing," I said as we walked down the Old Road. "I don't even *care* about him that much, anyway."

"Uh-huh," Gary said.

"Right? It's not like I actually developed real *feelings* for him or anything. It was just an infatuation that I can so easily get over. It didn't *matter*. It was never a *thing*."

"Right," Gary said. "Get over. Like you've been saying. For the last three hours."

"Because I don't need a man to define me," I said. "I am a strong, independent wizard. I'll be my *own* cornerstone."

"Don't need no mens," Tiggy said.

"*Exactly*," I said. "I *don't*. I have my boys with me, and we're going to go on adventures and do cool shit like fight manticores and discover caves and eat disgusting regional delicacies. Because I'm young and hung and full of magic."

"Sam," Gary said kindly. "I understand what you're saying. I really do. But let me give you some advice from the perspective of someone in a long-term relationship."

"You've been together for *five days*."

"And that's five days longer than you."

"Hey, buddy," Kevin said. "Just listen to him, okay? We both just want to make sure you don't make any rash decisions."

"I'm *not*. I'm grown up and every decision I make is the right one because I'm making it based upon all the feelings in my chest and brain."

"Kids," Gary said, shaking his head. "They want to grow up so fast."

"Remember when he was younger?" Kevin said with a warm chuckle. "He was at my keep and kept saying things like, *You can't take any of your stuff that's obviously important to you because what I say goes and I'm a giant dick-brained motherfucker.*"

"I'm pretty sure I never said that," I told them, but they ignored me. "And we were at your keep two weeks ago!"

"Pretty soon, he's going to want to go off on his own," Gary said, sounding upset. "Oh, Kevin. What are we going to do when he's ready to leave?"

"What is even happening right now?"

"Shhh," Kevin said to Gary, brushing their snouts together. "It's okay. You've been such a good mother to him. You'll see. He'll do good things. And if he doesn't, we'll be there to pick up the pieces because that's what parents do."

Gary started crying and pushed his face against mine. "You listen to me, okay?" he said, sniffing loudly in my ear. "You follow your heart because one day, it'll lead you home. You've been such a good son."

"Did you guys get high?" I asked them. "Like, super freaking high?"

Gary began to cry in earnest as Kevin rumbled low and licked the side of my face.

"Tiggy!" I yelled. "Help me! They've gone crazy. Save me!"

Tiggy looked conflicted as Gary sobbed in my ear and Kevin stroked his back and murmured soothing things to him. "We sad?" Tiggy asked.

"No—"

"*Yes*," Gary wailed. "Sam is growing up and he's going to move out and have orgies and do drugs and *it'll be all my fault.*"

Then Tiggy started crying and hugging me, begging me not to have orgies and do drugs. "No, Sam," he said, wiping his face on mine. "No mushrooms and gang bangs."

People on the Old Road gave us a wide berth as they passed us by, no matter how much I pleaded with them to rescue me.

The twenty-third morning.

I WAS a good distance into the Dark Woods, trying to find a spot to take a leak where I wouldn't be able to hear Gary and Kevin talking about how they were planning on adopting at least four Pomeranians. I thought I'd found the perfect tree and was giving good consideration to potentially rubbing one out after I pissed, when it happened.

"A*ha*," the Dark wizard shouted as he jumped out from behind the tree. "I bet you weren't expecting to see *me*."

"Um," I said. "I don't know who you are." There went *that* erection. Gods. Was it too much to ask for a little Sam time?

The Dark looked slightly offended. "Seriously?"

"Sorry," I said. "You all look the same to me."

"Rude," he said. "That's racist."

"Um. No, it's not. You and are I are the same race. If you were to ride a unicorn, that's racism."

"How is that racist?" he asked.

"Because it's mean," I explained.

"But that's not even the basis for—" He cut himself off and took a deep breath. "You know what? No. I've heard about you. You start talking and everyone gets confused and people start wanting to have sex with you and get turned into deck chairs."

I sighed. "It was supposed to be lawn chairs. And I think the stories about me are greatly exaggerated."

"So did you or did you not take down four of my brothers in the City of Lockes?"

"Oh. Well. That part was true."

"And did you or did you not send a pack of fire geckos after two more of my brothers?"

"Yeah. That was me."

"And did you or did you not kill Lartin the Dark Leaf?"

"No," I said. "I didn't."

"What?" he said.

"I didn't kill him."

"You did," he insisted.

"No, I didn't."

"Then who did?"

"My half-giant best friend."

"Oh," he said. "Well, same difference."

"Sort of, I guess."

"My name is—"

"Don't care," I said.

He glared at me. "Don't be rude."

I sighed. "Sorry. Go ahead."

"My name is Wan the Dark Hunter," he said, squaring his shoulders.

I waited.

He looked at me, clearly expecting a reaction.

I waited some more.

"So," he said, "that name should have inspired fear in you. You don't look very fearful."

I shrugged. "I don't know who you are." And I didn't. I'd never seen him before or heard his name. I thought he was probably a few years older than me. He was handsome, in a devilish way, his dark goatee trimmed perfectly, nary a hair out of place. He had tattoos on his arms and I recognized Dark marks, signifying he was at a higher level than the other Darks I'd faced. That was okay with me.

"Seriously?" he said. "Never heard of me?"

"Nope."

"That sucks," he said. "I thought I was really making a name for myself."

"Eh. What can you do?"

Wan rolled his eyes. "Of course you say it like that. Everyone knows who *you* are."

"That's not my fault," I said. "My mom says it's my face."

"What does that mean?"

"I guess I just have one of those faces."

"So you're saying that my face isn't good enough?"

"No," I said. "You're really cute." And he was. Too bad he was evil.

He flushed. "Shut up. No, I'm not."

"Yeah, you are. I like your goatee. It's very... trimmed."

"Thanks," he said, preening a bit. "I grew it myself." Then he winced. "Wow, that sounded awkward."

"It was pretty awkward," I agreed. "Adorable, though."

"Well. This has been just lovely. Maybe we could...." He closed his eyes. Took a breath. Opened his eyes again. "How in the fuck do you *do* that?"

"Yeah. I don't really know. Weird, right?"

"People fear me," he said.

"I don't."

"Most do."

"Oh," I said. "That's cool. So, like, are you going to monologue?"

His eyes narrowed. "Monologue."

"Villains tend to broadcast their plans and reasons when they capture me."

"I haven't captured you yet."

"Fair point," I said. "Are you going to try?"

"Lartin was my friend," he said, fingers twitching. I could feel his magic gathering.

"Really?" I said, arching an eyebrow. "That guy, man. What was his deal? All you Darks seemed to be all up in his shit."

"He was nice but he liked to hug for too long before his hands started to wander," Wan said. "He was one of the first Darks. His father didn't—"

"Oh no!"

"What?"

"I just realized I don't care. Are you done yet? You said you weren't going to monologue."

"I'm *not*."

"It's still monologuing when you do it on someone else's behalf," I explained.

"How has no one killed you yet?" he asked, sounding incredulous. "I've only known you for five minutes and I want to murder you."

"Rude," I said. "Don't lie. You want some of this."

He flushed again.

"Ha," I said. "No thanks."

"Honestly," he said. "All you do is talk. I don't see what the big deal is. You may not know me, but I've got the backing of the Dark wizards of the Dark Woods. Those that know me fear my name. I am a hunter, and you are the hunted. Your head will be mine."

"I am a hunter and you are the hunted," I mocked. "Gods. That was just awful."

"Hey!" Wan said. "That's rude. I worked hard on that."

"Well, yeah. But it's so cliché."

"You don't mess with classics, I guess."

"The Darks, right?" I said. "That's what you have?"

"Yes," he said, eyes flashing.

"Guess what I have," I said, smiling at him.

"What?"

"A dragon," I snapped and said, "*Kevin! Now!*"

I grinned and prepared for my friends (who were obviously listening in and waiting for me to give an awesome new catchphrase that I did like a *boss*) to burst through the trees and stand united against the Dark. Kevin would roar and fire would burst from between his teeth. Tiggy would smash his fists together and Gary would be shining in so much fucking glitter. It was going to be awesome.

And so, of course, nothing happened.

Wan looked at me warily. "What?"

"Sorry," I said. "Probably just a delay. Give it a minute."

We gave it a minute. Still nothing.

"Let's try it again," I suggested.

"Try what?"

"The whole *I have a dragon* thing," I said. "It'll work this time."

"You have a dragon," Wan said, sounding dubious.

"Yeah," I said. "Well, sort of. I think he's trying to be my dad now, which is weird."

"What?"

"I know, right?" I looked over my shoulder. Absolutely nothing. "So, blah, blah, blah. Guess what I have. *A DRAGON!*"

My voice echoed in the trees.

Nothing.

"For real?" I muttered. "Gods. Those assholes." I looked back at Wan. "Hold on just a second, okay? If he doesn't come, we can duel to the death or whatever."

"You're so weird," he said.

I grinned. "Thanks." Then, "*KEVIN!*"

"Yeah?" he finally called back through the trees.

"Can you come here, please?"

"Kind of busy, buddy."

"I'm not your *buddy* because you *aren't even my real dad*!"

"Sam," Gary called out. "That was mean. Say you're sorry."

"No!"

"Don't make me come over there," Gary warned.

"Gary, it's fine," Kevin said. "He just needs time to adjust."

"Sorry about this," I told Wan. "They have been in a monogamous relationship for nine days and apparently, two magical creatures together like that suddenly start acting like lesbian albatrosses and mate for life or something."

"Lesbian albatrosses," Wan repeated.

"You know, the birds? Notorious for monogamy and life partners. Like lesbians. I don't know. My life, right?"

Wan said, "How are you even a real person?"

I shrugged and said, "My parents boned and then I came out. How is anyone a real person? Boning. *KEVIN, GET YOUR ASS OVER HERE.*"

"Gods," I heard Gary complain loudly. "It's like puberty with him all over again."

"We'll get through it," Kevin rumbled, and I *finally* heard them start moving into the woods. "He can't be a dick to us for long. I'll tan his hide and maybe suck on his cock a little."

"So gross," I muttered. I looked up at Wan. "Don't listen to him. He's not my dad and he doesn't blow me."

"I don't even know what to think," Wan said.

I sighed. "I get that a lot. Okay, get ready."

"For what?"

"The whole catchphrase and awesome entrance thing. I'm not going to waste it just because Kevin is an asshole."

"I heard that!"

"You were meant to," I called back.

"Why is the ground shaking?" Wan asked. "And why does it sound like trees are breaking?"

"Don't worry about it," I said. "Just be ready to do your line."

"I think I'm going to go," Wan said, eyes wide.

"Oh, come on," I said. "Don't be like that."

"No, it's okay," he said. "I'm sorry I wasted your time. Please don't hurt me."

I rolled my eyes. "You Darks are a bunch of pussies," I said, and he *snarled* at me.

"You really want to mess with the powers of the Dark?" he growled.

"Wow," I said. "That was actually ominous and cool. I'm into this. Okay." I popped my neck and took a stance. I glared at him, curling my lip. "You may be the Dark, but I am the apprentice to Morgan of Shadows. I am Sam of Wilds, and I will kick your fucking ass." And then a breeze came and my clothes started *billowing*. It was *amazing*.

"I suppose we can do this," Wan said, raising his hands.

"Yeah," I said. "Well, I've got a *dragon*. Dammit! That didn't sound right. What the fuck, Wan? *You had one job*. Heh. Or you had *wan* job. Awesome."

Then Kevin, Gary, and Tiggy came up from behind me and Wan screamed in such a way that he totally lost all his goatee cool points. He turned and ran farther into the Dark Woods. I shook my head.

"What was that all about?" Gary asked.

"You guys need to work on your timing," I said. "Never again. I had the perfect setup with a cool line and a whole lot of epicness going on with the billowing, and you all just killed it."

I stalked away from them, muttering about how the help was never prepared when I needed them to be.

THE TWENTY-FIFTH day sucked because I missed Ryan something awful. Gary and Tiggy held me close as Kevin kept watch.

My heart was hurting.

THE TWENTY-SIXTH day I was angry.

THE TWENTY-SIXTH night, I was hurt *and* angry and made a really stupid decision.

THE THIRTIETH day found me back in Meridian City.

I left Gary, Tiggy, and Kevin on the outskirts. We'd passed through Old Clearing, and sure enough, the missing people had returned, telling stories of being kidnapped by a ruthless cult and fed more corn than they'd ever eaten in their lives. Of course, once they saw Kevin, they started shrieking, sure he was back to eat them this time. He assured them he would never do such a thing, that it went against his code (and his stomach), but this only proceeded to freak everyone out more, because dragons weren't supposed to talk.

We left Old Clearing rather quickly after that.

Not a huge loss, really.

But I made sure we stopped in Meridian City. Gary had asked me if I was sure, as if he knew what my plan was. Instead of answering, I told him I wouldn't be long.

"Sure," he'd said sadly.

And that's how I found myself once again standing in front of the Tilted Cross, Mama's medallion in my hand, smiling quietly at the bouncer at the front. It wasn't the same one as last time, but that was okay. He saw the medallion, nodded once, and opened the door for me.

There was a beautiful woman at the front desk, one that'd I'd never seen before. But she knew who I was from the way her eyes widened slightly before she smiled wickedly.

"Welcome to Mama's," she all but purred.

I said, "I need to see Moishe."

The smile faded slightly. "Oh? Conversation?"

I cocked my head at her. "Services."

"Hmm. I don't know if he does that anymore."

"He will if he knows it's me."

"Will he, now?"

"Magic has a taste," I said, leaning closer to her. She shuddered slightly as my breath fell on her cheek. "Or so he says. He wants it on his tongue. And I aim to give it to him."

"The great Sam of Wilds. How lucky he must be." She nodded and took a step back. "It'll be just a moment." She was up the stairs and out of sight before I could say anything more.

Mama's boys whispered quietly to one another as they watched me. Undoubtedly they'd overheard my conversation with the girl. They knew of Moishe's fascination with me. It was not a love thing, or even a like thing. It was, for lack of a better word, about lust. Though I didn't think it was for me personally. If Ryan had a magic kink, then Moishe had a power kink. I had both in spades. What better way to destroy my virginity than with someone who wanted what I had.

Or, at least, that was the plan.

Of course, it was never that easy.

"You foolish, foolish boy," Mama growled from behind me.

I rolled my eyes and turned around. "Figured you'd get here first."

She looked beautiful, as always. A long, onyx wig fell around her shoulders and back. Kohl-lined eyes, smoky and thick. Deep red lipstick, sticky and sweet. Her nails were short and black, the illusion of breasts cinched tight in a black and red corset. She wore knee-high riding boots over skintight silk leggings. She held a crop in one hand, smacking the leather against her other. She looked like she was going horseback riding. *Sexy* horseback riding.

She jerked the end of the crop under my chin, forcing me to look up into her eyes. The leather scraped against my skin. "What are you doing here, Sam?"

"I didn't ask for you."

"No. You didn't. But this is my establishment, and you should know better than anyone that whatever happens under this roof, Mama knows. Now. I'll ask one more time, because we're friends and I love you very much. You will answer me truthfully, or I'll tan your hide in front of my boys and you will *like it*." She dropped the crop from my face and reached out with a large hand, grabbing me by the wrist. She pulled me into a room where two twinks were sitting in front of a mirror, applying blush to their cheeks.

"Babies," she said, voice soft and kind. "Mama needs the room. You can use the mirror at the end of the hall to finish up."

"Yes, Mama," they both said, eyeing me curiously before leaving. Mama closed the door behind them.

"That's how rumors start," I told her. "They're going to tell everyone you've become a working girl again."

"Ah," she said. "Like I would actually charge you for anything."

I grinned at her as I leaned against the wall, crossing my arms over my chest. "You love me."

"I do, though I am having a difficult time remembering why just now." She sat on the recently vacated stool in front of the mirror and looked at her reflection. She brought a perfectly manicured pinkie up and brushed it across her lips, brushing away a flake of lipstick.

"Mama. It's not—"

"Cut the bullshit, Sam." Her eyes found mine in the mirror's reflection.

Fine. I could do that. "I'm here for Moishe."

"I gathered as much when Natasha came into my office and told me."

"Natasha has a big fucking mouth," I muttered.

"Where is your knight?" she asked.

"He's not *my* knight."

Mama rolled her eyes elegantly, because she could be no other way. "Hogwash and poppycock, that. He belongs to you more than he belongs to anyone else. He is your cornerstone after all."

I narrowed my eyes. "And just how the hell did you know that?"

She picked up a makeup brush from the vanity and brushed it under her eyes. "Didn't know for sure until right this moment. I suspected, but confirmation is always better."

"How do you know what a cornerstone is?"

She laughed. "Precious, I'm Mama. I know everything."

"Then you'll know he swore an oath to the Prince," I said. "An oath that binds him into marriage."

She sighed. "No. I didn't know that."

"It doesn't matter. I rescued Justin, now have a pet dragon father who licks Gary's butthole, and will be forced to attend the wedding of the century." I grimaced. "You know, I usually don't complain this much."

"A pet dragon father," she said, lips twitching.

"Yeah. Apparently I can talk to dragons. Or, rather, dragons can speak Veranian if I'm near. Magic is the shit, you know?"

"If I didn't have the Tilted Cross to worry about, I'd be following you wherever you went," she said. "The things you've seen and done fill my cold, crusty heart with adoration and envy."

"There's nothing cold and crusty about you," I said dutifully. And because there wasn't.

"I suppose not," she said. "The gods know I'm not getting any younger."

"And notice how polite I'm being by not asking the lady her age, even if she's given me an obvious in."

She gave me a shark's smile. "How lucky you have practiced restraint. I'd hate to see what you'd look like without testicles."

And so because I loved her, I told her everything. About the cornerstone business. About Ryan. About being force-fed coercion through corn. About cults and fairies and rescuing princes from ancient keeps. By the time I finished, my voice was hoarse and my heart was sore.

She was quiet for a time. Then, "Drowning in someone's skin will not help you forget the other."

I shrugged. "At least I'll feel wanted."

She turned to me then and stood. She reached out for me, her hands cupping my face, and I leaned against her touch. Regardless of how ruthless she could be, regardless of her own claims of being cold-hearted, she was still Mama to me. My fairy drag mother. The woman who had taught me to trust myself and my instincts. Morgan could teach me magic. My parents could teach me morals. Gary and Tiggy could teach me brotherhood. But Mama taught me that while life had sharp edges, it would only cut you if you allowed it to.

She said, "You *are* wanted. The heart that beats in your chest is the most wonderful thing I've ever been witness to. It hurts, precious. I know it does. But like all things, it shall pass and you will be all that much stronger because of it."

I hugged her then. She made a surprised noise at the back of her throat as this wasn't something she typically did. With anyone. But I was a hugger and she was my friend. Her arms came around me tentatively, her hands clasping at my back. She smelled of vanilla and clove. It was lovely.

She left, after a time.

Moments later, there was a knock at the door.

I opened it.

Moishe looked me up and down.

"Wizard," he said, his voice full of sex and magic. "I heard you asked for me. How may I be of service?"

I grabbed him by the collar and pulled him into the room, slamming the door behind us.

Later, I walked through Meridian City toward the gates.

I passed by a newsboy shouting out the headlines.

"*THE GOOD KING ANNOUNCES ROYAL WEDDING IMMINENT! PRINCE JUSTIN TO WED KNIGHT COMMANDER RYAN FOXHEART IN A MONTH'S TIME! READ ABOUT IT HERE FIRST! THE WEDDING OF THE CENTURY IS UPON US!*"

CHAPTER 26
Homecoming

I WASN'T surprised to find Morgan of Shadows waiting for us a mile outside of the City of Lockes, even though I hadn't spoken to him in days. The traffic on the Old Road had gotten heavier as we approached the city, and people continued to give us a wide berth, eyeing Kevin warily as he smiled at them, showing way too many teeth for anyone to feel comfortable around him.

One minute I was fighting the urge to run for the city gates that I could see on the horizon, and the next I felt a wave of peace wash over me. I took a stuttering step, stopped. Took a breath. Let it out slowly.

The crowd parted before us and there he stood.

Maybe I should have been embarrassed by my actions. Maybe I should have shown the slightest bit of decorum. I was the apprentice to the King's Wizard, after all.

But fuck that. I hadn't seen my mentor in almost three months. I'd faced things I'd never seen before. I'd been loved and broken. I'd eaten a shitload of corn laced with a truth serum.

So I don't know that I can be blamed for running full speed at him. I don't know that I can be blamed for the way my eyes burned when he smiled widely and opened his arms. I don't know that I can be blamed for the sound I made, that broken, wounded noise that crawled out of my throat when his arms wrapped around me. I felt his magic wash over me, and for the first time in weeks, I thought I was able to breathe. I let my forehead rest in the crook of his neck as he held me tightly.

He said, "I know. I know."

Because he did. He knew. He'd missed me as much as I'd missed him. This was the man who had rescued me from the slums with his pink shoes and exploding nipples. The man who had allowed my parents to follow us to the castle. The man who saw fit to give us a better life than our station dictated.

But most of all, he knew because he was my friend. One of my very first.

He knew how much I was hurting.

He knew what it'd cost me.

He said, "I am so very happy to have you home."

I nodded against his neck, not trusting myself yet to speak.

He said, "Your parents will be so thrilled. They have missed you so."

He said, "The King will never let you out of his sight again."

He said, "You've gone into the wilds and brought back a dragon. How unexpected. And how so very like you."

He said, "Hush, little one. Don't be sad."

He said, "I know, Sam. I know. But you must listen."

He said, "The Prince and Ryan arrived home two weeks ago."

He said, "They returned without incident on horseback to make up time on the road home."

He said, "Justin requested the wedding happen immediately."

He said, "The King wanted to wait for you."

He said, "The Prince agreed, but only just."

He said, "So I must ask of you the hardest task I've laid at your feet. You must be brave and strong and stand by my side at the wedding. You must honor your future king and the choices made, though your heart may be breaking. But you will *never* stand alone, because I will always be by your side. And once this impossible task I have asked of you is complete, I will take you away and we will see what we see."

He pushed my head up with his kind hands and brushed the tears from my cheeks with his thumbs. His eyes were warm, and I could see the love he felt for me on his face. And I loved this man too. More than I could say.

Morgan of Shadows said, "Can you do this, Sam of Wilds?"

And I said, "Yes," even though it felt like a lie.

He kissed my forehead, and I was *home*.

THEY GAVE us our moments, but as soon as I'd regained my composure, Tiggy and Gary bounded up, prancing around Morgan. He chuckled and hugged them both.

"I missed you, tiny wizard," Tiggy said, rubbing his face in Morgan's beard.

"It'll be nice to have intelligent conversation again," Gary said. "It's been difficult being the only intellectual amongst the group for weeks on end."

I rolled my eyes. "Because that's a real thing."

"It is," he insisted. "I am way smart and you guys are dumb and made me dumber because of it."

"No, *you're* dumb and Tiggy and I elevate you back to the level that could be considered functional."

"I help," Tiggy agreed.

Gary huffed. "I don't even know why I try with you two. It's obvious my breeding and social standing are far above your own and therefore I shouldn't even be associating with the two of you. Gods know why I do. You're *welcome*."

"What are you grinning at?" I asked Morgan, who stood beside us, eyes closed, looking more serene than I'd ever seen him before.

"The noise," he said, opening his eyes. "How I have missed the endless noise."

"I'm taking that as a compliment," I decided.

"You should," Gary said. "You don't get many of those."

"I have brooms," Tiggy said proudly.

"Oh look," a high-pitched voice rumbled. "There's a dragon. People should pay attention to him too. Like stupid wizards and unicorn sexual partners and half-giants who steal my brooms."

I rolled my eyes and looked back at Kevin, who was staring at us innocently.

"I don't know who said that," Kevin said. "It wasn't me."

"Morgan," I said. "This is the dragon. Kevin."

"Sam," Kevin hissed. "You're not doing it right. You *promised*."

"I'm not saying it!"

"Sam!"

"Grr. Fine! Morgan, may I present to you, the fearsome Beast from the East, the great creature who had a religion built up around him until he ate the leader, his holy dragon-ness... Kevin."

Kevin posed, wings spread, looking fierce.

The crowd that had started to gather around him said, "Oooooh."

"We practiced that for two days," I muttered. "Two. *Days*."

"Shhh," Kevin said. "Let them bask in me."

"You have found another one," Morgan said in awe, "that is exactly like the rest of you. How in the name of the gods do you *do* that?"

"Like the rest of us?" I echoed. "Bitch, please. I am my own man. I am an *individual*."

"Singular," Gary agreed. "Unique like a summer storm rolling over snowcapped mountains."

"My broom is my favorite," Tiggy said. "It is my broom and I love it."

"Bask in me," Kevin breathed. "*Bask*."

"You're right," Morgan said drily. "Absolutely nothing alike. I don't know what I was thinking."

"Are you done yet?" I asked Kevin. "You have to meet Morgan before he gets grumbly. He doesn't like being in sunshine too long."

"I don't get grumbly," he grumbled. "And I like my skin free of wrinkles."

"A few decades past worrying about that," I pointed out because I could and he needed it. He'd probably gotten very full of himself while I was gone. I couldn't let that happen.

"I'm so happy you're back," he said flatly. "Really."

"I know," I said. "I love you, boo. Kevin, stop posing and get down here!"

"But... they're *basking*."

I rolled my eyes. "I never should have told you about the cult."

"People make religions about me," he announced to everyone. "You may do the same."

"Ahhhh," they all said.

"Kevin!"

"Gods," he muttered. "Gary, control your child."

"*My* child? Oh, when he does something good he's *our* child. But when he starts acting like a whiny bitch, suddenly he's *my* child? Let me tell *you* something—"

"This is a thing now," I told Morgan. "Somehow, they got together and are convinced I am their child."

"I think I've finally reached the point where I no longer ask questions," Morgan said, looking up at Kevin. "I officially just go with the flow now."

"Dude," I said. "Right on. That makes my life easier."

"Sam, nothing about your life is easy."

"Right. But I have a talking dragon, so."

And Morgan just went with the flow.

I TOLD myself I was going to stroll triumphantly through the gates, my head held high because that was the only thing I could do. If Justin and Ryan were going to be waiting with everyone else at the castle, then I wanted to make sure they saw me standing strong, even if I didn't exactly feel it. I hoped they were far too busy planning a wedding to have time to stand around and wait for me to come home with the others, but knowing my luck, Justin would have them standing there front and center.

To say people gawked at us as we walked cobbled streets of the City of Lockes is an understatement.

Morgan told me the rumors of our quest were bordering on the ridiculous. Everything from me single-handedly battling a cult of Darks to taking down an army of dragons after I'd lost both legs and my right arm. ("How do they think I even got around after something like that?" "Very carefully.") Of course, no one really expected a dragon to return with us, especially one that had very recently kidnapped the Prince of Verania. Suffice it to say, people were curious and lined the streets as we made our way through to Castle Lockes.

"Everyone is staring at me," Kevin muttered. "I'm famous."

"Okay," I said. "Sure. Why not."

He lifted his head, his wings scraping against the side of a building, causing a scratch in the brick. "Oops," he said. "Sorry. Good people of Verania! I am a dragon. My name is Kevin. I ask that you bring me shiny things."

"No one bring him anything," I said.

"Don't listen to Sam. He's suffering from weariness from his travels. You should all bring me stuff. I'm not picky. I promise. It just needs to be expensive and shiny and pretty and covered in jewels and—"

"Kevin," Gary said.

"Yes, dear?"

"If you stop talking, you can have muffin later."

"How many muffins."

"The full batch."

"That's code for sex," I said to Morgan. "Do not go to their bakery."

Morgan covered his eyes with his hand and sighed.

We arrived at the castle gates without incident. The castle had never looked more beautiful. I had to stop myself from running full tilt toward it and hugging the stone walls. I didn't think Morgan would appreciate that.

"Well," Pete said, grinning widely. "Look who's strolling in triumphantly."

"Is there any other way to stroll?" I asked. "If there is, I don't know about it."

He pulled me in for a manly hug, patting my back three times and pulling away to grasp my forearms. "It's good to have you back, kiddo," he said. "It's been awfully quiet while you've been away."

"Can't have that," I said. "You keep everyone safe while I was gone?"

He rolled his eyes. "You know me. Fending off assassins and Darks left and right."

"I knew I could count on you," I said with a wink.

"Go on. Get out of here. We'll catch up later."

He understood, Pete did. He could probably see I was practically vibrating out of my skin. I had most of my family around me, but not the two who'd brought me into this world. And not my King. I needed to see them before I truly felt at peace. I didn't even think about Justin and Ryan then. I didn't care. I just wanted the last pieces of my puzzle put back together.

The gates rose at Pete's signal, and even before they'd cleared my chest, I was under them, not caring about decorum or my place.

The knights lined the walkway, standing at attention. Flags rippled in the breeze. The sun shone down from above. Morgan called from behind me, saying my name, telling me to slow down, but I couldn't. I just couldn't because I could *see* them. Waiting for me. My mother was talking with the King, my father standing at her side. The King said something to make her laugh, and I could hear it above all the noise and was reminded of growing up in the slums, of our little house where she would tend to her flowers and sing gypsy songs in a tongue that sounded of skylarks. There were others there too, but they were the only three I saw.

My father saw me first. One minute he was smiling faintly as his gaze wandered, and the next it stuttered and cracked as his eyes met mine. I saw his mouth move, and I knew, I just *knew* he'd said my name in that quiet voice of his because my mother stopped midsentence and looked at him, then out at me.

And she cried, "Sam!"

I ran.

I ran because I was home and they were my family.

I ran because I hadn't seen them in over two months.

I ran because I had gone out into the world with hopes and secrets and had returned with nerves exposed and skin twitching.

They laughed when they held me. Then we cried. My father's hand went to the back of my head, and my mother's nose brushed my cheek. My father said, "There you are," because he could, and my mother said, "My little boy," because I was.

I didn't want to let them go.

And so I didn't. For a time.

Then, "Sam."

My King.

I pulled myself away from my parents and turned to the Good King. He wore a quiet smile, one tinged with worry and sadness. I didn't like seeing that on him, so I schooled my face as best I could so he couldn't see the same mirrored in my own. I'd done what he asked of me. I might not have been his wizard, but he was still my friend. I couldn't blame him for anything.

He cupped my face in his great hands and pulled our foreheads together. He said, "You have done me a great honor, Sam of Wilds."

I reached up and curled a hand around the back of his neck. "And I would do it again," I whispered. "For you."

"Even after everything?"

"Even then."

"Anything. Anything you want. It's yours."

I shuddered out a laugh. "You don't mean that."

"I do," he said. "Because I know what this has cost you."

I had to ask. I had to. Even though everything told me to just walk away, I had to ask. "Could you make Justin release Ryan from his oath?"

My mother made a small wounded noise, but I couldn't look away from my King.

He was obviously pained when he said, "No, Sam. I could not."

"Then you can't give me what I want." I squeezed the back of his neck and pulled away.

He said, "Sam."

I smiled at him, forcing it to be as bright as possible. I raised my voice. "It is good to be home. Especially so much sooner than I expected."

"That may be so," a voice said from my right. "But you sure took your time getting back. Not all of us like to stand around waiting, Sam of Wilds. 'Tis a luxury you can't afford."

I closed my eyes and took a deep breath because if I didn't, I probably would have tried to curse the wizard of wizards.

"No penis noses," Morgan muttered as he walked up with the others in tow. "Whatever you do, do not turn his nose into a penis."

"No promises," I said, then turned to face the oldest living man in the known world.

Randall.

Unsurprisingly, he looked old as fuck. His eyebrows were eating his forehead. His nose hairs looked like they were staging an escape, curling out and around his nostrils. His beard was thin and scraggly, yellowed slightly around his mouth. Even his ears had more hair sticking out of them than was actually on his head.

He was older than anything else. He was whipcord thin. His liver-spotted hands shook slightly. His eyes were rheumy, sunken into their sockets.

And yet, the power that emanated from him was undeniable. It dwarfed Morgan's magic, until Morgan could have been nothing but a lowly street magician, swindling onlookers for coin by sleight-of-hand tricks. He was the greatest wizard in history. He'd seen and done things no other had ever been capable of.

And I had once turned his nose into a cock.

"Randall," I said, bowing my head in respect. "Your nose looks good."

Morgan groaned.

Randall narrowed his eyes as he took a step toward me. "Always with the lip, you are. If Morgan hadn't repeatedly sung your praises over the years, I would have had you up and over my knee a very long time ago."

"Kinky," I said. "Buy me dinner first."

"Sam," Morgan said. "For the love of the gods, shut your mouth."

"Sorry," I said, lowering my eyes. "It's been… a long trip."

Randall's gnarled hand curled over my shoulder and squeezed. I looked up and was surprised to see the smallest bit of kindness in his eyes. So, naturally, his mouth opened and ruined it. "I don't blame you, boy. If I'd gotten the shaft from my cornerstone, I'd be pissed off too. I don't know that I've ever heard of that happening before to any wizard, so you're forgiven for your lack of niceties." His eyes darted over my shoulder briefly and his mouth curled into mischief. "But you stink of elf, so it seems as if you've gotten back into the saddle, eh? Good for you." He chuckled to himself.

"Elf," came a low growl from behind me. "What. Elf."

Well shit.

"Oh *dayum*," Gary breathed. "I did not see that coming."

I looked back toward the castle entrance. There, only a few feet away, stood Prince Justin of Lockes and Knight Commander Ryan Foxheart. Justin looked regal once again, decked out in robes that were undoubtedly more expensive than my entire wardrobe combined. He looked like he would rather be anywhere else than standing here welcoming us home.

Ryan, though. Ryan, knighted out completely with his armor, shield attached at his back and sword sheathed at his side, looked furious. His hands were clenched, his shoulders squared and tense. He had dark circles around his eyes and his skin was pale, as if he hadn't had a good night's sleep since I'd seen him last. His gaze was on me, and I could see the anger in it.

Which did nothing but piss me off even more because whatever I did no longer concerned Ryan Foxheart.

I looked back at Randall and shrugged. "A friend of mine," I said. "Wanted a taste of magic."

"Did he now?" Randall said, ancient lips twitching. "How kind of you to provide him with a taste. Of your magic."

"Are they speaking in code?" Mom asked Dad, trying to be quiet but failing miserably.

"I don't know," Dad said. "I don't speak wizard."

"Neither do I. I feel like we've failed as parents."

"Nah," Dad said easily. "Look at him. He's adorable and knows how to put on his own pants. We did good."

"Those are some astounding qualifications," Randall said. "Seems about right for you."

"I am so happy you're here," I told him. "I promise to try and not make any part of you phallic in nature."

"That would be much appreciated. I have a wedding to officiate, after all. Wouldn't want history to repeat itself."

I immediately made plans to turn every visible inch of his skin into penises. It was foolproof and I would feel better. Therefore, it was a good idea. "Wouldn't want that," I repeated.

And because Morgan had trained me well, I schooled my face and turned back to my Prince, carefully avoiding anything having to do with Ryan. It didn't stop me from feeling his gaze boring into me. I bowed slightly at Justin. "I'm glad you made it back safely, my Prince. And I hear congratulations are in order."

Justin watched me coolly. "Yes. Well. I'm sure the next few weeks will pass rather quickly what with all the planning. It'll be a wedding no one will ever forget."

Rather than tell him that I would probably try and find a way to immediately forget it, I smiled thinly and said, "But of course. I am only pleased I was able to return in time to attend. I would have been devastated to miss the ceremony."

"I'm sure," he said. "And the gods only know that apparently nothing could get done without you here. It's the only reason it hasn't happened yet. Father insisted you be present."

"He honors me," I said, bowing my head again all the while wondering if there was a spell that would cause all of Justin's bones to melt. I was pretty sure there was. I thought to research it more closely. For my own peace of mind, of course.

"Yes," Justin said. "He does." His tone implied he didn't understand that in the slightest.

"My Prince," I said. "I take my leave of you. I'm sure you understand how tiring it was, having recently made the journey yourself."

He dismissed me with a wave of his hand.

I turned away without ever acknowledging Ryan.

"YOUR GRIMOIRE is sorely lacking," Randall told me a few days later. We stood in the labs, Morgan silent at my side while his former mentor proceeded to berate me and tell me how disappointing I was as an apprentice. "Have you not kept up with it at all in the time you were gone?"

I forced myself to calm before I did or said something stupid. "We found ourselves quite busy, if I'm being honest."

"That so."

"Yes."

"Because of all the times you got captured."

"That and the running for our lives," I agreed.

"Seems to happen to you often," he said, flipping casually through the Grimoire.

"I tend to spark a certain reaction amongst people who want to see me dead."

"Lartin the Dark Leaf."

"Eh. I don't know if he wanted me dead as much as he wanted to ransom me for pounds of gold."

"I wouldn't have paid it," Morgan assured me.

"And that's why you're my favorite," I said.

"And his death was the only way out?" Randall asked.

I shrugged. "For Tiggy, it was. He'd trussed us up in vermilion root, and Tiggy doesn't take too kindly to his family being threatened."

"Vermilion root," Randall said. "Fairy rings. Truth corn, as you call it. Maybe instead of learning how to be a wizard, you could start teaching people all the ways it takes for you to *not* be a wizard."

"Ha, ha, ha," I said, glancing at Morgan. "Randall's got jokes. I would have thought any sense of humor you had died centuries ago."

"He's always been funny," Morgan said.

"Really."

"I'm hysterical," Randall said, voice as dry as his skin. "You just fail to see it."

"I made your nose a dick," I said. "I see the humor just fine."

"Got those urges under control now, have you?"

"I'm twenty years old," I said. "Of course not. I'm made of hormones and an overactive imagination. Be thankful nothing else has been dicked out since you got here."

"I thank the gods every day for your restraint," Randall said, and I got the feeling he didn't mean that at all, the bastard. "The Grimoire, though. It is not something you can neglect, Sam. It is important to your education."

"I know," I said with a sigh. "But between the Prince and the godsdamn cornerstone bullshit, I haven't even thought about it. That's on me. I'd like to say I will make it a priority, but I can't make many promises until the wedding is done and over with. I'll be able to focus better then."

Randall studied me for a moment, then said, "Morgan, would you give us the room, please."

Morgan looked to argue, but Randall shook his head once. Morgan bowed slightly and left the labs, the door closing behind him.

"You're foolish," Randall said.

"Past the niceties already," I said. "That has to be a record."

He ignored me. "You are a foolish boy. You think too much. You talk too much. You're never serious. You fight your way with words more than the magic you were given. You argue with Morgan at every possible turn. You disobey direct orders. You think you know more than anyone else. And sometimes, I get the feeling you think you're above this. The training. The lessons. After all, what could two old wizards possibly have to teach you?"

I stayed silent, because the words hurt and because they were true.

"And yet," he said. He shook his head and traced his fingers along the Grimoire. "Your heart is bigger than anyone else's I've ever met. You are smart and fearless. You are talented and compassionate. You, by right, could be locked up in your room lamenting as to how unfair the world is, how unjust after everything you've done, but instead, you're here, head held high, listening to me at first talk shit about you, and then unfortunately gushing about your more tolerable qualities."

"Tolerable, huh?" I managed to say because Randall never said *anything* nice. About *anyone*. But especially me. I didn't even think he was capable of doling out compliments, even if they were slightly backward.

"Barely," he said. "And in small doses."

"You like me," I said, starting to smile, my fingers itching to hug him.

"Like is such a strong word."

"Admire."

"Tolerate."

"Adore."

"Endure."

"Love."

He sighed. "Why are you walking toward me?"

"Because I'm about to hug the fuck out of you," I said. "That's how we roll when we talk about feelings. We hug it out. For minutes. Fair warning: it's about to get awkward up in here."

"Sam, if you touch me in any way shape or form, I will hex you so that you have bloody, leaking pustules on your nether regions."

"I've changed my mind about that hug," I told him.

"Good decision. Now. Are you going to let this beat you?"

"What?" Because there were so many things. Darks. Ryan. Magic.

"All of it."

Of course he was all encompassing. "I want to say no."

"Then why don't you?"

"Because I *don't* know."

He rolled his eyes. "What *do* you know?"

"Honestly? Not as much as I think I do."

"I could have told you that. Let's start with something easy."

And then he began to smile at me and I knew I was in deep shit.

I HONESTLY never thought I'd get to say that I was on my back because of Randall. The thought alone was enough to make me cringe.

But here I was.

On my back.

Because of Randall.

"That looked like it hurt," Gary called out unnecessarily. "Especially that part when you got knocked back like ten feet. And then landed on the ground."

"Ow," I moaned. "Ow. Seriously. *Ow*. My body is not ready. It is *not ready*."

"Huh," Randall said. "Really didn't redirect the lightning that time, did you?"

"You're a big bag of assholes, Randall," I gritted out. "You flipping toe remover. I'll corrugate your metatarsals."

"Uh-oh, everyone," Gary said. "Sam is hurling nonsensical insults. That means he's pissed off. Watch out. Wouldn't want your feelings to be semihurt and confused."

"If Randall gets to shoot lightning at him," Kevin said, "then people should forgive me for knocking him into the side of a shed. I feel that's only fair. His mom and dad yelled at me for ten minutes. I felt sort of bad."

"Don't hurt Sam!" Tiggy growled, taking a menacing step toward Randall. "I smash you hard."

"He's not doing it on purpose," Morgan said, running his fingers along Tiggy's arms to calm the half-giant.

"Well, not *too* much on purpose," Randall said. "Sam, are you going to get up, or is this the part of the day where we lie down in the dirt?"

"Dirt time," I said, waiting for my limbs to stop twitching with residual electricity. "Definitely dirt time."

We were out at the sparring fields. The early morning fog was burning away with the rising sun. The Eighth Battalion was due out here in a bit to go through their exercises. Morgan told me that Ryan had delegated the training to another knight as apparently his sole focus needed to be on the wedding. Since that didn't sound like Ryan at all, I figured Justin must have had something to do with it. Ryan wasn't the type to delegate. He was dashing and immaculate, after all. I couldn't see him stepping down from his duties as Knight Commander now that he was finally back in the position.

Still, it made things easier, knowing I'd be able to avoid him yet again. In the week since we'd been back, I'd seen him once, briefly. I was in the gardens with my mother and he was moving toward the throne room and our eyes caught, stuttered. Held. I was the first to look away, resolutely so. When I looked back, he was gone.

It was better this way.

That and the fact that Randall hadn't left me alone even for a godsdamn minute, insisting that since he'd traveled all this way (and the bastard *still* wouldn't tell me how he beat me back to Castle Lockes), we might as well make the most of our time together. Which meant he followed me everywhere, berating me about my lack of focus, demanding that I explain to him the effects of the truth corn, requesting I list, in order, everyone single King's Wizard for the last thousand years.

In other words, he was being a pain in my ass. But I was so busy fighting the urge to punch him in the face that I didn't have much time to spare a thought for anything else.

Which is how I found myself woken up at the ass crack of dawn, told to get to the sparring fields immediately, only to be attacked the moment my feet hit the grass.

This was not going to be a good day.

…was the thought I had when I got knocked down for the sixth time.

"Are you sure you redirected the Dark's magic?" Randall asked, sounding amused as my appendages continued to spasm. "Because it doesn't seem like you can redirect much of anything right now."

"Maybe I just don't want to do it right away," I managed to say. "I'm just testing you to see if you still got it and all that. You do. Good job."

"How kind of you," Randall said. "To test me. Get up."

"I would," I said, "but apparently that much electricity tends to make muscles weak. Who knew?"

"Too bad his words couldn't actually physically cut someone," Kevin said to Gary. "His mouth would be his greatest weapon."

"I don't know if I want him using his mouth on Randall," Gary said.

"Oh my gods," I moaned. "Stop it. Bad thoughts. *Bad thoughts.*"

"I'll have you know I was considered quite the catch in my day," Randall said. "Did I ever tell you the story of the Morcadi triplets? Terrence, Theresa, and Trevor. All of them wanted a piece of my…"

"Not again," I muttered.

"…mind because everyone knows the mind is the most attractive organ on the body. However, the triplets didn't really understand the idea of individualism. When they did something, they did it together. And that included me. Why, I remember this one time, we decided to be sufficiently lubricated…"

"You're my hero," Kevin breathed. "Reveal to me your secrets."

"...on mulberry wine. The four of us held hands as we strolled through town, not caring that we were nude. You see, in those days, people didn't have problems with nudity. We always let our bobs and bits hang free because it as the *natural* thing to do."

"Déjà vu," I said. "Déjà vu and it's not any better the second time around."

"...and it didn't *matter* that Mr. McKlusky wouldn't do anything with his mouth but talk so we had to *improvise...*"

"I want to be him when I grow up," Kevin told Gary. "Triplets. *Triplets.*"

"Not in front of the children," Gary hissed. "They don't understand what we do behind closed doors."

"Or in the middle of the woods where everyone can hear you," I pointed out, finally able to push myself up.

"...and we never even really thought about whether or not we could bend that way. Unfortunately for Terrence, it turned out he could not and ended up with a sprain in his groin that hurt for days..."

"People wonder why I am the way I am," I said. "I tell them it's because I was always told to respect my elders and *these* are my elders."

"I am going to pretend that you meant that as a compliment," Morgan said.

"I didn't," I told him. "And this is pretty much all your fault. You found me."

"A decision I must live with every day," he said.

"...and that's how I ended up eating pie off the Morcadi triplets in the middle of a city fountain," Randall said, looking pleased with himself. "Now, Sam, if you please. Up and let us try again. Focus this time."

"I would like to," I told him. "But all I can focus on is how much it hurts when you electrocute me."

It happened three more times. And after each time, I found myself getting more and more frustrated at my apparent lack of ability to do something I'd already done before. It was embarrassing, especially in front of Morgan and Randall, the latter judging me harshly even though he never said a word about it. I knew what those furrowed eyebrows meant. Morgan, for his part, kept a straight face the whole time, though internally, he was probably bemoaning the fact that he ever knew my name.

I looked up at the sky, waiting for the seizing to stop, wondering just how I'd gotten to this point in my life. Granted, I supposed it was better to be constantly electrocuted by an old man whose nose I'd once turned into a penis rather than to focus on the penis of Ryan Foxheart that I would never have.

I know, I know. I could be philosophically poetic when I was morose. It's a gift.

"Maybe we should stop for the day," Gary said, as if he were actually doing something aside from watching me get knocked on my ass. "I don't know how much longer I can watch this sadness."

"Ah," Kevin said. "A mother's love knows no bounds."

"What the hell is wrong with the two of you?" I asked incredulously.

"I certainly didn't teach him that language," Gary said, frowning at Kevin. "What have you been saying around him?"

"Uh, yeah you did," I said. "The first day I brought you to the castle, you told me your room had better be nice because you, and I quote, 'Sure as shit wouldn't be staying in no crap shack. I'm a respectable fucking unicorn and my ass deserves only the finest of comfort.'"

"For fuck's sake, Sam," Gary said. "I don't talk like that. You bitch."

"The joys of parenting," Kevin said. "I never knew how wonderful it could be."

"My life is so weird," I muttered as I yet again picked myself up off the ground.

"Hi, Sam!"

"Hi, Tiggy."

"You okay?"

"Yes, Tiggy."

"Tiggy smash something for Sam?"

"No, Tiggy."

"Tiggy smash something for Sam."

He smashed one of the wooden sparring dummies.

"Thank you, Tiggy."

"Tiggy smash!" he bellowed and then proceeded to smash three more.

"Does he do that often?" Randall asked Morgan as they both watched splinters of wood fly into the air.

"Only when Sam or Gary gets hurt and or captured right in front of him."

"Ah," Randall said. "Lartin?"

"Lartin," Morgan agreed.

"And he wants to do that to me," Randall said as Tiggy ripped the head off one of the wood dummies and then drop-kicked it high into the air.

"Most likely," Morgan said. "He's showing remarkable restraint, isn't he?"

"Yes, remarkable," Randall said as Tiggy started growling and chewing on the arms of one of his victims.

And during Tiggy's Tirade of Destruction (capitalized, to make it important as it sounds), I felt my magic settle within me, more than I'd felt in days. I didn't understand how I'd suddenly overcome the blockage, but I wasn't going to argue. I felt almost like myself again, like I could do what I was supposed to do. Like I could be the wizard I knew I could be.

I looked up at Randall and said, "Again."

He must have heard something in my voice that hadn't been there before. He said, "Interesting how that works."

Morgan was looking toward the castle. "Maybe we should postpone this."

"A test is a test is a test," Randall said. "We just need to change the variables."

I didn't understand what they were talking about, but it didn't matter. I said, "*Again.*"

Randall moved quicker than he had before, quicker than a man of his age should have any right to. I was struck, for a moment, by what he must have been like at my age, or even Morgan's. There were stories, of course. One cannot live as long as Randall and not have been made into legend. Morgan had assured me many times that all of what I heard couldn't be trusted (the time Randall rode the Great White Dragon into battle against an army of Darks or how he'd once saved an entire mermaid kingdom by marrying their princess and therefore allowing the mermaid to assume her rightful place as queen).

But it was the stories that didn't get spoken aloud as often that I listened to the most. The stories not repeated by word or text with great relish.

How Randall had served a great king who had fallen into madness, brought back to sanity by the sheer force of Randall's will alone.

Of a darkness that rose beyond Verania's borders, a man bent on destroying all he could lay his hands on before Randall ended his life almost at the cost of his own.

And, if you dug further, you would find bare mention of Myrin. Myrin, who was never identified as man or woman, or even human at all. Myrin, who became Randall's cornerstone, who stood by his side, oft hidden in shadow. Myrin, who was Randall's great love. That last bit might have been a romantic talking, a wish to make the story more palatable. But regardless, I knew Randall's strength. I knew what a cornerstone meant. Regardless of who Myrin was, or what the relationship was with Randall, Myrin must have been an incredible individual to help Randall construct the level of magic he had.

Like now.

He moved with such grace, almost as if he were dancing. The movements of his hands, the muttering of the dark syllables underneath his breath as he called upon the lightning.

But this time was different.

Before, I could feel him holding back. I could feel the hesitation behind it, the need to make sure I wasn't seriously hurt. Beyond that, there was doubt. Doubt that I could even do it in the first place. Doubt that I had what it took. Doubt because regardless of what Randall thought of me, at that moment, he hadn't believed in me.

Now he did. Or, rather, he acted like he wanted to believe.

Or he just wanted to fry my ass for turning his nose into a dick.

That could be it too.

Because the sky above darkened, and there was a crash of thunder. For a moment, I thought his eyes glowed briefly blue. I considered it a very real possibility that I was about to die. There was a shout of warning from behind me, but before I could figure out who it could be from, Randall's lightning was called, arcing toward me, leaving burned trails in the grass. I thought *now now nownownow*, and it was like I was back on the dirt road near the Dark Woods. The Dark wizards standing in front of me, fire geckos bursting out from amongst the trees, the sounds of my friends escaping from behind me. My only thought was of their (*Ryan's*) safety, that they (*Ryan*) would have time to escape. That they (*Ryan*) would be clear and free and nothing could hurt them ever again.

The electricity struck my palm.

It curled up my arm and poured into my chest.

I had a lightning-struck heart and my *gods* did it beat.

And here it was again, this moment, this indefinable moment when I could so easily take this magic and make it my own. Take from Randall and keep it for myself. I could turn it on him, knock him around, fry him until his eyes melted in his sockets and his beard began to burn and curl into little heated black wisps of ash and smoke, and he would *know* who was the stronger of us, he would *know* who held the most power, and I would fucking *take it from him and*—

It wasn't who I was.

It wasn't what I wanted.

My magic wouldn't allow that. Not now. Not when it was settled.

(Because it said *ryanryanryanryanryan* and I thought nothing of it.)

And in the blink of an eye, I raised my other hand toward the sky and my heart expelled Randall's lightning and it *roared* above me, his magic mixed with my own, like we were in the middle of an electric storm unlike anything we'd ever seen. The sky flashed, and I thought maybe my eyes were glowing because it was *here* and it was *everywhere* and it was—

It was over.

The sun was shining.

The wind was warm.

I took a breath. Held it. Lowered my hand. Let it out slowly.

Found my center. How easy it seemed.

Opened my eyes.

The two wizards stood stock-still, Morgan's jaw dropped and Randall's gaze calculating.

"Well," I said with a cocky grin. "That was enlightening. Get it. *Get it*. En-lightning. It's funny. It's funny! Come on. Bah."

Gary groaned. "You don't *deserve* to have your clothes billow if that's what you come up with."

"Why?" I asked. "Would you say it was… *shocking*?"

"The fact that you can do what you just did is diluted when you open your mouth."

"Puns," Tiggy said solemnly. "Poor Sam and his puns."

I laughed because I felt *light*. I had done this on my own. I had done this without—

"What in the *hell* do you think you're doing?" an angry voice demanded from behind me.

I whirled around.

Behind me stood almost an entire contingent of knights. Dozens of them.

The Eighth Battalion, from the crest on their armor and shields. Even Pete stood with them.

They all watched me with wide eyes.

They weren't afraid, but it was close.

There isn't much distance between curiosity and fear.

Except for Pete. Pete just looked fondly exasperated, like he usually did.

But Ryan, though.

He stood in front of his knights. He still looked tired, and I wondered what was stopping him from sleep. I wondered what dreams he was having. I wondered why I should even care.

He also looked scared and angry and filled with such resentment, like he'd seen something that was an affront to him, that he'd been personally attacked.

Except it wasn't directed toward me.

No. Ryan Foxheart was glaring directly at Randall.

"Knight Commander," Randall said. "How lovely to see you."

"Did you just *attack* him?" Ryan asked, voice low. His hand was on the hilt of his sword still in the scabbard at his side. He took a step toward me, moving slightly to the left, keeping Randall in his sights. His knights behind him looked tense.

What a fucking moron.

Which is what I called myself when I felt my heart flutter slightly in my chest. Because *what*.

"Of course not," Randall said. "Sam will tell you the same thing when he's done being speechless. Which, I'll admit, is a good look on him. What you witnessed was a test. And I think he passed admirably. Don't you, Morgan?"

"You meddle too much." Morgan sighed.

Randall cackled loudly. "I regret nothing."

I finally found my voice. "What are you doing here?" I said to Ryan. It hit me then that this was the first time I'd actually addressed him face-to-face in weeks, and I couldn't even begin to grasp if it calmed me or pissed me off more.

Maybe both.

"I'm training my knights," he said, still scowling at Randall.

"Figured you'd be busy," I said, and *that* caused him to look at me.

"I have priorities," he said. "Responsibilities."

I grinned at him because I felt like being a bit of an asshole. "Oh. I'm aware of that. Don't worry about explaining yourself to me."

He frowned. "Why are you letting him hurt you?"

"Does it look like I'm hurt?"

"Your clothes are burned," he said flatly.

I looked down and he was right. There were scorch marks on my chest, and the cloth burned away, revealing reddened skin underneath. "Huh," I said. "Look at that."

"Are you trying to get yourself killed?" he asked.

I rolled my eyes. "Calm down. We're training. Just like you. You don't see me freaking out when someone comes at you with a sword."

"You'd freak," he said.

"Nope."

"You'd freak," he insisted.

"Hardly. You're dashing and immaculate, after all."

"That should not be a thing anymore," he said as the knights behind him began to snicker. "I get enough grief for it already."

"From your boys?" I asked. "Good. They should constantly give you shit. Wouldn't want that head of yours to swell." And, of course, since I hadn't meant to make that dirty, it came out way dirty.

Ryan flushed slightly and said, "No. We certainly wouldn't want that."

"Oh my gods," Randall muttered. "Are they always like this?"

"Constantly," Gary said. "You don't even know. It gets so much worse. They've always been like this."

"How is it that no one told them before now?" Kevin asked. "I would have said something just to make them stop."

"We're standing right here," I growled as Ryan flushed even further, causing me to *feel* things I didn't want to feel toward him. Charitable things. *Sexual* things. I was supposed to be pissed off at him and hate him forever (okay, maybe not *forever*, but for at least four years until I woke up one morning between two attractive men who'd I'd had a threesome with the night before and realized that I had moved on in a spectacular fashion).

"We can see that," Randall said. "Trust me, we can *all* see that. It makes you wonder where you went wrong." He glanced over at Morgan.

"Don't look at me," Morgan said, raising his hands defensively. "It's hard to train the obliviousness out of someone when apparently all they do is wallow in it."

"I despise all of you," I said.

"Hi, Sam!"

"Except for you, Tiggy. You're still my favorite."

Tiggy looked very smug at this.

"Maybe we should handle this," Kevin told Gary.

"Please don't," I groaned.

Gary glared at Ryan. "Maybe we should."

"Um," Ryan said.

Kevin reared himself up to his full height. For someone who thought he was my pseudofather and yet still threatened to suck me off on a regular basis, he was an imposing figure. The knights took a step back as one as he bared his teeth.

"You hurt my boy," Kevin rumbled. "Tell me why I shouldn't eat you right now."

"Not my real dad," I reminded him.

"Make sure you don't hurt your teeth on his armor," Gary said. "It'll be sort of like eating shellfish, I suppose. Crack the hard exterior to get to the meat."

"So bloodthirsty," I whispered in wonder.

"You wouldn't eat me," Ryan said.

"Wouldn't I?" Kevin asked. "Do you really want to test that?"

Ryan looked back at the knights behind him, like he thought they'd back him up.

Pete shot that shit straight down. "I don't expect you'll find much help back here, boy," he said. "Oh, excuse me. *Knight Commander*."

Ryan looked utterly betrayed as the knights smirked at him. I knew I liked them for a reason.

"I raised him to be a strong man," Kevin said, eyes narrowing. "To not take shit from anyone."

"You didn't raise me at all," I said, though no one was really listening to me anymore.

"And then *you* came along," Gary said. "And gave him a heart boner."

"That's embarrassing to hear someone say out loud," I said. "Though probably factually accurate."

"You don't touch his flower," Tiggy growled, taking a menacing step toward Ryan. "Tiggy smash your delicious face and make it hamburger face."

"Ye gods," I said. "This is turning brutal."

"You're a cornerstone," Morgan said. "Something revered and treasured. Except apparently you don't know how to act like one."

And that was all I could take. He wasn't theirs to berate. He was mine. They were my family but this was Ryan. "Stop," I said as Ryan took a step back.

Randall looked between the two of us. "All morning," he said. "I've been electrocuting him. Giving him just a mere taste of what he is capable of. And then the moment you turn the corner and come onto the sparring fields, I could see the difference. I gave him everything I could. He shouldn't have survived that."

"Um," I said. "Excuse me? I shouldn't have *what* now?"

"That might have been a little much," Morgan said. "You know. In case it hadn't worked."

"So little faith," Randall said. "I believed in him. Mostly."

No one seemed concerned that I was plotting their deaths out loud.

"Sam," Ryan said quietly at my side. "Are you all right?"

I opened my mouth to respond (and say what, I didn't know), but Randall beat me to it. "Away with you," he said. "We can handle it from here. See to your training with your knights and leave us be."

"But—"

"You have your priorities," Morgan said, not unkindly. "Your responsibilities."

"Your oath," I said without meaning to, and Ryan looked away.

"I know what I am," Ryan said. "I'm a cornerstone."

"Yes," Randall said. "You are. But you are not the only one. There will be others not bound as you are, and Sam will find them. Away, Knight Commander Foxheart. I won't ask again."

Ryan's jaw tensed, but that was all. His gaze flickered to mine, and I held it because I wasn't going to be hurt by him. I wasn't going to show on my face that my insides were screaming for him to fight back. To rally against Morgan and Randall. Against Tiggy and Gary and Kevin. Against all of them. For me.

He didn't, of course.

He called to his knights, even as some of them shook their heads. Pete looked annoyed, but he listened to his commander. They began to shuffle toward the far end of the sparring fields.

"You knew," I said as I watched him go. "You saw him coming and knew how my magic would react."

"Yes," Randall said simply.

"It won't be the same," I admitted. "With anyone else."

He looked sad at that. "I know. But it will be enough."

"Has this ever happened before?"

Randall could have played the fool. He could have lied. Instead, he said, "Once."

Morgan looked to speak, but Randall shook his head, once, cutting him off.

"And?" I asked.

"The man went Dark. He killed many people."

"What happened to him?"

Randall sighed. "I destroyed him. I destroyed him because I could not save him. He made a choice, and like with any choice, there were consequences. I was one such consequence."

"You're worried about me. Aren't you?" I didn't know if that made me feel good or even worse.

"Not yet," Randall said, and wonder of all wonders, he smiled at me. "You'll know when I start to get worried."

CHAPTER 27
Avoidance Is Key
to Maintaining a Happy Sam

"I'M WORRIED," Randall said a few days later while I worked on my Grimoire in the labs.

And because I hadn't stopped thinking about a single word he'd said, I freaked.

"I'm going Dark side, aren't I?" I said, sounding rather breathless at the horror of it. "I'll have to go live in the Dark Woods and be broody and start to monologue about everything. I'll try and trap people and then tell them all about my plans, thus giving them the means to stop me with, but I won't be able to do a thing about it because I won't have a fuck left to give! I knew this was going to happen! Why, just last night, I thought about taking the last strawberry scone on the plate even though I *knew* Gary wanted it. I thought to myself just how delicious that scone would be and how I wanted it in my mouth, and even though Gary asked if he could have it, *I didn't care*. I didn't care that my best friend wanted the last strawberry scone because I wanted it myself. I had to forcibly stop myself from taking it and lording it over him. I wanted to rub it in his face that it was *my* godsdamn scone. And don't get me started on my *other* devious plots that I have bouncing around in my head."

I waited.

Randall didn't say anything.

I sighed. "You're supposed to ask me about my other devious plots."

"I really don't want to," he said.

"Randall."

"Sam. You're monologuing."

"Oh. My. *Gods*. It's happening! It's *happening*. Randall. *Randall*. You have to kill me. You have to kill me before I lose control and come up with a ridiculous plan for world domination that relies on way too many moving parts and a completely ludicrous *deus ex machina* twist that makes no sense to the overall arc."

"So. Like. Your whole life. Basically."

I narrowed my eyes at him. "Are you seriously getting *sassy* with me right now?"

"I would never call myself *sassy*, Sam," he said.

"This is *serious*!"

"Sam. You're not turning into a Dark wizard."

"You just said you were worried!"

"I did. About what you're going to wear to the wedding."

"I… you… *what*?"

"And are you bringing a date? I think you should consider bringing a date."

"What the fuck—?"

"You are representing the King and Morgan after all. And by extension, me as well. Can't have you looking alone and slovenly. Why, the rumors alone in the Court would be egregious."

"Randall!"

"Yes, Sam. You may not be aware, but I am standing right next to you. There is no need to shout."

"I will turn your nose back into a dick, so help me gods."

He frowned. "Would that make you feel better? About the whole wedding thing? If it would, I wouldn't be adverse."

I gaped at him.

"Just don't make it so big this time," he said. "It was hard to officiate the ceremony last time when it kept falling in my mouth."

"I can honestly say that I wish I'd never heard those words coming from you," I told him.

"Can you do this?" he asked me seriously.

"Of course I can," I said. I even almost believed my own words. "I'm Sam of Wilds."

AND I thought I *could* do it. I really did. I told myself that the key to a happy Sam would be to handle my problems the way they should be handled. Maturely and responsibly.

So the solution was obvious.

Avoidance. Lots and lots of avoidance.

Now, let it not be said that I never faced certain... complications... head on. Many parties can probably attest that I often found myself in the thick of things, with no real idea as to how I got there (see gay fairy marriages and how every Dark wizard in existence seemed to want me dead). If someone I cared about was in danger, I'd fight my hardest. If I saw injustice, I tried to correct it. I spoke for those who could not, I helped those who could not help themselves, and I tried to be an all-around good person on top of it, regardless of the minor slipups I had where I ventured into morally gray territory.

However, when things got personal?

Well. That changed everything.

I offer the following evidence:

Five-year-old Sam said, "Hi, Mary. Why are you looking at me weird?"

Seven-year-old Mary said, "We should get married when we get older because I love you and you can stay at home and bake pie while I go to work at the mill, and I will have babies and you can raise them because my mom says that we don't have to follow normal gender constructs."

Five-year-old Sam said, "My mom is calling. I have to go. Bye. Oh, and I am moving to another country and if you see someone who looks like me after today, it's not me, just someone who looks like me and is not really me and is probably my evil twin so just ignore him forever."

And:

Nine-year-old Sam said, "We could be friends. I've always wanted to have friends."

Ten-year-old Monique said, "We can start as friends, I guess. And then you can be my boyfriend. You must tell me I am pretty every day and kiss me on the lips and say things about how you like my eyes."

Nine-year-old Sam said, "I don't want friends that bad. My mom is calling. I am moving. Boy who looks like me is evil. Avoid at all costs."

And:

Fifteen-year-old Sam said, "Who is that? Is that a new knight? What's his name? Why does he look like my dreams?"

The hornless gay unicorn named Gary said, "Oh, girl, you've got a good eye. That's Ryan Foxheart. Pulled up from the King's Army."

Fifteen-year-old Sam breathed, "I want to put my face on his face."

The hornless gay unicorn named Gary said, "Um. What did you say?"

Fifteen-year-old Sam said, "Nothing! Nothing. Um. I have to go. Upstairs. To… touch. The walls."

The hornless gay unicorn named Gary said, "Why don't you just go introduce yourself?"

Fifteen-year-old Sam said, "Nope. Nope, nope, nope. Good-bye."

So. There's a history there.

Granted, I'd never been in as deep as I was now.

Which made the avoidance that much more necessary.

And that much more ridiculously difficult.

Because it had been a *very* long time since there'd been a royal wedding. The King and the Queen had been twenty and seventeen, respectively, so the decades that had passed since then were a long drought for those that lived for such things.

And unfortunately, it seemed most lived for it.

The City of Lockes was transformed into the City of Rainbow Fucking Sunshine Because Everyone Is Celebrating Team Rystin. Banners were hung around the City, the profiles of Justin and Ryan flapping in the wind. Blooms of flowers were placed at almost every corner. Garland wrapped around the streetlights. Vendors set up carts on the roads, selling Completely Authentic Rystin Merchandise (which, shockingly, was not authentic at all and was most likely made in Meridian City by an aging factory worker and was in no way, shape, or form endorsed by anyone from the castle). All the hotels sold out within a day. I hoped Todd and his father were pleased. I spared a brief moment to appreciate the memory of Todd's ears.

But everyone was thrilled and merry and gay. There were smiles on people's faces, a skip to their steps.

Well, until they saw me.

Then there were the looks of sympathy, a slight wince to their faces because apparently *everyone* knew my business.

So.

Avoidance.

"Hey, Sam. How are you doing? Do you need to talk to—?"

"Nope!"

"Oh, Sam. Maybe you should just—"

"Nope."

"Hi, Sam. You don't know me, but I want to offer you my condol—"

"No, thank you."

"Sam. Forget Ryan Foxheart. My last name is Harding. Combine that and we'd be HaveHard. Doesn't that sound… erotic?"

"Nope!"

Avoidance became my mantra.

I told myself it would be easier to get over this entire shitstorm if I didn't have anything to do with Ryan and Justin leading up to the wedding.

With Justin, it worked out marvelously for the both of us because he seemed to be doing the same to me and was obviously far too busy with the wedding planners, discussing the food and clothes and decorations and music and lighting and vows and flowers—especially since my mother had looked at him, laughed, and walked away when he told her he'd be requiring her services. It was the first time in my life I'd appreciated a mutually beneficial arrangement I had going on with the Prince.

And Ryan?

Well.

Let me tell you about *that* motherfucker.

Avoidance is key to maintaining a happy Sam.

When problems of a lightning-struck heart are prevalent, avoid them until they go away all on their own.

Ryan did not get that memo.

While Randall was forcing me to elucidate, Ryan was right there, lurking like a fucking jackass in the corners.

"Can we help you?" Randall asked him once after he followed us into the library.

"No, no," Ryan said. "Just looking for… this book," he said, pulling one off the shelf. "To do… research."

Randall looked over and read off the title. "*Sex & Pregnancy: You Won't Actually Poke the Baby.* Huh. That's… light reading."

Ryan blushed, and it made me want to poke *his* baby.

Or something.

It was all very confusing.

"Yes, well," he muttered. "Can't be too careful." Then he fled.

"Idiot," Randall muttered, sounding strangely fond.

WHILE MORGAN and I were conducting our blood-on-shrooms experiment, Ryan just happened to need access to the labs to "continue the research" he'd done before he'd left the castle on the quest to rescue Justin. When Morgan asked Ryan to remind him just what that research had been seeing as how the wizard had *never* seen Ryan in the labs researching *anything*, Ryan mumbled something about poking babies and

some such and then accidently set his trousers on fire when he leaned against a
burner. It was very awkward (read: stimulating) because he was forced to take off
said trousers to avoid burns and apparently had forgotten that day to wear
undergarments, his top *just* long enough to preserve his modesty. Morgan sighed a
little. I died a little. Ryan fled.

"Shall we continue?" Morgan asked, rubbing his hands over his eyes.

"Oh my gods," I said because I couldn't quite compose my thoughts as I was
pretty sure I'd just seen a hint of Ryan Foxheart's balls.

"Sam?"

"Oh my gods."

"And I'm pretty sure the experiment is over for the day."

"Oh my gods."

WHEN GARY and I plotted our plans to follow the rumors of unicorn horns, Ryan
happened to be sitting at the table next to ours in the so-called War Room, obviously
doing his best to feign ignorance as we pored over the maps. It wasn't working. The
book he was holding in his hands was upside-down. It's like he wasn't even trying to
be subtle anymore.

"And just think," Gary said, far more loudly than what was actually necessary,
"after we get done with these ridiculous obligations your station requires you to be
present for—because let's be honest, that's the *only* reason we're still here—we'll
leave this place far behind and you, my young kitten, will find yourself a man of the
desert. Dark skin and dark hair. Big dick and awesome nipples. His name will be
Matta and he will take you into his desert dwelling before he goes into your desert
dwelling."

Ryan's hands tightened on his book.

"That was… unsurprisingly descriptive," I said.

"Shhh," the War Room librarian said. She had to be almost as old as Randall.

"Sorry, Griselda," Gary said, sticky sweet.

"Matta, huh?" I said. "Can his first name be Wassa?"

Gary stared at me blankly.

"Because then his full name would be Wassa Matta."

Ryan snorted loudly and covered it up with a very fake cough.

Gary knocked me off the chair. "You are not allowed to make jokes anymore."

"Shhh," Griselda insisted.

"Sorry, Griselda," Gary said. And then, "Hey, Sam?"

"What?" I said as I picked myself up off the floor.

"Do you know what I find fascinating?"

"What?"

"How knights apparently can read books upside down."

"Oh, mothercracker," Ryan said and then he fled the room.

"I taught him that curse," I said sadly.

"Shhh!" Griselda shouted at us.

"Oh calm the fuck down, Griselda," Gary snapped. "We're the only ones here, you ancient she-beast. You need to check yourself before you wreck yourself."

Griselda kicked us out of the War Room. I didn't blame her.

"NO, TIGGY," I said. "There were, like, two verses *before* he started singing about cheesy dicks and candlesticks."

Tiggy glared at me as we sat in the garden, sunning ourselves. There was the hustle and bustle of the castle around us as wedding preparations went on and on, but we didn't give a shit about that. Gary had decreed that Tiggy and I were so pale that we were haunting his dreams and forced us outside to get some sun.

"Dicks and sticks," Tiggy insisted. "Every line was dicks and sticks."

"I think you're misremembering, my friend."

"You dismembered," he grumbled.

"Not the same thing. One is forgetting. The other is getting your head chopped off."

"No," he said. "I use correct word."

I gasped and covered my heart. "Well I *never*. Are you *threatening* me, Tiggy?"

"Yes," Tiggy said, sounding smug. "Dicks and sticks."

"Fine. Dicks and sticks."

"And Knight Delicious Face."

"And Knight Del—wait, what?" I turned my head toward him, but he was propped up on his elbows, looking toward the castle. I followed his gaze and sure enough, there he was.

"I've never had a stalker before," I told Tiggy.

"I stalk you," Tiggy said.

"Erm. I don't think you do."

"Stalking is following. I follow you everywhere. I stalk you. I stalk you so hard."

"Tiggy, that's not—you know what? I am not even going to argue with you on that. You can stalk me all you want. In fact, I am honored to have you as my stalker."

Tiggy preened. "Pretty Sam. I'll hide in bushes and stare at you."

"Aww. You do that, buddy."

"Knight Delicious Face isn't subtle."

"You can't be called Knight Delicious Face and be subtle at the same time. It doesn't work that way." And really, he wasn't being subtle at all. I was rather embarrassed for him, if I was being honest. And annoyed. And angry. And slightly turned-on, though I was loath to admit it.

Because he was standing at the other side of the garden, pretending to be interested in whatever the florists were saying to him (pointing out different arrangements of flowers for the wedding, hired because my mother had flat out refused to participate—she's slightly vindictive, my mom is), but no one, and I mean *no one*, could miss the glances he kept shooting in our direction. It was getting to the point the florists were getting visibly annoyed with him because he obviously wasn't paying attention to a single word they were saying.

He looked over at us again as one of the florists started in again on the power of petunias.

Tiggy and I waved sarcastically because we were awesome.

"What a dick," I muttered.

"You love him," Tiggy said.

"No," I said. "I love only you."

"And Gary."

"And Gary."

"And Mom and Dad."

"Yes, and them."

"And Morgan."

"Sure. Lots."

"And the King."

"Yes, can't forget him."

"And Pete."

"Pete! My castle guardian."

"And Kevin."

"Stretching, just a bit."

"And Randall."

"That's not really true."

"You love Ryan," Tiggy said seriously.

"Motherfucker," I sighed.

"Dicks and sticks," Tiggy said.

"My whole life is dicks and sticks," I said.

Ryan looked at us again.

We waved.

Tiggy called out, "Knight Delicious Face. Find your balls yet?"

I choked.

The florists looked slightly scandalized.

Ryan made fumbling excuses and fled.

"Not yet," Tiggy said.

And then we made up many, many verses of "Cheesy Dicks and Candlesticks."

"SO, CHAMP," Kevin said, tossing the heavy twine ball back at me. "You have any crushes on anybody at school?"

"I haven't been in school for years," I said. "Since long before I met you."

He shrugged, the sun starting to set behind him. "I know it's hard, buddy. Having a new dad."

"What the fuck."

"I just want what's best for you and Gary. Your mom works hard, you know."

"First, Gary doesn't work hard. At *anything*. Second, he is not my *mom*."

Kevin nodded and caught the ball in his claws as I chucked it back at him. "All teenagers think the same thing about their parents."

"I'm *twenty*! Why are we even out here!"

"Bonding," Kevin said. "You said that we needed bonding." Then he leered at me, his lip curling, tongue snaking out between his fangs. "Or perhaps you meant bondage? Is that what you meant, pretty? You need me to tie you up and choke you on my dick? Make you scream as I twist your little nipples? Make you—"

"That's not what I meant at all."

The leer disappeared. "That's what I thought, sport. So, any boys or girls you want to get fresh with?"

"Get fresh with," I repeated.

"You know. Take to the dance, or whatever."

"The dance."

"Sock hop? I don't know what you kids call it these days."

"I think that being with Gary has made you both actually mentally disabled. Like your magic broke both of your brains the moment you fellated him."

"So much fellating," Kevin agreed. "Oh look, company."

I looked over my shoulder and sure enough, a small contingent of knights were coming out onto the sparring fields, even though I was absolutely *positive* there was no need for them to be here. Of course, Ryan was in the lead. Pete stood toward the rear, a look of amused exasperation on his face.

"Sam," he said, once they passed through the gates. The others headed toward the weapons shed, but Pete dragged behind them. Ryan almost was able to make it all the way to the shed without looking at me but failed miserably at the last minute.

"Pete," I said, ignoring Ryan completely. "Late training?"

He rolled his eyes. "It appears our illustrious Knight Commander felt we'd been slacking off recently."

"Is that so."

"Quite. And apparently, it couldn't wait until tomorrow, and we had to go to the fields right away. Been here long?"

"An hour or so."

"Funny, that," Pete said. "Right around the time the Knight Commander came up with this idea."

I rolled my eyes. "Go do knight things."

"Nah," Pete said with an easy shrug. "Getting too old for this shit. I'll just observe." He looked over at the dragon. "Kevin. Nice evening for a game of catch."

Kevin nodded sagely. "It is, Pete. Always a nice evening when I get to be with my boy."

"So that's still a thing, huh?" Pete asked me.

"No," I said crossly. "It is not a *thing*. It was never a *thing*."

"Forgive him," Kevin said, frowning at me. "He's a bit cranky tonight. I think he likes this boy from school, but I can't get a name out of him."

Ryan was apparently listening into the conversation like a creep, because he dropped a heavy long sword on his foot.

Everyone stared at him as he grimaced. "It slipped," he said.

"Oh boy," Pete said. "This just gets sadder and sadder."

"And I have absolutely no idea what you're talking about," I said.

"Ah," Pete said. "We're at avoidance."

I grinned at him. "There's nothing to avoid because there's nothing there."

Pete sighed and shook his head fondly. "So what boy does he have a crush on, then?" he called out quite loudly to Kevin.

Ryan tensed.

"Don't know," Kevin said, tossing me the ball again. "But you can sure as shit bet I'm going to meet him before he takes Sam out. Instill the fear of the gods in him, I will."

"Your life is so weird," Pete said to me.

"Right?" I said.

"Hey, Sam," one of the knights called out. He was handsome in a rugged sort of way, all charm and a wicked glint to his eyes. I thought his name was Nat or Nate. "You ain't seein' anyone, right?"

"Right."

"I could take you out," he said, looking me up and down. "Show you a good time."

"Yeah?"

"Yeah. You, me. Candlelight. See where it goes."

"I think I have a good idea of where it might go," I said. "You just licked your lips. Lasciviously."

"Think of the other things I could lasciviously lick—"

"Get in line," Ryan snarled at him.

Nat or Nate winked at me and followed orders.

The knights started going through their paces. Ryan called to Pete, but Pete rolled his eyes and waved him off. "I'm retiring in four months," he said. "I don't have time to be a part of your weird flirting."

Ryan sputtered and then fled to the other side of the sparring fields, his knights following and laughing behind his back.

"They think he's an idiot," Pete said as he watched them go.

"The knights? Why?"

Pete shrugged. "For what he did to you. They think he made the biggest mistake of his life and give him shit for it. Nobody fucks with Sam of Wilds."

I gaped at him as he walked away, whistling a jaunty tune.

THE WEEK before the wedding, I was in the gardens with my mother, helping her weed and water her flowers. It was good work, hands dirty and smelling of earth, muscles in my back and arms burning. We were back in the secret parts of the garden, the area where few ever ventured. Ryan and I had been here once, speaking of wishes and stars.

"*Mamia* loved her flowers," my mother said, tending to the crocus and the tulips. "She could grow them year-round, even in the snows. She kept a greenhouse, the first of its kind. She built it herself, refusing help from the men and women. She said it was hers, and as the *rom baro* of our clan, she would lead by example. She understood helping others, but also showing that one could stand on his or her own feet."

"I'll meet her one day," I said.

She smiled at me. "Of course you will. You are a part of her just as much as I am. I may not be allowed back, but you will be."

"Do you regret it? Choosing Dad over your *roma*." Because when all else was stripped away, that is what had happened. Mom had fallen in love outside of her *roma*—her clan—which was expressly forbidden by gypsy law. She'd been outcast, shunned by her people when her choice had been made clear. She had chosen to follow my father instead of her own people. But my mother was always clear in the fact that there was never animosity after she left, and that her mother had held her tight and whispered in her ear how proud she was of her daughter, how wonderful she thought she was, how sad she was to see her go.

"No," she said simply. "Not ever."

"How did you know it was the right thing to do?"

She sat back on her knees, a smidge of dirt on the tip of her nose, a light sheen of sweat on her forehead. I thought she'd never looked more beautiful than she did at that moment.

She said, "I didn't."

"What?" Because *what*?

"I didn't know it was the right thing to do."

"But. You and Dad always...." I trailed off because I didn't know how to finish. I always thought that what had existed between the two of them was sure and strong, even from the beginning. To find out there was doubt really threw me.

"I was young," she said, smiling quietly. "So sure I knew more than *mamia* as to the ways of my heart. And I knew that I'd already given my heart away to your father. That was never in question. From the moment I laid eyes on him, I was his and he was mine."

"But?"

She shrugged. "But you can never be sure, Sam. No matter how hard you wish something to be so, there's always going to be risk involved. I knew that if I followed him, I would be cast out from the *roma*. I would have the man I loved. I would lose my family. Or, I could stay with the *roma* and never see Joshua again. The choice was easy for me. Even if I didn't know it was the right one at the time."

"Now?" I asked.

She looked down at her flowers, fingers grazing along the petals. "Now," she said. "Now I know it was the right choice. Hindsight can be a wonderful gift, Sam. Or a terrible curse."

"I don't know what to do," I admitted. "I just.... Mom. I don't know what to do."

She reached out and took my hand in hers. She said, "Sam, I—"

I never got to hear what she would have said then, because we were interrupted as Ryan pushed through the low-hanging trees and stumbled into the rear garden. He looked harried, eyes wide, hands shaking. He saw my mother and me and took a step backward. "I'm sorry," he said. "I didn't know anyone would be here. I'm sorry. I'll just...." He turned, shoulders stiff, back toward the entrance.

"Ryan," my mother said and he stopped. Took a great breath. And then another. And then another.

She asked, "Are you all right?"

"I'm fine," he said, though it wasn't believable at all.

"You're not fine," she said with a frown. "You're shaking."

"I'm just tired. It's been a long few weeks."

"I can imagine."

"Why are you here?" I blurted out.

He tensed even further but didn't turn around. "I needed a place to go," he said. "To get away. Just for a little while."

"And you came here," I said. "Because my mother showed you this place."

"Yes," he said.

"Good," I said. "I hope it helps. Mom, I have to go."

Now he turned. He said, "You don't have to leave. You were here first. I can—"

"You need it more than I do," I said. "It's fine."

"Sam," my mother said. "Are you sure?"

I looked her in the eye and said, "Sometimes, you know what's right, even when it hurts you the most. Just… keep him calm, okay? He doesn't have… I don't know. Sing him a song from *mamia*."

She looked to her flowers and nodded.

I stood and went to pass Ryan. Of course, he reached out and grabbed my arm, fingers curling around my bicep. I didn't look at him. He didn't look at me. But he held on tight, his body a solid, warm line against mine.

He said, "You don't have to go."

"I think I do," I said.

He said, "I don't want you to go."

I said, "And that's why I have to."

"Sam."

"Stay here," I told him. "Listen to my mother. She will keep you safe for now."

I pulled away, and Ryan let me go.

I didn't look back as I fled.

My lightning-struck heart thundered in my chest.

I never asked what they spoke about.

TWO DAYS later, my dad said, "I like getting drunk with you," the noise of the tavern rolling all around us.

I grinned at him, knocking our beers together. "And I like getting drunk with you." Though, I wasn't anywhere near as drunk as he was. Apparently, the stout he'd been slamming back was pretty strong.

"I'm so glad we had you," he said, his smile a little sloppy. "So glad you're what came out of me and your mom."

"Dad. Gross. What the hell."

"Right, right. Sorry. You know I don't drink very often."

"You're such a lightweight."

He scowled at me. "I am not. I'm a big man. A huge man! That's what your mother says."

"*Dad*!"

He grimaced. "Sorry, sorry. It's the beer."

"Yeah, maybe no more beer for you."

"You touch my beer, I'll make sure Kevin is your new dad."

"You wouldn't dare."

"Try me, spawn of my loins."

I didn't touch his beer.

"Now," he said. "Man-to-man talk."

I took a long drink because I needed it for whatever was going to come out of his mouth. "All right," I said after I'd drained my mug and signaled for a refill. "Hit me."

"You love Ryan."

Wow. "You sure didn't ease into that one."

His nose wrinkled in disgust. "I mention Ryan and you talking about easing into things? Sam, there are some things a father should never know."

"Oh my gods."

"Not that there's anything wrong with that," he said. "You know I don't care who or what you ease into, as long as it's consenting."

"Oh my gods. What do you mean who or *what*?"

He shrugged. "I dunno. I don't discriminate. You put it where you want. Ryan. A fairy. A tree."

"Oh for the love of—"

"Sam!"

"What!"

"You love him."

I sighed. "Yeah. I guess I do."

"And he loves you."

"Maybe. Not enough, apparently."

"Fuck him."

"That was the whole idea and *why did I just say that to you*!"

"I know about sex, Sam," he said, rolling his eyes. "Your mother and I—"

"If you love me, you will not finish that sentence."

He closed his mouth.

"I love you too," I said, patting his hand.

"I just don't like it when you're sad," he said. "And you've been sad for a while now."

"Yeah," I said. "I guess. But isn't that all part of growing up? Your first isn't always going to be your last."

"It was for me," he said, "and I want it to be for you."

That stung and made me feel warm all at the same time. I was so happy my parents found each other like they did. "It's okay, Dad. I'll figure it out. I always do."

He reached up and grabbed the back of my neck, pulling me until our foreheads touched. "There's someone out there for you," he said. "Someone who will love your hair and your words and your eyes and the way you still scrunch up your nose when you're thinking hard on something. He will love you for all of the things that you are and all of the things you aren't. He'll love you beyond all reason and will be convinced that you hung the sun and moon. He will see the stars and wish for only you. Someone will love every single part of who you are, and my gods, I can't wait for the day to meet him to tell him thank you."

"Yeah?" I asked hoarsely.

He squeezed my neck. "Yeah."

And I believed him because he was my father and he would never lie to me about such things.

He pulled away, smiled at me. And then the smile slid away and his eyes narrowed. "*You*," he snarled.

"Eep," I said, sure my father had lost his mind.

But he wasn't looking at me. His gaze was over my shoulder, and before I could turn around, he was reaching past me and grabbing hold of someone. I felt them collide with my back and I almost fell off my stool at the bar. Whoever my father had a hold of was dragged around me as my father stood.

It was Ryan.

Because of course it was.

"I am so not up for this right now," I groaned. The barkeep looked like he was about to intervene, but I just waved him away. "It's cool. Just my dad and my… Ryan." Wait. "Not that he's *my* Ryan or anything. He's his own Ryan. Nobody else's. Except for maybe the Prince. Yes. That is the Prince's Ryan and my dad and everything is cool."

Everything was not cool.

My dad was furious. (And drunk.)

Ryan looked resigned to whatever fate my father would bestow upon him.

I was sure this would end in bloodshed, one way or another.

So imagine my surprise when instead of kicking Ryan's ass, my father pulled up another stool, sat Ryan down between us, and ordered him one of the regional beers on tap.

All in the space of about five seconds.

"I don't even question things anymore," I said.

"Good," my dad said. "It'll make things easier." He turned his glare back at Ryan. "Now you will sit here. You will drink this beer. And you will be happy about it."

Ryan drank his beer without question.

"Now," my father said. "What are you doing here?"

"Besides following me," I said.

"I'm not following you," he said weakly.

"Uh-huh."

"I'm not!"

"So you just happened to be in the same place that I am. Again."

"Maybe you're following me!"

"Yeah, because I have so many reasons to want to see your stupid face."

"Oh please. You think my face is delicious."

"Children!" Dad barked at both of us.

We were sufficiently cowed.

"Ryan, you will tell me why you're here," he said. "Sam, you will let him speak, and then, when he's finished, you may resume your back and forth that is supposed to be snarky banter but is in actuality snarky foreplay."

"*Dad*!"

"More stout please," my father said to the barkeep. "I'm going to need it with these two idiots."

"No more for him," I said. "He's cut off."

"*You're* cut off," Dad said as the barkeep filled his mug.

"You guys are so related," Ryan said.

"Shut up," I said. "We are not." Then, "Wait. Yes we are. But shut up."

"Are you drunk?" he asked, sounding amused.

"No." I was. "I'm not at all." I was pleasantly buzzed. "Sober as a kitten."

"Sometimes," my dad said, "you don't make sense when you speak, but that's okay because I love you anyway."

I said, "I make sense. And I love you too."

"Regional beers are awesome beers," he said, taking another drink. "Now. Ryan. Speak."

"He's not a dog," I grumbled. "Mostly."

"It's my bachelor party," Ryan said. "Next door at the hotel."

"Ah," Dad said. "And how is that working out for you?"

"Okay, I guess," he said, looking down at his hands. "I had to get out of there for a bit."

"Uh-huh."

I was annoyed, and I couldn't quite figure out why. "Why wasn't I invited?" I said, sounding sufficiently outraged.

Ryan snapped his gaze up to mine. "Would you have even gone?"

"Well, no. But still. Semantics. And rude."

"I wanted to invite you," Ryan said. "But I chickened out. It's mostly just knights. Some army buddies."

"That's...." I didn't know what that was. So I decided on "Weird."

"You make me weird," he grumbled.

"Were there strippers?" Dad asked sympathetically. "Strippers also make things weird."

"My dad is a lightweight," I explained.

"This much is true," Dad said.

"So," Ryan said, "pretty much like you, then." I thought I saw the hint of a smile.

I rolled my eyes at him. "No. I can handle my booze."

"I've seen you handle your booze. That's not handling."

"No reminiscing," I warned him. "That'll just make me leave faster."

That almost smile disappeared. He looked away again. "Yeah," he said quietly. "Okay."

"Both of you shut up," my dad said. "Because I'm about to lay some truth on you."

"This is probably going to be awkward," I told Ryan.

"I'm used to your family's awkwardness," he said and his knee touched mine briefly.

"So much foreplay," my dad grumbled. "Okay. Truth time. You ready?"

"Bring it, Pops."

"You," Dad said, pointing at Ryan a little unsteadily, "are a fucking dick."

"Whoa," Ryan said.

"Dude," I breathed. "That's my *dad*."

"And *you*," Dad said, pointing at me, "are pretty damn awesome."

"Ha!" I said.

"But you're also a fucking dick."

"Hey!"

"S'true," Dad said. "And what do you get when you put two fucking dicks together?"

"I don't know if I like where this is going," I said.

"Absolutely *nothing* because you're choosing to be fucking *dicks* instead of fucking each other's dicks!"

"Dude," I said. "What."

"He is so your father," Ryan said, sounding rather awed.

"Truth time, boys," Dad said. "Life is all about chances. It's all about these little moments that add up to greatness. And there are times when you have to grab greatness by the balls and say, 'Hey! Greatness! I've got your nuts and you can't do a single godsdamn thing about it!'"

"This is going in a direction I did not expect," I said.

"I am mercurial," Dad said.

"Oooh," I said. "Word porn."

"You're being stupid," Dad said to Ryan. "So fucking stupid. You have the chance. The little moments. The greatness. You just need to grab some balls and never let go."

"I don't know quite what you're telling me to do," Ryan admitted.

"I don't think anyone does," I said.

"You'll figure it out," Dad said. "Now. My son is going to take me home so my wife can yell at me for getting drunk and pretend to fight off my advances even though we both know that old-people sex is awesome sex."

Gods. "So many lines have been crossed," I groaned.

"Do you guys need help or...." Ryan looked unsure.

I shook my head. "Go back to your party. I'm sure they're missing you."

I didn't look at him again before I grabbed my father and fled.

When we got to the street, I put my arm around my father's waist and said, "That hangover you're going to have tomorrow? Penance, my friend. Pure, magnificent penance. And I shall be there with bells on. Literal bells."

My dad just laughed and laughed.

TWO DAYS before the wedding, I stood in the throne room, watching as the King regally posed next to a stained-glass window. I had the easel set up a few feet away from him as I studied him closely, wanting to make sure I got his likeness just right.

"Oops," I said.

"Oops," the King said. "What oops?"

"Okay, so, how would you feel if you looked like you had boobs?"

"Is that a hypothetical question?"

"Hypothetically... no. More like that's what I painted somehow and will now be a part of the finished product because I don't know how to fix it. Nor do I know if I want to."

"Am I busty?"

"Very. You also have three of them."

"Good. Proceed."

"Excellent," I said, putting more puce on the canvas, because if there was one thing the world needed more of, it was puce. "I am such a good painter."

"Well," the King said. "Let's not get ahead of ourselves."

"You should hire me to do all the royal paintings."

"I could never ask of you such a thing. For all our sakes."

"I should teach others how to paint."

"The arts would weep at such a thought."

"Oops," I said.

"Oops?"

"So, hypothetically. Okay, that was a lie. It's not hypothetical. I painted you to be as big as the Great White and you're destroying Meridian City like a giant monster. My muse is obviously a surrealist and I must follow her into the artistic abyss."

"Am I breathing fire?"

My eyes widened. "You could be. I have so much puce."

"Make it so."

He let me focus for a while, the sounds of the castle bright and loud around us. The throne room looked immaculate, banners hung and chandeliers polished. Many had thought the wedding would happen in the church, but apparently Ryan had refused, saying he didn't follow any specific religion. I didn't know what, if any, arguments had come from that, but it didn't matter in the long run. One, I didn't care (mostly). And two, the King had agreed to host the wedding in the throne room, followed by the biggest ball of the season. It would be a magical day for all those involved.

And unfortunately, I was a part of that magic.

I didn't have to do much. My job was to stand up in front and look pretty next to Morgan and keep my mouth shut. The King would speak, and Randall would speak, and then the ceremony would happen and everyone would live happily ever after.

I might have put far more puce than was actually necessary.

The King must have seen my artistic outlet for what it was and asked, "Are you okay, Sam?"

"Of course," I said.

"I've known you a long time."

"You have," I agreed.

"I know you very well. Better than most."

"You do."

"I'm glad you agree. So then maybe you can also agree that I can tell when you're lying."

"Drama king," I muttered.

He turned to look at me.

"Stop moving!" I snapped at him. "You'll ruin the painting and no one will forgive you because this is a masterpiece that will be treasured for generations."

"Normally, I would only feel the need to encourage any pursuit you feel is necessary," he said. "I don't know that art is one of them."

"You say that only because you haven't seen this yet."

"How many breasts do I have in your painting?"

"Three."

"And how many do I have in real life?"

"What? You don't have any—oh, I see what you did there. It's called artistic license."

"Sam."

"I'm fine."

"You're not. And it's okay not to be."

"Thanks. I wouldn't have known that otherwise." I winced. "Sorry. That came out wrong."

His lips twitched. "You could be pooping in buckets for taking that tone with me."

"Yeah, yeah. You're the mighty King and all that."

"I could even have your head."

"Sure. Because *that's* a thing you do."

"Could see a return of it. A good old-fashioned beheading in the courtyard."

"My blood would cause a revolution."

He smiled, looking far less regal and all the more awesome. "Of that I have no doubt."

He watched me and waited. He knew me very well.

I sighed. "I'm fine. Or, I will be."

"Will you?"

I put down the paintbrush. "I will. Because there's no other alternative."

"There is," he said. "You can be not fine. That is something you're allowed to do."

"Is it?"

"Yes."

I took a step around the easel so he wouldn't come toward me and be able to see the work in progress that would be hailed for centuries as a modern marvel. He watched me approach with curious eyes. He was smart, my King. "I have to be."

"Why?"

"Because if I'm not, I'm of no use to anyone. And if I'm of no use to anyone, then I might as well be back in the slums."

He shook his head. "Sam, how can you possibly think it's not okay for you to *not* be okay?"

"Because I'm Sam of Wilds," I said, though it was beginning to sound like an excuse. "I'm always okay."

He stepped down from the platform where he'd been posing for me. His hands came down onto my shoulders and gripped me tight. He said, "You're Sam of Wilds. But you're also human."

"I know."

"You don't have to have the answers to everything."

"I know."

"Do you?"

I rolled my eyes.

"I worry about you, sometimes," he admitted.

"Why?"

"Because you've built up this shell around yourself. This exterior made up of sass and wordplay. You wear your heart on your sleeve, but you've disguised it so that only those that are close to you can ever hope of seeing it. You show so much without actually showing anything at all."

I swallowed past the lump in my throat. "That your expert opinion, doctor?" I asked, cringing as soon as the words left my lips.

"Sam," he admonished lightly.

"Sorry," I muttered, looking away.

"I would fix this for you if I could."

"Would you? Because that would be at the expense of your son."

He looked troubled at this. He appeared to choose his next words carefully. "I don't know that Justin is in this for the same reason you are."

"I'm not in anything. That much has been made clear." I almost told him about what Justin had said at the dragon's keep, about feeling he was trapped in the shadow of his father and myself, that he'd felt forced to make a decision. But it wasn't my place. I could not speak for the Prince. Whatever issues there were between them were just that: between *them*. Not me. The King had already told me he could do nothing to break the oath Ryan had sworn to Justin, much like no one else could break the oath that Ryan had to the King.

I really fucking hated oaths.

The King said, "I don't—"

"Did you *paint* this?" an incredulous voice asked from behind us.

I turned and looked over my shoulder.

Ryan stood in front of the easel, looking horrifyingly amused as he studied my painting. I hadn't seen him since the night of his bachelor party a few days before. His hair had been cut in advance of the wedding, looking more regal and coifed versus his usual floppy mane. He still appeared exhausted, but he was biting his bottom lip and I realized he was trying not to laugh.

I narrowed my eyes at him because the last time I checked, he was *not* an art critic.

"Yes," I said. "It is a work in progress. You can't judge it until it's completed."

"Oh," he said. "I'm not judging."

"Uh. Hello. I have eyes and I can see your face. You are so judging."

"No, no," he said innocently, eyes wide. "I would never think to judge something of this... caliber. There's a lot of... red."

"It's called puce," I said.

"Ah. Because that makes it better."

"Don't be jealous of my talent. It's unbecoming of you."

He looked up at me, unable to hold back the smile any longer. "I don't know that jealous is the right word. Horrified, maybe."

"Horrified?" I said with a scowl. "There's nothing horrifying about it!"

"You gave the King breasts," he said. "Three of them."

"Yes, well. It's commentary on the state of postmodern feminism."

"Uh-huh. And the chest hair he still seems to have?"

"He's very manly." I looked back at the King who was gazing back and forth between Ryan and me with a thoughtful look on his face. "You're very manly," I told him.

"Thank you," the King said. "I don't know if I want to see the painting."

"Traitorous lies," I said.

"So he's a manly feminist?" Ryan asked.

"That's a thing," I insisted. "Everyone knows that's a thing."

"I don't think that's a thing," the King said.

"You don't get to have an opinion," I told him. "You're just a king of an entire country who has an infinite amount of responsibility and a wealth of knowledge far beyond my own and are pretty awesome. You wouldn't know anything about it."

"How I treasure you," the King said, smiling quietly at me.

"The feeling is mostly mutual," I said. "Art appreciation notwithstanding."

"Is he toppling Meridian City?" Ryan asked, still studying the painting. "While shooting fire from his mouth?"

"It's me taking a strong standpoint against consumerism," I said.

"You're profeminist and antiestablishment."

"Exactly."

"By having the King being a three-breasted monster shooting fire."

"See, when you say it like that, it makes me start to regret my life choices."

He didn't stop the laughter that time, the smile now as wide as I'd ever seen it. "*That's* the thing that causes you to regret your life choices. Nothing else. *That.*"

And it hit me then. How close this was to being like things once were. When I could harbor my secret love in my secret heart and banter back and forth for hours on end. My magic was an underlying current that was saying *yesyesyesyes* and *moremoremoremore*. It felt good. It felt right. I felt whole.

And I couldn't have it.

It's why the avoidance had been key. But somehow, Ryan had wormed his way back in.

And gods, how I loved him for it.

How I hated him for it.

I said, "Opinions aside, you've encroached upon a private discussion. Perhaps you should find someone else to bide your time with until your nuptials instead of wasting mine."

It was as if I'd slapped him. There was shock on his face. Then pain. Then anger, whether at me or himself or the situation, I didn't know. I told myself it didn't matter. I had to do what I had to do to protect my head and heart, and if it meant being crueler than I ever thought I could be to Ryan Foxheart, then so be it.

He took a step back.

I turned away from him in what was obviously a dismissal.

He said, "Sam."

I said nothing.

I heard his footsteps echo in the throne room as he fled.

The King watched me for a moment. Then, "I told you something once. On the night of his promotion ceremony."

"You told me many things," I muttered, ashamed of the way I'd just acted. Ryan deserved it. Maybe. But that didn't mean I needed to act like he did.

"I told you he doesn't smile. Not a real one, anyway. Not one that's not forced or for show."

I remembered that. I remembered because I'd thought how odd that was as I'd seen him smiling several times that day alone.

"Until you," the King said, sounding as sad as I'd ever heard him. "I don't know why I didn't see it before. Especially since it was right in front of me. But anytime he smiles, anytime it's real, it's because of you. He lights up brighter than anything I've ever seen."

"Is that supposed to make me feel better?" I asked, unable to keep the bitterness out of my words.

"No," he said. "I don't suppose it is."

"Fix this."

He looked stricken. "I can't. He made the oath of his own volition. He's a knight. It's what's expected of him."

I nodded once and turned to walk away.

Before I got two steps, he said, "I tried."

I stopped but didn't turn around.

"I tried, Sam."

"I don't understand."

"I asked Justin to release Ryan from his oath."

"Why?" I managed to choke out.

"Because I wasn't lying the day I told you that I thought of you as a son. And my heart breaks for you. Your pain will always be my pain, and it is sharp within me. I wanted something better for you, but I've failed. I'm so sorry, Sam."

I spun back around and threw myself at him. His arms came up and he held me close.

I couldn't find the words to say how I didn't blame him. I couldn't find the words to say how much I loved him. I couldn't really find any words at all, so I just held him for a very long time and hoped he understood all the things that were not said.

CHAPTER 28
A Brief Interlude

I GLARED up at the stars while I lay on the grass in the secret garden.

"You're fucking jerks," I told them all. "Seriously. What the hell."

The stars didn't reply. But then, they were stars, so. Pretty much expected.

They still twinkled like assholes, though.

"I hope you all blow up. You know what? You probably are *already* blown up and it's just taken your light thousands and thousands of years to reach here. So ha fucking ha. You're dead now and all I'm seeing are your last gasps." I sighed. "I'm sorry. That was rude."

Because it was. It wasn't their fault Ryan was getting married tomorrow.

It was Ryan's fault. And Justin's. I mean, who makes an oath to a prince to honor a dead and cherished mother?

Rude.

And very sweet. And beautiful. And lovely. And just like the selfless bastard.

But also rude.

I scowled at the sky.

"It's cool," I told the stars. "I'll find someone else. And it'll be awesome and I'll be all, like, Ryan who? I've got a new cornerstone. His name is Juan Carlos and he's an exotic accountant. Or something. Mental note. Think of better exotic jobs in the future. Like... actuaries. Dammit. Why can't I think of something exotic off the top of my head? Exotic. Exotic. Go! Juan Carlos is going to be an exotic mortician!" I groaned. "That doesn't even make sense."

"Who're you talking to?"

I squawked like an indifferently tall man.

Ryan laughed quietly to himself.

"Dude," I sighed. "Seriously. The stalking."

He stopped laughing. "I wasn't. Not this time."

I looked back up toward the stars and cursed them in my head. "So you admit to the other times."

"Mostly."

"You can't mostly stalk someone. You're either all in or not."

"Ah. Well."

"Stalker," I muttered.

"Not this time," he said. "I didn't know you were out here."

I snorted. "Yeah. Okay."

"I didn't. I just needed...."

"Needed...."

He sighed. "I needed to get away. For a little bit."

"Okay."

"You don't want to hear this."

"You're right. I don't."

The silence that followed was awkward. Him standing above me while I refused to look at him was awkward. Everything about this was awkward.

Of course, I couldn't keep that to myself. "You're awkward. This is awkward."

"I know."

"It's like you're my ex that I've seen for the first time since we had our really bad breakup."

"Is that what it's like?"

"Sure," I said. "But it sucks because it's like we're exes without having any of the benefits of not having been something before we were exes."

"Benefits?"

"You know," I said. "Butt sex."

He choked.

"Or other things," I said quickly. "Because it's not all about butt sex."

"Thank the gods it's just not all about butt sex," he said faintly.

"But you see what I mean? Awkward, but no benefits of having gotten there."

"I suppose that's my fault."

I laughed. "Yes. I suppose it is."

"I don't expect you to understand."

"I don't," I said. "And I don't care to anymore. I'm done fighting. Aren't you done fighting?"

He didn't answer.

"I'm done fighting," I said again. "Fighting you. Fighting for you. Fighting against you. I'm done. It makes things easier."

"What things?" he asked quietly.

I raised my arm and waved my hand toward the stars. "This. These things. Everything."

"That's... all encompassing. As usual."

"Like a tornado."

"Uh. Sure? Are you drunk?"

"Not this time. Maybe tomorrow night. No offense, but Gary, Tiggy, and I will probably get drunk and besmirch your name a bit."

He took a step toward me. I refused to look at him, but I could still see him in the periphery.

"Besmirch, huh?"

"So much besmirching," I said. "You don't even know how besmirched you'll be."

"I think I have an idea," he said. "I traveled with you three for weeks. It'll probably get a tad vicious." He took another step. Like he was aiming for subtlety. Nonchalance. He was failing miserably.

And it was getting dangerously close to reminiscing again. That wouldn't bode well for my Plan of Not Caring. Nothing ruins Not Caring like Willful and Fond Reminiscing. I hoped he hadn't capitalized the plan in his head yet. "Eh," I said. "I won't let it get too bad. Maybe some choice curse words here and there but nothing too bad. I won't hex you or anything."

"Could you do that?"

"Probably. I don't really know what I'm capable of anymore."

"Lightning," he said and took another step.

I sighed. "Yeah. I've been through worse. Randall just likes to try and get a rise out of me."

"It looked like he was trying to kill you."

"Nah. He knows I'd come back and haunt his ass. He wouldn't dare."

"What did it feel like?"

I was starting to get irritated. "Gods, sit down if you're going to stay here. Stop hovering. You're making it worse."

"You aren't going to run?" he asked, a light tease, and I had to remind myself that *I didn't care.*

"You're the one that's been running lately," I said.

That shut him up right quick. He sat down next to me, carefully maintaining a slight distance like I was a cornered, skittish animal. He huffed out a breath, then lay down on his back, looking up through the thin canopy of trees above.

And because I was probably a masochist, I asked, "You ready for tomorrow?"

I felt his eyes on me as he turned his head in my direction. "Are you serious?"

"What? I can't ask questions?"

"I don't know."

"You don't seem to know a lot of things."

He groaned and rubbed a hand over his face. "Gods, you confuse me."

"Oh dear."

"You infuriate me."

"My bad."

"Yes, Sam," he snapped. "I'm ready for tomorrow."

"Sounds like it."

"You're a dick."

I laughed. "Yeah. I know. If you'd like, I can go back to pretending you don't exist."

"Would that be easier?"

"For who?"

He didn't answer. Instead, he said, "Did you ever think you'd get here?"

"Where?"

"Here. Where you are now. I… back in the slums, I always figured I'd stay there. I'd work there. That I would die there."

"That's… sad."

"And yet that's how it is for most people born there."

"I don't know," I said. "Maybe. I spent a lot of time thinking of ways to get us out of there. Wishing for something to happen. I never thought I'd… well. I don't know what I thought was going to happen. But no. I never expected this. To be here. Where I am."

His arm brushed against mine, whether by accident or not, I couldn't tell. But I had learned very quickly that very little happened by accident when it concerned Ryan Foxheart. "I never hoped," he said. "I never wished. I never dreamed. Not until you."

"Ryan—"

"Listen. Please, can you just listen?"

"I already know what you're going to do. I can recognize the tone in your voice. I don't need you to justify anything to me. I don't want you to."

"I'm not trying to justify anything."

"Then what are you trying to do?"

"Have a conversation," he said, pouting slightly. I refused to find it adorable.

"No," I said. "You're trying to explain yourself. Why you pledged your oath to Justin. You did it for your mother. You did it because you got out and she didn't. You did it for her, because you thought that's what she wanted for you, and you could never go back on your word because of how much you loved her. I get it, Ryan. I get it, okay? I know why you're doing what you're doing. I hate it, and I think I sometimes hate you, but I get it. I do. Okay? I promise. I do. If you need my blessing, have at it. It's yours. Do what you have to, because in the end, you'll have to live with yourself. Not me. Not Justin. Just you." By the time I finished speaking, my voice was hoarse and my hands were shaking. I didn't even have the sense to stop him when he reached over and curled his fingers in my own. His grip was tight and warm.

He tugged on my hand gently, but insistently. I turned over on my side as he was silently asking me to do, facing him. His position mirrored mine. His eyes searched my own. He opened his mouth once, then closed it. Then, "I meant what I said."

"When?"

"When I told you that the only thing I wished for was you."

"You bastard," I whispered. He took our joined hands and brought them to his face. I felt the brush of his lips against my skin, and I fought against jerking my hand away. "Do you want to know what it felt like?"

"What?"

"The lightning."

"I don't—"

"It hurt. At first. It wasn't like the first time when we were running from the Darks and the fire geckos. It was so easy then. So easy to take it in, wrap it around my heart, and then send it away. I didn't understand why I couldn't do it again. Why it wasn't working."

His face was so close to mine. I could feel his breath on my skin.

"And then something was different. Morgan and Randall knew why. I didn't. Maybe I should have. I just felt it. In my bones. In my blood. It whispered to me and said that everything was going to be all right. That I could do this. That I could do what they were asking of me. And then Randall gave me more than he should have. Far more than I should have been capable of handling. But it didn't matter because the moment it touched my skin, I knew it was different. That *I* was different. I knew I could do this. I knew what I was capable of. I took it in and it wrapped itself around my heart and it was scary and devastating and wonderful all at the same time. It felt of *power* and *strength* and I could have kept it there. No matter how much it hurt. I could have kept it there for myself. But it wasn't mine to keep. It wasn't mine to hold. So I let it go. I let it go and I didn't understand. Why it felt so familiar. The electricity crawling along my heart. I didn't understand at first. But I do now."

"What is it?" he whispered.

"It's you," I said, not able to look away. "It's how I feel when I'm with you. How I think I've always felt. You're my lightning-struck heart. It doesn't matter about the cornerstone. It doesn't matter about who I am or who you are. Not to me. I think it would have always been this way for me. Even if we had never escaped the slums. Ever since the beginning. Ever since I've known you, you've struck my heart, and now I have to let you go because you're not mine to keep. I need someone that I can be strong for. But I need someone who can also be strong for me."

"Sam," he croaked out, his eyes bright and wet.

And I'd said enough. I'd had enough. Much like Randall's lightning had arced along my heart, Ryan did the same. The only way forward was to expel him from me because he wasn't mine to keep.

And because I would never get another chance, I brought his hand to mine, brushing a kiss against his knuckles. I said, "I think I love you."

I let him go.

I pushed myself up.

I looked up at the stars, but I did not make a wish.

And then I left him there in my mother's secret garden.

CHAPTER 29
The Lightning-Struck Heart

"WELL," GARY said, as he posed in front of the floor-length mirror in my room. "Today should be a fuckton of shits and giggles."

"That was sarcasm," Dad explained to Tiggy. Tiggy still hadn't quite got the hang of sarcasm yet, even though Gary had made it his singular mission.

"Got it," Tiggy said, frowning in concentration. "Fuck shit giggles sarcasm."

"Tell me I look pretty," Gary demanded of Kevin, who was sticking his large head through the window. We were lucky my room was at the back of the castle so that Kevin could actively participate in discussions of a serious nature, like telling Gary he looked pretty.

"You are like the sun and the moon combined to make a creature so astoundingly beautiful that the world can't even contain its—"

"Oh my gods," I groaned as I lay on my bed. "Gary, make him stop."

"Never," Gary said. "This is probably as close as I will ever get to looking like a princess so I expect to be treated as such."

I looked over at him and tried not to laugh because he would find ways to eviscerate me. Gary had gotten it into his head that his mane and tail needed to be permed for the wedding, and he looked like two gigantic cotton balls were consuming him from either end. They were adorned with dozens of fresh flowers and his hooves had been painted blue and silver to match the flowers. I wanted to tell him I thought he looked like he should be working for Mama, but I valued my testicles so I kept my mouth shut.

"Exactly like a princess."

Gary narrowed his eyes. "I can tell when you're being sarcastic, Sam Haversford. I'll have you know that big hair is in this spring. Everyone has it."

"Gary, no one else in this room has it."

"I would have big hair," Mom said. "But I don't have the lady-balls to pull it off."

"I have lady-balls," Gary said. "I'm a fierce fucking princess."

"You look like you pooping snowmen," Tiggy said.

I laughed until I cried. Which, on a day like today, I sorely needed.

Gary glared at me.

I laughed harder.

It felt good.

So when the knock came at the door, I was as ready as I could ever be.

My mother fussed with my dress robes, brushing off invisible things so she could calm me (and most likely herself).

She leaned in and kissed me on the cheek. She whispered, "We get through today and then we'll move on to the next. I am so proud of you, my son."

I hugged her close.

Pete waited for us on the other side of the door. He smiled quietly at me, his armor shining, the decorative sword and scabbard fastened at his side. "Morgan and Randall are waiting for you in the lobby. The ceremony will begin shortly."

I nodded and let the others out before I followed. I looked back at Kevin. "They've opened the Great Doors to the gardens," I told him. "There should be more than enough room for you there."

"Should I light something on fire?" he asked. "Like Justin? Or the wedding party?"

"No fires," I said. "This wedding is going to go smoothly and then we'll get drunk and I'll be sad and then tomorrow, I'll wake up and start again."

"I am also proud of you, my son," he said seriously. "In addition, your ass looks great today."

And that was something I would never get used to. "Ew, and you're still not my dad," I called out, closing the door behind me.

I could hear the thrum of people seated in the throne room. The King's Court, the heads of state, dignitaries from across Verania. At last count, there was to be over a thousand people attending the wedding of Grand Prince Justin of Verania to Knight Commander Ryan Foxheart. They'd all been seated earlier, waiting for the procession. The King would speak, Randall would speak, and we'd all sit in stifling heat wishing for death. I could hardly wait.

I descended the staircase to the lobby and saw my family waiting for me. Morgan looked stately, his robes a deep burgundy, his beard newly trimmed. Randall looked like an ancient pimp, his robes a bright green that I was sure Justin was going to take great offense to. He wore a large hat with a wide brim. A purple feather stuck out the top of it. I thought it was awesome.

"About time," Randall grumbled. "You'd think it was *his* wedding day by the way he was dallying."

"Hello, Randall," I said. "Make sure your women give you your money so you don't have to pimp slap them."

Gary snorted. It came out violet and chartreuse, and I thought it paired with the flowers in his mane very well. Only a gay unicorn could match his uniquely visible sarcasm to his floral accessories.

Randall narrowed his eyes. "And what foolishness do you speak of now?"

"Nothing," I said. "Tell me, Randall. What street corners are yours, because I don't want to overstep my bounds."

"I'm onto you, boy," he said. "You think you're being clever, but I'm onto you."

"Ah," I said sympathetically. "It's hard out there for a—"

"And this is probably indicative of how today is going to go," Randall said with a sigh.

"Is it?" Mom asked. "This certainly bodes well for today's events."

"I don't think that's quite what he meant," Dad said to her.

"I'm maintaining a positive outlook," she said. "Denial is such a comforting place to be."

"Well," I said to Morgan, "I *tried* to get drunk first, but *some* people wouldn't let me." I glared at my parents. And Tiggy. And Gary. "You know I'm much more tolerable when I'm intoxicated."

"Wizard Spaghetti Face," Tiggy reminded me.

"Okay, that was *one* time. And Betty and I *bonded*."

"You called her a sexy grandma," Gary said.

"In my defense, I'd had a lot of wine."

"And you think that makes you tolerable?" Randall asked me. "Canoodling with elderly ladies?"

Canoodling, I mouthed at Gary, who just shrugged.

"Maybe we should consider a bit of a reeducation of your young apprentice," Randall said to Morgan.

"Please don't hit me!" I said, cowering away from him. "I'll have your money by the end of the week. I *promise*, Randall. I've always been your best girl."

"I fear it's already far too late," Morgan told Randall. "Run. Save yourself."

"Sam," Randall tried again, "I know that today is going to be difficult—"

I scoffed, cutting him off. "I'm fine."

They all stared at me.

"What?"

"Sam," Mom said. "It's okay to *not* be fine."

"Good to know," I said. "I'm fine. You all act like I'm going to break down in inconsolable tears or do something stupid like interrupt the service when it gets to the whole *speak now or forever hold your peace* thing."

"Well," Gary said.

"I'm *not*. I wouldn't do that!"

They looked slightly guilty, and I suddenly had a very bad feeling.

"And none of you can say a damn thing either."

"Yeah," Gary said. "Okay. Sure. Get right on that, kitten." He batted his eyelashes at me, and I was almost ready to coo at him when I realized he was wiling me with his ways.

"You foul temptress," I hissed at him. "How dare you try to woo me with your powers of beauty! I shall not be tricked!"

Gary preened. "Did you hear that, everyone? Sam says I have powers. Of *beauty*."

"None of you can say a godsdamn thing," I said, making sure to glare at each of them in turn. "We are not going to ruin someone else's wedding day just because he should be marrying me instead as I'm obviously way cooler and have good teeth, awesome cheekbones, and a sunny fucking disposition."

"His disposition isn't very sunny right now," Gary whispered to Tiggy.

"Oxymoron," Tiggy said.

"Well said," Gary replied. "He *is* a moron."

"You lucky you pretty." Tiggy said, burying his face in Gary's ridiculous mane. "Feel like bubbles on my nose."

"Listen to me," I snapped. "You all need to keep your mouths shut! There will be *no* talking. Well, except for Morgan because I think he's supposed to talk. And Randall, since he's officiating the entire ceremony. They can talk. None of the rest of you can."

"I can talk if I want to," Dad said, looking slightly defiant.

"I'm *serious*," I said.

"Dear," Mom said. "Look. He's serious. That's his serious face."

"You've made that same face since you were three," Dad said. "That's how we knew you were serious."

"Like the one time he was six and came home to tell us he was seriously going to kiss Derek?" Mom said.

"Or that other time he was almost eight and said he was seriously considering opening up a business to sell toast and hats and wouldn't I like to invest?" Dad said.

"Or when he was ten and he told us that he was *seriously* upset because we wouldn't let him jump off the roof naked to test the wings he'd made out of a bedsheet and couldn't we just see how *serious* he was?"

"You were a very strange child," Randall said.

"I am nothing but a product of my upbringing," I said, frowning at my parents.

"Thank you," Mom said, beaming.

"And you're welcome," Dad said.

"You're lucky I love you," I told them. "Because otherwise I'd be ordering you to the dungeons for treason for telling the naked roof-jumping bedsheet story."

"Pooping in buckets is a small price to pay to be able to tell that story," Dad assured me. "Especially when I get to tell the part about how you were bare-ass naked when you were trying to argue with us."

"If you try that now," Gary said, "I bet you'd win more arguments."

"Please don't try that with me," Randall said. "I don't know how much shockingly pale skin I can handle."

"Gods," I muttered. "How did we even get here?"

"That's a question I find I ask myself often around you," Morgan said, patting my arm.

And then the announcement horns flourished brightly and all conversation ceased. Pete poked his head back out into the throne room. "We're about to begin," he said. "Joshua, Rosemary, if you could follow me please. I'll show you to your seats."

"I can't believe the King got Justin to agree to allow you and Tiggy in the ceremony," I told Gary. "I thought for sure he'd nix it."

Gary rolled his eyes. "I told him it was considered the greatest of fortunes to have a unicorn and a half-giant walk down the aisle together. That it would bring him and his marriage luck and prosperity."

I was slightly put out. If that was true, I would have hoped Gary and Tiggy would have instead refused to even show up.

"Stop pouting," Gary said. "I just made that up so you wouldn't have to stand there by yourself looking sad and alone and afraid and sad."

"And handsome," I said.

"Let's not push it."

"Said the talking cotton balls," I muttered under my breath.

"What?" he asked sharply.

I smiled sweetly at him.

Mom and Dad kissed me on the cheek before following Pete through the Great Doors.

We lined up in front of the door in order of our entrance. Gary and Tiggy, then myself, then Morgan, with Randall following up in the rear. Ryan and Justin were being kept in separate rooms on either side of the lobby. Ryan would enter first, followed by the King and Justin.

Gary was whispering something to the Royal Announcer and I knew that it was probably nothing good. I tried to kick him in the ass, but his tail was so curled, I couldn't seem to find it.

"Tiggy said it looked like he was pooping a snowman," I whispered to Morgan who covered his mouth to hide the laughter.

Randall smacked us both on the back of our heads.

The Great Doors were pushed all the way open.

A thousand people stood as one, and the throne room fell silent.

"Ladies and gentlemen," the announcer called, voice echoing off the stone. He was reading from a card. "Introducing, the most fiercest unicorn in existence, Mrs. Kevin the Dragon, aka, Gary."

Gary coughed loudly.

The announcer rolled his eyes.

Gary coughed again.

"Gary the Magnificently Beautiful who is universally adored by all and whom everyone aspires to be because he is so amazing," the announcer said, sounding aggrieved.

"Oh my gods," I muttered.

"Thank you!" Gary said quite loudly. He began to walk down the plush red carpet toward the throne. "Hello," he said, bowing his head at those standing on either side of the aisle. "Hello there. Hi. Ooh, girl, that hat is to *die* for. Work it. Hi. Hello. Salutations. Honeybunch, you're at least fifty, not twenty. Cover up just a little bit more. This is a wedding, for fuck's sake. Keep it classy. Hello. Hi. Oh goodness. Greetings. Oh my *gods*. That *scarf*. Where did you get that *scarf*? *Really*? At Medacio's? The one off Grover Street? You know, I went there once and the service was just *terrible*. The salesgirl was just *rude* and I complained and got a twenty percent discount. Gods, what was her name? Leslie? Cochina? Mai Ling Wong? I don't remember. It's not important. But I just *swore* I wouldn't go back there after—what? Oh. Right. Sorry. Sorry, everyone! Sorry. I tend to forget what I'm doing when I'm talking about scarves. It's a sickness, I dare say. Hi. Hello. Good afternoon. Hello. Hi. Hi. Hello."

He finally reached the throne.

"Tiggy," I whispered. "I swear to the gods, you better get next to Gary as quick as you can and not stop. Do you understand me? No stopping to talk to *anyone*."

"But Gary said—"

"Tiggy!"

"Tiggy never gets no fun," Tiggy grumbled.

"We'll have fun later," I promised him, though he didn't seem to believe me.

"Presenting," the announcer called, reading from another card, "at nine-and-a-half feet tall, weighing in at six hundred forty-seven pounds. He is revered as a giant of impeccable taste and immaculate grooming. He's—okay, I'm not going to finish this."

"Say it!" Gary shouted.

The announcer sighed. "He has captured our hearts, filling us with love and joy and we are better off because he exists. Ladies and gentleman. The half-giant, Tiggy."

Tiggy startled everyone by running as fast as he could, not stopping until he stood next to Gary, who looked slightly alarmed. He turned back toward me and said, "That fast, Sam?"

Everyone looked back at me.

"Yes, Tiggy," I said, barely resisting the urge to bury my face in my hands. "That was fast."

"I fast," Tiggy said. "Sam said fast and I *fast*. I don't get fun, but I *fast*."

"Sam wouldn't know what fun meant if it jerked off on his face," Gary said.

I groaned because did he have to say it so *everyone* could hear?

The announcer switched to his next card.

"I will literally give you *anything* if you don't read that," I pleaded with him.

"Can't help you," he said, shrugging in apology. "Gary already threatened me with Unicorn Rage."

"That devious bastard," I said, trying not to be impressed. "That works on everyone. You know, I'm really starting to regret that I can't sweat angry glitter."

The announcer shrugged. "Yeah, it can be intimidating. Sorry about this, Sam."

"Go ahead," I said, waving my hand at him. There was really nothing else I could do.

Gary smiled evilly at me.

"Ladies and gentlemen," the announcer called. "It is with great honor that I present to you a man loved and treasured for his wit and charity, but maybe not for the way he dresses himself. He looks respectable right now because of Gary. If it weren't for Gary, he would look like a homeless ruffian whom you would think was probably out to steal your wallet. So, thank you, Gary, for the specimen you see before us. We are all in your debt. Sam is currently single and any and all inquiries for a good roll in the hay can be made attention to Gary and Tiggy. Sam likes magic and long walks in the forest. For some reason, he likes ears that stick out. He also likes... seriously? Gary, come on! Oh for the love of—He also likes butts, so please have a nice one. Feel free to attach an etching of your butt so that we may review it for quality. I give you the wizard... Sam of Wilds."

"Apprentice!" Gary yelled. "It says wizard *apprentice*. Gods. Good help is so hard to find these days."

"They just tried to pimp me out," I said, sounding completely awed. "Why does that always happen in this room?"

"Remember," Randall murmured from behind me, "I get ninety percent of all your take. Don't make me slap you. You Randall's girl, now."

"Oh my gods," I moaned. "Please let this be a nightmare."

But it wasn't, and after Morgan shoved me in a not-so-gentle fashion, I walked down the aisle. Tiggy kept waving at me as I approached and Gary smirked at me even as I wondered what it would be like to shove my boot up his ass. I was about halfway down the aisle when I spotted someone who I hadn't even expected to be here.

She stood next to the aisle, her dress expensive and perfect as always. She cooled herself with her exotic folding fan, the handle clearly inlaid with gold.

And she was glaring at me as I approached, even though she technically didn't know me.

Well. Not *this* me.

Even with all that I'd faced, dragons and Darks and cultists and fire geckos, she was still my most mortal of enemies.

And today was her victory day.

The president of the Ryan Foxheart Fan Club Castle Lockes Chapter.

Lady Tina DeSilva.

My fluttering heart hardened in my chest.

I wasn't in control of how this day would end.

I was losing the one thing I wanted.

But this. I could control *this*.

I curled a nasty smile at her.

Then I realized I wasn't dressed as Mervin, and her eyes widened as I looked positively murderous.

And I found I didn't care.

I wouldn't be going back to the damn meetings.

I was no longer a Foxy Lady.

From here on out, I was a SamGirl4Life.

I paused briefly when I passed her.

She scoffed prettily.

I dropped my voice to Mervin-like levels and murmured, "My muffins were *never* dry, you abhorrent wench."

I winked at her.

Her breath hitched.

Her eyes widened.

She hissed, "*You.*"

"You'll never prove it," I snapped quietly at her and continued on.

I felt better. Getting the last word to a sixteen-year-old girl can do that to you.

"Do I even want to know why a little teeny-bop looks like she wants to eat your flesh?" Gary asked when I reached the front.

"We're enemies," I said. "Mortal enemies."

"Of course you are, kitten. Only you would be mortal enemies with a teenage girl."

"Don't let her looks fool you. Her countenance hides nothing but evil."

"I wonder at you, sometimes."

"You're in so much shit," I growled.

"Worth it."

"What are you guys whispering about?" Kevin asked. "Is it secrets? I love secrets." I looked over my shoulder to see his head shoved through the Great Door, chin resting on the floor.

"Tell you later," I said.

"You better," he said. "I wouldn't want to have to spank you, son."

"Boo," Gary said. "Stop hitting on our baby boy."

Everyone was staring again.

"Not my parents," I said for all to hear. "My mom and dad are right there."

Mom and Dad stood and waved.

"We're the parents of his heart," Kevin said.

"Shut up," I said. "No, you're not. And that doesn't even make sense. Stop making it weird and gross."

"Don't talk to your father that way," Gary said. "You're grounded."

"Can we please move this along?" I asked. "Seriously."

"He's got his serious face," Mom called to the announcer. "He's serious."

Morgan and Randall were presented without fanfare, and then I pretty much forgot everything else that existed because Ryan entered the throne room.

To say he looked handsome would be an understatement.

It wasn't as if I'd never seen him in his full knight gear before. I had. Several times. But maybe it was because today was important, that it was so monumental that it just felt different. Of course, since it was Ryan Foxheart, I wouldn't be surprised if the gods themselves were shining down upon his broad shoulders because everything about him *shone*. His armor, his shield, the scabbard at his side, his skin, his *hair* (seriously, what the fuck? How did he have *shiny hair*?). *Everything*.

And I couldn't take my eyes off of him.

But that was okay.

Because he couldn't take his eyes off of me.

Not once did he look away through that long walk down the aisle.

Not once did I avert my eyes for any step he took.

For a moment, I allowed myself to imagine he was walking toward me. That it was *my* wedding day and he was shining just for me.

It was a good dream. A frivolous dream.

I swallowed past the lump in my throat, trying to control my breathing.

It almost worked.

He reached the throne. Mere feet away.

He stood, facing me.

I was over him. I was done with this.

I wanted to beg him to stop this.

I wanted to never see him again.

I wanted to wake up every morning with him curled around me.

And then the King and Justin were announced.

The King looked resplendent, his robes accentuating his powerful frame, burgundy and gold, the edges trailing behind him on the floor. He was smiling quietly at his subjects, but there was something else in his eyes that I couldn't quite make out. He moved more stiffly than I'd ever seen him before.

Justin. Well. Justin on the other hand, looked regal and amazing as always. Perfect hair, perfect smile, perfect everything. Even if he was wearing—

"Is that bitch wearing white?" Gary hissed in my ear. "Who does he think he's fooling? There is nothing pure and virginal about him. Even his *boots* are white. Oh my gods. The *travesty*. The tabloids are going to have a field day with this. Who wore it better? Prince Justin or this homeless hooker."

I coughed, trying to cover up the hysterical laughter. I didn't want to draw any more attention to myself than already had been. It wasn't my day and I knew Justin had the power to make my life a living hell, more so than he'd already done. But Gary was right. Justin was not pulling off the blushing groom he was trying to portray.

This was confirmed when I saw Tina practically swoon as he walked by on the King's arm. Since I knew Tina absolutely had no taste whatsoever, I felt remarkably relieved.

"Ryan," Gary whispered. "Shouldn't you be looking at your future husband walking down the aisle rather than staring at Sam like an asshole?"

Ryan flinched and blushed. His eyes darted toward Justin and the King, and he swallowed with an audible click in his throat.

"That's better," Gary murmured. "Wouldn't want you to miss any part of the best day of your life."

"Oh snap," Tiggy said.

"Oh snap indeed," Randall muttered.

Morgan just sighed and I knew he was regretting all of his life choices.

I smiled softly at the King when they reached the throne. Justin ignored me completely, a determined look on his face. He stood near me, facing toward Ryan. Ryan paled slightly as Justin reached out for his hand. He glanced at me again. I kept my face blank.

The King turned toward his subjects. "I'll keep this brief as today isn't about me. Today is about love between two people. Two people who are pledging loyalty and devotion to one another for the rest of their lives. Two people who will one day take my place upon the throne, knowing they do so in complete honesty and transparency."

Oh, that magnificent bastard.

"I remember," he continued, then stopped. Shook his head. Cleared his throat. When he spoke again, his voice was a rougher. "I remember when I stood in this very room years ago looking upon my beloved. It was one of the happiest days of my life, knowing that I would get to look at this beautiful person for the rest of her days. And I did. There may have been days when we didn't see one another. Days when commitments led us far from home, priorities that required our attention. But there was never a day that my Queen was far from my thoughts. She left this world far quicker than I had ever thought possible, but the time we shared together has kept me warm these many years later. For her, I would do it all over again.

"And that is what love is. Even when you're hurt. Even when you're angry. Even when you think you can't take another step, love is what keeps you going. If you can love, then you can overcome anything that may rise against you. And it should be love that helps guide your actions because it will show you truth. It will show you beauty. It will show you compassion. And these traits, these insights, are the mark of a king. Without it, one can never hope to rule with a firm and kind heart."

He took a breath and looked at Justin. "And so today, I give my son, Grand Prince Justin of Verania, to Knight Commander Ryan Foxheart in the hopes that he will have all the moments his mother and I had. You have my blessing."

The King stepped back.

Randall stepped forward as the audience took their seats.

"Now," Randall said. "I must ask before we proceed. Prince Justin, are you here of your own volition and peace of mind?"

"Yes," Justin said, voice strong and clear.

"Knight Commander Foxheart, are you here of your own volition and peace of mind?"

Ryan was staring at me over Justin's shoulder....

I narrowed my eyes at him and jerked my head toward Randall, trying to get him to pay attention.

The audience tittered quietly.

"Knight Commander," Randall said again.

Ryan looked startled. He turned his head toward Randall. "Uh. I'm sorry? Can you say that again?"

"Oh my gods," Gary muttered.

Randall's lips twitched. "Of course. Are you here of your own volition and peace of mind?"

"Uh. Yes?"

"Is that a question?" Randall asked.

"Yes."

"It's a question."

"Er. No. I'm here."

"Of your own volition."

"Yes."

"And peace of mind."

"Ha-ha," Ryan said weakly. "Uh. I mean yes. My mind is in pieces." He paled further. "I mean, my peace of mind. It's peaceful."

What the hell?

"Good to know," Randall said. "I'm glad that you're so... peaceful."

Justin's shoulders were tense. My hands were clammy.

"Now," Randall said, raising his voice to carry out around the throne room. "We gather here today to join the Prince of Verania to the Knight Commander who will one day stand as King Consort. They have both spoken and have agreed they are here of their own volition and peace of mind. Before we begin the ceremony joining these men in a bond not easily broken, there is a question I must ask."

I knew what was coming. I made sure to glare at my family in quick succession to get my point across. They mostly ignored me. Except for Gary. Gary rolled his eyes at me. What a dick.

And then Randall asked his question, and I swore all the world held its breath.

"Should anyone here present know of any reason why this couple should not be joined in holy matrimony, speak now or forever hold your peace."

The room was completely silent.

I felt a sad sort of relief as I looked down at my feet.

Well, until Randall spoke again. "Anyone at all?"

Silence.

"Does anyone in this room have *any* reason that they shouldn't marry?"

Silence.

"Nobody. Nobody here has *any objection* to this union?"

Oh my fucking gods, I was going to *murder* Randall when this was over.

"Not a single person has any—?"

"I object! Holy *mothercrackers*, do I object!"

The voice rang out, echoing around the throne room.

The audience gasped.

Gary choked.

Tiggy growled.

Morgan sighed.

I snapped my head up.

"Say again?" Randall asked.

"I object," Knight Commander Ryan Foxheart repeated, looking straight at me.

"And why do you object?" the King asked gently.

"Because," Ryan said, eyes darting to the King. He swallowed thickly. "I don't love Justin. My heart belongs to another."

The audience gasped again.

"Oh my gods," Gary snapped at them. "Stop doing that. It's not like that's a surprise or anything. This is already dramatic enough as it is given that we're at a *wedding*. Stop adding to it."

"I'm sorry," Ryan said, looking at Justin again. I couldn't see the Prince's face, but I could see his hands curled into fists at his sides. "I never wanted it to come to this. I let it go too far. And it's my fault. I should have put a stop to this long ago. Justin, we can't go through with this. It's not fair. To either of us."

"Fair," Justin repeated. "*Fair.*"

I think I was going into shock. I leaned over and whispered to Gary, "Um. What's going on?"

Gary looked amused. "I'm pretty sure Ryan just called off the wedding because he wants to sit on your smile."

"Whoa," I breathed. "I am so into that."

"You made an *oath*," Justin said through gritted teeth. "You swore your fealty to me."

"I know," Ryan said. "And I shouldn't have. I thought I was doing the right thing. I thought it's what she would have wanted. But... I did it before I knew what I know now. Not that that's an excuse. I shouldn't have let it get this far. For that, I am truly sorry." He took a deep breath. "I ask you to release me from my oath."

"I won't," Justin said.

"Oooh," the crowd said.

"Justin," the King said with a frown.

"You don't love me," Ryan said quietly. "And I don't love you. Why would you do that to yourself? Justin, there is someone out there for you. Someone who is far better than I could ever be. Someone who will love you as your mother loved your father. That person can't be me."

Justin laughed bitterly. "Love. Why does it have to be about *love*? I gave you what you wanted. I gave you a place in this castle. You would become King Consort. You would be the force of so much change, hundreds if not thousands of lives, and you're willing to throw that away because of *love*?"

"Yes."

"*Why?*"

"Because," Ryan said, eyes flicking to me, "my mother told me that I had to follow my heart in all things. I thought I was. I thought I'd done what was right. But then I looked upon the stars and I wished for the one thing I wanted more than anything else. I didn't believe it could ever come true or ever be mine, but then I held his lightning-struck heart, given freely and without reservation. And I would gladly treasure it for the rest of my days."

The audience sighed dreamily. Except for Tina. She looked like she had dysentery. Explosively so.

"He talking about Sam?" Tiggy whispered to Gary.

"Yes, he is," Gary said, voice teary. "That motherfucker just gave my heart a boner. Well played, Knight Delicious Face. Well played."

"I can say no," Justin said. "I can hold you to your oath."

"You can," Ryan agreed, sounding surer. "But you wouldn't."

"Why wouldn't I?"

"Because that's not who you are."

"Justin," the King said quietly, "release him from the oath. It's the right thing to do."

"I...."

The blood pounded in my ears.

"Godsdammit," Justin snapped. "Fine. Ryan Foxheart, I release you from your oath to me. Because of *love*." He rolled his eyes. "Worst day *ever*."

"Holy shit," I said rather loudly. Which, of course, caused everyone to look at me. "Er. Um. Hi." I waved awkwardly. I leaned over to Gary. "What the fuck is going on?" I hissed in his ear.

"I'm pretty sure you're about to get plowed like a field," Gary whispered back.

"I'm *what*?"

"Sam."

I looked back up. Justin stood next to the King, who had his arm around the Prince's shoulders and was whispering quietly in his ear.

Ryan, though. Ryan was looking right at me.

Gary shoved me toward him.

"You bitch," I growled over my shoulder.

"Love you," he said with a grin.

I stood in front of Ryan. If I wanted to, I could reach out and touch him. And gods, I wanted to, but I wasn't quite convinced yet that this wasn't some cruel dream that I would soon wake up from.

"That's my boy!" Kevin called out from behind us. "That's my *boy*."

"Kevin," Gary snapped. "You're ruining the *moment*. Our son will *never* forgive you if you mess this up."

"Why is that a thing?" Randall asked Morgan.

"Haven't had time to study it," Morgan said. "Frankly, I don't know if I want to know. I go with the flow now."

"That just means you've given up understanding your charges."

"There was no hope in understanding them."

"Ah," Randall said. "Reality's a bitch, ain't it?"

"What are you doing?" I asked Ryan hoarsely.

"I couldn't do it," he said, sounding nervous. "I couldn't go through with it. Not now."

"So you waited until the moment you were about to get *married*?"

"Uh. Yes?"

I was slightly pissed off. "Who the fuck *does* that?"

"Yeah," Justin said. "Who the fuck."

We both glared at Ryan.

He started sweating. "Well. I guess. Maybe. I did?"

"You're an asshole," I said.

"The biggest asshole," Justin said.

"Gigantic asshole," I said.

"I'm losing my heart boner," Gary said to Tiggy.

"I know," Ryan said.

"What the fuck?"

"I know."

"No. Seriously. What the fuck? You were *minutes* away from getting married."

"I'm aware," he said drily. "I am standing right here, after all."

"So much sass," I said. "How can you be sassy right now?"

He shrugged. "Someone told me once I'm the God of Sass."

I narrowed my eyes at him. "You think you're funny."

"Sometimes."

"I'm not just going to fall into your arms."

"Okay," he said. Then, "How about now?"

"My heart boner is getting chubbed up again," Gary said.

Ryan reached out and grabbed my hand. I thought about pulling away, but his skin against mine felt like something akin to relief. Beautiful, wonderful relief and I thought maybe I trembled with it.

He took a step toward me, and I could feel his heat. His eyes were wide and clear, and I felt trapped by them. He squeezed my hand. "Sam."

"You're an asshole," I said.

"I know. I'm sorry."

"You don't get to be an asshole."

"I know. I need you to listen to me. Okay?"

"Why?"

"Because I need to say what I should have said to you many times before."

I could only nod.

"Achieving full heart boner," Gary said. "Heart boner is imminent."

Ryan took a deep breath and let it out slowly. He said, "Sam, it's always been you. It's always been you because I lo—"

And that's when a group of Dark wizards burst into the throne room, led by Wan the Dark Hunter.

"Aha!" he cried. "The element of surprise is *ours*!"

People in the audience screamed and began to push their way toward the sides of the throne room. The knights moved in front of them, taking defensive positions.

"Oh for fuck's sake," Gary said. "Seriously?"

"Sam of Wilds," Wan shouted. "I am here to avenge the death of Lartin the Dark Leaf. He was a nice and strange man whose father—"

"No," I snapped. "You do *not* get to monologue during Ryan's love confession."

The Darks stared at me. "His what?" Wan asked.

"In case you couldn't tell, I was about to be told how wonderful I am and how much I am loved and how I am the greatest thing in his world and he worships the ground I walk on and that I also have great hair and my sex puns are the funniest things ever. He was also probably going to kiss me and I was considering making it a little dirty even though we have an audience."

"Oh shit," one of the Darks said to another, and I recognized them as the ones that had been chased away by the fire geckos outside of Tarker Mills. "They finally got their act together."

"I told you they would," the other said. "You owe me coin."

"Bullshit," the first Dark said. "You literally said they would do it before the wedding."

"Oh my gods, would you stop saying *literally*?"

"I thought he was marrying the Prince?" Wan asked.

"Plans changed," I said. "And because I fucking deserve it after all the shit I've been through, you're going to shut the fuck up and let me have this fucking moment. When he's finished, I'll deal with you. Do you understand?"

"I don't think—"

"Do you understand?"

"Eep!" Wan said. "I mean, yes. Yes, I understand."

I glared at him until I was sure he was going keep his mouth shut. Then I turned back to Ryan, who was watching me fondly. "Sorry about that," I said. "You may continue."

"Can I?" he asked, smirking just a bit. "Wouldn't want any more interruptions."

"There won't be any," I said. "Proceed."

"Well apparently I'm supposed to say you're the greatest thing in the world and I worship the ground you walk on."

"That's a good start," I said.

He closed the distance between us, his chest bumping against mine. "And your sex puns are the funniest thing ever. You also have great hair."

"That's good," I managed to say. "That's real good."

"And I think you're pretty wonderful."

"Yeah? This is working for me. A lot."

He grinned. "I think there was one other thing you wanted me to say."

I nodded, not trusting my voice.

Ryan reached up, cupping my face in his hands. He searched my face for something, and he must have found what he was looking for, because he said, "You're my lightning-struck heart, Sam of Wilds. I love you more than I could ever say."

And then he kissed me.

It wasn't like the first kiss atop the dragon's keep. That one had been born of desperation and longing. No. This kiss spoke of sweet relief, of a future that I hadn't thought would ever be possible. As his lips moved over mine, my magic sang and thrummed along my skin, and I wondered if this is what it felt like to be cherished, to be held in such wonder that it was breathtaking.

His tongue dragged along the seam of my lips and I opened for him. I felt the scrape of his teeth and his fingers tightened on my face. My hands were on his hips and I held him close.

He pulled away only to kiss my cheeks. My nose. My chin. And then he rested his forehead against mine and we breathed each other in.

"So," he said.

"So."

"Sorry it took me so long."

"S'okay. You can make it up to me."

"Yeah?"

"Yeah."

"I love you," he said, kissing me sweetly.

I couldn't stop the smile that grew on my face even if I'd wanted to. "Because I'm awesome."

He rolled his eyes. "Yes, Sam. Because you're awesome."

"Good," I said. "I love you too, even if you are an asshole."

"Heart boner," Gary moaned. "Throbbing heart boner."

"We should probably deal with the Darks so we can get out of here," he said, running his thumbs over my cheeks.

"Yeah? Where we going?"

He blushed.

"Oh," I said. "*Oh.* Yeah. We should definitely go do that. We should go do the hell out of that. Many times. Like, I'm so down with that. You have no idea."

"Make sure to get the money up front," Randall whispered. "I need my cut."

Morgan sighed again and shook his head. Poor guy. He'd had a long day.

"What they doing?" Tiggy asked.

"Well," Gary said. "When a knight finally pulls his head out of his ass at the last possible moment obviously staged for dramatic purposes and admits that he loves a wizard's apprentice, they go into their room and do a special hug that—"

"Butt sex," Tiggy said.

"Yes, Tiggy. Butt sex."

"Go, Sam!"

"Thank you, Tiggy." And because I could, I kissed Ryan again. It was awesome. I felt him smiling against my lips, and I didn't think this day could get any better.

Then Wan cleared his throat. "So. We're still standing here. In case you were wondering."

"That so?" I said, pulling away from Ryan and turning toward the Darks.

Wan squared his shoulders. The Darks behind him stood in formation. "Sam of Wilds," Wan said. "You murdered Lartin the Dark Leaf. He was a great wizard who liked pinecones and eating fried fish while wearing slippers. We have come here to exact our revenge and—"

"Okay," I said.

"Okay?" Wan asked.

"You want revenge. I'll let you try."

"You will," he said, eyes narrowing in suspicion.

"It's the least I could do," I said. "After all, you were the ones who had the foolproof plan to infiltrate Castle Lockes on a royal wedding day when a large contingent of the King's knights would be present, not to mention the two most powerful wizards in the known world, a pissed-off unicorn, an angry half-giant, a dragon, and my boo." I blew a kiss at Ryan. He rolled his eyes and pulled out his sword.

"Don't call me boo," he said as he tried to stand between me and the Darks.

"Mini-muffin?" I said, shoving him to the side.

"Gods, Sam."

"Honeybear?"

"I've changed my mind," he said. "I take back the love confession."

"Too late," I said. "We have, like, a thousand witnesses. You're stuck with me pretty much for forever."

He shook his head. "Still taking it back."

"Heart boner gone," Gary muttered.

"So you see," I said, looking back at the Darks, who were not quite as confident as they had been before. "You pretty much done fucked up, son."

"We can take you," Wan said, brow sweating.

"You sure about that?" the King asked, shrugging out of his robe. He reached behind the throne and drew out a longsword, double fisting it and grinning. "I look forward to it."

"Well," Justin said, catching two swords in either hand thrown to him by a knight. He flourished them both. "At least this day didn't end in a total crapshoot. Killing something will probably make me feel better." He stood next to his father, coolly gazing out at the Darks.

"Pretty sure," Wan said weakly.

"We need you to be *positive*," my dad said, pushing his way out of the crowd and coming to stand amid the knights. He cracked his neck from side to side, popping his knuckles, the heavy muscles in his arms bunching.

"So maybe think very carefully before you act," my mother said, sliding out to stand next to my father, eyes glinting as she took a defensive stance, bouncing lightly on the balls of her feet.

"So," I said, all eyes coming back to me. "You picked a pretty bad day to fuck with Verania. Kevin! Make me billow!"

Kevin sucked in a great breath and blew a stream of air at me, causing my robes to billow around me in the breeze.

"Do I look badass?" I asked Ryan.

"Dashing and immaculate even," he said, bumping my shoulder.

"Awesome," I breathed. "Now I just need a catchphrase."

"Oh, here we go," Gary muttered.

"Got it!" I said. I glared at the group of Dark wizards standing before us. "It's time to turn off their lights and leave them in the dark. Permanently."

Everyone groaned. Literally *everyone*.

"That wasn't very good at all!" someone in the audience cried.

"Keep working on it," Dad said.

"Or don't," Mom said. "That works too."

"Good job on that one," Randall said to Morgan. "You must be so proud."

"Hey," Morgan said. "I had nothing to do with that. I'm just as embarrassed as you are."

"It's like we've taught him nothing," Gary said to Tiggy.

"He slow," Tiggy said. "It okay."

"He tries so hard," the King said, winking at me.

"Obviously not hard enough," Justin said, flourishing his swords again. Like a douchebag.

"I thought it was good," Ryan said. "Sort of."

"Thanks, boo," I said, beaming at him. "I'm glad you get it. Unlike the *rest* of these idiots who wouldn't know awesome even if it punched them in the dicks."

"I should hope not," Mom said. "Seeing as how I don't have one."

"Last chance," I told the Darks.

"Bring it," Wan said and I felt the heavy weight of magic permeate through the room.

I smiled at him. "I was hoping you were going to say that."

The people of Verania roared.

THE BATTLE lasted two minutes and thirty-six seconds.

No one died, not even Lady Tina DeSilva. Much to my chagrin.

The Darks never stood a chance.

CHAPTER 30
Butt Sex Is Pretty Darn Wonderful

HE CROWDED me up against the door to my bedroom after closing it behind us. His breath was hot against my neck as he pressed his chest to mine. His lips trailed along my jaw, and I might have made a noise or two that I will deny until my dying day.

"This," I gasped, "is very unexpected."

I could feel his smile against my cheek, the scrape of his teeth near my ear. "How could any part of this be unexpected? It's been a long time coming."

My hands found their way to his hips and curled into his trousers. I was trying to gather the courage to move my fingers to the buttons on the front, but was having difficulty forming even the simplest of thoughts. "Well, you were about to be married not a few hours ago."

He snorted. It felt gross. And awesome. "There is that."

"Unexpected," I said again as he bit my earlobe.

"We've been dating for weeks," he said. "It's just that neither of us realized it."

"That doesn't count as dating if we didn't know about it."

"It does," he insisted.

"When was our first date?" I asked, somehow resisting the urge to grind up against him. I was already half-hard, and if things kept going the way they were, it was going to become a noticeable problem very, very quickly.

"Antonella's."

I laughed. "You mean my date with Todd."

He pulled back and scowled at me. "That was our date and you know it. And don't you say a damn word about his ears."

"I was such a dick to Todd," I said. "But then so were you."

"I wasn't a dick," he said, going back to doing whatever he was doing to my neck and ears.

"Dude," I said. "You so were. You should send him a letter of apology."

"Sam, do you really want me to stop what I'm doing and write a letter of apology to Todd?"

"I didn't mean right this second *oh my gods do that again*."

And he did, swirling his tongue on my ear and pressing himself harder against me. The handle to the door was digging against the small of my back, but I really couldn't find a fuck to give about that because Ryan was truly, truly talented.

"Now," he said, his voice low and rough. "You are going to go into the bathroom. You are going to bathe. When you're finished, you're going to come back out here. There will be no need for clothing. Is there any part of that is unclear?"

"Not a single word," I breathed.

"Good. I'll be back shortly. Don't keep me waiting, Sam." He leaned in and kissed me, dirty and wet. Somehow, he managed to make us trade places and before I knew it, he was out the door and gone.

"Um," I said. "What the fuck?"

I stood there for a few long minutes, unsure of what had just happened, or what would be happening. The fact that he'd given me a few direct orders that had done nothing but made my dick harder than it'd ever been was something I wasn't even remotely ready to deal with.

There was a frantic knock on the door.

I opened it quick, sure he'd already come back. "That was fast. Couldn't wait to come back and fuck me—*Gary*."

Gary stared at me. "You're still wearing clothes."

"What? Did you think I wouldn't be? Why the hell would you knock on the door if I wasn't going to be wearing—never mind. I don't even want to know."

He pushed his way past me. "Where's Ryan?"

"He ordered me to get naked and bathe and then left."

Gary stared at me some more. Finally, "Today has been a very strange day."

"I still have an erection because of it," I admitted.

His lips twitched. "Kitten, some things are obvious."

I looked down and sure enough, there was my penis, very evident through the trousers. I covered myself with my hands. "Oh my gods," I muttered. "Get the fuck out! I have sexy orders to follow!"

"Sexy orders?" he repeated.

"Sexy orders," I agreed. "Though I can't quite figure out why I need to bathe. Shouldn't we be already down with the boning?"

"Sam," Gary said, sounding very patient. "We were just in a battle. You are dirty."

"So?" I asked. "Why would he care? It's not like he's going to...." My eyes went wide.

"There it is," Gary said.

"He's going to put his mouth on me!"

"And his tongue," Gary said.

"Gary!"

"Oh boy."

I started stripping off my clothes. "He wants some of this!"

Gary closed his eyes. "That may be so, but I don't want to see it."

I scowled at him. "I had to listen to you and Kevin role-play naughty unicorn. You can fucking deal."

Gary sighed, sounding extraordinarily put out, but he followed me into the bathroom anyway.

A servant had already been up ahead of us in the room, and the bathtub was filled with water that still steamed. Violets and lemongrass floated along the surface. I shucked my trousers off and stepped into the water, hissing as it reddened my skin.

"Okay," I said to Gary. "Advice time."

"Go," he said.

"What do I suck on first?" I asked, taking a bar of soap made of goat's milk and flaxseed oil and rubbing it against my armpits vigorously.

He choked. "I am so not ready for this."

"It doesn't *matter* if you are," I told him. "This is happening. In less than a day, I've gone from being sad and despondent and still pretty awesome to having a super fucking hot boyfriend who is about to ravage me in ways I never thought were possible and *you better tell me what I need to suck on*!"

"Yikes," Gary said. "There really is no need to shout."

"I might be freaking out a bit," I said.

"No shit."

"So?" I lathered up the soap in my hands and then scrubbed my feet. I didn't expect anyone to be licking my toes in the near future, but I didn't want to rule out the possibility. I didn't think I quite knew what was considered foreplay and what was considered kink yet. I figured I'd get better with practice, but I didn't want to make the mistake of saying something like, "Oh, this is nice, now is second base where you eat my feet?"

"Gary! What do I need to do with my mouth!"

"His penis," Gary offered.

"His penis," I said, brain melting. "Like. What. And just. Whoa."

"Sam? Sam. Oh for the love of the gods, did I break you?"

"No," I said. "I'm just. Just."

"Thinking about Ryan Foxheart's penis," he said helpfully.

"What if he's huge?" I asked.

"What if he's tiny?" Gary asked with wide eyes.

"I would love him anyway," I decided.

"Aww," Gary said. "I only threw up a little bit at that."

"You're not helping!" I said, soaping up my hair. "If you're going to be sassy, get the hell out. Wait. Why are you even here?"

"I came to make sure you weren't nervous," Gary said. "It's not every day that your flower gets eaten."

"I'm not nervous," I said nervously.

He rolled his eyes. "Of course not. You only got everything you've wished for over the years and now you're about to find out just what a prostate does. Of course you're not nervous."

"Best friends are mostly awesome," I said. "This is not one of those times. And stop calling it my fucking flower. I am not some fair maiden being wooed. I am a fucking wizard's apprentice about to have hardcore gay sex. I am a motherfucking *man*."

Gary grinned at me. "Yeah, you'll be fine. Remember two things."

I nodded, because I just knew he was going to impart words of impeccable wisdom upon me that I would treasure for the rest of my life.

"First," he said. "You don't ever have to do anything you don't want to do. If you are uncomfortable, if something hurts, you tell him to stop and he will. If he doesn't, you curse his fucking ass, find me, and I will murder him. Are we clear?"

"My loved ones are extraordinarily violent," I said. "Deal. What's the second thing?"

"When you're finished," Gary said, "you have to tell me every single detail. I want to know *everything*."

"Everything?"

"Everything," he said. "You're about to get porked and I want to know what kind of sex face he has."

I grimaced. "Nothing about that sentence was even remotely sexy."

"Wash your taint, kitten."

And so I did.

When I felt I couldn't be any cleaner, Gary handed me a towel and I wrapped it around my waist. The mirror was foggy, and I wiped a hand across it. My reflection was wide-eyed and looked slightly manic. "Crap. I have crazy face."

"Only a little bit," Gary said.

"That wasn't as helpful as you thought it was," I said.

"You got this, okay?"

"That was a little better."

He snorted, and it came out eggshell white and olive green. I would have though it pretty if I wasn't unsuccessfully trying to make my crazy face go away. "Sam," Gary said quietly, hooking his chin over my shoulder and watching me in the mirror. "It's going to be okay. Ryan loves you, and he's going to take care of you."

I shrugged. "I know." Because I truly did.

"And you are going to live happily ever after."

"You think?" I asked, trying not to get my hopes up.

"I know it," he said. "And I came to tell you I told you so."

"I love you," I told him. "You know that, right?"

"I know," he said, pressing his lips against the side of my head. "I love you too."

"Good. Feel better?"

"You know what? I do. It's going to be fine. I'll just—"

A knock at the door.

"—go out of my *fucking mind because he's here*."

"Well," Gary said. "I tried. Sam. It's been lovely. Have fun. Make sure you press up right behind his balls before he comes. It'll feel really good."

"Wait, *what*!"

"Toodles!" he called over his shoulder, heading for the door, leaving me to my doom.

I heard the door open. Then, "Well, I'll be. Ryan Foxheart. Now *this* is unexpected."

"Gary," I heard Ryan say. "Everything okay?"

"Peachy," Gary said cheerfully. "Sam is finishing up in the bathroom. While he's in there, you and I can chat for a minute."

"I can hear every word you're saying!" I called out.

"Ignore him," Gary said. "He's naked in front of the mirror admiring his nipples."

"That's... nice," Ryan said, sounding rather breathless.

"Sweet molasses," I muttered.

"So, quick word. You love him?"

"Yes." No hesitation.

"You going to hurt him?"

"Not intentionally."

"Hmm," Gary said. "I'll allow it, Ryan. Can I call you Ryan?"

"Don't you normally?"

"Wonderful. Ryan. If you hurt him, Tiggy and I will tear you to pieces and bathe in your blood. Your soul will be torn from your body and we'll trap it in an enchanted urn. I will then light the urn on fire and Kevin will eat it. Soon, you would be nothing but a pile of dragon shit. Are we clear?"

I groaned quite loudly.

"Oh, listen," Gary said. "Sam sounds like he's practicing."

"He sounds... practiced," Ryan said.

"Ew," Gary said. "Is that your sex face? I am getting kind of grossed out just being here right now. It's like my children are about to bone."

"There are so many things wrong with that sentence!" I shouted at him.

"We're clear," Ryan said. "No dragon shit, and we'll be good."

"Not *too* good, I hope," I heard Gary purr.

"Yep," I said. "Time to leave. Bye, Gary! Bye! Thank you! Bye!"

"Rude," Gary said. "But also acceptable. I'll leave you to it. Sam, I expect to see you in the morning with tales of your flower being devoured."

I ran out of the bathroom, but he was already cackling his way out the door. I slammed it behind him, flicking the heavy lock for good measure. I began to plot his timely demise for the millionth time since I'd known him and had a pretty good scenario in my head involving a vat of acid when I realized I was standing next to Ryan Foxheart wearing nothing but a towel.

He'd changed too, wearing a light cotton shirt that clung to his skin. Loose-fitting trousers hung at his waist. His feet were bare, and I found that strangely adorable. His hair was wet, as he must have bathed as well. His eyes were on me, dark and heated, and I swallowed thickly. A trickle of water rolled down his throat to his collarbone, and I wanted to chase it with my tongue.

So I did.

There was a sharp intake of air as my tongue flicked out against his throat, tasting the droplet, licking up the path it left. I followed it up and my cheek brushed against his and our lips met, slick and hot as he kissed me. His hands came up to my hair, fingers digging and tugging gently as he worked his mouth over mine. His tongue slid wetly over my lips and I groaned, opening my mouth. He took it as invitation and I was pressed again at the door, my back against the wood, his front against mine from head to toe.

I didn't stop myself from grinding into him this time, and I shuddered when I felt an answering hardness. There was electricity in the contact, and my skin felt stretched taut and hot. He kept one hand in my hair, pulling my head back as he sucked lightly on my throat. He dropped his other hand down against my chest, fingers trailing until his nails scraped against my right nipple. I gasped when he pinched the skin lightly. "Okay?" he murmured against my lips.

"Yeah," I said. "I'm so fucking okay right now."

He chuckled. "I have plans."

"Do you?" I asked, opening my eyes, his face inches from my own.

"Yes," he said, resting his hand on my stomach. He brushed his groin against mine again, and I trembled at the touch. "I'm going to take care of you. I promise. I'm going to make sure you won't—"

"I didn't have sex with Moishe," I blurted out, unable to stop myself. "I just… wanted you to know. I didn't have sex with him."

He closed his eyes and took a stuttering step back, and for a moment, I thought maybe I'd done something wrong. Granted, it was probably not the best to be speaking about sex with another person (or lack thereof) when you're about to get funky with someone else, but I couldn't let that stay hidden. I couldn't let him think otherwise. Everything was on the table now. No more hiding.

"But," he said. "You…. Randall said. He could smell the elf on you."

"I was going to," I said, trying to force the words out. "I went there. To Mama's. To let him take from me what he wanted. I was so fucking pissed off at you and I wasn't thinking clearly and I… I don't know. I just thought that maybe. Maybe I would feel better to have someone want me."

"But you didn't."

"No. He came in the room. He kissed me and his hands were on me and it felt wrong. I just. I couldn't do it so I told him to stop. He did. I left."

"Sam," he said, breathing heavily.

"Yeah?"

"Lose the towel."

I acted without thinking. I pulled the towel off. Dropped it away.

He was on his knees even before it hit the ground. His callused hand circled the base of my dick, and he licked the reddened tip. I groaned, my back falling against the door. There was no warning then, when he took me in his mouth, cheeks hollowed and eyes fluttering closed. He sucked down the length of my cock and my hips jerked at the slight sting of teeth, the swirl of his tongue. His nose brushed against my pubes and he held it there, my cock knocking against the back of his throat. I wasn't big by any stretch of the imagination, but I wasn't small either, and the fact that he took me down in one smooth go of it was almost enough to knock me on my ass.

I didn't know what to do with my hands, and so I kept them curled in fists at my sides. That is until he grabbed my right hand as he bobbed up and down, taking it to the top of his head, curling my fingers into his hair. It was still wet and I looked down, my fingers disappearing into the locks. I watched as spit leaked out the side of his mouth, his lips stretched. His eyes opened and he looked up at me before sliding back up and off. "It's okay," he said. "You can. I can take it."

"Can what?" I said roughly.

His lips were wet with saliva when he said, "You can fuck my mouth. I'm good. Come on. You can do it."

If that wasn't the hottest fucking thing I'd ever heard anyone say, then I didn't know what was. I ignored the strange curl of jealousy that rolled in my stomach, knowing I wasn't his first or second or third. He could do this because he'd done it before. I pushed it away, though, before it could get any further (*JustinJustinJustin*). He wasn't mine then, but I thought he might be now, so I let it alone and nodded down at him.

His mouth went back to my dick, and I pushed experimentally into his mouth, a shallow thrust. He waited for me to go at my own pace, but his fingers tightened on my hips and I knew he wouldn't wait for long. I tugged on his hair and he moaned, muffled around my cock. It vibrated in my skin and my balls tightened.

I pushed forward again, farther this time, fingers against his scalp. The slide of his tongue was wet on the underside of my cock, the minute flick of it against the slit almost making my knees buckle. I thrust again, pushing as far as I could go, his throat constricting and loosening as I pulled out and pushed back in.

I'd never felt anything like it before, the wet heat. The feel of his head in my hands. His nails digging into my hips and ass. One of his hands came up and he tugged gently on my balls and I thought I would shoot off right then, but I was able to stave off, though I wouldn't last much longer.

"Stop," I finally gasped. "Just stop and—"

He pulled off immediately, his lips swollen. He wiped his face with the back of his hand and there was something amazingly erotic about him, this powerful knight, fully clothed and on his knees while I stood nude above him, my dick wet with his spit.

"I was going to come," I said. "I didn't... not yet. I want."

He seemed to understand my babbling because he stood swiftly, kissing me again. There was a slight bitterness on his tongue and realized I was tasting myself in his mouth. I chased after it, my hands curled around his nape as he rubbed up against me, finding friction and rutting into it.

"Naked," I muttered against his mouth. "Why aren't you more naked?"

"That what you want?" he asked me, kissing me again, then backing away. His eyes roamed hungrily up and down, taking in every inch of me. My first instinct was to hide, to cover myself, the heat of embarrassment crawling up my neck. But there was nothing cruel or mocking in his gaze. Quite the opposite, really. He looked as if he wanted to reach out and touch, but was stopping himself from doing so.

"Yeah," I said. "That's what I want."

He nodded once.

The shirt came off first and I remembered the day in the river, watching him bathe, the sun setting behind him on golden skin, the flex and pull of tissue and muscle. It was on display here again, except we were alone and in my room. Then felt like a dream, hazy and bright. Here, the sun was almost down and the colors were muted. Candlelight flickered behind him, shadows dancing along his arms and shoulders.

"The rest," I said.

He moved slowly then, and if I put too much thought into it, I might have said he was performing. His hands went to the front, unfastening each button with nimble fingers. He pulled the trousers open, his pubic hair darker than the trail on his stomach. He brought his hands to his hips, inching the trousers down. I could see the base of his dick, then the length, then the ruddy head as it sprang free. It was slightly thicker than my own, and curved toward the right. I wondered at the weight of it, my fingers itching to reach out and touch.

He slid the trousers down his legs, bending over but never taking his eyes off of me. His thighs were covered in light hair and were corded with muscle. He let the trousers fall to his feet. He pulled himself back up to his full height. Lifted his right leg, shook his foot free. Did the same with the left. Kicked the trousers away.

And just stood there.

I said, "I'll be honest. I'm pretty sure I want to write sonnets about your dick."

He gaped at me.

"Dammit," I said as I winced. "That sounded sexier in my head."

He snorted and shook his head. "It was still pretty sexy. Sort of." He brought his arms over his head, clasping his hands and stretching back. Muscles bunched and contracted all over him, the light from the candle moving over his skin as if it were made to do only that.

"You're doing that on purpose," I said hoarsely.

"What?" he asked, cocking a teasing eyebrow.

"That," I said, waving my hand at him up and down. "With your whole... *thing*. You're posing."

"Am I?" he asked, taking a step back away from me.

"Dashing and immaculate," I insisted, taking an answering step toward him, not even caring anymore that I was completely naked and with a ridiculous erection.

"You don't say?" Another step back.

"It was nice," I admitted.

"*Nice?*" he said, sounding smug. He took another step back, and he was almost at my bed. "You think it's *nice*? A minute ago, you were getting ready to rhapsodize about my dick. Now it's *nice*." The backs of his thighs hit the edge of my bed, and he sat down on it. He put his hands on the mattress, forearms flexing as he pushed himself back on the blankets. I tried not to stare as his balls bunched under his dick, dragging along my bed. "*Nice*," he said.

"I like nice," I said, voice just above a growl.

"I know," he said. "Do you remember what I said the night we first danced?"

"You said many things. I wondered if you would ever shut up."

He laughed. "I told you I wasn't nice."

"I'm nervous," I said, cringing slightly.

His face softened. "Sam."

"What?"

"In a minute, you're going to come over here, okay?"

"Okay."

"You're going to kiss me."

"Okay."

"You're going to touch me and I'm going to touch you."

"Okay."

"And then you're going to fuck me on your bed."

My mouth went dry.

"Sam?"

"Yeah," I managed to say.

"Did you get all that?"

"Yeah."

"Come here."

I have no shame in admitting that I pretty much ran the rest of the way to the bed, jumping and landing on top of him. The laugh that came out of him was an awesome sound to hear, and his hands went to my back, fingers trailing down to the top of my ass, the full length of my body pressed against him. His breath was on my face as he smiled up at me, eyes sparkling in the candlelight. They reminded me of stars and I remembered my wish from that day in the secret garden, where I wished that I had someone to call my own, so I could show him why I was made for him.

And here he was. Ryan Foxheart, Nox that was. My cornerstone.

"You're mine," I said in awe.

His smiled widened. "Yeah, Sam. Yeah."

I kissed him then.

Later, I watched him stretch himself out, his fingers glistening with oil, his breath hitching as he instructed me to slick myself up. His hips were propped up on pillows. I could barely take my eyes away from the sight before me, watching his fingers disappear into himself, stretching but trying to fuck into himself too, but not able to get the right angle.

After that, time slipped gently. I remember his hand on my cock as he guided me, his legs around my hips. I felt the resistance of his ass and the pull of the muscle around my cockhead. There was a flash of immense heat as I pushed farther. He groaned underneath me, his eyes closing, chest rising and falling in rapid breaths. He pressed a hand against my stomach when my hips met his ass, stilling me, telling me to wait.

I told him I would. For him, I would. For him, I would do anything.

Eventually, he nodded.

I gave a shallow thrust and he opened his eyes, staring up at me. I pulled out farther, my length dragging inside him. I pushed forward again and he said, "Sam. Sam, please. Go."

And I did. It took me a moment to find a rhythm I could work with. I went to my knees, bringing his right leg straight up and over my shoulder, his ankle at my ear. His left leg stayed curled around my back, the foot near my ass. I rolled my hips up, fucking him deeper. I picked up the pace then, kissing his calf, the bone of his ankle as he moaned underneath me.

We lasted longer than I thought we would, given the months of pent-up frustration. Sweat dripped down my back and his pupils were dilated. He was breathing heavily when his hand went to his dick and he began to jack himself off. I changed the angle slightly and his eyes flew open and he said, "There, there, *there*."

I could feel the magic under my skin and there was the haze of gold and green, and it whispered to me, telling me that I was *here*, that I was finally *here*, home, home at last. I cried out as he clenched around me. He said my name when he came all over his chest and stomach. I fucked him through it and when his hand dropped away, I pulled out and he sighed as I jerked myself off above him, once, twice, three times before I came on his dick, the spunk dripping down onto his balls and falling onto the bed.

His chest heaved as he stared up at me, dazed.

I said, "Holy fucking gods," as I panted.

The smile that followed felt like a wish upon the stars.

"SHIT," I said, sometime later when I thought I could speak again.

"Hmm?" he said, fingers brushing through my hair. I'd decided that lying on his chest and listening to his heart beat was just about the best place I could ever be.

"I forgot to press below your balls when you came like Gary told me to. He's going to be so pissed at me."

"Oh my gods."

"Remind me to do it next time."

"Oh my gods."

I rolled my eyes. "You sound way too much like me."

His laughter rumbled in my ear and I thought that maybe wishing upon the stars was the greatest thing I'd ever done.

EPILOGUE
A Destiny of Dragons

IT HAPPENED, randomly, some weeks later. To say that it was unexpected is an understatement.

Granted, I'd gotten the both of us captured again.

Totally not my fault, by the way.

"It is totally your fault," Justin said.

"Not really," I said, frowning down at the fairy ring rising up from the dirt around my feet. "Okay, maybe just a little bit. To be honest, I'm a little bit embarrassed that I keep getting stuck in the middle of a magic mushroom circle."

"Yeah," Justin said. "I don't think that's the only thing you should be embarrassed about."

"If it makes you feel any better," I said, ignoring his obvious ire, "the last time this happened, Ryan was molested by a tree."

He gaped at me.

I wiggled my eyebrows at him.

"You know what?" he said. "That does sort of make me feel better."

"Good. It should. It should make everyone feel better. What happens now?" I shrugged and looked through the trees of the Dark Woods where Justin and I had been sent on a quest for Morgan (and by "quest" I mean the King and his Wizard conspired to force Justin and I to spend time together in the name of bonding—those sneaky bastards). "Either the mushrooms will grow feet and will lead us deeper into the woods, or Dimitri will appear."

"Your ex-boyfriend?"

I scowled at him. "He's not my ex!"

"That's not what Ryan said."

"Ryan doesn't know what he's talking about. Ever."

"That really explains why he's with you, then."

"Oh my gods," I said, eyes wide. "You're sassy!"

"No I'm not."

"Sassy," I insisted. "Or bitchy. I don't know if I can tell the difference."

"Sometimes," Justin said, "I think about what it would be like if you'd been born without a voice box."

"Dude," I said. "Whoa."

"Sam," Dimitri said, appearing out of nowhere with his tiny naked body and his tiny groomed mustache. "How lovely to see you again."

"Dimitri," I said. "You've really got to stop this. Kidnapping is not wooing."

"This is your ex," Justin said. "Him."

"He is not my ex!"

"I'm his ex," Dimitri said, fluttering over to Justin.

Justin grinned evilly. "This is just marvelous."

I groaned. "You are not allowed to use this against me. Ever."

"You're going to be so used," Justin said.

"Can I watch?" Dimitri asked.

"Gross," I said. "Shut up. Don't even."

"I can't believe you were going to get gay fairy married," Justin said.

Dimitri scowled. "Hello. We just call it *married*. And I'm a *king*."

Justin rolled his eyes. "And I'm the Prince of Verania."

"That sounded kind of douchey," I said. "The both of you."

They glared at me.

"Prince Justin?" Dimitri asked. "Weren't you with the knight last time?"

"I was," Justin said. "And then *he* turned into a home wrecker and broke up my wedding and stole my husband-to-be."

"That is sort of true," I said. "Except for the parts where it's not. Which was most of it."

"I tried to marry him," Dimitri told Justin. "His unicorn kicked me in the face and then they ran away."

"That sounds about right," Justin said. "I'm sorry you've been subjected to the horror that is Sam of Wilds."

"Still standing right here," I said. "With my feelings."

And then it happened. The most unexpected thing.

"Why didn't you just kill him?" Dimitri asked. "Surely it would have been easier to chop off his head than let him steal your man."

"That seems extreme for something I really didn't do," I said. "And stop giving him ideas, Dimitri."

Justin let out a long-suffering sigh. "I can't kill him, no matter how much I want to."

"Why?" Dimitri asked.

"He's a pain in my ass," Justin said. "There are days when I can't stand the sight of him. He's too mouthy, opinionated, and he made my fiancé fall in love with him by just existing. People worship the ground he walks on while turning their nose up at me, even though I am the king-in-waiting and he is but from the slums."

"And he still has his head because…." Dimitri said.

"Because he's my wizard," Justin said. "And we're going to be together for a very long time."

My jaw dropped.

"Huh," Dimitri said. "I think I'm attracted to you."

Justin snorted. "Not going to happen. I am staying free of men for the foreseeable future."

"You," I breathed. "You *like* me."

"Not hardly," Justin said wearily.

"You seriously *like* me."

"That's not even remotely true."

"We're going to be best friends," I said in awe.

He sighed. "I knew I should have chopped off your head."

"Dimitri," I demanded. "Lower your fairy ring this instant. I am having so many feelings right now and I need to project them onto the Prince."

"If you do that," Justin growled at Dimitri, "I will punch you in your tiny face."

"He won't," I said. "I won't let him. Lower the godsdamn ring."

"Sorry," Dimitri said to Justin. "Sam and I were almost married. That bond never goes away."

"There is no bond," I said, even as the rings lowered.

Justin took a step back away from me.

"I'm going to awkward hug the fuck out of you," I warned him.

"You stay right where you are," he said, holding up his hands.

"No. You just said we're going to be friends forever and that you want to go get coffee with me and gossip about boys while eating pastries."

"I didn't say *any* of that!"

"It was implied!"

"There were no implications!"

"It's okay," I told him as he backed into a tree. I opened my arms wide as I stalked toward him. "I hear all the things you can't say because you're emotionally stunted and need me to bring out your softer side through the fiery depths of your man pain."

And then I hugged Grand Prince Justin of Verania.

His arms stayed resolutely at his side as I laid my head on his shoulder, my nose near his neck. "This is nice," I said.

"This is *not* nice," he growled.

"It is," I said. "You just don't know it yet."

"This is hugging against my will. This is assault."

"If you hug me back, it'll be over quicker. You smell like moonbeams and cookies."

"Oh my gods," Justin said.

"You're *my* moonbeam cookie—"

His arms came up around me and held on tight. Really tight. To the point I was having trouble breathing.

"You're too good at this," I wheezed.

"Shut up," he said.

"Do you want to talk about feelings now?"

"Sure. I feel like I want to murder you."

"That's good," I said. "Getting it all out. I feel like I want to go get matching haircuts with you and tell people we're brothers from another mother."

"I feel like you two should kiss," Dimitri said. "Because this shit is hot."

"Is he masturbating?" I whispered to Justin.

"I don't even want to look."

"He ruins things," I said.

"So do you," Justin said. "Can we be done now?"

Not wanting to upset this delicate balance, I only held on for three more minutes.

By the time we left the Dark Woods, Justin had a promise from Dimitri to convene soon to discuss a new treaty with the Dark Woods Fairies and I had a new best friend, even if the new best friend denied it vehemently and said we were casual acquaintances at best.

"SO," RYAN asked me a few nights later as we ate a quiet dinner in my room. "I have to ask you something." He sounded a bit nervous.

I swallowed the salted pork calmly, put down my fork, wiped my mouth with a napkin, and said, "I can't marry you just yet. I think we should date first for a while."

His eyes went wide. "I wasn't going to ask you to marry me!"

I grinned. "No shit, dude. Though I'm almost offended by how much you're freaking out."

"I'm not freaking out!"

"Um, your face is red and suddenly sweaty and you just bent your fork in half."

"It was already like that when I got it," he said, dropping the fork onto the table.

"Wow," I said. "You're a really fucking bad liar."

"I am *not* a fu—"

I glared at him.

"—mothercracking bad liar," he said instead. Because he had to think of the *children*.

"Pretty bad," I said. "But I'll marry you one day. It just won't be today."

The smile that formed then was as wide as I'd ever seen it. It was like getting hit in the face with a puppy made of ice cream and good dreams. "You will?"

"Yeah," I said, sounding slightly strangled.

"You just bent your fork," he said smugly.

"What? No, I didn't. It came like this."

"Uh-huh."

"It did," I said. "I watched them craft it. Your smile didn't make my balls tingle at all."

"That's… I don't know what that is."

"Classy," I said. "Classy is what it is. Just think. You get *allll* of this. For *years*." I leered at him, sure it was more sexy than rapey.

He grimaced slightly. "I may not have thought this through as well as I should have."

I tried to unbend my fork. "This is the worst proposal ever."

"I'm not proposing!"

"I know," I said. "I'm just saying if you were, this would be the worst proposal ever. First asking me to marry you and then insulting me."

"Oh please," he scoffed. "When I ask you to marry me, you're going to be sobbing in joy because I'm awesome. And you still need to work on your leering. I was worried for a moment you'd put something in my drink and I'd wake up tomorrow sore and smelling like you but not remembering how it happened."

"We may be spending too much time together," I said. "Because that sounded way too much like something I would have said."

"Better than you spending all your time with *Justin*."

"Hey," I said. "You leave him alone. He is a best friend in training."

"Which is *weird*."

"It's not weird." I gave him my fork so he could eat and started to unbend the other one.

"Sam, it's kind of weird."

"Okay," I admitted. "Maybe a little bit. But since you left him at the altar—"

"For *you*."

"—*at the altar*," I said loudly, "he's had a bit of a change of heart. He's back on track in his relationship with the King, he doesn't look angrily ill every time I walk in the room, and I think I almost convinced him the other day to let me send him on a date."

"With *Todd*."

"He has these awesome ears," I said, as if he didn't know. Because he *should*. *Everyone* should.

"I would not be sad if Todd lost his ears in an accident," Ryan grumbled.

"Oh my gods!"

He looked slightly startled. "What!"

"You were *jealous*. The *whole* time!" It hit me, every now and then. These little epiphanies that burst through the gigantic cloud that was my obliviousness at the affections of Knight Commander Ryan Foxheart. Little moments that I remembered about our interactions before I knew he wanted to fuck me stupid that should have given it away, but didn't because I was so convinced I never stood a chance.

"I was *not* jealous."

"You were!" I crowed. "You wanted to *murder* him. I gave him a *hand job* in front of you! Well. Sort of."

"To be fair," Ryan said, "he looked like the type that I could easily murder."

"You want my babies," I said.

He sighed. "I chose this," he said to no one in particular. "This was my choice."

"You're welcome. This is still the worst proposal ever."

"Sam!"

I nodded. "I know. I don't have any idea how we got here either. You were saying?"

"I don't even remember now."

I reached over and patted him on the hand. "You'll think of it, boo. I have faith in you."

AND HE did, that night, when we were curled around each other, sweat and spunk drying on our skin. It was actually really disgusting, but I couldn't find it in me to give a fuck. Especially since Ryan's legs were tangled in my own, his soft cock resting on my thigh. It spoke of intimacy, even if I was starting to get itchy.

I was drifting lazily when he said, "How do I do it?"

"Do what?" I asked, brushing my nose against his ear.

"Become your cornerstone."

And that woke me right the fuck up. "What?"

"Your cornerstone, Sam. Is there some kind of ritual? Do we have to dance naked in the moonlight with Randall after he covers us in arcane symbols made from yak's blood?"

"Sex makes you stupid," I said fondly. "And awesome, but mostly stupid."

"I'm serious, Sam. Okay. Not about the naked dancing with Randall."

"I should hope not. If you were, I would begin to question a few things."

He pinched my side. "Be serious."

"Yeah."

"So?"

"It's...." I trailed off, unsure of how to explain it. I thought back to all the things Morgan had taught me, that Randall had hinted at. Of bonds made and the magic borne of it. "You know what a cornerstone is."

"A foundation for which to build your magic."

"It's more than that. A cornerstone determines how the rest of the stones will be set. How the entire building will be constructed. It's the most important piece and without it, there would be discord. Chaos. And magic is the same. Without the cornerstone in place, it'll grow wildly. Out of control. Exponentially so until one day, it's a disfigured thing with no rhyme or reason, slowly eating away at the user."

"The Darks," he said quietly, tracing a finger along my chest.

"Yeah," I said. "They're unstable. They don't last, not for long. They're not meant to. But they forsake the idea of cornerstones because to have one is to admit a need most aren't comfortable with."

"Which is?"

"You aren't the reason I have magic," I told him, kissing his forehead. "But you would be the reason it's defined. And if what Morgan and Randall believe is true, if I am more powerful than anything else out there, then you'll be the most important cornerstone to exist."

"Whoa," he said. "Holy crap. I'm *amazing*."

"And of course that's what you took from that," I said. "But yeah. You are. Though I'd tone down the smugness. You already think you're dashing and immaculate. Can't have your self-esteem get *too* high."

"They wrote that in the paper," he said. "So you know it has to be true now."

"Ugh," I said. "I changed my mind now too. I'm going to take Justin's place and go on a date with Todd. At least his ears are—"

And that's all I got out because one moment I'm curled up against him, and the next I'm flat on my back, him propped up over me, the candlelight flickering on his face as he scowls down at me.

"Hey, boo," I said.

"You're not going to go on a date with Todd," he snapped.

I rolled my eyes. "No shit."

"Because you're mine now."

"That should not be as hot as it is."

"Say it."

"Oh my gods. Seriously. Like half a chub just from that alone."

"Sam."

"Yeah, yeah. No date with Todd."

"Because you're the prize that I won," he said, smirking at me.

I groaned and shoved him away. "I can't *believe* I even said that."

"I can," he said, leaning his head down and kissing me on the chin. "It seems like something you would say."

"Asshole," I said.

"Already put it there," he said. "Twice."

I gaped at him. "Did you just… what. I. Sweet molasses. I don't. Did you just make a *sex pun*?"

Ryan frowned. "I don't know if you understand what a pun is."

"Marry me," I demanded.

"Sure," he said with a shrug. "I can do that."

"What?"

"What."

"You just agreed to marry me!"

"I know. You just asked me to."

"But. I don't. What the hell is going on?"

He rolled his eyes. "I don't think you ever really know."

"We're still going to date first," I decided. "You owe me so much for all the shit you've put me through."

"Put *you* through? What about when you—"

"You waited until your wedding to someone else to announce your feelings for me."

"Dammit," he said. "I am never going to win an argument because of that."

"Never."

He collapsed down on top of me, miles and miles of naked skin pressed against my own. I could barely breathe. It was awesome.

We were quiet for a time, just the brush of lips and fingers.

Eventually, I said the only thing I could. The only thing that mattered. "You don't have to do anything. To be the cornerstone. Or, rather, you don't have to do anything more. I don't need to love you for all the things you could be. I already love you for all the things you are. So no. There's no special ceremony. No dancing naked covered in yak's blood. Randall doesn't need to approve and Morgan doesn't need to agree. My magic already knows you like I do. It's known you for years. One day, and one day soon, it'll just happen because that's what you are to me. And I was made for you, you know? I wished for this even before I knew what it was, and I am happy it's you. And I'm going to spend the rest of my days showing you why."

"Sam," he said. He sounded as if he was in awe of me, and I knew I was in awe of him, so I kissed him then, relishing the feel of his lips against mine, knowing that this was it. My magic sang because like the stories of old, of whimsy and fancy-free, this was my ending.

My heart was lightning-struck and it beat for him.

This was it.

This was my happily ever after.

AND IT was.

For three days.

Because of *course* that was the way my life went.

After all, there was still finding Gary's horn, finding Tiggy's family, getting captured by more Dark wizards, taking the Trials, pissing off Randall when I turned his fingers into dicks, finishing my Grimoire, meeting my mother's *roma*, learning just how bendy Knight Commander Ryan Foxheart was while fucking him in the most unusual places we dared to take our pants off in, discovering that, yes, I did quite like rimming, and last but not least, finding out in the middle of all of this that I was somehow the center of a thousands-year-old prophecy that named me as the sole owner of a destiny intertwined with the dragons of Verania who I would lead in a battle against some ridiculous Dark wizard who would most likely monologue at me until my ears bled.

Yeah.

I was annoyed too.

Seriously.

Fuck my life.

Because this ain't over. Not by a long shot.

It's one thing to be told you're awesome. It's a whole other thing to be told you have a destiny of dragons.

But that... well.

That's a story for another day.

When TJ KLUNE was eight, he picked up a pen and paper and began to write his first story (which turned out to be his own sweeping epic version of the video game *Super Metroid*—he didn't think the game ended very well and wanted to offer his own take on it. He never heard back from the video game company, much to his chagrin). Now, over two decades later, the cast of characters in his head have only gotten louder, wondering why he has to go to work as a claims examiner for an insurance company during the day when he could just stay home and write.

Since being published, TJ has won the Lambda Literary Award for Best Gay Romance, fought off three lions that threatened to attack him and his village, and was chosen by Amazon as having written one of the best GLBT books of 2011.

And one of those things isn't true.

(It's the lion thing. The lion thing isn't true.)

Facebook: TJ Klune
Blog: http://tjklunebooks.blogspot.com
E-mail: tjklunebooks@yahoo.com

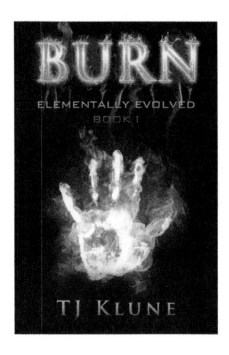

Set in a world that closely resembles our own, *Burn* is a story of redemption and betrayal, of family and sacrifice, which leads to the greatest question of all: how far would you go to save the ones you love?

Fifteen years ago, Felix Paracel killed his mother with fire that shot from his hands. Since then, he has hidden from forces bent on exploiting him and his fire and wind Elemental abilities. But Felix's world is about to change, because he is Findo Unum—the Split One—and his coming has been foretold for generations.

Though Felix's arrival brings great joy to the Elemental world, it also heralds a coming darkness. No one knows this better than Seven, the mysterious man who rescued Felix from that horrible fire years ago and then disappeared... who now has returned to claim what's rightfully his: Felix's heart. But even as Felix begins to trust Seven and his feelings about his place in the world, the darkness reveals itself, bringing consequences no one could have predicted.

http://www.dreamspinnerpress.com

Five years ago, Benji Green lost his beloved father, Big Eddie, when his truck crashed into a river. Everyone called it an accident, but Benji knows it was more. Even years later, he's buried in his grief, throwing himself into managing Big Eddie's convenience store in the small-town of Roseland, Oregon. Surrounded by his mother and three aunts, he lives day to day, struggling to keep his head above water.

But Roseland is no ordinary place.

With ever more frequent dreams of his father's death and waking visions of feathers on the river's surface, Benji finds his definition of reality bending. He thinks himself haunted; by ghosts or memories, he can no longer tell. Not until a man falls from the sky, leaving the burning imprint of wings on the ground, does Benji begin to understand that the world is more mysterious than he ever imagined—and more dangerous. As uncontrollable forces descend on Roseland, they reveal long-hidden truths about friends, family, and the stranger Calliel—a man Benji can no longer live without.

http://www.dreamspinnerpress.com

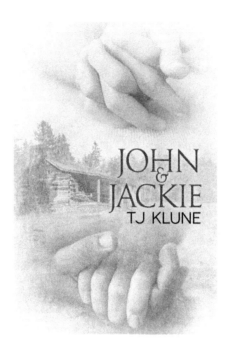

John and Jackie first laid eyes on each other when they were twelve years old. Now, seventy-one years later, Jack prepares to give his beloved husband the ultimate gift. Before he does, they'll relive five key moments from their younger lives together over the course of a single afternoon. From their first meeting and first kiss to the violence of an abusive father and the heartache of growing up, these moments have defined who they have become. As sunset approaches, John will show the depths of his love for the one man who has made him whole: his Jackie. They'll soon learn there is no force more powerful than their devotion to one another.

http://www.dreamspinnerpress.com

Do you believe in love at first sight?

Paul Auster doesn't. Paul doesn't believe in much at all. He's thirty, slightly overweight, and his best features are his acerbic wit and the color commentary he provides as life passes him by. His closest friends are a two-legged dog named Wheels and a quasibipolar drag queen named Helena Handbasket. He works a dead-end job in a soul-sucking cubicle, and if his grandmother's homophobic parrot insults him one more time, Paul is going to wring its stupid neck.

Enter Vince Taylor.

Vince is everything Paul isn't: sexy, confident, and dumber than the proverbial box of rocks. And for some reason, Vince pursues Paul relentlessly. Vince must be messing with him, because there is no way Vince could want someone like Paul.

But when Paul hits Vince with his car—in a completely unintentional if-he-died-it'd-only-be-manslaughter kind of way—he's forced to see Vince in a whole new light. The only thing stopping Paul from believing in Vince is himself—and that is one obstacle Paul can't quite seem to overcome. But when tragedy strikes Vince's family, Paul must put aside any notions he has about himself and stand next to the man who thinks he's perfect the way he is.

http://www.dreamspinnerpress.com

Three years ago, Bear McKenna's mother took off for parts unknown with her new boyfriend, leaving Bear to raise his six-year-old brother Tyson, aka the Kid. Somehow they've muddled through, but since he's totally devoted to the Kid, Bear isn't actually doing much living—with a few exceptions, he's retreated from the world, and he's mostly okay with that. Until Otter comes home.

Otter is Bear's best friend's older brother, and as they've done for their whole lives, Bear and Otter crash and collide in ways neither expect. This time, though, there's nowhere to run from the depth of emotion between them. Bear still believes his place is as the Kid's guardian, but he can't help thinking there could be something more for him in the world... something or someone.

http://www.dreamspinnerpress.com

Bear, Otter, and the Kid survived last summer with their hearts and souls intact. They've moved into the Green Monstrosity, and Bear is finally able to admit his love for the man who saved him from himself.

But that's not the end of their story. How could it be?

The boys find that life doesn't stop just because they got their happily ever after. There's still the custody battle for the Kid. The return of Otter's parents. A first trip to a gay bar. The Kid goes to therapy, and Mrs. Paquinn decides that Bigfoot is real. Anna and Creed do… well, whatever it is Anna and Creed do. There are newfound jealousies, the return of old enemies, bad poetry, and misanthropic seagulls. And through it all, Bear struggles to understand his mother's abandonment of him and his brother, only to delve deeper into their shared past. What he finds there will alter their lives forever and help him realize what it'll take to become who they're supposed to be.

Family is not always defined by blood. It's defined by those who make us whole—those who make us who we are.

http://www.dreamspinnerpress.com

Tyson Thompson graduated high school at sixteen and left the town of Seafare, Oregon, bound for what he assumed would be bigger and better things. He soon found out the real world has teeth, and he returns to the coast with four years of failure, addiction, and a diagnosis of panic disorder trailing behind him. His brother, Bear, and his brother's husband, Otter, believe coming home is exactly what Tyson needs to find himself again. Surrounded by family in the Green Monstrosity, Tyson attempts to put the pieces of his broken life back together.

But shortly after he arrives home, Tyson comes face to face with inevitability in the form of his childhood friend and first love, Dominic Miller, who he hasn't seen since the day he left Seafare. As their paths cross, old wounds reopen, new secrets are revealed, and Tyson discovers there is more to his own story than he was told all those years ago.

In a sea of familiar faces, new friends, and the memories of a mother's devastating choice, Tyson will learn that in order to have any hope for a future, he must fight the ghosts of his past.

http://www.dreamspinnerpress.com

IMMORTAL

AMY LANE

http://www.dreamspinnerpress.com

CPSIA information can be obtained
at www.ICGtesting.com
Printed in the USA
BVOW11s1536080617
486273BV00006B/82/P